RICKET

Book Two of the Star Watch series

Written By

Mark Wayne McGinnis

Cover design by:
Eren Arik

Edited by:
Lura Lee Genz
Mia Manns

Published by:
Avenstar Productions

Print Book ver :
ISBN-10: 0-9861098-7-8
ISBN-13: 978-0-9861098-7-4

To join Mark's mailing list, jump to
http://eepurl.com/bs7M9r

Visit Mark Wayne McGinnis at
http://www.markwaynemcginnis.com

Foreword

Quick Tip:

For those using web-enabled e-readers, or have access to the web via a PC you can now refer back to the author's website for illustrated floor plans of The Lilly's and the Minian's various decks and compartments, as well as those of another vessel called the Parcical.

More ship diagrams will be added over time. Throughout this book, the various little icons (such as the one below) are provided as a quick reminder of this option—simply click on the ship icon to jump to the Explore The Ships website diagrams:

Chapter 1

CAP-RIM Star System
Decommissioned Spacecraft Repository

"She's slowing and entering the shipyard, Captain," Mc-Neil reported.

Jason knew the captain of that vessel would do just that ... it was a smart move. Hundreds of decommissioned freighters and tankers, and just about every other type of space-faring vessel, were marooned in this graveyard for the old, obsolete, and discarded.

Jason said, "*Minian* ... announce General Quarters, ship-wide."

He heard the *Minian's* AI over the PA, telling the ship's crew to report to their respective battle stations.

"I recommend we slow down too, Cap ... he's not worth the risk," Gunny said.

Jason ignored her. "Helm, are we gaining on her?"

"Yes, sir ... we've gained on her ... but not by much."

"Kick it up faster, McNeil!" Jason ordered, giving a quick, over-the-shoulder glance toward Orion.

Jason watched the overhead display's three-hundred-and-sixty-degree view, as massive structures passed by them at an alarming speed. "If you have to, enhance forward shields."

"Already at max," Orion said, not hiding her unease at the

new situation.

"Captain, the *Carrion*'s headed for that space between the mining vessels," McNeil said. "She'll be boxed in until she comes out the far side."

Jason saw it, too. The *Carrion*, less than half the tonnage of the *Minian*, was headed for an opening between four monstrous, five-mile-long ships. It would be a tight squeeze for the *Carrion*, but definitely a tighter fit for the *Minian*, double the other ship's width. "Go above the mining ships and catch the *Carrion* on the other side. Kick it up, Helm!"

McNeil brought the nose of the *Minian* up, with mere feet to spare. "Our ass is dragging; we're going to lose some paint on this one, sir."

"Shields are holding," Orion added.

The bridge shuddered and everyone grabbed something to hold on to. The *Carrion* was now hidden from view and, instinctively, Orion inserted a logistical, icon-based segment to the display above them.

"Shit!" Jason said as he watched the alien battleship emerge from the other side, immediately turning away from the *Minian*'s current trajectory.

"We're going to have to slow some in order to make the next course change, sir," McNeil said.

Jason stayed quiet. He didn't want to lose that ship. Captain Mar Oswaldo, known as Captain Oz, was an amazing tactician. Jason had done a little research on the Darion Cartel's most famous captain. He'd avoided capture by the Alliance, the Craing, and numerous other independent militaries for at least eight years now. Captain Oz was like Earth's famed Manfred von Richthofen, the Red Baron, the First World War German flying ace. Oz had never been defeated in space combat. It was rumored he'd destroyed over two hundred adversary ships—from small destroyers to a Craing dreadnaught caught off-guard. Jason knew, firsthand, that was not an easy feat.

Currently, Captain Oz was farther from home than was typical. The recent defeat of the Craing Empire had, no doubt, contributed to these more enterprising, far-reaching attacks. Jason had to give the Darion Cartel, the planetary system of thirty united planets that Oz was commissioned by, the credit. The cartel operated within its own laws. They sneered at the term space piracy, since they only invaded sections of space that were, in their view, within their own spatial borders. And that was true: At one time there was a Darion Empire—spanning close to two hundred light-years in distance—but that was a millennium ago. Just as the Roman Empire on Earth crumbled away over time—so had the Darion Empire.

But ten years ago, things started to change. There was a shift in attitudes among both government and populace … undoubtedly brought on from the Craing's invasion. With the Darion Cartel a mere shell of what the Darion Empire had been a millennium earlier, the question arose … if the Darion Empire had stayed strong—stayed together, would the Craing have been able to defeat them so easily? A reunification of mind and spirit had forged a fresh emergence of patriotism. Countering the Darion Cartel demanded more and more Craing military resources and an abundance of Craing vessels were destroyed. Eventually, the Craing simply learned to keep to the periphery of the planetary system and leave the Darion Empire alone for the most part.

Now, the Darion Cartel was a force to be reckoned with. Methodically, the cartel kept expanding its borders in all directions. Their military was growing, too … as quickly as they conquered an adversary they recommissioned that enemy's vessels into their own fleet. The single biggest contributing factor to the cartel's recent success was Captain Oz. Capturing him, or, if necessary, killing him, would provide a significant blow to the Darion Cartel's growing momentum.

Star Watch was given carte blanche to handle the audacious Captain Oz as Jason deemed necessary. But Jason's current, near-frenzied pursuit of Oz was far more personal. Two weeks earlier to the day, a small planetary system located at the edge of Sector 22—called Airigo 5—was attacked by Captain Oz. Tranquil, peace-loving individuals were unnecessarily killed in the thousands when the *Carrion* strafed numerous government buildings within the capital city. It was an unnecessary assault since no resistance—no military force—had ever been rallied.

But the real reason behind Jason's consuming hatred for Captain Oz was the subsequent death of General Taft. An emissary from Earth, General Jonathan Taft had been a close friend of his father's, as well as his own. An elderly man, he'd become more of a diplomat than a military man at that late point in his life. He'd been dispatched to Airigo 5 to open up negotiations for an Allied presence, a new space station, within their system. When Jason relayed the sad news to his father, now living back in San Bernardino, California at the family scrapyard, via video link—his father broke down. The show of such strong feelings took Jason completely by surprise. Typically, the admiral was anything but emotional ... the news had hit him hard. His father made one simple request ... *"Get the one responsible, Jason ... get him and kill him."*

"We've got a visual on the *Carrion*, Cap," Orion said.

The *Carrion* had entered a particularly dense section of space, holding only a few large vessels, but many others smaller in size, like cruisers, transport vessels, and unmanned drone ships.

"She's making a path," Orion said.

The *Carrion*'s plasma cannons were now firing non-stop—blasting obstacles into small fragments.

"We'll need a bigger swath than what he's made in order

to follow him, Orion."

"I'm on it," she said.

Jason felt the subtle vibration from the *Minian's* big guns as they came to life. Above, on the overhead display, the hulls of lifeless crafts were exploding, one after another, all around them. They were finally making headway—consistently closing in on the smaller ship.

What do we have here? Jason asked himself, his brow furrowed.

The *Carrion* had done the unexpected: She'd slowed and come about.

"She's positioning for a fight," Orion said. "Oz must know that he's overwhelmingly out-gunned … what the hell's he thinking?"

"Full stop, Helm," Jason said, rising to his feet, his eyes glued to the display.

"I don't like this," Orion said, her voice a mere whisper.

"Me, neither … Get us out of here! Phase-shift—"

Jason's words were cut short by multiple high-yield explosions impacting both sides of the *Minian*. Off in the distance, on their one side, were the remnants of a fractured space station; on the other was a massive space-crane. Both gargantuan structures had been fitted with plasma weaponry … a whole lot of weaponry. How the *Minian's* sensors had missed seeing them was just one of Jason's concerns.

"We've got missiles coming in from a whole lot of other ships now, Cap."

But Jason already knew this, having seen the approach of too many small red icons to count up on the overhead display. *Where did they all come from?*

"I don't think I've ever seen so many missiles directed at any one target … us!" Orion added.

The *Minian* shook and jolted with each repetitive explosion impacting on her shields. "Phase-shift system offline, Captain," McNeil shouted over the noise.

"Bring all guns active, Gunny! Shred anything within ten thousand miles of here."

"Guns are faltering … shields holding, but falling fast … they're down to thirty percent," Orion said.

Lieutenant Commander Perkins, the XO, rushed onto the bridge, looking rattled, but he knew enough to keep his mouth shut. He took a seat behind the command chair.

Jason watched as the open space around the *Minian* became filled with thousands of streaks of bright green and blue plasma fire. It had been a planned trap, obviously. The firepower assembled here was at a level he didn't think possible. It must have taken them many weeks of preparation.

"Starboard drive just went offline … now the port drives, too … we're not moving any time soon," McNeil said.

But Jason was only half-listening. On the display, he watched as the *Carrion* leisurely turned one hundred and eighty degrees on her axis—the ship's drives coming alive in a burst of white-hot energy as she proceeded to leave the area.

"Incoming message from the *Carrion*, Captain … just one word," Seaman Gordon nervously said from the comms station.

Jason waited for it.

"*Gotcha.*"

Jason gritted his teeth. *I'm going to get that son of a bitch if it's the last thing I do.*

"Hull breaches reported on decks five, eight and twenty-three."

"Come on … take out those guns, Gunny!" Jason ordered, his frustration rising.

"They've erected shields in front of both the space station and the crane. There's no way we're going to bring them down before our own shields are gone, Captain."

Jason didn't answer for several moments. Then he turned toward Orion: "There's no way they're able to shield anything other than the inward-facing sections of those two structures ... right? As is ... the amount of power that would be required is staggering." He didn't wait for an answer, facing Perkins. "XO, get Grimes and her pilots dispatched to their fighters. Make sure that she has them phase-shift directly from the flight bay, to ensure they're out of the line of fire. We'll take out those guns from their backsides."

"I suggest we deploy the fighter drones as well, sir," Perkins said.

"Agreed."

Between the seventy-five Caldurian fighters, and the three hundred unmanned drone fighters, the firepower—soon to be brought to bear on the far side of the space station on one side, and the crane on their other side—was profound. The main question Jason pondered: Were they deployed before the *Minian*'s shields were completely depleted?

All eyes were on the overhead display. New, bright yellow icons were now added to the mix. Like bees swarming, they converged on the two targets.

"Shields failing fast, Captain. Ten ... now down to eight percent," Orion said, her voice ominously calm.

Jason knew that was not a good sign—she sounded resigned to an inevitable fate. "Don't throw in the towel just yet, Gunny," he said, with more gusto than he thought himself capable of.

"Incoming hail, Captain. It's Lieutenant Grimes."

"Put her through, Seaman."

"There are shields placed at the far side of the station, too, Captain. Not like those on the inward side, facing the *Minian*, but enough to hinder our attack."

Jason shook his head. Was it really going to end like this? Damn! He couldn't believe he'd been so easily bested by Oz … he had to give him his due … he'd certainly covered all the bases. If they got out of this alive, he'd never let that happen again. He contemplated an abandon ship order but there would be too little time, now. It was do or die …

"I've directed the drone fighters to enter the space station from a small, unshielded opening at the bottom. Too small for our manned fighters, but I think the drones can manage it."

"How about the crane? What are your pilots reporting over there?"

"Slow going on that one, sir."

Orion cut in, "Cap, the *Minian*'s guns did the trick. The crane has been neutralized."

Jason confirmed the good news with his own eyes and, sure enough, the big space crane was completely destroyed.

"All our guns are now directed toward the space station. Its shields are falling fast," Orion said.

"Get those drone-fighters out of there and have our pilots back off."

Jason sat back down in the command chair and watched as the space station suddenly went quiet. It too had been neutralized. "Any crew or pilot casualties?" Jason asked.

"None, Cap … but the damage to the *Minian* is substantial."

"Get repair crews started immediately … get Ricket and Granger to help with the drives. Nix that," Jason said, suddenly remembering: "Ricket is on a field trip to the Mansan Core system for the day. Perkins can work with Granger in Engineering instead. I also want continuous perimeter patrols by our fighters. Come on, XO, you're with me … let's go check out the damaged areas."

Chapter 2

Mansan Core System
Planet Eriok; Port City

Ricket sat quietly on the corner of a closed equipment transport locker, one of five he had arrived with. He and the others were situated beneath a canvas tarp. A mild breeze kept the bright blue fabric above them flapping in a constant state of agitation.

"Unfortunately, the physics do not support what you are attempting to do here, I'm afraid," Ricket said, doing his best not to insult Silgin Burak, the Port City engineer. "Perhaps if we take a step back and reevaluate what it is you're trying to accomplish—"

Burak cut him off, "No! No stepping back bullshit …" he said, making no attempt to hide the sneer on his meaty round face. The humanoid city worker was short and sweating profusely, prompting Ricket to breathe strictly through his mouth to avoid smelling the man's sour body odor.

Ricket was keenly aware the atmosphere around him had changed. The other eight Eriokians, wearing similar olive-green overalls, had the same hostile expression on their faces. The visit was supposed to be an Alliance gesture of good will. It wasn't like this Mansan Core system planet ranked high on the priority list for Star Watch … there were hundreds of requests for the Alliance's newly formed Star Watch policing/marshaling service.

Ricket glanced over to the *SpaceRunner*, parked three hundred and sixty-two feet to the north. Rising heat waves from the midday sun gave the vessel a shimmery, dream-like quality. For the first time, Ricket hoped Leon Pike, the space ship's captain, was keeping tabs on the situation below.

Ricket brought his attention back to Burak. "I am here to assist you. But the amount of power necessary for that type of plasma ray ... well, it needs to come from somewhere. The geo-thermal source currently in use has only one-third the capacity of what is required."

The Port City engineer stood, his arms crossing over his barrel chest. Ricket looked up at him, then over to his companions. It became obvious that Burak and the others already knew that, as no indication of surprise or indignation lit their faces. Ricket was unsure what, exactly, was going on here. He'd arrived three hours earlier with Leon, Hanna, and the mecher, the seven-foot-tall robot from Trom, for what was intended to be a simple, one-day field trip—to provide both technical know-how, and some customized plasma weaponry, to Port City. Then the *SpaceRunner* would phase-shift back to the Sol system, to Jefferson Station, later today.

"Perhaps I should return to my ship. We can take a break ... start again in an hour. Would that be acceptable?" Ricket asked.

Burak said, "Stay where you are, Craing."

Ricket didn't take offense at being sneeringly called *Craing* by Burak. Born on the planet Craing, he *was* a Craing, all 4"1' of him; but he was also so much more: Over two hundred years old, he was infused with countless nanites and Caldurian tech-devices that provided him with incredible sensory capabilities. And right then, he detected sudden, massive amounts of energy, five hundred feet to the west of their little encampment.

Ricket sent a NanoCom message to the mecher, who was, undoubtedly, still sitting at the controls of the *SpaceRunner*: "Get away from here!"

That was the entirety of the message Ricket sent before another vessel suddenly came into view. He had detected the unique energy signature of an impending phase-shift, something that happened very infrequently. Other than select Allied vessels, such as the *Minian*, the *Assailant*, and the *SpaceRunner*, and various fighters and shuttles, this technology—the capability to instantly phase-shift from one place to another, within thousands of miles, could only be coming from one source— the Caldurians, the originators of the technology. The *Minian*, in fact, was also a Caldurian ship.

The vessel loomed high and broad. Like the *Minian* and *The Lilly*, the vessel was black, with a smooth matte finish. Unmistakably Caldurian in design, she had similar lines to *The Lilly* but was more egg-shaped. Perhaps this was the latest replacement model for that class of vessel, Ricket thought. The spacecraft had two sets of stubby, angled-back wings on each side and two extremely large observation windows set high and far back on the hull. Perhaps it was the two large eye-like portals or maybe it was the overall design of the ship, but it was definitely an imposing, almost ominous, ship to behold.

The Port City engineers quickly scattered and only faint traces of Burak's foul body odor remained behind. Ricket, not moving from his perch, continued to observe the events going on around him. He noticed the Caldurian ship's nose was pointed toward the *SpaceRunner* and, in that same instant, detected another familiar energy signature—that of a powerful plasma cannon being energized. In a burst of bright blue light, the Caldurian ship fired its primary weapon. What remained of the *SpaceRunner* looked more like a dark cloud … she had been atomized.

Ricket brought a hand to his mouth. He'd just witnessed the death of Leon and Hanna.

A gangway appeared beneath the Caldurian vessel and three tall beings, one following the next, descended the ramp. Ricket recognized they were of Caldurian heritage; they looked similar to the one Caldurian crewmember on board the *Minian*: Granger.

Now standing, frozen in place by what he had just witnessed, Ricket watched them approach. Using every aspect of his advanced internal devices to assess the situation, he still felt scared, unsure what to do next. Ricket was not a warrior, although he significantly appeared more like one than he once did, before meeting Captain Jason Reynolds two years earlier. He was well aware that in order to survive the present situation, only his intellect would save him.

The three Caldurians walked beneath the tarp and stopped several paces in front of him. The difference in their height became very apparent.

"There was no need to fire on that vessel—killing those still on board. Our purpose here only had peaceful motivations," Ricket said, with unbridled indignation.

Tall, dressed similarly in black spacer's jumpsuits, they looked akin to the Craing, possessing angular heads and large eyes. *An attractive species*, Ricket thought. They were now communicating amongst themselves. Their advanced NanoCom devices allowed them to talk through singular mind-based conversations—more akin to telepathy … something his own nano-devices were yet incapable of. But with the most recent advancements to his nano-devices, he could, at least, hear them.

The closest of the three was saying, "Is this the one? I expected … something … other than him."

The other two smiled and appraised Ricket, like they were observing a bug ... a science experiment.

"He is listening to us ... he's partially modified our own technology," the Caldurian in the middle said.

The closest one, apparently the leader, talked aloud, using his voice: "Your comrades are not dead, but I suspect you already know that."

Ricket did know that. He'd just detected their life-form readings a moment earlier, so they must have phase-shifted away safely. He also detected the mecher was still with them.

"Then, you are aware they are currently pointing weapons at you?" Ricket lied, unsure if that were true.

"You are Ricket, yes?"

"I am."

"We have much to discuss ... come with us. Your friends are now on board our ship."

Ricket verified for himself that what the leader said was, in fact, true. They had been phase-shifted aboard.

"What do you want with us ... with me?" Ricket asked.

"You will be coming with us. Away from this realm."

Ricket was well aware that the Caldurians were, for the most part, travelers of the multiverse. In fact, a whole faction of their society, the *progressives*, had migrated to some other dimensional realm years ago and rarely returned to their original realm.

"What do you want with me?" Ricket asked again.

"Rest assured, nothing that will cause you any physical pain." The Caldurian leader nodded his head, gesturing toward his ship.

Although the response didn't answer his question, Ricket didn't see another option open. He could, possibly, activate his battle suit and phase-shift elsewhere, but could he get away in the few seconds it took for his suit to initialize? Where could he go that these advanced beings wouldn't find him? And what about Leon and Hanna? Since they were now on the Caldurian vessel perhaps it was best to go along with their demands—at least for now. There was another consideration too: He was more than a little excited to see the inside of their vessel. No doubt, it contained the absolute latest in Caldurian technology. He briefly wondered if he would be allowed to update his own internal devices. A feeling of excitement came over him as he walked with the threesome toward the vessel.

As they ascended the ramp, Ricket realized they'd certainly gone to a lot of trouble; the request for assistance by Eriok's Port City, the meeting with the engineers, was all a ruse. *Why not contact me directly?*

At the top of the ramp, Ricket experienced a slight electrical charge rove over his entire body. He'd passed through an environmental field similar to that on board the *Minian*, alleviating the need for airlock chambers. They walked some distance before entering a DeckPort, then exited out its other side into a surprisingly expansive space. In the distance, Ricket heard voices … specifically the mecher's. "I am designated as Trommy5 … I am a mecher from the planet Trom …"

Leon and Hanna were being held within separate confinement cells, behind light aqua-colored energy fields.

Ricket then realized only the pudgy leader was still with him—the other two must have DeckPorted to another section of the ship. Another Caldurian, broad-shouldered and older than the others, was waiting for him.

"Welcome, Ricket, my name is Hobel."

Before Ricket could answer, he heard a familiar voice coming from behind the Caldurian.

"What the hell have you gotten us into, Ricket?" Leon Pike yelled. "Did you see what they did to my ship?"

The Caldurian named Hobel wore an all-white, single-piece uniform, with four blue stripes on each of his sleeves. He tapped at a virtual control panel on the bulkhead, next to the confinement cell, and Leon's voice went silent. Ricket noticed three SuitPac devices were lying on a nearby console. Ricket quickly assessed his surroundings. His excitement grew as he observed what could only be described as awe-inspiring. Very little here had actual physical form: 3D virtual holographic displays surrounded them. He reached out his hand and touched a nearby, quasi-transparent, blue-hued virtual console and was surprised that it felt solid. His internal sensors detected a slight energy fluctuation as his fingers followed the contours of the structure ... *this is simply amazing!*

The Eriokian, whom Ricket earlier thought was the leader of the Port City engineers, brushed past him and placed a fourth SuitPac on the console. *When did he take that away from me?* Ricket wondered.

Hobel waved the other one away with a casual gesture of his hand. He waited for him to leave the compartment while continuing to stare down at Ricket.

"You can relax, you have no reason to fear me."

"Why have you taken us captive? What do you want with us?"

"All your questions will be answered in due time. For now, rest assured—you and your friends are safe."

Ricket's eyes moved to his comrades standing behind force fields. Leon was silently yelling something, silenced within his cell. Hanna stood at the back of her own enclosure, arms folded beneath her breasts, glaring angrily at Ricket.

The ship lurched slightly. Apparently, they had departed Eriok.

Hobel's expression became contentious. "Unfortunately, Ricket, you will not be leaving the *Parcical* ... not within your lifetime. You should come to terms with that here and now."

Chapter 3

Sol System, Jefferson Station
The Minian, Captain's Ready Room

Jason entered the captain's ready room, finding half the seats already filled. At the far end of the table sat Admiral Dixon, a middle-aged, silver-haired officer with a strong Southern drawl, which often disarmed even those who opposed him. But he was no country bumpkin. Dixon was as sharp as they came and more than once stood behind Jason's father when support within the ranks of the Alliance was hard to come by. He respected and liked the man. It was Dixon who'd called the meeting and it was he who'd personally selected those in attendance today.

Jason knew why he was here. What happened yesterday, in the Mansan Core system, was appalling. He'd been so caught up in the chase that he'd been bushwhacked. Worse, he'd nearly lost his crew—close to twelve hundred men and women—and nearly lost the Alliance's most prized warship, the *Minian*. Losing her to an enemy faction would be disastrous.

Jason nodded toward Admiral Dixon and was rewarded

with a friendly smile. A few more late stragglers hurried to their seats, then the room became quiet. It suddenly dawned on Jason that his junior officers were purposely avoiding eye contact. *So this is what it's like to lose the respect of my crew.*

Jason cleared his voice. "Thank you, Admiral Dixon. Welcome—"

Admiral Dixon cut him off, putting up a hand and gesturing for Jason to hold up. He rose to his feet, walked around the table, and stood at Jason's side. "Captain Reynolds, if you would indulge me for a moment, I'd like to address your junior officers."

"Of course ... the floor is yours, sir."

Dixon's friendly demeanor evaporated. His gray-blue eyes turned icy cold. "You all really screwed the pooch yesterday. What a clusterfuck. I've reviewed the reports, including the AI bridge feeds. I thought I was watching one of those old Keystone cop movies."

The room stayed quiet as the attendees stared down at the table like scolded children.

"Your captain was given specific orders to apprehend, or kill, Captain Mar Oswaldo. The Alliance does not issue such orders lightly. You want to blame your captain for the shit-pile you found yourselves in ... well don't ... at least, not completely. Your captain is effective only to the level of support he's given and that support was near non-existent. Staff-Sergeant Orion, who was responsible for tactical on the *Minian*'s bridge during the altercation?"

Orion looked up and caught Jason's eye, then looked at the admiral. "I was ... am ... responsible for the tactical station, sir."

"Why wasn't the trap detected?"

"Sir, there were no sensor readings of any kind coming from either the space station or the space crane ... they were both dead quiet, Admiral."

"Were they? Are you sure?"

Again, Orion's eyes flashed toward Jason before she answered, "Sir, all I can do is work with the readings—"

The admiral was shaking his head and Orion stopped talking.

"You had a wide array of options available to you, Staff-Sergeant Orion ... granted, I'm not as tactically current as you are, but according to the AI, there were still sixteen, both long- and short-range, in-depth sensor fields available to you ... that information had already been processed, but it wasn't checked. You relied strictly on what, I understand, are referred to as tactical *fast scan* screens ... low level cursory threat evaluations. Now, I've had the opportunity to review those other, missed, readings and with the assistance of a Jefferson Station tactical officer, I was able to verify that there were, in fact, energy spikes coming from both the space station and the space crane. They were very small ... but they were there."

Jason wasn't going to let the admiral publicly flog Gunny. "Admiral, when you're in a battle situation, there's simply no time—"

Admiral Dixon waved away Jason's protest and turned his attention to Ensign McNeil. "Ensign, you were at the helm during the altercation?"

"Aye, sir."

"Let's move ahead to the point where the *Minian* was drawn into the trap; the moment when your captain gave the order for you to get the ship out of there. Then he ordered you to phase-shift away."

McNeil looked nervous, like a young boy being scolded by a school principal. "Aye, sir. The phase-shift system was one of the first systems taken out ... there was no way—"

Dixon took a step closer to McNeil and, putting his hands on his hips, his face stern and his eyes unforgiving, said, "Yes, you are one hundred percent correct, Ensign. The phase-shift system was down at that point. But the drives were operational. In fact, you had several seconds before the drives were taken out. Let me ask you this, Ensign … how far can the *Minian* travel in the span of … say … five seconds?"

Jason watched McNeil's face as the young man mentally calculated the question.

"At that point the only direction open to us was the way we'd come in and backing out."

Dixon raised his brow and waited for him to continue.

"If I had acted immediately, instigated a full reversal of both drives and auxiliary thrusters, we might have been able to clear the trap," McNeil said, looking apologetically toward Jason.

Dixon put a consoling hand on the ensign's shoulder and moved on to the young man sitting next to McNeil—Seaman Gordon.

Jason gave McNeil a reassuring nod and brought his full attention to Seaman Gordon. An identical twin, both he and his brother had freckled faces and bright red hair. Like McNeil, Gordon looked as if he were going to pee his pants.

"Seaman Gordon, you were on the bridge comms, correct?"

"Um … Yes, I was, sir … Admiral, sir."

"At the point Captain Reynolds initiated pursuit of the *Carrion*, were you monitoring space chatter?"

"Aye, sir … that's part of my duties … to listen for other vessels in the area."

"That's very good, Seaman Gordon. You're also instructed to listen for AI audio prompts, correct?"

"Aye, sir."

Jason saw Gordon's face fall. What the admiral was referring to was the comms channel audio beeps, intended to prompt the comms technician to review sub-channel comms. The spectrum was almost limitless and could be quite a time-consuming process. In high-stress situations it would be difficult to check each and every AI prompt.

"I had the opportunity to review the AI audio prompts and what I discovered was quite interesting ... would you like to know what you missed, Seaman?"

"Aye, sir."

"The *Carrion* sent a sub-channel communication to both the space station and the space crane. It was that same communication which triggered the attack on both the port and starboard sides of the *Minian*."

"That's enough, Admiral," Jason said, rising to his feet. "I'm not going to let you interrogate my crew ... to second-guess their every action or decision."

"Don't get your panties in a wad, Captain. Sit down!"

Jason did as he was told and realized all eyes were on him.

"Can anyone tell me what the point is to this inquiry?" Admiral Dixon asked no one in particular.

The voice came from the far end of the table. Jason had avoided looking at her up until then. "That no one person, not even the captain, was fully responsible for what transpired in that space repository."

"Thank you, Dira ... that's exactly right. Should your captain have made better decisions? I suspect so. But he did the best he could with the information provided him. I'd be hard pressed to find a single one of you on the bridge yesterday who didn't screw the pooch in some way or another. Own it and learn from it. And one more thing ... next time, don't be so ready to point fingers. Now, I need the room ... everyone return to your respective stations."

Jason felt Dira pat his arm as she moved past him and out the door. Jason waited for the last of his crew to leave before speaking. "That wasn't necessary, Admiral. I didn't need defending … in the end, what happened was my own damn fault."

"You're damn right it was!" Dixon, now seated next to Jason, looked as angry as he'd ever seen him. "Let me be perfectly clear here … Star Watch is a pilot program. Do you have any idea how many in the Alliance want to pull that ship away from you for their own directives?"

"I imagine quite a few."

"Yeah … quite a few … and then what do you do? You bring her back safe? NO! You had to be towed back to Jefferson Station … the *Minian* all beat to shit. I've been in non-stop meetings with fleet admirals, Alliance dignitaries, even the president, asking how you were so easily caught with your pants down around your ankles."

What the admiral said was true—Jason had no excuse. His assumption that the *Minian* was undefeatable, mixed with a blind desire to take down Captain Oz, was inexcusably short-sighted. He'd take whatever punishment the admiral threw at him—but he didn't want to lose command of the *Minian*. Until then, he hadn't realized how much he wanted to keep command of her. The admiral spoke up again: "Where is Ricket, Jason? You're going to need him to get this vessel back in fighting form."

It took a moment for Jason to jump tracks. "Ricket … he's … we don't know where he is. He was on a day-mission to the Mansan Core system, assisting with Eriok's planetary defenses."

"Did he make it there, has he reported in?"

"Yes … Ricket and his team made it to Port City, and began work on the planet's surface."

"His team?"

"Captain Leon Pike and Hanna delivered Ricket there in Pike's small trader ship, the *SpaceRunner*. But we've heard nothing from them in over twenty-two hours. I need a ship, sir. We need to find Ricket and the others."

Admiral Dixon stared flat-faced at Jason. "You want another ship?"

Jason didn't answer. He knew the question was rhetorical and, at that point, saying less was probably better than saying too much.

"I don't think it's a good idea to separate you from your crew at this time. You have some issues to work out. So what you need is an off-duty ship without a crew. How many of those do you think we have lying around?"

Jason was well aware there were quite a few. The long war with the Craing had finally ended and thousands of warships were being mothballed. Jason knew enough not to say anything.

"Take your father's ship. It's not scheduled for redeployment for another week. The crew is on leave. It is, actually ... just by chance ... stationed here at Jefferson Station. But listen to me, Jason: The vessel already has a crew ... and the assigned captain fully expects to board a functional, still in one piece, spaceship. Don't ruin another perfectly fine ship."

His offer surprised Jason. Next to the *Minian*, the *Assailant* was the most powerful warship in the Alliance fleet. She also possessed an advantage that no other Allied vessel did. She had cloaking capability—was able to go invisible visually so even the most advanced sensors couldn't detect her.

"I don't expect to need her for more than a day ... two, at the most. Rest assured, Admiral, she'll be as good as new when we bring her back."

Admiral Dixon let out a breath and nodded, although his expression didn't convey confidence in what he was hearing. "Leave the Caldurian behind ... Granger ... he can direct repairs on the *Minian* while you're gone."

"Thank you, Admiral."

"Go ahead and take a day, maybe two, to locate the *Space-Runner* and to find Ricket. But take the rest of the week completing your previous directive. I want Captain Mar Oswaldo in custody ... or eliminated, if absolutely necessary."

"Yes, sir."

"Until you do, Star Watch's effectiveness will come into question. I can't have that."

That was music to Jason's ears ... he needed a second opportunity to grab Oz. He'd been duped once ... that wasn't going to happen again.

The admiral continued, "One more thing ... I'm well aware of your actual rank, Jason. There comes a time when we need to come to terms with our full responsibilities. Admirals don't command warships, Jason ... they command fleets."

Jason let that sink in for a second before answering, "With all due respect, Admiral, the day I'm required to ride a desk is the exact same day I retire from Star Watch, and from the Allied fleet command."

Chapter 4

```
Sol System, Jefferson Station
The Assailant, Captain's Ready Room
Office
```

It took the rest of the afternoon for the crew and supplies to be loaded onto the *Assailant*. They'd be leaving Jefferson Station first thing in the morning, at 06:00 sharp. That would give him five hours of sleep. Sitting in the dark, at the small desk in the captain's office, there was one more thing Jason wanted to do before hitting his bunk. He waited for the connection to be made. The display suddenly came alive and his father's face filled the screen. With no less than three days' silver stubble, plus several black grease streaks on his one cheek, Jason was fairly certain what chore his father had just been pulled away from—he'd been under the hood of his partially restored 1949 Ford F-pickup.

"Son?"

"What time is it there, Dad?"

"How the hell should I know? These days I get up when the sun comes up. What's wrong … you okay?"

The admiral seemed to be adjusting to retirement at the family scrapyard in San Bernardino, California, as well as could be expected. Perry Reynolds, now in his mid-sixties, was captured two months earlier and badly tortured. The degree to which he had suffered wasn't completely known … his father hadn't volunteered to discuss it. But that arduous time spent with Lord Vikor Shakrim stole something from the Allied Fleet Commander. He wasn't the same … he'd lost his edge. He'd taken the suggestion to retire in stride, offering up no objections. That alone was out of character for his father and demonstrated how affected he was by his ordeal with the vicious Sahhrain leader.

"I'm fine … just wanted to check in. How's the '49?"

"Waiting on parts … in the meantime, I'm working on a Studebaker Commander convertible."

Jason thought about that. He knew every inch of their three-football-field-sized scrapyard property. "We don't have a Commander in the yard."

That remark evoked a smile from his father. "We do now. One was dropped off two weeks ago."

"You bought it?"

"What if I did?" his father replied, somewhat indignant. He turned his back to the laptop camera and Jason could see him refilling his coffee cup in the kitchen.

The truth was, Jason and his father would never have to pinch pennies—both were awarded multi-millions of dollars for their contributions during the Craing war.

His father continued, "The previous owner, a guy older than me living in Reseda, was recently killed by a horde of peovils. His wife let me know it was available for the right price."

"I'm looking forward to seeing it. What color is it?"

Again the smile. "Canary yellow … she's a sweet automobile, in fine shape. Doesn't run for shit … but I'll get her going."

"I'm sure you will, Dad."

His father took a sip of the hot coffee and stared back at

Jason, assessing him. "Out with it."

"I'm fine. Can't a son check in with his old man once in a while?"

"Take some time off … you can help me with the Commander."

Jason nodded. "I will … soon. You look good, Dad. It's good to see you again."

"Stay in touch." The connection was gone but Jason continued to stare at the screen. Two arms slid around his shoulders and chest from behind. Dira brought her lips down to his neck and gently kissed him. She turned him in his chair and slid into his lap—her arms encircling his neck. Now facing him, she kissed him on the mouth.

"When did you sneak in here?" he asked.

"I checked with the AI to see if Boomer was asleep … figured you could use a little TLC tonight."

She kissed him again and he felt the tip of her tongue begin probing and exploring his mouth. He felt his passion for her grow where she straddled him. He slid his hands down her back, realizing she was completely naked. He cupped her two firm bottom cheeks and, in one fluid motion, lifted her up and stood. Her legs wrapped around his waist.

"Where do you think you're taking me?" she whispered—her lips lightly brushing his ear.

"I'm taking you to my bed, woman."

"Oh … but I'm not a woman … I'm not even human … so what you're doing is very, very dirty."

Jason kissed her, harder now, and carried her down the narrow hallway and into his quarters. He brought her down to the bed and released her. The overhead lights were dimmed to the point he could just make out the contours of her slender form, lying on the bed beneath him. Her light violet skin, her breathtaking beauty, gripped his heart. He watched as her hands came up and covered her breasts—as if timid or embarrassed by her own nakedness. He knew she wasn't, not in the least. But she knew how to tease … how to draw him in. Jason undressed, never letting his eyes veer from hers. Then, slowly, he lowered himself onto her. She guided him into her—into that special place no human woman possessed. Her fingers tugged at the back of his head, grabbing two fistfuls of hair. As their lovemaking grew in intensity, her grip tightened—pulling his head back to the point he wanted to scream out. Her own escalating moans grew in intensity, forcing her to free one hand to cover her mouth. Soon, together, the muscles in their arms … their legs … their abdomens, tightened … went rigid … and they drew each other in, desperately, closer and closer, until there was no space between them … until they were one.

★ ★ ★

Jason entered the *Assailant's* bridge and was reminded how small it was compared to the *Minian*. The bridge crew was already there, and going through their pre-departure routines. He caught Orion's eye: "We good, Gunny?"

"We're good, Cap … going to find Ricket?"

"Damn right … first thing on the agenda."

"Let me guess what the second thing is …" a voice said from behind them. Billy Hernandez stood at the back of the bridge and shrugged. "Well, she's not what we're used to, but the ship has its plusses … I guess."

"Yeah? Name one," Orion said.

"She's operational … whereas our other ship seems to have … well … a few mechanical problems."

Jason took his seat midway inside the small bridge. Like the bridge itself, even the chair seemed cramped. He wondered how his father'd managed to sit there, with his substantially-larger derriere.

There was a large, curved step down in front of the command chair that ran the width of the bridge, where Billy chose to sit, holding a steaming cup of coffee.

Jason waited for the question he knew was coming. Billy was Jason's closest friend and together they'd fought side by side—first on Earth, as Navy SEALs; then through the Craing wars in space, in multiple alien worlds. He was the officer-in-charge of their onboard military contingent—now commonly referred to as Billy's Sharks.

"You do know I had to leave two-thirds of my people on-station, don't you, Cap?"

"We're all making sacrifices, Billy," Jason said, looking around the bridge.

Billy lowered his voice, "What the hell happened yesterday? You losing your edge? Perhaps married life's made you soft?"

"I'm not married yet … and this isn't an appropriate conversation for the bridge." Jason saw Orion, faced away from them, give a subtle nod.

Billy scooted closer, then crouched down right next to the command chair. "It's not like Ricket to simply disappear like that. We'd all be hard-pressed to find anyone more conscientious than that little alien. Something's wrong, and I don't like what I'm … well, what I'm thinking."

Jason had nothing to add to Billy's remark. He'd not been able to think of anything else all morning. He was responsible for the three individuals on that mission, and Ricket was as close a friend to him as Billy. If something catastrophic had happened to him it would be a tremendous loss. Although he didn't know Leon Pike or Hanna very well, he'd come to respect them both. Neither were bound to the *Minian*, but both had opted, at least for now, to stay and lend their support.

They'd become an invaluable resource running reconnaissance into civilian territory. Leon's ship, the *SpaceRunner*, was an impressive, fast, vessel.

"Where are we starting the search?" Billy asked.

"At the last place we heard from them … Mansan Core system … a nondescript little planet called Eriok."

Billy stood up to leave.

"Hey, how large a contingent of Sharks do you have, Billy?"

"Around five hundred—plus or minus a few. Oh, and about thirty-five Tahli warriors, in training."

Jason lowered his forehead into the palm of his hand. "Sorry about that, Boomer can be—"

"It's not her … trust me on that. What she can accomplish with that shield-thing of hers is nothing short of amazing. No … the men requested that she train them. It's she who set the limit at a thirty-five person class size. All my guys want the training."

Jason knew Boomer was continuing with her Kahill Callan training. She'd kept in contact with several Blues within the Dacci system, and with one Kahill Callan master, in particular. How she continued with her own training, virtually, Jason wasn't quite sure.

Billy left the bridge.

"Captain, the *Assailant* is good to go," McNeil said, from the forward, port side of the bridge.

"Seaman Gordon, request clearance to pull off."

"Aye, Captain."

While Jason waited for station clearance, he opened his virtual notebook and ran through his crew roster, levels of supplies, weaponry status and ammunition stocks, and, specifically, all red flagged items. Even with the *Minian*, there were always issues … problem areas. Some were fixable, such as broken light fixtures or plumbing problems; others, inherent in the design of the ship, required finding new ways to cope with each issue. Jason's eyes locked on one such red lined item: the cloaking system on the *Assailant* had a tendency to trigger itself off, arbitrarily causing the ship to suddenly become visible. Jason remembered his father complaining about that in the past and what a nuisance it was. Jason used his internal NanoCom to hail Bristol.

"Yeah?"

Jason let out an exasperated breath. The young junior science officer had maintained a wiseass attitude for as long as he'd known him. "I want you up on the bridge," Jason said. "You'll be filling in for both Ricket and Granger on this ride."

"Um … give me a few minutes. Still haven't taken care of the three *S*s."

Jason rolled his eyes and cut the connection. Bristol was referring to Shit, Shower and Shave; he'd undoubtedly caught Bristol still lounging in his bunk.

"We've been granted clearance to pull away, Captain," Seaman Gordon said.

"Helm … take us away from Jefferson Station."

"Aye, Captain."

Ten minutes later, Bristol entered the bridge. He walked to the station next to Orion and made a face. She looked over at him and pointed to another station, on the opposite side of the bridge. "Whoever configured this layout was an idiot," he muttered aloud to himself. He passed in front of Jason without acknowledging him, taking a seat by himself at the open station.

"Bristol, I want you to take a look at the ship's problem with the cloaking system."

He nodded his head. "It's probably not a problem here on the bridge."

"I didn't mean right this second … when you can, though."

"No problem, Captain."

His reply was about as congenial and respectful as Bristol ever got. Jason and Orion exchanged a surprised look between them.

McNeil said, "Captain, our request for an interchange wormhole has been granted. It's forming now, forty-six thousand miles ahead, before our bow. The outpoint will bring us within five hundred thousand miles of Eriok, sir."

Jason saw the multi-colored spatial aberration already taking form on the forward bridge screen. "Take us in, Helm ... true and steady."

Chapter 5

Open Space, Nearing Arkwane
Parcical, Ricket's Quarters

Leon moved to the front of his confinement cell, right up against the bulkhead. He could feel the energy field emanating inches from his face. "Hanna? You there?"

There was no reply. Earlier, the Caldurian commander had done something—making it impossible to verbally communicate. He'd obviously instigated some kind of *mute* function. But Leon thought that had been turned off when he was later able to converse with another Caldurian, an underling, who'd asked him if he was hungry.

"I'm here," came her soft voice. She, too, must be right up against the bulkhead.

"I'm sorry I got you into this. I'm going to get us out of here … I promise."

She didn't answer. The truth was, he didn't know Hanna all that well, even after two months. What started off as a whirlwind romance in their first few weeks together had suddenly quelled ... had changed to a strictly business relationship. He'd been aware she had been wrestling with something, even conflicted, but she didn't want to talk about it. And perhaps that was for the best. After all, he wasn't a damn shrink. If she wanted to discuss some personal issue, she could very well make some effort to do so.

They did work well together and she was far more competent than most men he'd partnered with, in some business ventures, over the last few years. He tried to think of the best word to describe her ... was it *cunning*? Perhaps that was too harsh. No, cunning actually did fit her cool and detached demeanor. He'd witnessed her ability to manipulate others, mostly males, with a feigned vulnerability when dealing with arrogant, domineering types—such as dignitaries or officials. But she could just as easily bring her sexuality into play. Leon had also witnessed her flirty side—watched as unsuspecting potential adversaries were drawn into her web, becoming putty in her hands. Had he too been manipulated? Had she become bored with him once the conquest was made? Or, perhaps it was the complete opposite ... his aloof go-with-the-flow attitude had driven more than a few women to distraction. He'd been told more than once he wasn't relationship material ... whatever that meant.

"I'm sorry," she said. Her voice was so faint he wondered if he'd heard her correctly.

He brought his head closer to the bulkhead.

"I've had some issues to contend with ... internal stuff ... are you there?" she asked.

"I'm here." Now she wanted to talk. He could see how their separate confinement cells made it easier for her. The wall ... the isolation. "Stalls?"

"Yeah ... that and other things. My brother getting killed

37

started it all. Forced me to take a different look at my life. Who I was … where I was going."

"You can go wherever you want, Hanna, that's the good news. If you want, I'll take you … or you can set off on your own. It's nice having choices."

Leon waited for her to answer, then wondered if she'd already stepped away.

"Sorry about your ship," she said. "I know how you loved her … the *SpaceRunner*."

"Yeah, well that bastard out there owes me a new ship. I figure this one will do just fine."

He heard her laugh on the other side of the wall.

"Then hurry up and get us out of here," she said.

★ ★ ★

Surprisingly, Ricket was given free rein to roam the Caldurian vessel at will. He wondered, at first, if he should take offense at that. Was he so inconsequential a threat, compared to Hanna and Leon, that the Caldurians felt there was no need to incarcerate him? But he did determine that wasn't it at all: They needed him for something and they needed him to do it willingly.

This vessel, Ricket learned, was called the *Parcical* and she was actually larger than he'd first estimated, about the size *The Lilly* had been. It had five primary decks and several sub-decks. He currently sat on Deck 4, toward the ship's stern, where the confinement cells were located—as well as a small laboratory and the ship's Medical facility, including four advanced MediPods—and another compartment, which Ricket hadn't yet figured out. The ship was roughly shaped like an egg and there was much to catch the eye since almost everything solid was actually virtual … simulated matter. That gave some

38

things—like bulkheads, consoles, and some of the deck plating—a soft radiating glow. The effect was almost ethereal and Ricket found it quite soothing.

The craft would easily hold several hundred, but there was but a mere skeleton crew presently manning the ship … a number he estimated to being fifteen total Caldurian crewmembers—although there were several dozen security forces on board. Hobel, their commander, held the officer's title of *Omni*, equivalent to the rank of Captain and sometimes Admiral on Earth.

At present, both Leon and Hanna were asleep in their respective cells. Ricket had seen the hostility in their eyes, figuring—since he was free to come and go as he pleased—that he had probably changed allegiance, maybe in order to save his own hide. *That's fine, let them think that*, Ricket thought. Until he had things figured out, he needed the freedom to investigate, and he needed access to Hobel … the one with all the answers.

A noise behind him had Ricket look back. He recognized Norwell, his own equivalent of a science, or technical, officer on board the *Parcical*. He was a pleasant enough Caldurian, but a bit too chatty for Ricket's liking.

Norwell stopped in the corridor and held out an open palm. "Would you come with me, Ricket?"

"What is it you require, Norwell?"

"Nothing to be afraid of; this way, to my workshop." He was old—perhaps one hundred and ten or twenty, which even for a Caldurian was pretty old. He was stooped and shuffled his feet as he walked. Ricket caught up to him just as he meandered into a nearby DeckPort. He knew the old Caldurian's workshop was on Deck 2 and he emerged onto that deck, nearly walking into the ever slow-moving Norwell.

Ricket hadn't entered the workshop before for it was one

of the few off-limits compartments. Seeing it now, Ricket was reminded of his own workshop on an upper deck of the *Minian*. Here, too, countertops were strewn with an assortment of devices and contraptions of varying sizes. Ricket was like a child in a candy store. It was almost too much to take in; he turned and saw something familiar lying across the furthest worktable—Trommy5.

"You have the mecher here," Ricket said.

Norwell joined Ricket at the robot's side. A cavity at the top of its head exposed a myriad of circuitry inside.

"Interesting … you've removed its primary personality tab," Ricket said.

"Terrible design. These bots are unstable … surprised they can stay up on their feet at all."

Norwell shuffled over to the middle of three large, wall-mounted devices. Ricket knew they were smaller versions of the phase synthesizer device located on the *Minian*. Norwell waved a hand in front of the device and the three separate-looking devices merged into a single larger version. A virtual door opened, exposing a small compartment about the size of a standard home oven. Inside it sat something metallic and oblong. Norwell reached forward but suddenly stopped himself.

"Would you … please?"

Ricket stepped in close and reached in to retrieve the item for Norwell. Once he had it firmly in both hands, he hefted it out and stood there. "Where do you …"

"Oh … sorry, Ricket. Here, place it right here, next to the mecher."

Ricket did as asked and set the heavy item onto the workbench. Not having a flat side, it wobbled around a bit. "Why did you completely reproduce a new head?"

Norwell tilted his own head as he looked down at his

handiwork. It was an identical mecher head.

"Easier to start from scratch than repair or modify inferior designs." Norwell used a tool on the workbench to pop the top of the newly manufactured head. He found a tiny thumbnail-sized card, or tab, on a raised shelf and placed it into the circuitry of the newly created head. He then brought his attention over to the original mecher, and, using another tool, loosened a restraining clamp on its neck area and lifted the head away, then placed it down onto the workbench.

"Please hand me the new head, Ricket."

Ricket again did as asked and watched as the old scientist configured the new head onto the mecher body with surprising dexterity.

Norwell reached across to the far side of the metal body and depressed a somewhat hidden button there. The mecher's eyes came *alive*, turning yellow. Ricket watched as the robot went through its internal initialization routines, then processed its current environment. After running through a quick threat assessment, it was ready to be commanded.

"Sit up, Trommy5," Norwell commanded.

The mecher used its arms to sit up, while letting its legs swing down.

"I feel different," Trommy5 said.

"I should think so. Much of your processing and micro-interface has been upgraded. You're smarter and more nimble. Why don't you hop down from there and walk around for us?"

Trommy5 did as told, landing with a heavy thump onto the deck, with neither a teeter nor a wobble. The robot then proceeded to move about the workshop with an ease and fluidity uncommon for even the most sophisticated bots. "I feel different!"

Norwell and Ricket exchanged glances. "Perhaps saving the personality tab was an error in judgment," the Caldurian scientist said with a slight smile.

"Ricket … can you tell me where Captain Pike and Miss Hanna are located? I would like to show them my new capabilities."

Norwell interjected, "They are resting, Trommy5. They are not to be disturbed. You are not to leave this workshop unless given permission by either me or Omni Hobel."

It was then Ricket realized Trommy5 had just been configured with Caldurian NanoCom tech. Ricket, peeking into the mechanical being's neural network, checked to see if its admin-level programming had been secured. It hadn't been … everything was still in an unlocked mode. He glanced over to Norwell, who was disposing of the older mecher head into what Ricket surmised was an access panel that led to an incinerator.

"What will you do with it?" Ricket said.

"The bot head?"

"Yes."

"Probably phase-shift it into the MicroVault."

Ricket was familiar with the technology. Virtually anything could be phase-shifted into one of the vaults, nearly microscopic in size, and stored in there indefinitely. On a vessel as small as this one, adequate storage space was at a premium. By placing items—some as large as the ship herself—into the onboard MicroVault, they could be accessed as needed or required without taking up any space.

"Is that what you'll do to me and Captain Pike and Miss Hanna?"

The question seemed to discombobulate the old science officer. While he continued putting his tools away, and moving things from one location on the workbench to another, Ricket could hear him muttering to himself. Finally, he said, "I would not do that. I have spent sixty-five of your years searching for you. You, Ricket … are my inspiration."

Ricket didn't know how to respond to that—how to address such a bizarre comment. So he didn't try. "And Leon and Hanna?" But Ricket had already figured that much out for himself; they were being held captive as insurance. Insurance that Ricket would do as he was asked. What he hadn't known, up until that moment, was that it was Norwell who had incited the kidnapping. The whole setup was his doing. But why?

"They need to be released at once, Norwell."

"That is not possible. They will eventually be placed into stasis and stored in the MicroVault."

"No. I will not help you this way … I will self-destruct … I will overload my neural interface. A simple process."

That got Norwell's complete attention. "You would not do that … I don't believe you."

Ricket remained expressionless. "Why don't you tell me what you need from me? Why you have gone to so much trouble."

"I thought that was explained to you." Norwell faced Ricket and suddenly he looked all his years. "As advanced as Caldurian technology has become, there is one technology that has eluded us. Without the ability to fully understand and master that technology … our Caldurian way of life is in jeopardy."

Ricket did his best to digest Norwell's comments, then it hit him—the Zip Farms. The *Minian,* and most other Caldurian vessels, used them as a means to travel into the multiverse. This technology was developed on Alurian, a planet in the Corian Nez constellation system, one hundred and thirty light-years from Earth. Caldurians had only discovered the technology eighty-nine years earlier. A vessel the size of the *Minian* required a number of Zip accelerators—the locomotive-sized pieces of equipment which made up a Zip Farm.

"I'm confused," Ricket said. "The Caldurians have countless vessels, moving in and out of the multiverse … surely, you have mastered a way to reproduce this technology. How else—"

"Originally, we came into possession of twelve Alurian ships of varying sizes. And, like you said, we simply cloned the ships' Zip accelerators … creating varying-sized Zip Farms as needed."

"So what's the problem now? Are they no longer working correctly?"

"They work perfectly. That is not the issue. It's the interface to the multiverse itself. It has been altered … whether by natural, or some other means, we are unsure. What we do know is that we no longer have the proper *key* to unlock the passageway into the multiverse realms …"

"So you're saying all Caldurian vessels are marooned within their current realms? Including this one?"

"That is correct."

"Are you the only one … trapped here?"

"Oh, no … there was enough time for a small fleet of Caldurian ships to transport into this realm … our home realm. We are in transit to rendezvous with them, as we speak."

Ricket was getting a bad feeling. "What is the fleet doing here … what is their objective?"

"I believe the answer lies within a Caldurian ship … one with one of the original Alurian Zip Farms. Obtaining this ship will be a requirement before we can begin work. The fleet will commandeer that ship—and by force, if necessary."

Ricket connected the dots. "The *Minian*."

Chapter 6

Mansan Core System
The *Assailant,* Gymnasium

B oomer, stretched out on her back with her arms over her head, stared up at the ceiling. She heard a string of swear words coming from her left.

"I had this working perfectly fine back on the *Minian* … why didn't you just leave it alone?"

Boomer turned her head and saw Bristol, working across from her in the gym compartment, crouched down next to the portable hologram projector-*thingy*. She tried to remember what he'd called it.

"What's that thing called again?" she asked.

"It's just a projector," he answered irritably.

She made a face at him. Boomer was sure he'd called it something else, a more complicated-sounding name. "Are you almost done?"

Bristol sat cross-legged on the mat, an open toolbox at his side. The projector-*thingy* lay in several pieces on the mat and she wondered if he'd be able to put it all back together again. She was already late for her meeting, and said, "It's not very sturdy. Shouldn't you be able to carry the thing from one place to another without it breaking apart?"

"It's delicate. It needs to be handled gently … you must have banged it on something."

Actually, she had. She'd bashed it entering a DeckPort on the *Minian*. It was just a glancing blow, but she thought she'd heard something come loose. "I'll be more careful from now on."

Bristol fitted the final piece onto the projector and secured it with two screws. He flipped a switch—instantly, a bright blue, glowing, quasi-transparent sphere encircled the projector, as well as Bristol. The holographic image was distorted by Bristol's disruptive presence.

Boomer jumped to her feet and clapped her hands. "You did it! I love you, Bristol!"

She saw movement in the hologram. "Ah, can you step outside of the sphere, Bristol?"

"You mind if I get my toolbox first?" he snarled, making sure he slammed its lid shut as loudly as humanly possible. He hefted it up and stepped away from the hologram. Both Bristol and Boomer observed the bearded man, now standing patiently before them. He wore a tan *Shadick*—the simple loose-fitting nomad's attire a Tahli warrior master wore. A single blue circle could be seen on both his sleeves, indicating he was a Master of the First Degree: a feat taking twenty years, or more, to accomplish. There were three levels a Tahli warrior master could aspire to in the art of Kahill Callan: Master of the First Degree … Master of the Second Degree … and Master of the Third Degree. He bowed toward Boomer and nodded his head in the direction of Bristol. Bristol returned a quick wave of his hand and left without another word.

Boomer bowed, then straightened. "May I approach, Master Sahhselies?"

He smiled, bringing up his enhancement shield, and assumed the Kahill Callan defensive stance. "You will attack first, Boomer … remember what you learned last time. Do not make the same fatal mistake."

She sprang up, and forward—the shield strapped to her left forearm angled toward her opponent. She had progressed to the point she could utilize the shield to do multiple things at once. Its curved three edges emanated their own unique distortion waves, which she used to help propel herself higher into the air; the front, or face, of the shield initiated the powerful energy weapon that looked similar to a bright plasma beam, but actually were highly concentrated distortion waves, which the one wielding the shield could influence through mental kinetic manipulation. The more skilled the wielder of the shield, the more powerful, and accurate, were the weapon's uses.

Boomer was a natural with the shield. Over the last few months, she'd advanced in her training to a point she now found frustrating. She had little problem defeating any of the Kahill Callan masters presented to her by Prince Aahil Aqeel. He had been nearly killed in a spectacular battle recently, against Lord Vikor Shakrim. Eventually, Shakrim was bested, but Prince Aqeel's injuries were serious enough to require him months of convalescence. Up until now, Boomer had yet to be trained by a more skilled opponent than Master Aqeel.

Master Sahhselies' holographic form moved swiftly within the confined space. Like Boomer, he too was using a practice enhancement shield. He dodged her advance and struck his shield forward in three quick thrusts. Boomer easily blocked the incoming waves, spun around, and delivered a back-spinning heel-kick high enough to cross through the master's chin. A blow that would have put him onto his back had her kick not been virtual and holographic. He countered quickly with his own forward kick, followed by two more kicks—one low, toward her exposed front knee, then one high up, close to her right ear. She blocked both with her shield—seeing the blows coming—and already formulated a reprisal before he'd completed his maneuvers. *Is that the best you can do?* Boomer thought impatiently.

In a surprise move, he suddenly cartwheeled backwards, sweeping distortion waves down at her from an angle. Boomer had anticipated Sahhselies to continue moving forward and was, instead, struck across the abdomen by holographic distortion waves. In a real fight, she would be dead. *Crap! I didn't even partially block his attack.*

Boomer flexed her fists into tight balls and clenched her jaws. "I can't believe I fell for that!" She bowed toward the Kahill Callan master, giving him due respect and appreciation. She hated, yet loved, being bested: Hated it, because she was highly competitive; loved it, because she'd learned something new. He would never be able to pull that particular move on her again. In fact, she'd use his fancy move on her own students, later that day.

Master Sahhselies bowed, brought his hands together as if in prayer, and quickly walked away.

"Wait … Master Sahhselies … we've only just started!" Boomer briefly wondered if she'd said or done something to offend the Kahill Callan master. She stomped her foot down hard on the soft mat beneath her.

She saw movement off to her right. It was Dewdrop, her droid, hovering and coming closer to her.

"I told you to wait in the corridor. You're distracting, when you hover around me."

"Boomer?"

She turned to see Prince Aahil Aqeel's holographic representation, standing three paces in front of her. He looked thin and a mere shell of the warrior he'd been before his fight with Shakrim. But he was alive and seemed to be recovering. He was wearing a light gray *Shadick*, with two blue circles on its sleeves. Boomer's affection for her master became evident by her ear-to-ear smile. "Master! I'm so happy to see you … you're walking … are you here to continue my training?"

That brought a smile and chuckle from Aqeel. "No, I am not quite ready for that. I've come to you for a different reason, Boomer." His expression turned serious, and his stare was somewhat disconcerting.

"What … what is it? Are you dying?"

"No, Boomer … I'm not dying … please just stop talking long enough for *me* to talk."

She nodded, heeding his words.

"I'm very proud of you, Boomer. I want you to know that. Although young in chronological terms, you are old in spirit—way beyond any of us. What you have accomplished in your short lifetime is staggering. The truth is, your training to become a Tahli warrior began long before I met you … I suspect you have always been a warrior at heart. You cannot be anything but that, for that is who you are."

Boomer felt her cheeks flush and burn with embarrassment. She didn't know how to respond to what he was saying. She didn't feel she'd done anything all that spectacular. She was, after all, her father and mother's daughter—she'd seen bravery from both, more times than she could count. How else was she supposed to act?

He added, "I look forward to continuing your training. You have much to learn: finesse and subtlety, to name only a few attributes. But you are no longer a novice … you must be recognized for the accomplishments and strides you have exemplified."

Boomer's eyes moved, first left then right. People were

streaming into the small gymnasium from both sides—everyone staying close to the bulkheads, and off the mat. Again, she felt heat flush her cheeks. *They're here for me ... to honor me!* She now recognized what was happening. Dewdrop, close by her side, was holding something in its short outstretched arms. Beyond her, she could see her father and Dira, leaning against the bulkhead; and Billy and Orion ... Bristol ... just about the whole crew—were all smiling at her.

Aqeel said, "Boomer, it is with great honor I present this simple Tahli warrior *Shadick* to you."

Boomer tasted salt from sudden tears even before she realized she had started to cry. She held her arms out to accept the *Shadick* from Dewdrop, and only then noticed there was a simple blue circle on one of the exposed sleeves. Her jaw dropped open, though no words escaped her lips. Today was her birthday ... she'd mistakenly surmised they'd all convened here, Prince Aqeel as well, to wish her a happy one. But this was far more important an occasion than that.

"As of this moment," Prince Aqeel continued, "you are now a Kahill Callan Master of the First Degree. And perhaps even more importantly, the Council of One has bestowed upon you a most precious, and special, honor ... you will be recognized by both Blues and Sahhrain alike as a true Tahli warrior. Now, Boomer ... Tahli warriors are given new names ... a name that exemplifies true dignity and heroism. I asked your father, Captain Reynolds, to assist me in that regard. He suggested Lion Heart ... which, translated into Dacci, is Tahhrim Dol. You, Boomer, are now called *Master Tahhrim Dol.* You honor me, all of us, with your true lion heart. Thank you."

Boomer clutched the light garment close to her chest and, biting down on her lip, hoped the pain would stop her tears. She tried to think of something an eleven-year-old Kahill Callan master, a Tahli warrior, would say: "Well, did someone bake me a cake?"

As the holographic image of Prince Aqeel faded away, others around her moved forward. Her dad was the first to wrap his arms around her. He kissed the top of her head and said, "I'm so proud of you, little one." He pulled away and looked down at her with a wide smile.

"I wish Mom was here ... I really miss her."

"I know you do ... she'll get to see this on vid-feed. You can call her tonight."

Dira, now at her side, was kneeling down next to her. "I want to give you this," she said, holding a small necklace out for Boomer to see. Hanging at the end of a thin gold chain was a gold lion.

"It's attacking ... see how it's leaping ... its claws are out!" Boomer said, not taking her eyes from the only piece of jewelry she'd ever been interested in. "I'll never take it off ... thank you, Dira. I love it."

"There's a lot more presents waiting for you in the mess ... and cake, too," her father said.

Boomer smiled and took in a big breath. She felt overwhelmed ... and something else. What was it? She looked up at her father, suddenly needing to tell him something. She pulled at his sleeve. "Dad!"

"What is it, Boomer?"

"It's Ricket ... he's in trouble. He's in a lot of trouble."

Chapter 7

```
Mansan Core System
Planet Eriok; Port City
```

Grimes brought the shuttle lower, circling high above Port City.

"Nothing on sensors, Captain," she said.

Jason continued to take in the landscape below just the same. "Put us down at the *SpaceRunner*'s last known coordinates, Lieutenant."

"Yes, sir."

Part of Jason knew time was of the extreme essence ... that mere moments counted. Even before he'd seen fear sprout suddenly into Boomer's eyes, he, too, had felt some strange unease: like someone frantically knocking at a door ... but you can't see or hear them ... you don't even know where the door is.

Grimes put the *Perilous* down in an open field. Out the forward observation window Jason spotted the small encampment.

Jason stood. "Stay with the ship ... this shouldn't take long." He made his way into the shuttle's cabin and motioned for the others to get up and get moving. Jason had handpicked this team. Not too large a contingent, but one that would leave little doubt they meant business.

Jason was the first to head down the rear gangway. Billy Hernandez soon followed, then Sergeant Jackson, one of the biggest, meanest-looking men Jason had ever met. The three men, holding on to multi-gun rifles, waited for the last member of their small team. Traveler, the seven-foot-tall—one-thousand-plus-pound rhino-warrior, descended the ramp, his heavy hammer clenched firmly in one hand.

News of Ricket's disappearance had a profound effect on the crew. Jason had discovered over the last twenty-four hours that Ricket had affected many lives, in many different ways. For Jason, Ricket was as close as his own brother ... closer, actually. But Jason was surprised by Traveler's reaction when he heard Ricket was missing. Rhino-warriors, Jason knew from years of interacting with them, don't show emotion in the same manner humans do. Heartfelt pain often exhibited itself in outbursts of anger ... even violence. Jason wasn't present at the rhino encampment, within HAB 170, on that particular occasion, but apparently one less domed habitat was evident. So affected by the news about Ricket, Traveler pummeled the large dome residence into dust with his heavy hammer.

The four headed off, toward what Grimes described as an access tunnel into a subterranean pumping station. The outer blue tarp flapped in the early morning wind. Five chairs—one turned onto its side—and several large containers sat at the perimeter of the site, but it was five large lockers which captured Jason's attention. They were Ricket's ... he'd seen them in his workshop.

"Those lockers look like—"

Jason cut Billy off: "Yeah, they're Ricket's. He spent last week preparing all this equipment for a Port City engineer."

What was his name? "For Silgin Burak."

"We must find this Silgin Burak," Traveler said, looking toward the far horizon.

Jason, Jackson, and Billy joined Traveler's side.

"This is one ugly planet," Billy said.

Jason couldn't argue with that. Gray skies and a dull, colorless landscape surrounded them.

"And flat," Jackson added, "like Kansas."

Jason was being hailed. "Go for Captain. What do you have, Lieutenant?"

"Captain, there's a small settlement to the east. Sensor readings tell me there are twenty-seven locals there … I think it's some kind of barracks. Probably all sleeping since their life-icons are lined up in neat little rows."

"Send me the coordinates; we'll check it out." Jason triggered the SuitPac device on his belt and, within two seconds, he was completely encased head to toe in an advanced, Caldurian-tech, battle suit. The others initiated their own suits right after him. Jason, seeing the coordinates for the barracks on his HUD, selected the *group phase-shift* option and phase-shifted the four of them away as a unit.

In a brilliant white flash they appeared eighteen miles eastward, appearing on the outside of the fifteen-foot-tall fencing of vertical metal bars—which encircled the entirety of the compound.

"Eriok's version of quonset huts," Jackson said.

Jason was thinking the same thing. No less than ten cylindrical buildings made up the little compound on the other side of the fence. And there was security … of a sort.

"What the hell are those things?" Billy asked.

"Dogs?" Jackson said.

"Naaah. Too big … and look at the tails," Billy added.

Jason thought they looked more like small kangaroos—

kangaroos with fangs.

Three of the beasts, noticing their presence, were now standing at the fence. Jason gave Traveler a quick nod and the rhino-warrior ripped apart the fence's metal links as easily as if they were made of paper.

The pack of fanged kangaroo-*wannabes*' number had grown to near twelve.

"See ... they bark like dogs," Jackson said, still trying to make his point to Billy.

The animals were making a terrible racket and they had begun to attack. One by one they rushed forward, their heads low and teeth bared. Jason felt jaws repeatedly clench and release at his ankles as he crossed through the hole in the fence. Although their suits protected them, it was an annoying experience just the same. Traveler kicked one of the beasts, sending it ten feet into the air. They scurried away from Traveler and concentrated more on Jason, Billy and Jackson. Because of their somewhat, though remote, similarity to dogs on Earth, Jason couldn't bring himself to hurt them, and evidently, Billy and Jackson shared the same sentiment.

Traveler turned to Jason. "Start here?"

Jason looked for a doorway but couldn't see one nearby. "Sure, good a place as any."

Traveler used the business end of his heavy hammer to make an entrance into the first quonset hut's siding. The noise was loud enough to frighten off the animals and send them into hiding.

Traveler was the first to enter the building. Jason inwardly smiled—as far as first impressions would go, he couldn't imagine a more frightening sight than a seven-foot-tall, battle-suit-clad rhino-warrior. His four-hundred-pound hammer was icing on the cake.

Jason counted eight humanoid life signs on his HUD. As

they entered, the eight scurried from their cots in surprise, obviously used to the racket of the animals. All eight were dressed in the same white boxer-like shorts and Eriok's version of a wife-beater undershirt.

"Up against the wall ... all of you. Move for a weapon, or make any quick movement, you'll be stunned. It's a very unpleasant feeling ... one you don't want to experience," Billy said.

They did as instructed, raising their hands without being told.

They looked unkempt and grimy in their stained underclothes; Jason briefly wondered if they were an accurate cross-section of the people of Eriok. They stood side by side at the wall and nervously looked at their captors.

"We're looking for Silgin Burak," Jason said.

They quickly glanced between each other but held their tongues. Traveler raised his hammer several inches.

"Two buildings down ... Burak's two buildings down."

"Jackson, keep an eye on these fellas while we check out the other barracks."

"You got it, Cap."

Jason, Billy, and Traveler hurried out through the ragged opening in the siding and rushed toward the barracks, two buildings away. Halfway there, they came to an abrupt halt. Jason realized the pack of vicious kangaroo-dogs weren't the only security at this compound.

"Hired muscle?" Billy asked.

"Probably. Definitely not human," Jason replied.

There were four of them and Jason's earlier assumption that Traveler's appearance would be traumatic to all the locals might have been incorrect. This foursome was equally frightening, if not more so. The shortest one was ten feet tall—the tallest, and biggest, was another foot above that. Their legs were thick as tree trunks … sequoias … and their arms were long and sinewy. They had faces only a mother could love: Mouths without lips explained the constant streams of dripping saliva, and their yellowed, cracked teeth constantly moved inside their jutting jaws. The clincher was a single large eye, placed mid-forehead. The giant Cyclops had pinkish hide covered in …

Billy said aloud, "Their warts really complete the picture … don't you think?"

Traveler grunted. Clearly agitated, bursts of steamy snot puffed from his flaring nostrils.

Each monstrous-looking beast held a weapon. Jason's HUD indicated they were plasma-based rifles.

Behind the Cyclops a group of Eriok men had gathered.

"We're here to speak with Silgin Burak … there doesn't need to be any trouble here. We're looking for our shipmate. We're looking for Ricket. Just tell us where he is and we'll be on our way," Jason told them.

One of the locals—pudgy and partially bald—stepped forward. What hair he lacked on the top of his head was made up for by numerous black tufts of chest hair, billowing out from the top of his wife-beater undershirt, as well as from under his armpits. He smiled and looked confidently complacent. "I think you've found yourselves in a bit of trouble anyway." In a defiant gesture, he pointed his chin in the direction behind Jason.

Four more! For some reason, his HUD hadn't detected them. He'd seen it happen before; technology only did so much … then, one by one, life-icons of the now eight Cyclops showed on his HUD. Database updated.

"You Burak?"

He raised his furry brows. "Who's asking?"

"Captain Jason Reynolds … Star Watch. Answer the question."

"You found me. But I have nothing to tell you. Best you leave here and don't come back. From what I understand, those creatures eat their prey."

"Where's Ricket?"

"Nowhere you'll ever find him."

That was all Jason needed to hear. He'd already reconfigured his multi-gun to its highest, most-lethal, setting. He shot the tallest of the Cyclops in the face. He'd aimed for the eye, but was off by at least an inch to its right.

A blackened scorch mark did nothing to improve its looks, and it didn't kill it either. In an instant the air was filled with streaks of crisscrossing plasma fire. The Cyclops' weapons were, technologically, far inferior to their own ... but the Cyclops were an amazingly robust species. Their hides were like armor.

Traveler rushed for the big one; in three strides, hammer held high over his head, he attacked. The Cyclops took the brunt of the blow high up on its chest. There was a sickening sound, a thud mixed with the sound of cracking bones and tearing flesh. The hammer came away, leaving a three-inch-deep indentation.

The Cyclops staggered but stayed on its feet. It flipped its large rifle around and used it like a bat, swinging it widely toward Traveler's head, but missed by a mile. Traveler did something Jason had never seen him do before—the rhino's version of a head-butt. Traveler dove headfirst, horn first, into the Cyclops. The point on his horn entered the beast's chest where his hammer had made an indent. The Cyclops died where it stood.

Jason hailed Jackson. "Need you out here, big guy."

"On my way," Jackson replied.

Jason turned toward Billy, who'd yet to engage any of the Cyclops. "You got this?"

"We got this."

Jason located Burak. He stood in the middle of a small crowd, his arms crossed over his chest.

Jason phase-shifted over, and in the blink of an eye stood directly in front of the oily little man. He took ahold of Burak by the upper arms and phase-shifted again.

When he released him they were standing beneath the blue tarp, eighteen miles to the west. Burak lost his balance and fell on his backside, landing on one of Ricket's big equipment lockers. Now fear replaced the smug expression on his face.

"What ... what do want from me?"

"We're going to have a little talk, just you and me. If I detect even the slightest measure of dishonesty, I'll start breaking bones. Fingers, arms, legs ... one by one, they're going to break." Jason opened his visor so Burak could more clearly see his eyes ... his resolve. Burak's body odor nearly bowled him over.

"Start from the beginning, Burak ... leave nothing out."

Chapter 8

Mansan Core System
Planet Eriok; Port City

B urak had ten broken fingers, a broken arm, and a split lip. Jason watched him twitching—curled into a fetal position on the ground. Jason was disgusted with himself—with the level of violence he'd inflicted on the Eriokian engineer. But he'd gained enough information from him to know who was responsible for the abduction of Ricket, Leon, and Hanna. Jason, having retracted his battle suit several minutes earlier, now felt a cold chill, which had nothing to do with the gusty breeze flapping the overhead tarp. Could their kidnappings be the start of his worst fears coming true? Were the Caldurians, the universe's most advanced beings, back and on the attack?

Jason answered an incoming hail and heard Billy's voice. "What's up—"

"Need your help back here!"

Jason quickly grabbed his multi-gun and phase-shifted back to the compound. Apparently, these Cyclops were far tougher than he'd thought. Four of the big beasts lay dead on the ground. The other four were embroiled in hand-to-hand battle with Traveler, Billy and Jackson.

Anger, and the same stone-cold resolve, flared in Jason. The eight creatures were gifts from the Caldurians—protection—for doing their part in the abduction. Burak had used the term "brought out of storage"—like these monsters had sat on a shelf somewhere, just waiting to be put into action by the Caldurians.

Jackson seemed to be faring the worst. Granted, up against two of the creatures, he certainly was holding his own. Jason quickly flipped through his multi-gun munitions options on his HUD. Ricket constantly made adjustments—updates to both battle suits and weaponry. *Where'd he ever find the time?* And, sure enough, a new option appeared … something called *Spreader.*

Jason selected the option and fired into the back of the big beast. With each pull of the trigger a low velocity pellet sputtered out. *What kind of bullshit is this?* He was about to switch back to a more conventional option, when he noticed something happening on the Cyclops' broad upper back. The three pellets were drilling deep into its thick outer hide; three dark purple spidery webs were growing darker and spreading outward. Something was happening to the beast's circulatory system; veins and arteries began bursting, at an increasing rate. Suddenly, the Cyclops ceased fighting Jackson. Flinging its two long arms backwards, it was trying to stop what must be debilitating, agonizing pain.

Jackson gained the opening he needed. He used the stock of his multi-gun, like a battering ram, to repeatedly pummel the Cyclops in the throat.

Jason fired more pellets into the other three Cyclops. Within two minutes, they each became self-absorbed, frantically trying to extricate the horrific little pellets from their bodies.

★ ★ ★

Twenty-six engineers were rounded up and placed under guard in one of the barracks buildings. Apparently, Burak had been the primary contact with the Caldurians. Billy and Jackson continued to grill the other engineers, but nothing new was learned. Jason instructed Dira to phase-shift down from the *Assailant* and attend to Burak. He knew she was not in favor of some of his tactics: to say torture of any kind was against her principles would be a gross understatement.

Burak was still on the ground when Dira assessed his injuries. Jason perched on the corner of one of Ricket's equipment lockers and watched her work.

"Did you get what you needed from him?" she asked, not looking back at Jason.

"It's hard to know … to know what you *don't* know. But I think he spilled what he knew."

"So where is he? Where's Ricket and the others?"

"His story goes like this: a Caldurian vessel landed here three weeks ago. They were friendly and enthusiastic about making the engineers' lives here better. The engineers were also shown where rare mineral deposits lay underground, and given the equipment to mine them. They were also given special gifts—land-based vehicles, weapons, and the promise of a spacecraft, in due time. And all that was required in exchange was for the engineers to bring Ricket, as well as the *Minian*, into Eriok space. The engineers were fearful of a reprisal by the Alliance, so the eight Cyclops creatures were delivered to them for added protection."

"Are the Caldurians close by? What exactly do they want?" Dira asked, injecting a needle into Burak's upper arm.

"He said he didn't know, and didn't care to know," Jason said.

Dira suddenly slapped Burak's face, startling Jason almost as much as Burak. She leaned in close to the injured engineer, bringing her face within inches of his own. Her voice was quiet, almost soothing, but emotionless. "You have three minutes to live … perhaps less. You've been injected with Sacrilum 99. Undoubtedly, you are beginning to feel the effects of the drug, as it's starting to reach all your major organs. It takes a full three minutes for your organs to turn to mush. Do you feel the burn yet?"

Jason watched as Burak, lying on his back and staring up at Dira, definitely felt something. His eyes widened to the size of dinner plates and he began to whimper.

"I want you to know, Mr. Burak, that Ricket is a very special friend of mine. I don't ordinarily condone using such tactics. You now have two minutes and … sorry, I forgot to ask, do you have anything you'd like to say?"

The engineer nodded frantically. "Anything. I will tell you anything … all I know … hurry!"

"Where are Ricket, Leon, and Hanna?" she held up a new injection device for Burak to see. "It's the antidote. One minute and thirty seconds left before you are beyond help."

His eyes frantically darted from Dira to Jason, finding no sympathy from either. "They mentioned Arkwane. Might be a planet … or maybe a system? Maybe it's …" Suddenly Burak's words trailed off, his eyes bulged wider. "Oh my god, I feel the burning! Give me the antidote! Please … I'm dying."

Jason watched Dira's seemingly calm demeanor. He didn't think she had it in her to continue on like this.

"Is it a planet or a system? One minute …"

"A planet!" he yelled. "I remember the leader, one called Hobel, required something from below the surface … said they'd be back. So it had to be a planet … right? It has to be!"

Dira stood and looked down at Burak for a moment before joining Jason on the equipment locker.

Burak stared up at her, dumbfounded. Jason was curious too—wasn't she going to give him the antidote?

She smiled at Jason, a mischievous glint in her eye. "Vitamin B12 ... it has a tendency to burn when given in high doses."

"Good work! That's two things I hadn't gotten from him; a planet name and the Caldurian leader's name ... Hobel."

"And I didn't have to break any bones to get it. Maybe you should bring me along more often, huh?"

★ ★ ★

Both Billy and Jackson needed to spend several hours in the *Assailant's* only MediPod. Traveler, probably, too, but there wasn't one large enough on board to accommodate his girth. Jason entered the bridge and took a seat in the command chair.

Orion said, "Got nothing from the AI on anyone named Hobel in the database ... also, in general we have very little on the Caldurians. I got ahold of Granger, back at Jefferson Station, and he said he knows Hobel and wanted me to give you a message: Be very cautious around that one ... if we come into contact with him, watch our backs."

"Good to know. And the planet?"

"That, most definitely, was in our database. Arkwane is one of five planets, located in a nearby system; it is totally aquatic ... no land masses at all."

"What would they want there?"

Orion smiled. "Here's the thing: the inhabitants—to me they look like mermaids or mermen—are fantastic farmers. Incredible sea-bottom crops grow there year-round. The planet supplies food staples to dozens of other worlds."

"Okay ... interesting, I guess. But why would the Caldurians be interested in that?" Jason asked.

"Something else Granger said. We know the Caldurians are fascinated by alien cultures ... alien worlds. I mean, to the point it's a cultural obsession ... like football or soccer in some countries on your planet. Caldurians collect alien world species, to a degree we never realized before."

That does make sense, Jason thought. Both *The Lilly* and the *Minian* had Habitat Zoos. "So you're saying Hobel is looking to add to his collection? He's on Arkwane to pick up a few mermaid specimens?" Jason asked.

"Granger thinks it's more likely he's doing some preliminary research, for either an existing, or a future, habitat. Habitats are extremely difficult to create. For one thing, as you know, the habitat is a virtual duplication, or clone, of some real-world environment. But to survive within the multiverse, it must be completely self-contained. Some HABs, like HAB 12 on *The Lilly*, required external influences ... like those feeding drones ... and some manipulation of the wildlife and ecosystems."

Jason knew all that. He'd spent enough time with Ricket, who was also fascinated by habitats. "So this Hobel is taking time out from his kidnapping ventures to play with his latest toy ecosystem?"

Orion shrugged. "It's just a guess, but I think it's a good one."

Jason turned forward. "Seaman Gordon, let's request an interchange wormhole that will put us no closer than one light-year's distance from Arkwane."

"Aye, Captain."

"Gunny, kick in the *Assailant*'s cloaking system."

"We're already running cloaked, Cap."

"Sir ... the wormhole is forming off our starboard bow, and it should be fully formed within twenty seconds."

"Helm, take us in, soon as it's stable enough."

"Aye, Captain," McNeil said.

Bristol entered the bridge and took his seat off to the left. He looked at his station's display and snorted.

"Something of interest, Bristol?" Jason asked.

"I've heard about this planet and their ..." Suddenly Bristol looked embarrassed and stopped talking.

Jason was going to finish Bristol's sentence for him and say *mermaids*, then remembered the young junior science officer was gay. *Maybe he'd heard stories about the mermen?*

"Entering the wormhole now, Captain," McNeil reported.

It took less than four seconds to emerge out its distant side. "Status, Gunny?"

He already knew this was a busy space corridor. Thirty or more ships were visible on the forward display.

"Shipping vessels, mostly, Captain. Two are luxury space-liners. Definitely, it's a major thoroughfare, of some kind."

"Captain, we're being scanned!" Orion said, all her attention refocused on her board.

"I thought we were cloaked?"

Bristol moved to her side and said, "It must have turned off while we were within the wormhole ... the damn thing's flaky as shit."

"We already knew that it was flaky, Bristol. Damn it! That's why I specifically asked you to fix the thing," Jason said, exasperated.

"We've got company," Orion said. "Looks like four Caldurian vessels are approaching from deep space ... warship class ... each one as large as the *Minian*. Their weapons are charging, sir."

Chapter 9

Open Space, Nearing Arkwane
Parcical, Ricket's Quarters

Ricket rarely slept—long ago, he had manipulated his internal nanites to adjust the levels of melatonin in his bloodstream, as well as another hormone called norepinephrine. But on this particular evening he'd slept deeply. He was given small, but adequate, quarters on the second deck. He sat up and rubbed at his eyes ... his internal clock told him he'd been asleep for close to four hours: a seeming eternity in Ricket's world. He got to his feet and relieved himself in the adjoining head. By the time he made his way up to the *Parcical*'s fourth deck, he knew something was very wrong. Hanna's and Leon's confinement cells were both empty. Ricket spotted a young Caldurian crewmember he knew as Barkley and approached him.

"Barkley … can you tell me where the two human prisoners were taken?"

The Caldurian, holding an equivalent rank of Seaman, nervously looked in the direction of the two empty cells, then back at Ricket. "I'm not supposed to talk to you."

Ricket continued staring up at him.

He said, "Deck 2 … the MicroVault compartment," before hurrying off.

Ricket pondered that information for a moment, quickly remembering there was a locked compartment on Deck 2 … one he hadn't been given access to. He rushed into the nearest DeckPort and emerged on Deck 2. Without breaking his stride, he continued heading toward the bow, via the primary corridor, then made two left turns down two smaller corridors. Seeing movement up ahead, Ricket ran forward.

"Stop! Please stop!"

The group of five, two humans and three Caldurians, paused, and looked back toward Ricket. He recognized Hobel. The two Caldurians with him were armed, their weapons pointed at Leon and Hanna. By the time Ricket caught up to them, Hobel had instructed the guards to keep the prisoners moving.

Out of breath and sounding frantic, Ricket said, "I will not help you if my friends are harmed."

Hobel glanced down at Ricket but didn't slow up his pace.

"I've never known Caldurians to be barbaric … you're an advanced people—"

Hobel cut him off mid-sentence: "Ricket … they will not be harmed. It is for their own wellbeing, as well as the crew's, that they are placed into long-term storage. I'm sure someone of your intellectual level understands the need for efficiency."

"Let them go … why keep them on board this vessel at all?"

"They may be of importance to us … perhaps for negotiation purposes later on."

The guard in front of the group opened an energy hatch, then, stepping aside, waited for Hanna and Leon to proceed forward. Ricket noticed their hands were tied behind their backs, bound securely in glowing red virtual handcuffs.

"You better think of something, Ricket," Leon said.

Hanna remained quiet. Her resigned sad expression cut right into Ricket's heart.

"I'll get … both of you … out of this, I promise," Ricket said.

The six entered the circular compartment. As much as Ricket was terrified for what was about to happen to Leon and Hanna, he was equally exhilarated seeing the surrounding area's technology. Hobel must have observed Ricket's rapt expression.

"This is the MicroVault access terminal."

The compartment was surrounded by a circular, three-hundred-and-sixty-degree virtual window. Looking up, he saw the same virtual window was extended up overhead above them as well.

"What you're looking at, Ricket, is the virtual contents of just one of the MicroVaults on board this vessel. In reality, everything you see is scaled down to molecular-level size. This representation is for our visual reference only. We can both observe and search everything stored within the vault this way … although it is much more efficient to simply have the ship's AI locate needed items by their designated catalogued identifications."

Ricket quickly digested Hobel's words. What he was currently looking at, out the curved virtual window in front of him, was miraculous. Like looking into a ginormous, ultra clean, ultra white storeroom. Items hovered weightless in the air, and were all contained within three different sized containers: small, about the size of a large shoebox, medium-sized, which Ricket guessed to be about ten foot by ten foot, and much larger, which were off in the distance and Ricket, from this perspective, could not guesstimate the size. He saw row upon row of items of every sort, spanning out to some distant horizon that seemed miles away. Close to where they were standing was the first of many ten-foot-square containers holding some kind of animal or creature that was bright purple and reptilian looking. It was lying on a padded platform and monitoring devices, such as those found on the *Minian's* Medical compartment, indicated its heart was beating, along with some other life-affirming functions. Next to the creature, in an identical container, was some kind of transportation vehicle, though not the same scale size as the creature. Everything here was scaled down, no matter what the actual size was, to fit within each ten-by-ten-foot container. Four containers over, Ricket viewed something that nearly took his breath away. It was the *SpaceRunner*! Leon's ship wasn't destroyed after all.

"My ship! You stole my fucking ship and stuck it in this vault," Leon yelled. But the anger in his voice was belied by his expression, which couldn't hide the relief, the flaring renewed hope he felt, upon seeing the *SpaceRunner* again.

"As you can see, they will not be harmed. Stasis is a … what you would call … a humane treatment." The Caldurian captain moved closer to the curved window and swiped his hand sideways. The virtual storage vault, everything visible on the other side of the window, spun around fast, making it impossible to see anything. He used his fingertips to slow down the spinning to a crawl. The perspective within the virtual storage space had now completely changed. Then, using his hands in a wide, expanding gesture, he zoomed the virtual image to an undefined point in the distant horizon.

"You might find this particularly interesting, Ricket. These are cloned Zip accelerators. As you can see, we have plenty of them."

True to Hobel's statement, Ricket saw fifty or so of what would normally be huge locomotive-sized devices lined up in matching, large-sized, containers. "You will be assisting Norwell with these ... once we have an original accelerator in hand, you will be able to make all necessary alterations to bring these units into operational status."

"Are you talking about the Zip accelerators on the *Minian* again?"

"I am ... and we are close to acquiring her. I assure you, I can't stress the importance of that ship."

"Well, good luck with that, asshole," Leon sneered. "Don't forget what that ship's captain accomplished when bringing down the Craing Empire. He made them his bitch ... and he'll do the same thing to you."

Ricket and Hanna looked at Leon, surprised at his outburst. But perhaps more of a surprise to Ricket was Hobel's look of unease. Apparently Captain Reynolds' exploits in space were common knowledge among the Caldurians ... even those inhabiting the multiverse.

Hobel stood at a virtual pedestal which, only seconds before, hadn't been present. *He must have accessed it through an internal nanotech*, Ricket thought. Hobel tapped at a display and within another few seconds a virtual energy hatchway opened up nearby.

"Take the prisoners inside and make them comfortable," Hobel ordered the two guards.

Now that's interesting, Ricket thought. He'd no idea the MicroVault could be physically accessible by the crew of the *Parcical*. He watched as one of the guards stepped into the virtual hatchway, leaving the MicroVault's access terminal; instantly, he could be seen—now a small figure, standing off to the side, within the MicroVault.

One by one, they all walked through the hatch, arriving into the glaring white world of the vault.

Ricket, Hanna, and Leon exchanged glances, spinning on their heels to take in the enormity of what they were seeing. So many different items; Ricket had no idea what purpose they served—organisms in tubes; creatures; weapons; even odd items of clothing ... it was almost too much to comprehend.

Again, Hobel somehow summoned up another virtual pedestal and began to tap at the small screen. Two containers appeared at the end of a nearby row. As he tapped some more, life support and monitoring devices came into view, appearing at the end of both containers.

"I implore you ... please do not do this," Ricket said to Hobel.

Hobel briefly looked toward the guards and nodded. The guards raised their weapons and fired. Both Leon and Hanna lost consciousness immediately, but neither fell, nor even slumped, sideways. *This is all virtual,* Ricket reminded himself. The basic rules of physics were obviously different here. The guards slung their rifles over their shoulders and effortlessly tilted the prisoners' bodies—from a vertical standing up position to a lying-down, horizontal position. The two weightless bodies were repositioned in respective containers: First, Leon's body, then Hanna's, were lain onto padded platforms. They looked to be sleeping, and appeared to be fine, from Ricket's perspective. The guards next attached a small round device onto the two foreheads, then rejoined Ricket and Hobel. Their work was done.

"It's time for us to leave now, Ricket. There's only a twenty-minute window of safety ... for any of us to maintain consciousness within this realm."

Ricket joined Hobel and the two guards as they headed toward the energy hatch. He took another look over his
shoulder at Hanna and Leon. Part of him wondered if the
two would be spending eternity here, within a space probably
smaller than the head of a pin.

Chapter 10

Open Space, Commerce Corridor Near
Arkwane
Assailant, Bridge

Jason queried Bristol, again, in regard to the *Assailant*'s flakey cloaking system and what he was going to do to get it operational.

The skinny junior science officer had no quick reply. He sat at his station and picked at a blemish above his right eyebrow.

"One of those vessels has a lock on us, Captain," Orion said.

Jason was well aware that the *Assailant* was no match for one Caldurian warship, let alone four. Hell, a fleet of one hundred ... two hundred ... Allied warships would find their hands full with that lot.

"Phase-shift us as far away from here as possible, Helm."

"Cap ... our cloaking device just initiated ... we're now invisible to them," Orion said.

"Shall I still phase-shift us elsewhere, Captain?" McNeil asked.

Jason watched the forward display. Orion put up a logistical view but the four Caldurian vessels weren't showing up.

Like the *Minian* and *The Lilly* before her, Caldurian tech made the ships nearly invisible to scans and sensors.

"No ... ease us out of here, Ensign. Slow and steady; keep our drives cool ... and no comms activity either, Seaman Gordon."

Jason continued to watch the display. The logistical view, used earlier to see the four ships, was replaced with a magnified feed of open space. Tracking boxes surrounded and moved with the alien ships, doing a commendable job keeping track of them, considering they were as black as space itself.

"They've lost their lock on us, sir," Orion said.

Ensign McNeil looked over his shoulder at Jason. "Orders, Captain?"

Jason wasn't sure. How would they ever locate the missing trio in such a vast spatial wilderness? Their only lead was that the Caldurian ship, the *Parcical*, which had abducted Ricket and the other two, was en route to Arkwane; the Eriokian engineer who'd provided that one bit of information had done so under extreme duress. But there was still another opportunity to glean information—and one that was far more accessible.

"Bristol?"

Bristol looked up from his panel.

"Is there a way to cloak our battle suits?"

He scrunched up his face in an exaggerated expression but then looked as if he'd just thought of something new. "Actually ... Ricket's been trying to do that ... it's been one of his pet workshop projects."

"Did he manage to make it work?" Jason asked.

Bristol shrugged. "I know he was close. I remember ... there was a timeout problem. He could cloak a battle suit for a little while, then it would pop back into view."

"What's a *little while* mean? Like two or five or ten minutes? It makes a difference."

Again, he gave a shrug. "I can look at one of the suits on his bench and see what's happening with it."

"Hurry … in fact, you've got permission for within-ship phase-shifts. Go!"

Bristol stood, depressing the two small side tabs on his belt's SuitPac device. His battle suit initialized and he flashed away.

Jason brought his attention back to the convoy of four, mammoth-sized, Caldurian vessels. "Follow them … keep a safe distance back, but stay with them, Helm."

"Aye, Captain."

★ ★ ★

Boomer moved between three rows of Sharks. Fifteen men were in the class—all well over twice her weight and far stronger than she would ever be. The gym was hot and humid from sweaty perspiration. The pungent smell of body odor was nearly overpowering; still, there was no place Boomer would rather be. Learning Kahill Callan was the most fun she'd ever had. But teaching its strict discipline to others was an altogether different challenge … she felt a strong sense of responsibility … to the martial art itself as well as to her masters. Not taking it lightly, she did her best to honor both them and her students. Still, one simple fact remained … she was only a kid. At first, she had been embarrassed teaching grownups, until Prince Aahil Aqeel offered her the perfect advice: "Don't try to be anything you are not. Embrace being an eleven-year-old … revel in it." And so she did. Soon any trace of embarrassment had fled.

She observed the stance of every Shark; adjusting, where needed, the position of their training enhancement shields and its relation to their upper bodies and the mat beneath their bare feet.

"Billy, why do you keep holding the shield so close to your chest? Hold it more like this," she said, demonstrating the proper shield position.

"Yes, Master Tahhrim Dol," Billy said.

A short snicker came from the front row and Boomer knew exactly where. Donaldson. He was the youngest one here, other than herself.

"What's wrong with you, Donaldson? You have a problem taking directions from a kid?"

Donaldson, still wearing a smirk on his face, didn't even try to hide it.

She let it go. "Okay, at my signal, let's try the complete *Jarta*, from the beginning stance." She moved from the middle of the mat to the side. She clapped once and watched.

She studied the men as they all moved in unison. In synch, they thrust their shields forward in three abrupt motions, then, swinging their left legs behind them, turned their bodies ninety degrees counter clockwise. Immediately, the Sharks used their shields' edge in a tilted, swiping motion to propel themselves six feet into the air; up there, they used the opposite edge on their shields to counteract their forward progression. The precise move was an addition she'd made to Master Aqeel's Jarta—one she'd perfected over the last few weeks. The men, suspended in the air for two full seconds, flipped their feet backwards, over their heads, and landed gently on their feet.

Seeing all fifteen Sharks complete the fast-moving martial arts routine with relative ease and precision filled Boomer with the impulse to clap her hands and cheer. Instead, she simply said, "Good! Now let's break into pairs."

She watched fourteen Sharks break into pairs—except for Donaldson, who was odd man out.

"I'll pair with you, Donaldson," Boomer said.

Again the smirk came.

She waited.

"Yes, Master Tahhrim Dol," he said, his tone of voice exaggerating her title.

Boomer scanned the other pairs, noting that all were properly standing in a beginning combat stance. "Choose who will attack," she said, loud enough for everyone to hear. She pointed to Donaldson. He nodded, and she clapped once.

As much as she wearied of Donaldson's disrespect, the guy could move. Both he and Billy were the class superstars, although Rizzo, who'd attended a previous class, was equally good. Donaldson charged forward, using a combination similar to the Jarta move they'd each practiced, and, with three quick thrusts of his shield, sent low-powered disruption waves in her direction. She easily blocked them, ducking low to one side. Surprisingly, though, he anticipated her movements and she felt warmth as his shield's disruption waves hit her left cheek. Instinctively, she used her shield to cartwheel backward, countering with her own blast to Donaldson's chest.

He burst out laughing and clutched his chest. "Damn! How is it you always beat me? You beat everybody!"

Boomer bowed to her opponent and waited for him to return the formality. He did so, and she returned his smile. "Well, that time you got me." She pointed to her cheek. "If your shield wasn't a trainer, I'd be standing here with half a face."

"And try explaining that one to the captain, Donaldson," Billy said, two rows over. Boomer heard a familiar sound in her ear—she was being hailed. She saw Billy bring two fingers up to his own ear ... he too was being hailed.

"Dad?" she inquired.

"Come to the ready room ASAP ... little one."

★ ★ ★

Boomer arrived in the ready room four minutes later, still wearing her Shadick. Dressed similarly, Billy was right behind her. The conference room was partially filled. Jason sat in his usual seat at the head of the table, closest to the door. Bristol was there and so were Orion and Rizzo.

"Have a seat," Jason said, all business. "I have a mission for you."

Boomer beamed. "Me too?"

Jason stared at her for a long moment before answering: "Yes ... you too, Boomer."

Billy asked, "What do you have in mind?"

"Something I probably shouldn't be attempting ... especially with my eleven-year-old daughter. This particular mission requires stealth, and will uniquely match a Tahli warrior's ability."

"What is it ... what are we doing, Dad?"

"There are four Caldurian warships close by, similar in size to our own *Minian*. I want to see their captains sitting in our brig ... all four of them!"

Billy raised his furry brows and smiled. "You ... um ... think that might be a bit ambitious, Cap?"

"Uh huh ... it's pretty bold, Billy. But we have a unique situation close at hand. We're in near proximity to those four ships and we're cloaked. If we're going to rescue Ricket, Hanna and Leon, we need intel. Find out where the hell they've been taken. We only have one shot at this, so we might as well go big. Between the four captains, I'm hopeful at least one of them holds the information we need. They will also serve as our own hostages ... they take our people ... we take theirs."

"How's this going to work, Captain?" Orion asked.

"You will remain on the bridge ... but your involvement here will be crucial, because timing will be everything. You'll be phase-shifting the teams, both in and out. None of us will have time to mess with setting new phase-shift coordinates … or any of that stuff."

"I'm still not clear how this will work," Rizzo said.

Jason nodded and looked at Boomer. "You've played tag before, right?"

"Oh yeah … I rock at tag."

Jason said, "Good, because this far-out venture will be just like that. Two teams … Boomer and I will make one team, and Billy and Rizzo will make the other; each team will infiltrate two ships."

The room went dead quiet.

Jason continued, "Look, Bristol assures me that he can provide us with new prototype battle suits that can stay cloaked up to sixty seconds."

"A whole whopping sixty seconds! Wow, Bristol, you've really outdone yourself with this one," Rizzo muttered sarcastically.

"Hey … it's Ricket's design. I don't understand how it'll work even that long," Bristol replied, defensively.

"We phase-shift in, grab the captain, and phase-shift out. What could be more simple?" Jason asked.

"Then why do we need two-man teams?" Rizzo asked.

"One will be the grabber who physically snatches the captain … the second one provides extra protection … in the event something goes wrong."

"I'm your protection?" Boomer asked.

"Yep … I've seen you with that shield … you move like greased lightning."

"I guess I'll be the grabber on the second team," Billy said, with a shrug.

"Where do you plan to put the captured captains?" Orion asked. "It'll need to be a fairly large space. Folks phase-shifting in and out all over the place can be a dangerous situation."

"What do you think?" Jason asked. "The *Assailant*'s hold? Or maybe the flight bay?"

Orion said, "The hold could work. We can have armed Sharks posted around the perimeter."

"You know, don't you, something typically goes wrong with impromptu plans like this, Cap. You sure you want to take on all four captains?" Billy reconfirmed.

"If we're going to do this, I want those four ships off kilter ... all four of their bridge crews running around like monkeys set loose at a circus."

Boomer giggled at that, then became serious when she looked at Billy and Rizzo. "I want two hours of practice in the hold ... with real enhancement shields."

"This isn't fair ... when do I get trained to be a Tahli warrior?" Orion asked.

"I promise that you and I will be trained by Master Tahhrim Dol ... but not today. Okay, everyone—we all know what we have to do. Three hours till *go time*."

Chapter 11

Open Space, Commerce Corridor Near
Arkwane
Assailant, Hold 2

Hold 2 on the *Assailant* was a large, seventy-five by nine-ty-foot space. The area's surrounding thick compos-ite-material bulkheads were pretty much indestructible ... at least, for their immediate purposes. Orion was all set—sta-tioned on a narrow, cantilevered sub-deck, fifteen feet above the deck of the hold, where she could see everything going on down below, while still being out of the way. Jason, standing below on the hold deck, could see her up there, seated at her makeshift station, double- and triple-checking all her settings.

"How's it looking up there, Gunny?"

"I'll still need a few minutes, Captain."

Billy entered the hold first, leading the way for the ten armed Sharks who followed close on his heels.

"Form a perimeter around the hold," Billy told them, ges-turing with his finger in an overhead circling motion.

Jason exited Hold 2 and entered Hold 1, on the other side of the corridor. In there, in an area exactly the same size as Hold 2, were four people: Sergeant Jackson, Chief Horris,

Dira, and Lieutenant Commander Perkins.

Jason, earlier, used masking tape strips on the decking to section the hold into four equal-sized areas. At present, the four crewmembers were grouped together in the middle of the hold, talking.

"Okay … team captains … go ahead and assume your respective bridge area positions."

The four separated to stand in the middle of their sections. Jason smiled. "Remember, you're surprised when things start to happen. Feel free to fight back … do the unexpected. That's why we're here, doing mock simulations, right? We need to be prepared for anything."

Jason looked at each one, getting nods back; Chief Horris smiled broadly, obviously having more fun than the other three.

"When is this happening, Jason? I have a patient in Medical," Dira asked.

"It could be one minute from now, or ten." With that, he left Hold 1 and returned to Hold 2. He glanced up at Orion and was rewarded with a *thumbs-up* signal. Bristol was seated next to her, looking bored as usual.

Rizzo, Boomer, and Billy silently waited within Hold 2; their battle suits initiated, each stood well apart from the others, an enhancement shield on their left forearms. Jason felt a bit left out—like not yet a part of a secret club. He *really* needed to schedule time with Boomer to begin learning the basics of Kahill Callan.

"This is very simple. I don't expect trouble, nor problems of any kind. A few practice sessions will increase our odds of success." Jason initiated his own battle suit, then stood in the open space, opposite Boomer. She smiled back at him, looking more excited than he could remember. She lived for this stuff.

"Remember, everyone … you'll be phase-shifted into

Hold 1. You and your teammate will be cloaked." Jason glanced up at Bristol, assured he'd provided them the new cloaking-capable battle suits. "You have about sixty seconds before you become visible ... that's thirty seconds per bridge jump ... but you should be well away from those Caldurian ships by then. This will be a quick, *grab and go*, exercise. We'll have an open channel—Gunny will be listening, in case anyone runs into trouble. Any questions?"

They shook their heads.

"Okay, then. Bristol, make us invisible."

Jason watched as Boomer, Billy and Rizzo disappeared. "Okay ... phase-shift us all now, Gunny!"

In a flash, Jason phase-shifted into Hold 1. He was in Chief Horris' section. The big man was truly surprised, seeing the dual flashes. Jason and Boomer being cloaked from the chief's sight made it easy for Jason to rush forward and wrap his arms around him.

"Got him," Jason said aloud. In a flash, he and Chief Horris appeared back in Hold 2. He noticed other flashes going on around him. He let go of the chief. "Ready!" Jason said. Within two seconds, he was phase-shifted back into Hold 1. This was Dira's section. He saw her and moved to grab her, but she somehow dodged away, running to the far side of the taped-off section. Jason moved fast to grab her but, once again, she eluded his clutches. He saw his mission timer closing in on the one-minute mark. He heard Dira laugh, which sparked a flash of irritation. She was too difficult to catch. *Damn!*

Jason and Boomer suddenly became visible. Dira's hands covered her mouth, as she began to laugh. Suddenly, two arms wrapped around her from behind, and Boomer yelled, "Got her!" The three were phase-shifted back to Hold 2 by Orion.

Jason, looking around, could see the other groups were there already, waiting for him, along with their abducted *cap-*

tains. Jason raised his visor and looked up at Orion and Bristol. "How was that from your perspective?"

Bristol spoke first. "A clusterfuck."

Orion said, "It could have been better."

"Did you two have problems?" Jason asked, looking at Billy and Rizzo.

"I bumped into Rizzo ... sent him sprawling on that first phase-shift. Other than that, it went pretty good," Billy said.

Rizzo had a question: "Why does the protector need to be invisible? It's confusing, not knowing where your other team member is."

"Yeah, one of the two being visible would make for a good diversion, while the invisible one grabs the captain," Billy added.

Jason turned his attention to Dira. "Okay ... spill it ... how did you know where I was?"

He could see she was close to laughing again. "The deck plates in Hold 1 don't fit right. Every time you took a step, I saw them wobble. I knew exactly where you were."

"And one more thing," Orion said, "even though I'm up here and tracking your icons, it gets real confusing hearing everyone say *ready* or *got him*. Be better if you said something like, *Jason has captain*, or *Billy has captain* ... that way, I'm less likely to make a mistake."

"Everyone back to your positions ... we'll keep trying until it's perfect."

They practiced again—this time Boomer and Rizzo stayed visible, and Jason and Billy spoke their own names aloud, once they'd made their grabs. On this run, Jason grabbed Sergeant Jackson; he got cute, pushing Jason's arms away when he was caught, but in the end it worked out better. The only mishap was he'd become visible again at the last moment, which wasn't a big deal since he'd already taken ahold of Jackson at that point.

They tried the maneuver another four times, until both teams came in with five or ten seconds to spare on their mission timers.

Jason thanked his volunteer helpers, waiting while Dira, Chief Horris, and Perkins returned to their scheduled duties.

"Gunny, do you have the four bridge coordinates configured for our phase-shifts?"

"As well as possible. Those four ships are practically invisible to my sensors, even at this close range. I'm forced to use the coordinates from the *Minian* as a reference … it's the best I can do."

"That should work," Jason said. He noticed Jackson had rejoined the Sharks positioned around the periphery. "Sergeant, be ready for anything."

"We'll be ready, sir."

Boomer splayed her hands out and raised her shoulders. "So are we going to do this now, Dad?"

"Everyone ready?" Jason asked.

They all said yes.

Jason looked up toward Orion. "Make us invisible, Gunny."

Billy disappeared from view. Jason noticed he couldn't see his own arms or legs. "Phase-shift us now, Gunny!"

The next instant, Jason saw Boomer flash into view before him. They were standing in the forward section of a Caldurian bridge, which looked remarkably similar to the *Minian*'s. He spun toward the command chair. No command chair. In fact, there were no chairs here at all. A klaxon began to bellow loudly all around them. *Movement.* Identical to Boomer's droid, Dewdrop, five hovering droids appeared on the bridge. With remarkable speed, the droids spun about to face them … actually, to face Boomer. Simultaneously, access panels on their upper torsos opened and stubby plasma weapons emerged. Jason, using his suit's integrated wrist plasma guns, began to fire.

As plasma fire erupted all around them, Boomer dove both up and sideways over a console to come up behind two droids. She thrust her enhancement shield forward, and bright purple distortion waves pounded into the droids' backs. Both droids were propelled high into the air, to the far side of the bridge, where they careened into the bulkhead. Neither got back up.

Jason continued firing his wrist weapons until the other droids went down on the deck.

"You okay, Boomer?"

"I'm good," she said, looking around the bridge, not knowing just where her dad was standing. At that point, a full minute had elapsed and Jason popped into view. Boomer looked at him with a confused expression. "Where's the captain?"

Jason gestured for Boomer to hold that thought. "Orion … what's going on with the other ships? There were only droids present here."

"Went like clockwork," she replied. "We have two Caldurian captains on board, currently being held in Hold 2."

Jason checked and saw his mission counter had reset to zero. He was good to become invisible again. "Go ahead and cloak me, and phase-shift us to the last ship's bridge."

"They'll be waiting for you … you won't have the element of surprise."

"We'll be fine."

A second after Jason was cloaked, Orion phase-shifted them both. They flashed onto the last ship's bridge and, to no one's surprise, the Caldurians were ready for them. Boomer, already on the move, cartwheeled high in the air, firing off distortion waves in multiple directions.

There were no less than fifteen armed Caldurians, all standing at the ready on the bridge. There were also five droids. Boomer, visible, held everyone's attention and was drawing fire. The ship's captain, the only one dressed in all white and barking orders, stood at the rear of the bridge, close to the exit. Jason reached him in two long strides, but before he even put a hand on him, he screamed out, "Gunny ... get Boomer the hell out of here, now!"

He saw Boomer flash away just as his hands grabbed a firm hold on the Caldurian captain's upper arms. A mixed expression of surprise and fury transformed his face.

"Jason has the captain," he yelled.

★ ★ ★

The *Assailant* possessed only one operational holding cell within the ship's cramped brig. All three abducted Caldurian captains stood at the energy field, looking both indignant and red-faced.

Jason stood outside their cell, arms folded over his chest, listening to their demands to be released. He'd already heard them make numerous threats of reprisal, throwing more than a few insults targeting the warmongering, sub-intelligent human race. He gave them no indication their comments bothered him. He simply waited for them to calm down and shut up.

Eventually they did, and Jason spoke up: "You can make this a difficult process or a simple one."

The demands and insults started up again and Jason waited. Finally, having heard enough, he raised a hand. "Let me speak ... if you want to be returned back to your ships ... let me speak."

Once they quieted down, Jason began again: "We are more than ten light-years' distance from your ships, and we are cloaked. There will be no rescue forthcoming. You are in deep trouble, and only *you* are in the position to save yourselves. Your lives may be spared ... maybe ... if you cooperate. If you do not ... you each will experience a terrible, painful, prolonged death. I promise you that."

Jason knew he was piling it on pretty thick, but he deemed it necessary. In reality, he had no intention of hurting these three. At the most he would repeat the poison antidote charade Dira had used on the Eriokian engineer. But time was not on his side. No sooner had he returned from the mission and ushered the three abducted captains into their cell than Jason had been pulled away to a meeting with Admiral Dixon. The older man's face was projected onto the overhead display in his ready room.

"Captain Reynolds."

"Yes, sir ... good to see—"

The admiral talked over him. "This isn't a social call, Captain. There's a big problem with the Cadacci."

Jason eased down into his chair and let out a breath. He knew what the admiral was going to say, even before he voiced it. The Cadacci were a small, rodent-like species. They were annoying and demanding ... but harmless, for the most part. Their planet was only a stone's throw from the CAP-RIM Star System—the same star system where Captain Oz and the *Carrion* were creating havoc on an epic scale.

"I believe your primary directive was to bring Oz to justice ... one way, or another. So when I received notice you were thirty-five light-years away ... obviously still in pursuit of your lost crewmembers ... I was surprised. Did I not make myself clear?"

"You did, sir. Things have escalated. There's a small fleet of Caldurian vessels—"

Again the admiral cut Jason off. "The Caldurians are not our enemy! I don't care about the Caldurians."

"I'm just saying ... this is more than simply recovering our crew—"

"Look, I am not Admiral Reynolds, whom you had no

trouble manipulating. Your days doing what you want ... when you want ... are over. I gave you an order and I expect you to follow it."

The admiral stared hard at Jason, letting the silence underline his point. "Now, go get Captain Oz. Then, you can try to find Ricket. Thank you, Captain Reynolds."

"Yes, sir," Jason replied, but the screen had already gone black.

Jason brought his attention back to the here and now ... brig. He watched as fear was now taking a firm hold on the three Caldurian captains. He instinctively didn't like them ... didn't respect them. Perhaps because they weren't battle-hardened officers—unlike the dedicated combatants within his own Allied forces. Those who'd fought against the Craing— some for decades. No, these Caldurians, though full of bluster and arrogance, didn't actually have any real chops—they were simply military figureheads.

"Look ... I have zero time to waste on you. Who will be the first to start talking? Who will be the first to avoid unnecessary pain and suffering?"

Big and ominous-looking, Sergeant Jackson arrived at Jason's side. "On my way to the mess, thought I'd see if you needed any assistance."

His timing couldn't have been better, Jason thought. Neither had planned his presence here, but the way Jackson was now staring straight at the three prisoners—even he was a bit intimidated. The three Caldurian officers seemed to visibly withdraw and shrink. Jason answered, "Maybe, Sergeant ... now that you ask."

Chapter 12

Open Space, Near Arkwane
Assailant, Brig

The three captains looked so much alike that Jason had a hard time telling one from another. Not using their rightful Caldurian names, he was corrected on three separate occasions.

"From now on, you, the one on my left ... I'm calling you Larry, and you ... the bossy one on the right ... you're Moe." He was the only one with hair—a few black locks at the top of his head. "And you ... the clown in the middle ... you're Curly."

They looked back at Jason, mystified.

Jason turned and signaled the brig guard, sitting at a desk down the corridor, to disable the cell's energy shield.

"Do me a favor, Jackson, go take a seat behind them."

Sergeant Jackson took three long strides, brushing past Moe and nearly knocking him over, to straddle the toilet behind the captives. The Caldurians glanced around at Jackson, then faced Jason. The energy field returned and Jason took a half step closer.

He figured he'd start out with an easy question. "Why was one of your ships piloted solely by droids?"

Moe was first to speak up: "Every Caldurian fleet has a droid-only vessel as part of their spacecraft contingent. It's usually the first ship—sent into troubled conflict zones, or to those unexplored regions of space suspected of posing higher levels of danger to us."

Jason thought that was probably a safe tactic—but also chicken-shit. He suspected the Caldurians had become very adept at doing things in safe mode.

"Where is my science officer? Where is Ricket?"

Moe, Larry, and Curly exchanged glances. Again, it was Moe who answered first: "What we know is limited. I can tell you he is extremely important to the survival of our people. To our society."

Sergeant Jackson stood up tall. Like a skyscraper, he loomed ominously above the much shorter captains.

Larry piped up, "They're being held within the *Parcical*."

Moe and Curly looked toward Larry with disgust.

"Thank you, Larry … you will be the first to return to your ship. That is, if you continue to be useful to us. How do we find this vessel … this *Parcical*?"

"It is a Rogue Class ship … our most advanced vessel. Smaller in size to ours, but it cannot be infiltrated. The security provisions imposed by the AI are impossible to breach. You won't be able to board her, like you did the four Master Class ships."

Jason, never having heard the term before, suspected the *Minian* was considered a Master Class vessel as well, and briefly wondered what type of class *The Lilly* had been considered.

"Tell me how to skirt the security measures. What would that AI need to allow us access onto the ship?"

The Three Caldurian Stooges shook their heads in unison.

Jason waited while the tension within the little holding cell grew palpable. Jackson chose Curly, the officer in the middle. He grabbed a fistful of the white uniform at the nape of Curly's neck, lifting him up one handed. Both Curly's hands came up as the makeshift noose tightened around his throat. His face quickly turned red and was on its way toward an ugly shade of purple.

"I think I might know!" Larry yelled.

Jackson lowered Curly to the deck, releasing his grasp enough for him to gulp in several deep breaths, though his hand remained on Curly's shoulder.

"You would need one of us, a captain-level officer. But, even then, the AI would probably detect something wrong ... detect the increased bio-levels. She'd smell the fear."

"Don't worry about that right now. We'll find a way to deal with the AI. Tell me, where is the *Parcical* now?"

"Probably still on Arkwane," Moe said.

"The water planet? Why? What's there?"

"Recently harvested crops. This time every year, we ... The Caldurian people have an affinity to Palm-Stalk. Replicators, no matter how advanced, don't do that crop justice. Fresh, naturally grown Palm-Stalk is our primary staple. The *Parcical* is picking up enough stores of the harvested plant to last us another year."

"How large a vessel is this *Parcical*?" Jason asked, imagining the ship to be many miles long—something that would dwarf even a Master Class ship.

"Rogue Class vessels are small. But they are structured to store a near-infinite amount of Palm-Stalk ... or anything else, within their MicroVault systems."

"Huh? How large is this vault?"

All three captains seemed confused by his question. Moe said, "It takes up no physical space at all. It's a virtual vault. A vault residing within the multiverse."

Of course, Jason thought. It would be similar to a Zoo's habitats.

"How long will the *Parcical* remain on that planet?"

"We are scheduled to stay in Arkwane space for three days. Two of those days have since elapsed."

"So what's planned after that?"

The three Caldurians again became tight-lipped. Jackson placed his other hand on Moe's shoulder.

"To take back the ship, the one you call the *Minian*," Moe said. He let out a breath and looked resigned, as if he'd come to some kind of mental decision. "As you know, Caldurians move within the multiverse with relative ease. Very little time is spent here, within this particular realm. Although it is … was … our home, we far prefer others. With the exception of collecting Palm-Stalk, and other essentials, we rarely return here. Recently, our vessels have experienced difficulty making the transition from one realm to another. We fear, even now, that we may be marooned here … here within this realm."

"You pride yourselves on being the brightest race in the universe … why can't your scientists figure that one out?"

"The same technology is integrated into everything … all our advances utilize multiverse transmutation. Habitats, phase-shifting, DeckPorts, virtual storage of munitions … everything is based on the same technology."

Jason knew where he was going: Zip accelerators. Found on the *Minian,* and apparently on other large Caldurian ships, they were necessary for traveling into the multiverse. Ricket had explained to him that the Zip accelerators, located on the *Minian,* came from Alurian … a planet one hundred and thirty light-years from Earth—part of the Corian Nez constellation. The Zip technology was Alurian, not Caldurian.

Moe continued, "Zip accelerator technology has been

duplicated, scaled down from the massive units found within Master Class vessel Zip Farms, to tiny, simplified, near-molecular-sized units, which are used for other devices … including our own internal nanotech." Moe then gestured toward his head. "So far, only the larger Zip accelerators have exhibited such malfunctions but our scientists assure us that it is only a matter of time before all our Zip accelerator technology will be similarly affected."

Moe looked at Jason with an expression that conveyed the irony of it all. "I've already detected that you have the same internal technology—albeit, several generations behind ours. You too will be affected. Ultimately, both our, and your, mortality is at stake here."

Jason let that sink in. His entire crew, Dira, Nan, the kids, were dependent on their internal Caldurian nanotech devices.

"What is it you need?"

"An original, not replicated, Zip accelerator … such as the one on the *Minian*."

"Why not just ask? It's a problem we are all faced with … why not work in concert with us?"

Moe didn't answer. Curly and Larry stayed quiet as well.

Then the reason hit him, and Jason knew exactly why. "All your advances … your subsequent dominance over those you encounter … is based on that technology. Sure, you've been able to integrate it into miraculous devices. Been able to exploit it in ways that are truly amazing. But your society doesn't fully understand the technology … at least, not completely. What would happen if someone else … another society … figures it out? Hell, they could hold that over you. Replace you as the dominant player." Jason chuckled at the thought of that. "You assholes."

It was starting to make sense. Yes, they needed the *Minian* and the original Zip accelerators. But they needed *some-*

thing more, as well. Someone smart enough to be free of the Caldurian mindset—outside the box. Ricket! If anyone could figure out old Alurian technology, since that society no longer exists, it would be Ricket.

"You'll permit us to return to our vessels now, since we provided you with all the information you asked for." Moe stared across at Jason.

"Maybe. But certainly not before we get our people back. I suggest you put your heads together and come up with a better way for us to infiltrate that ship ... the *Parcical*."

★ ★ ★

Jason sat in the dark, in the ready room office, waiting for Admiral Dixon to come to a decision. The truth was, Jason was prepared to disobey his orders, if need be. Thinking about it, there was a good chance Dixon too had nano-devices embedded within his gray matter. If so, his mortality was also at stake.

He caught the admiral at dinner ... *or was it lunch there?* He was eating at his desk and chewing. And thinking.

"Damn ... are you sure about all this? That those Caldurian captains were telling you the truth?"

"I'm sure, sir."

"Well, that does change things. No matter what havoc Captain Oz continues to cause, it seems our own technological superiority is at stake, and that takes precedence. Not to mention, the many lives within Star Watch and select fleet personnel."

"Not to forget the acting-president of the United States," Jason added.

Dixon glared back at Jason, knowing full well, not only was Nan his ex-wife, but immensely important to the U.S.'s, and Earth's, future recovery from the recent Craing war.

"Fine. You'll stay on mission in the Arkwane system. You have three days. No more. There are reports coming in that Captain Oz's fleet could travel as far as Earth. We don't want another attack in our backyard. Although, he'd be crazy, going up against the might of the Allied … and U.S. fleets. Jason, I want to be kept in the loop … get me updates no less than twice a day. Is that understood, Captain?"

"Perfectly, Admiral. And I won't forget about Oz … I have unfinished business with him."

The connection ended and Jason was somewhat satisfied he'd gained the admiral's limited support. Three days would be tight. He rubbed his tired eyes—he needed sleep. He rose and left the ready room, exiting the officer's suite, and headed toward the bridge.

Perkins was seated in the command chair.

The onboard AI announced, "Captain on deck."

Perkins stood and relinquished the chair.

"What's the situation, XO?"

"We're still running cloaked, and in high orbit over Arkwane. We haven't been scanned and there's no indication the Caldurians, or the Arkwanians, for that matter, know we're here."

"And the *Parcical*?"

"Impossible to tell for sure. If she is there, the vessel must be invisible to sensors … all our scans have come back negative."

Jason looked around the *Assailant*'s cramped bridge at her smaller nighttime, grave-shift crew.

"One of the Caldurian captains mentioned they were here to pick up a load of something called **Palm-Stalk**. I wonder if that narrows things down any?"

Army Ranger, Sergeant Gail Stone, was seated at Gunny Orion's station. Six feet tall and thin, she wore her platinum-blonde hair crew-cut short, except for her bangs, which angled down across her forehead, nearly covering her eyes. The effect was dramatic and eye-catching, which, Jason figured, was her intention. She turned in her seat, using her fingers to push her bangs away and secure behind one ear. "I wish I had that tidbit of information four hours ago," she said, then spun back to her board. Her fingers moved quickly as she entered something; soon, her head could be seen nodding up and down. "Of course ..." she exclaimed aloud. She turned back around. "That stuff, *Palm-Stalk*, practically covers the entire planet's ocean floor. It's their main crop. What's interesting, though, is not all gets harvested at the same time. There are only three submerged harvesting stations in use currently." She pointed to the forward display.

Jason saw the quickly revolving, bright blue planet. Arkwane was similar to Earth, having white wispy clouds and royal blue oceans, but there were no patches of brown or green, or even gray. Three areas on the planet were circled in red, and within each circle was a much smaller black circle, about the size of Africa on Earth.

"Those are the harvested areas, and the specific stations for those crops," Sergeant Stone said pointing, looking proud of herself.

"Good work, Sergeant. Now tell me at which station sits the *Parcical*?"

She continued to study the screen. Her bangs, breaking free from their ear-hold, hung over her eyes. Stone made no attempt to move them back as she stood and approached the display. She raised an arm and pointed at the center-most pair of circles: "Here, Captain. She's sitting right here."

"How do you know?" Perkins asked before Jason could.

"Crops are disappearing and at an astounding rate ... a whole acre at a time. Not simply moving from one location to another, but completely disappearing. That's some heavy-duty tech causing that."

Chapter 13

Ocean Floor, Arkwane
Parcical, Norwell's Workshop

Ricket was given several tasks to perform by Norwell over the past twenty-four hours. Relatively simple ones, Ricket suspected they were merely tests of some sort. Norwell wanted to learn, first hand, what Ricket was capable of. His first task was to troubleshoot a malfunctioning replicator—one of three—mounted inside the workshop. He found the problem and had it operational within thirty minutes. His second task was to assess what was needed to get his own internal nanotech devices updated to the latest Caldurian standards. He determined that the upgrades would require micro-hardware modifications, as well as a complete flushing of his internal nanites. Apparently, the billions of nanites currently attending to his bodily needs were far too antiquated to update.

Norwell, looking over Ricket's findings, agreed with Ricket's assessment, and whisked him away to the ship's small Medical compartment, where he spent about an hour in a MediPod device far more advanced than anything he'd encountered before. At first, he was reluctant to undergo the procedure. Would he somehow lose himself during the process? What would Norwell implant within his physiology? Would he forever be at their calling, no more than an organic droid ... the Caldurians at the controls? But Ricket was provided exact details of the procedures—what would be done to him, down to the smallest detail. After reviewing the MediPod's instruction set, Ricket recognized he had little to fear. In fact, he became excited at the prospect of adding far more capabilities to those he currently possessed ... even with his own *jury-rigged* modifications. Gaining increased internal sensors, enhanced diagnostic capabilities, and better overall cognitive functioning, he would also be provided with the latest communications package. In the end, the procedure was a complete success.

Ricket's third and final task was to design a new hand-held sensor device—one that could detect if something was replicated, or was, in fact, an original. Although a far more difficult task, Ricket designed the device within several hours, and had it ready to send to the ship's phase synthesizer.

As Norwell, sitting at his workbench, reviewed the sensor device design, Ricket watched the elderly Caldurian. Norwell was dying. Ricket had suspected the scientist of being ill before, but now, with his newly installed array of sensors, he was able to probe the Caldurian's physiology. What he found was both interesting and disturbing: Embedded within his brain was a ticking time bomb, and it didn't take a genius to understand the implications. The device had served only one primary purpose—controlling Norwell. Control him, keep him from leaving, make him do what he was directed to do. Briefly,

Ricket wondered if such a device was subversively inserted into his own brain, but he dismissed it. The device would be simple to detect, just as he'd done with Norwell.

Norwell's ticking time bomb was at the end of its cycle. Leaking radiation was at toxic levels, and even though his internal nanites were doing their best to compensate, they were quickly becoming overtaxed. Norwell, from Ricket's assessment, had less than a week to live.

Norwell spoke without looking up from his work. "I sense you've been probing around in my head." It was a statement, not a question.

"I apologize, it was insensitive of me," Ricket said.

Norwell turned in his seat and gazed at Ricket. He looked old and tired. The slightest smile crossed his thin lips, and he said, "You have questions. You want to know why."

"Yes."

"It's complicated. It wasn't necessary—I've always been dedicated to my work … to my people. But fear affects judgment. The Caldurians are an amazing race … we are caring, and devoted to the natural order of things. An empathetic society, we abhor conflict and war. For the most part, our advanced Caldurian technology has allowed us near-perfect existence across numerous realms of the multiverse."

Ricket already knew that to be true, but he quietly listened, sensing Norwell's need to formally express his thoughts.

"There are but a handful of great minds left among the Caldurian people. I am one of them. But in their fear of losing one of their most important intellects, they have inadvertently killed him. As you've undoubtedly discovered, the device implanted in my brain has become caustic to my system. And no, it cannot be removed or tampered with. It cannot be repaired."

"I am sorry, Norwell. Are you in much pain?"

"Yes … much pain, and I am tired."

Ricket did not know what to say. He felt sad for the old Caldurian.

"We have been watching you for many years, Ricket; some you know about. The Caldurian you call Granger observed you undetected, and there were others. So when this latest development began to emerge, the faltering of the Zip accelerators ... it was determined that in addition to acquiring the *Minian*, you would be abducted and convinced to lead our technological efforts into the future. You will take my place as the Caldurian Science *Omni*: a most auspicious and revered position."

Again, Ricket was caught off guard and became tongue tied. Flustered, he looked away.

Norwell continued, "The third task I gave you ... the design of a new sensor device."

"Yes, to detect if something was replicated; or was, in fact, an original. Was it not to your liking? I could reevaluate my design and—"

Norwell raised both palms, gesturing him to stop. "Ricket, the design is fine. What took you thirty minutes ... from imagining, to design, to be ready for phase synthesis has stumped the Caldurian science community ... including me, for more than thirty years."

Ricket looked at the small *virtual* tab, lying on the workshop counter. It held the design code for the device. He picked it up, weightless in his fingers, then placed it back down on the counter.

"I cannot stay here. I cannot do what you need me to do, Norwell. My home is with the crew of the *Minian*." He searched for a better phrasing: "I have lived two hundred and thirty-six years. I have held esteemed positions among my people, the Craing. I was Chief Scientist ... even emperor, at one time. I lost my way ... lost my soul to technology, but found it again with the help of strangers, now friends, both figuratively and literally. After two hundred and thirty-six years, I have a family. There is nothing you can say or do to me that would cause me to desert them. Nothing. I am sorry."

"I too am sorry, Ricket, as sorry as I am for my own plight. You will not be allowed to leave ... not ever. You might not have an embedded device implanted in your brain, but technology, being what it is at this point in time, made that unnecessary."

Ricket quickly reviewed the code on the updated nano-tech procedure. Racing line by line, as fast as any AI could, he mentally assembled and disassembled the embedded, elegant and intricate, programming. And there it was, hidden in plain sight: Two lines of code that diametrically opposed each other. Two simple lines of code, innocuous, that for all intent and purpose, were no different than the ticking time bomb embedded in Norwell's brain.

"I did not see it. Clever ... very clever," Ricket said. "This was your program ... I see your technique, the artistry in the language ... in the programming. It was fine work, Norwell."

Moisture welled in his eyes and a single tear wet the old scientist's cheek. "I am sorry ... more than you will ever know. I should not have done this to you. As ordered ... I placed the same shackles, which have tormented me for so many years, onto you. And, unfortunately, your plight, should you not stay here, on board the *Parcical*, would still be the same. Your death won't be instantaneous ... but there will be degradation of the nano-devices, as they become toxic—soon raging infections, which will be painful and irreversible. Here, Ricket, is your home, for as long as you live."

Ricket reexamined Norwell's internal code and instantly knew that Norwell's attempt to imprison him would be relatively easy for him to extricate. He would not tell this to Norwell ... no need to disappoint the dying scientist.

Chapter 14

```
Open Space, Near Arkwane
Assailant, Captain's Quarters
```

At 0400, Jason had no sooner rested his head on the pillow than the ship's klaxon began to wail a call to battle stations. In less than two minutes, he'd dressed and returned to the bridge.

"What the hell's going on?"

Out of breath, Orion too ran into the bridge and quickly moved to the tactical station, sitting down next to Sergeant Stone.

Stone said, "Captain, there are twelve Master Class Caldurian vessels now moving into local space. Four are the same ships we encountered earlier. We only got visual confirmation of their presence after you'd left the bridge."

"I understand, Sergeant. Hand everything over to Gunny; you're relieved until your next shift."

Jason could see the young tactical specialist didn't want to miss any of the coming action.

Orion said, "She can stay, if she wants. I could use her help keeping a visual on so many hard-to-track targets."

"That's fine then."

Perkins relinquished the command chair, as the rest of the early-morning shift began filing in, replacing their counterparts. One after another, a fresh bridge crew took over.

"There!" Sergeant Stone yelled, startling Jason and everyone else on the bridge. "Did you see that? That glimmer, at the planet's outer atmosphere?"

"What? What are you talking about?" Jason asked.

"It was only for a second, but I saw the perfect contour of a cloaked vessel, just now leaving the planet. Egg-shaped ... and she was moving fast. Definitely a ship. The *Parcical* ... I just know it."

Jason looked to Orion for confirmation.

"I didn't see it ... but I'd go with Stone's evaluation ... I trained her ... she's pretty good."

The two females exchanged quick smiles and bumped fists.

"Tell me we're still cloaked and nobody knows we're here," Jason said.

"Affirmative on that, Captain. Nothing on comms," Seaman Gordon said.

"Captain, there's an interchange wormhole forming two million miles off our stern. All vessels in our area are moving in that direction," McNeil reported.

"Can we catch them ... go through it, along with them?"

"Not without phase-shifting, sir."

Jason didn't like that option—that could possibly make their presence known to the Caldurian fleet.

Gunny must have read his thoughts. "They know we're here, somewhere, Cap ... we dropped in on four of their ships and abducted three of their captains."

"Let's wait until their last ship enters the mouth of the wormhole. Only then, phase-shift in, following behind it."

"Aye, Captain."

There was no way Jason was going to lose sight of their twelve ships. Somewhere in that mix was the *Parcical*, and maybe even Ricket.

Two of their massive ships had already passed through the wormhole; the other ten were rapidly converging behind them. Suddenly Jason realized he hadn't attempted to hail Ricket directly, via his NanoCom, for several hours. He brought two fingers to his ear and tried hailing him. Almost immediately, he heard Ricket's voice—sounding distant and hollow.

"Captain! You must warn Jeffer—" The connection was cut off.

All eyes were on Jason. "Did you get Ricket?" Orion asked.

"I did, but he was cut off. It sounded like he was telling me to warn Jefferson Station." Jason pointed to Seaman Gordon. "Get on the horn … let them know they may have company."

"Aye, Captain." Seaman Gordon nodded and quickly turned back toward his station.

The last of the Caldurian vessels could be seen entering the mouth of the wormhole.

"Phase-shifting now, Captain," McNeil said, and everything flashed white.

The display suddenly changed; they were now at the mouth of the gaping wormhole. The final Caldurian ship was already gone from view.

"Good job, McNeil, you timed that perfectly. Extremely close, but perfectly."

"Wormhole is collapsing, Captain," Orion said.

By the time her words were spoken, the *Assailant* had already entered—was safely within the space anomaly's grasp.

Then, just as quickly, they exited the wormhole.

In the far distance the bright blue planet Earth appeared, looking small and vulnerable. Their current distance from Earth was about five times the distance between the Earth and moon—or somewhere near a million miles. Between their ship and Earth were a dozen mile-long vessels, and somewhere, too, a significantly smaller cloaked vessel—the *Parcical*.

"Hail coming in from Jefferson Station, Captain."

"Put it on screen, Seaman Gordon."

Admiral Dixon's worried, line-creased face filled the display. "Captain Reynolds, what the hell have you done? If you're responsible for bringing that fleet—"

Jason cut him off. "We had nothing to do with their arrival. We're cloaked and they haven't observed our presence. We simply followed them here. Admiral … listen to me … they're there to grab the *Minian* … you need to phase-shift her out—"

The admiral cut Jason off, "No! She's in no shape … she's a mess. All her navigation and propulsion systems are offline."

"Get me Granger!" Jason barked, not having time for an argument. The *Minian*'s phase-shifting ability was neither a part of the propulsion nor the navigation systems, and he strongly suspected Dixon to be clueless about such details.

The admiral looked indignant, ready to put Jason in his place; instead, he looked away to talk to someone nearby. A moment later, Granger's face took the place of the admiral's on the display.

"What is it, Captain Reynolds?"

"A fleet of your brethren are here in local space, and from the looks of it, ready to take back their ship. Can the *Minian* be phase-shifted away … like right now?"

Granger immediately shook his head, then stopped, as if considering something else. "It will take me twenty minutes to reconnect the interface. Alone, I don't think I have time."

"How about if I sent you a little help?"

"Do it!"

Jason scanned the bridge. Of course, Bristol wasn't there. That would be too easy.

"I'm already on it, Cap … he's in the mess," Orion said. "I've forwarded the *Minian*'s bridge coordinates to him."

"Helm, phase-shift us closer in to Jefferson Station … close enough for Bristol to phase-shift onto the *Minian*."

"Yes, sir … that will take several consecutive phase-shifts … but I'm on it, Captain."

Jason realized he'd been holding his breath and forced himself to breathe. Including the Craing, there had never before been such a powerful, imposing, alien force within this close proximity to Earth. The Caldurians were not known for any ruthlessness—he couldn't recall an instance where they had arbitrarily attacked another without provocation. But what the three Caldurian captains confessed—if they had told the truth—was that the Caldurians might just be desperate enough to do something out of character. If so, the base at Jefferson Station, and any Allied or U.S. fleet asset stationed there, was in jeopardy. Hell, Earth was in jeopardy.

Several bright flashes occurred and Jefferson Station filled the forward display. Jefferson Station, and its adjoining Allied fleet base, was always an impressive sight. Details of the sprawling space base became more apparent as they approached. Sited closer to the moon than Earth, four sprawling military platforms for the Allied combined fleets could now be seen; dozens of moored warships idled there, scheduled for maintenance for one thing or another. But it was Jefferson Station that held their full attention. As the recognized seat of the Alliance, most major decision-making policy took place there. The station went up against all preconceived, conventional design principles, but with that said, it appeared beautiful and inspiring, yet immense and intimidating at the same time. Jason had spent some significant time there over the last few months, but still, upon seeing it again, he found it captivating. There was the center hub disk, or saucer, spanning a thirty-mile radius, where the primary station's populace conducted business and resided. Encircling the hub, almost twenty miles out, was a thick outer ring, which had ten constantly rotating, encircling, round rings spaced evenly along the structure. Jason thought the smaller perpendicular rings looked somewhat like little Ferris wheels.

Orion said, "There are several Alliance meganaughts, five dreadnaughts, and one hundred and twenty heavy and light cruisers in the immediate area."

The *Minian*, clearly visible to them now, was secured to the outer station ring.

"Captain, Bristol has phase-shifted onto the *Minian*'s bridge."

"Thank you, Gunny. What's the ETA of the inbound Caldurian fleet?"

"If they don't phase-shift, like we just did, about ten minutes."

"Sir, it's Admiral Dixon again," Seaman Gordon reported.

Jason gestured toward the forward display and waited for the crusty officer to appear.

"I hope you understand the predicament we're in, Captain. We're mobilizing our assets and preparing for battle."

"Well, that's a big mistake, Admiral. You need to stand down and remain with the status quo ... don't do anything ... anything at all ... that would be construed as aggressive."

"I don't take orders from you, Captain. I think you've forgotten your place. We're calling all forces to battle stations; we're certainly not backing down from an obviously hostile invasion of our sovereign space."

"Don't be stupid, Admiral! Just one of those Caldurian vessels will mop the floor with our fleet assets, let alone twelve."

Admiral Dixon's face darkened several shades of red, his building anger clearly evident. "Damn you, Reynolds. You're on report. As of this moment I'm relieving you of your command. Helm officer ... I'm ordering you to bring the *Assailant* into a directed berth. Captain, report to my office when you arrive."

The feed went black. McNeil turned in his seat and faced Jason. "Orders, Captain?"

Jason had to smile at that. He thought about their situation and rose from the command chair. "I have no intention of following the admiral's orders. Any of you are free to leave the bridge if you wish to stand with Admiral Dixon."

No one made a move toward the exit.

"Captain, Allied and U.S. fleet assets are on the move. All manned vessels within the area have been ordered to their battle stations," Orion said.

"Somebody give me a live visual feed of the *Minian*'s bridge," Jason said.

When the live feed came across, Jason's heart sank. Virtually every console was torn apart, exposing inner circuitry and cables. Only Bristol's legs could be seen, protruding beneath the ship's forward, right-helm station. Tempted to ask them their progress, he resisted the impulse, knowing they were working as quickly as possible. Any distraction would only hinder their progress.

Low but excited murmurs were heard coming from the tactical station.

"What is it, Gunny?"

"Sergeant Stone thinks she knows where the *Parcical* is."

Jason saw Stone nervously look up from the board before her, to Orion, then over at him. "What do you see, Sergeant?"

"Another glimmer ... I think it happens just prior to, and just after, phase-shifts. When other Caldurian vessels arrive and depart there's always a bright white flash. Only it seems this one particular ship momentarily glimmers, instead. You have to be looking out for it to see it. Fortunately, I know what to look for."

"Well ... where is it then?" Jason asked impatiently.

Stone replied, "She's in close ... ten miles out from the

Minian's starboard side. She jumped ahead of the rest of their fleet."

"Captain, four Allied dreadnaughts … the *Cornice*, the *Atlantic*, the *Bridgestone*, and the *Shire* have moved into a line. They're powering guns," Orion shouted.

"Gordon … put me on the screen of every local Allied and U.S. vessel. Do it now!"

It took five seconds before Gordon said, "You're live, Captain."

Jason took a half step closer to the forward display. "I am Captain Jason Reynolds … I'm sure most of you know who I am. What you don't know is that I also hold the fleet rank of Rear Admiral. Bridge commanders, you need to stand down … right now! We cannot go up against twelve Caldurian vessels. Do not … I repeat … do not engage the approaching Caldurian fleet. Hold your positions and wait for further orders from me."

Jason was well aware he'd just torched his career. Not only had he disobeyed the direct orders of a superior, he'd blatantly incited fleet-wide mutiny. *Screw it.* What was happening *now* was far too important to worry about the rules.

"The Caldurian fleet has picked up speed, Captain. ETA is less than five minutes, before they reach the line of Allied dreadnaughts," Orion said.

Jason saw Perkins hurrying into the bridge, making a beeline for him.

"I've been instructed to relieve you of your command, sir."

"Thank you for the update, XO." The two officers held each other's stare for several long beats, as the bridge went quiet. Jason had always found Perkins' *go by the book*, risk-adverse style of command irritating. More than once, he'd wanted to tell his second-in-command to grow a pair, but he hadn't, because the man was the perfect counterpart to his own *off the book* command style. As captain, Jason probably played things far too loose; he definitely took far too many risks. No ... he needed Perkins' careful, measured influence, at least sometimes. But right then wasn't one of those times.

Perkins spoke first. "Message delivered, sir. What can I do to help?"

"Help Gordon on comms. He's inundated with fleet-wide requests."

As Perkins joined Seaman Gordon's side, Jason kept his eyes focused on the *Minian's* bridge. Bristol, now standing, was talking to Granger. Holding two fingers up to his ear, Jason heard Granger's incoming NanoCom hail.

"What's your status, Granger?" Jason asked.

"We'll attempt to phase-shift within the next minute or two. Stand by."

Damn, a minute or two, right now, is like an eternity. "Hurry," was all Jason could say.

"The *Cornice* and the *Atlantic* have moved from their positions. They're letting the fleet pass through. Looks like you made an impression on the fleet commanders, Captain," Orion said.

Perkins spun on his heels. "Captain! Jefferson Station ... they've sided with the admiral. I can hear their chatter."

The forward display now showed a wide, external view of Jefferson Station. Plasma fire was erupting from no less than twenty on-station cannons. Bright red energy streaks crisscrossed open space, heading toward the incoming Caldurian fleet.

Somehow, during the action, Jason didn't initially notice that the *Minian* was no longer parked alongside the outer ring of the space station. Did Bristol and Granger manage to phase-shift her away?

Sergeant Stone said, "It was the *Parcical* ... sir. There was no phase-shift. Both the *Minian* and *Parcical* are gone."

Before Jason could respond, the first of many explosions in space occurred. Before their eyes, they watched the Caldurian fleet of twelve Master Class ships return fire. Jason, like everyone else on the bridge, stood paralyzed—unable to do anything but watch as the station's outer ring took the initial plasma blasts. The firepower that these newer Master Class warships were inflicting upon the Alliance headquarters was beyond terrible ... it was catastrophic. Huge segments of Jefferson Station's outer ring were floating free among thousands and thousands of smaller, fractured sections—among that debris, Jason knew, were many bodies ... some, even now, dying a horrible death within the icy vacuum of space. *God, let that be the end of it ...* Jason thought. But it wasn't the end. If anything, the Caldurian fleet increased their barrage, turning what remained of the other ring, the larger sections, into nothing more than space dust.

Hearing her rapid intake of a breath, Jason was aware of Orion, now standing at her station. "How can they do this? Why?"

Jason was afraid to move, afraid to even breathe ... hoping that the Caldurians would be satisfied with the devastation they'd already caused. The station's central saucer still remained. Tens of thousands of people were still alive ... would live to see tomorrow.

After a long period where no more plasma fire came from the Caldurian fleet, Jason was close to letting out his own breath and relaxing just a bit. But the bright plasma fire erupted again, and in one more simultaneously choreographed show of ruthless power, Jefferson Station's massive central saucer was atomized by an explosion the likes, the intensity, that Jason had never experienced before.

Chapter 15

Sol Solar System
Assailant, Bridge

Silent, shocked astonishment was soon replaced by voices expressing emotional outrage. Jason watched as the twelve Caldurian Master Class ships methodically moved away, passing Earth's moon, until the black vessels were no longer visible against the equally dark backdrop of space.

Jason's fists tightened—his knuckles turning white—as he stood perfectly still. He vowed he'd have his revenge on the Caldurians ... Once again, and unequivocally, Earth was at war with an alien race.

"Captain!"

Jason turned, seeing Orion standing by his side. *How long has she been there? How long have I been lost in thought?*

"Captain ... some of it's still there ... look!" she said, pointing to the display.

Behind a space cloud of debris, continuing to flash with hundreds of smaller, micro explosions, was what remained of Jefferson Station. About one-fifth its original size, a ragged segment of the inner saucer was now visible.

Perkins and Gordon were at the comms station, seeming overwhelmed by the increased level of inbound communications.

"Have Sergeant Stone give them a hand," Jason said to Orion.

Perkins, two fingers up to his ear, turned toward Jason from across the bridge. He looked white as a ghost and ready to throw up—pretty much like others of the crew. Jason went over to his side.

"Captain … fleet commanders are requesting orders. They want to assist in rescue searches for possible survivors."

Jason looked toward the display. *Could there be any?* "Have you made contact with anyone? Is someone still alive on the station? Survivors?"

"Yes … the section that remains does contain crew barracks … some of the *Minian*'s crew were temporarily on duty at the station. I talked to the ranking officer … a Lieutenant Kline."

"Wait … hundreds of officers were stationed there … generals and admirals … ambassadors and dignitaries, from the far outer reaches of the Alliance."

Perkins stared back at Jason, obviously not knowing what to say. Jason, feeling a hand on his shoulder, turned to see Billy behind him. He regarded his friend's familiar reassuring face.

"Walk with me," Billy said.

Jason, looking disoriented and confused, simply stared back at Billy. Others on the bridge had taken notice. The bridge was going quiet.

"Come on … let's go," Billy said, gesturing with his chin toward the exit.

"Um … now? I don't know … go now? In the midst of all—"

"Now, Jason."

Jason followed his friend off the bridge and into the central corridor away from all the concerned faces of the bridge crew. Once clear of the bridge entrance, Billy suddenly stopped in his tracks and spun around, facing Jason.

Jason looked blankly back at Billy.

"You're in shock. If you could see what I'm seeing, you'd know what I'm talking about."

Jason didn't argue with him. He shook his head repeatedly as if hearing something in his head; voices he didn't want to listen to … didn't want to accept. He looked down at the deck … at his boots.

"Look at me, Jason!"

Jason refused to meet Billy's eyes. He spoke quietly, barely above a whisper: "Billy, I … I killed all those people … might as well have pulled the trigger myself."

Billy's face twisted in an expression of undisguised anger. Without warning, he hit Jason with a roundhouse right, lifting him off his feet and knocking him down, onto his ass. His fist still raised, Billy loomed over Jason, looking ready to throw another punch. "I'm only going to say this once, so listen up … not only did you not cause any of those deaths … you probably saved many thousands of lives. Had an Allied vessel fired on the Caldurians, she, too, would have been destroyed. Hell, they might have let loose, destroying every ship in local space. You're being touted as a fucking hero. Personally, I think that's going a bit overboard, but what do I know? Listen to me, Jason: You're going to get off your ass, go into your ready room, and notify Washington what's happened here. Then you're going to contact your father."

"My father?"

"Yes … he may not be one hundred percent, but he's still plenty effective. You'll need his support up here."

Jason still wasn't getting it.

"Jason … Captain … you are now *the* ranking Allied Forces officer. You're the man and you better get up, off your ass, and start acting like it." Billy held out his hand and waited, unblinking, for Jason to reach up and take it.

★ ★ ★

Thirty-eight minutes later, Jason was back on the *Assailant*'s bridge. The crew's eyes tracked his movements as he assumed his seat in the command chair. Perkins, standing next to Gordon and Stone at the comms station, and Orion, seated at tactical, all stared back at him.

Earlier, Jason had done exactly what Billy, not so subtly, told him to do. He'd rushed into his ready room and called the White House. He spoke to Nan, relaying all the horrific events that had transpired, and watched her expression turn from professional concern to pure shock.

"You're telling me it's gone ... Jefferson Station has been obliterated? All those on board ... dead?"

Nan's hands covered her mouth as she stared at Jason and slowly absorbed the impact of what he was telling her.

"I know this is a blow ... a terrible, terrible blow ... but we'll make our way through this tragedy, Nan."

"And the *Minian* ... she's ... she's gone too?"

"Yes. She is gone."

He watched Nan as the news sank in. No longer looking straight into the camera, her eyes lost their focus. Slowly her head shook—the weight of the devastation closing in on her.

"Hey, Nan ... we ... you ... have some big decisions to make now. But we'll get through it."

Her eyes locked on Jason's. She was all business again, though fury raged in her eyes. "You don't understand, Jason ... the summit ... it was being held up there, at Jefferson Station."

"What summit? You're not making any sense."

"They're all gone. Not only were all the ranking officers from fleet command there ... all the U.S. commanders from

Earth … generals and admirals … the Joint Chiefs, for God's sake! They were in attendance for the annual Joint Chief's summit. Usually, it's held here, in Washington. I was scheduled to arrive there this morning too, but Mollie suddenly came down with the flu. She threw up on my dress on our way out the door. We were about to head out again when you called."

Jason was processing the fact he'd almost lost Nan and Mollie when she continued: "Jason, as Rear Admiral, clearly the most experienced officer in Allied space, you are now the Alliance's ranking superior officer. You know, don't you, the president of the United States doesn't command the Allied forces?"

Jason nodded. Billy had alluded to the same thing, but it hadn't fully sunk in. "Yes … I do know that, Nan."

"Good. So let me ask you, Admiral Reynolds, are we at a state of war with the Caldurians? Is that what you're informing me of?"

Jason didn't answer right away; but he didn't need to ponder the question, or weigh the pros and cons. Thousands of men and women, citizens from other worlds throughout the Alliance, were brutally killed; no warning—no attempt made to work things out through negotiations. Of course they were at war. But was that even realistic, considering the Caldurians typically operated far out of reach … from some other realm within the vast multiverse?

"We are at war, Nan. A war we cannot win without spacecraft like the *Minian*. We need that ship—we need her technology." Jason then realized something more—Granger and Bristol, working on the *Minian's* bridge, were now also gone— but, he hoped, still alive.

"Nan … I'm going after them. Without that ship, we're not only at the mercy of the Caldurians, we're at the mercy of every uprising faction within the galaxy."

"Just tell me what you want me to do."

"Heads of state within the Alliance need to be contacted. All other members, too, need to be told what has happened up here. My next call is to my father; he'll manage things here, in space, in my absence."

"Stay in contact, Jason. We cannot afford to lose you … not now, with everything falling apart."

Jason called his father, who took fifteen minutes to get to the comms unit. When his face finally appeared, Jason noticed his father's two- or three-days-old stubble had progressed into a full-on white beard. Streaks of black grease across his face made him look like a character from a movie.

"What the hell's so damn important? Can't you simply leave a message, like normal people do? Don't you know you can't stop in the middle of a transmission rebuild?"

"Dad … listen to me: I need to speak to you as admiral-on-duty right now, okay?"

"What is it? What's happened?"

"The Caldurians … they've taken out Jefferson Station. They have the *Minian*."

"Jesus Christ … the summit … are you telling me that all the superior officers … Joint Chiefs—"

"All gone, Dad. Listen, I need to get back to the bridge. Things are held together only by a thread up here. I need your help and I need it now."

"Of course. I need to shower first, but I can be in space within an hour."

"One more thing, Admiral. You'll be reporting to me … not the other way around."

★ ★ ★

Jason brought his attention back to the bridge. Orion, facing him, looked concerned.

"Okay, Gunny ... bring me up to speed."

"There are four hundred and twenty-one survivors living on the station. In addition to that saucer section, there are three separate, outer-ring segments, also containing people. Of those alive, eighty-nine are injured. Dira and her team phase-shifted directly onto the saucer and are currently attending to the most critical. She mentioned she tried to hail you but you didn't answer."

"Been pretty busy, Gunny. What does she need?"

"MediPods ... she says a good portion of the injured will probably die without one."

There had been close to a dozen of them on Jefferson Station; Ricket had them especially configured for the station's hospital, which was now, of course, gone. "There's a handful on Earth, used for treating *peovils*. You'll need to contact the Pentagon to track them down."

"I'm on it. What's our next move, Cap?" she asked. The bridge crew stopped what they were doing to also look toward Jason.

He looked at the forward display, at the blackness of space. "Any indication the Caldurians called up an interchange wormhole, or phase-shifted?"

"No ... in fact, they're still out there. I sent a probe out after them. Figured you had your hands full. They've left this solar system but are still relatively close."

"Good. To answer your question, we're going after them and we're going right now."

"Comms ... dampen our outgoing communications. Helm ... ensure we're still cloaked and get us on a matching course. Let's catch them! And watch the heat of our drives. Stealth is the name of the game from here on out."

Chapter 16

Open Space, 1.2 Billion Miles from
Sol Solar System
Parcical, MicroVault Terminal

Ricket stood within the confines of the *Parcical's* Mi-croVault access terminal and felt a level of frustration surpassing anything he could remember. He felt useless and now millions … billions of lives would be irrevocably affected. Losing *The Lilly*, months earlier, was a devastating loss to the Alliance. And now this: the loss of the *Minian*! How would that affect the Allied worlds' very survival? And what of the ship's crew … his friends?

Hobel, Norwell, and Ricket stood before the wrap-around display, viewing the section of the MicroVault that had been allocated for its latest addition, the Minian. She hovered in there, in the glaring whiteness of virtual storage, and didn't look real. The once-huge spacecraft looked more like a child's toy.

Norwell was at the pedestal. His brow furrowed as his fingers moved quickly over the small virtual display. He looked up toward Hobel and said, "The ship made the transition into virtual storage unaffected."

Hobel's strained expression relaxed somewhat, and Ricket saw him take in a deep breath and expel it noisily out. Apparently, the whole process was far more dangerous than he'd previously assumed.

Norwell said, "There is a … an issue … Omni. There are two life forms present. On the vessel's bridge."

"Human?"

"One human and one Caldurian."

Ricket watched the exchange with interest. Granger had to be the Caldurian, since he was the *Minian*'s lone Caldurian crewmember. He wondered who the human was.

"They will not survive much longer within that miniaturized virtual environment. One option is to simply let them expire … their bodies will not cause any issues," Norwell explained.

"No! They must be saved … I insist," Ricket said adamantly.

Norwell and Hobel looked down at Ricket, as if noticing him standing there for the first time.

"I'm sorry, Ricket. That was insensitive of us," Hobel said. The Omni looked to Norwell and nodded his head in a gesture that said *please, take care of this.*

★ ★ ★

Ricket had thrice visited the small *Parcical*'s Medical compartment, each time finding Granger and Bristol still unconscious on their gurneys. This time, though, they were awake and sitting up. A male medical tech was attending to a gash on Bristol's forehead.

"It's fine! You checked it like two minutes ago. Back off, dude!" Bristol noticed Ricket standing in the doorway. "Ricket?" The smile on the young science officer's face was genuine. He looked relieved. "What is going on … where the hell are we?"

"I will explain everything … as best I can … soon." Ricket turned his attention to Granger.

The tall Caldurian sat on the gurney, his arms folded across his chest, with a bemused expression Ricket could not quite read. "And how are you, Granger?" he asked.

"Well … I'm alive. For how long, only time will tell. The progressives aren't exactly my allies. You know I didn't leave under the best circumstances."

Ricket was somewhat aware of Granger's past situation. Several years ago he and other crewmembers commandeered an advanced Caldurian vessel, the *Minian*, to flee from one multiverse realm in order to return to this one. He would, Ricket imagined, be held responsible for his past crimes, now that he was on board a Caldurian military vessel.

Bristol reached up and pulled a tethered piece of equipment down for closer examination. "The tech here is ridiculous … years … decades more advanced than even that found on the *Minian*."

Ricket simply smiled.

"How much of this thing is even real?" He tapped at the bread loaf-sized device with his fingertip.

"You will find much here is virtual, Bristol. They've mastered the technology for providing tactile feel and simulated mass, even true weight characteristics, for what, in actuality, is nothing more than complex programming."

"Uh huh … you can feel it … like a tingle when you touch

things like this ... whatever the hell it is." Bristol brought his attention back to Ricket. "Where's the *Minian*?"

The answer came from Hobel, who'd just entered the compartment: "The *Minian* is fine. She is stored within this vessel."

"Bullshit. That's impossible."

Taken aback by Bristol's outburst, Hobel looked to Ricket.

"Bristol rarely filters what he is thinking," Ricket said. "It may take a while for you to get used to him and his ways."

"I'm sitting right here, Ricket. If he has a problem with how I talk, fuck him. As far as I can tell, I was just abducted ... right?" Bristol, now looking directly at Hobel, asked, "What do you want from me? Why am I here?"

"I want nothing from you. I was content to let you die on board the *Minian* until Ricket insisted we bring you both here, on board the *Parcical*."

Hobel moved to the side of Granger's gurney and said, "I wondered if you'd ever be apprehended ... I doubted it, but I wondered just the same."

Ricket watched the exchange and noticed something interesting: There was a striking similarity between the two Caldurians. He found himself looking from one to the other—noticing the intricacies of their features—the same thinness at the bridge of their small noses; the same cleft at the center of their prominent chins. Some similarities were evident too beyond the merely physical: They wore similar expressions—the same downturn to the corners of their mouths and the same raising of their brows. *Are they brothers? Cousins?*

"You were the brightest, had the most potential," Hobel said. "Then you dishonored yourself. I figured you would return again to this realm, perhaps live among a faction of the *originals*."

Ricket didn't see how that made any sense. There were two major factions of Caldurians—the originals and the progressives. The originals lived here, in this realm; they existed more like nomads now, traveling the galaxy in what were referred to as Crystal Cities. The originals did not share the same belief that crossing into an alternate multiverse realm was acceptable. To them, it was some sort of Caldurian sacrilege. The progressives, on the other hand, were far more technologically advanced, more willing to break free from the bindings of old myths and religious doctrines.

"That's ridiculous ... I wouldn't have been accepted, nor did I want to be accepted, by any of those remaining original colonies. Many died off, anyway. I witnessed the fate of that dwindling group of Caldurians, personally. No ... instead, I made a home for myself among a diverse collection of people in this realm."

"I'm sure you have."

"So what will you do with me? Take me back? Execute me?"

"Don't be so dramatic, Granger. Yes, at some point you will need to make restitution, but you do know corporal punishment among our kind has been outlawed for hundreds of years. You know that."

"And you know, as well as I do, that as you travel within the multiverse you're altering things that should not be changed."

Hobel waved off the comment, as if it were a trivial matter. "But in the end, Granger, you may have just saved our species from a devastating fate. We originally thought the *Minian* was destroyed by a phase-shift anomaly, in a time and dimension far removed from this one."

"So what? I'm sure you have a shitload of such ships," Bristol butted in.

Hobel ignored him. "We only discovered the *Minian* by accident, when we returned from searching for new sources of Palm-Stalk."

Ricket said, "Bristol, it's not so much the *Minian* that they are interested in … it's the Zip Farm, the individual Zip accelerators. On the *Minian*, one of the earlier Master Class ships, the technology for their accelerators originally came from Alurian, a planet in the Corian Nez constellation system."

"Yeah, I know all that … they're like a hundred and thirty light-years from Earth. The Caldurians jacked the technology from them, and probably killed off all the Alurians in the process."

Hobel spun toward Bristol. "Caldurians do not arbitrarily *kill off* anyone!" But he cut his response short and Ricket knew why: the recent destruction of Jefferson Station. If that wasn't arbitrarily killing, what was? Hobel looked flustered. It was clear he was deeply affected by what happened there. It seemed also clear that Hobel probably wasn't responsible for giving the order to attack. Ricket decided he would keep the information regarding the station's demise from Bristol. At least for the time being—no sense agitating him further. It was evident he was already beginning to grate on Hobel's nerves.

"I understand from Ricket that you are quite intelligent, Bristol—that you understand alien technology nearly as well as he does. I already know Granger has a great mind. So the three of you will be tasked with finding a solution to our mutual problem. The doctor has cleared you both … you will start immediately."

"I'm not doing anything for you. Take me back to Jefferson Station," Bristol retorted, touching his forehead and noticing the open gash was no longer there.

Hobel said, "That's impossible, Jefferson—"

Ricket quickly cut Hobel off. "Bristol, please assist us. It is not for Hobel, or the Caldurians; … it is for any of us that utilize Alurian technology. Norwell, this ship's science officer, suspects our own nano-devices may eventually be affected too, since their technology is based on original Alurian science."

Bristol raised his hands in exaggerated futility. "Really? Again! Didn't you have something like that happen a few years ago ... internal nanotech was a ticking time bomb, ready to take a dump in your heads?"

"Yes and no ... this is different," Ricket told him. "Nothing is going to explode or self-destruct. But the functionality of these devices may be impaired. There's no way to know what will happen. And the problem isn't with the technology, per se—it's the inability of the technology to adjust to any new spatial changes, to the nanoscale alterations that occur in time and space within the universe ... or multiverse. Apparently, according to Norwell, the *Minian*'s Zip accelerators do adjust to spatial changes and continue to operate perfectly. It's only the duplicated, or cloned, devices, such as the Zip accelerators on other ships, even this one, that do not seem to adjust adequately. This problem has caused Caldurian ships to lose the ability to travel between multiverse realms. So we must discover why this is so and provide the necessary fixes."

"And I'll be allowed to return to Jefferson Station afterwards?" Bristol asked, looking at Ricket.

"Yes ... Or probably rejoin your crew under Captain Reynolds," Ricket said. He then turned to Hobel. "One more condition—once we've helped you, the *Minian* will be returned to the Sol solar system."

Bristol swung his feet off the gurney and slid down to the deck. "Yeah ... that's like non-negotiable, man." Bristol then looked over to Granger. "And Granger gets a free pass on all the shit he pulled with you guys several years back."

Ricket was surprised to see Hobel actually considering Bristol's words. Granger's eyes, too, were locked on Hobel, waiting for his response.

"Agreed. You have my personal promise," Hobel told them.

Hobel's eyes stayed on Ricket with an expression that said far more. Ricket himself would never be allowed to leave.

"How do we know he'll keep his word?" Bristol asked.

Irritation flared on the Omni's face. "Caldurians take great pride in their honesty. Such questioning of our integrity is offensive and I personally will not stand for it."

Bristol shrugged, "Whatever. I guess we'll get to work then."

Chapter 17

Open Space
Minian's Zip Farm, within the *Parcical*, MicroVault

Ricket, Granger, Bristol, and Norwell filed out together from the *Minian's* 12th floor DeckPort and headed across the corridor, entering into the expansive Zip Farm. Ricket still found it amazing that yes, they were on board the *Minian*, but the *Minian*, like themselves, was a mere molecular version of itself—stored within a MicroVault on board the Parcical. Two armed Caldurian guards, from the *Parcical*, followed close behind, taking up positions near the entrance.

The Zip Farm compartment was one of the largest on the vessel. Ricket found it uniquely dissimilar to the rest of the ship because Alurian technology was all around them—from the gigantic black and oily locomotive-sized Zip accelerators, lined up in parallel rows, to the somewhat old-fashioned console interfaces, sited along the forward bulkhead.

"We have twenty-two minutes. I suggest we make the most of our time here," Norwell said.

"Where do we start?" Bristol asked, looking up at the nearest towering Zip accelerator.

"Each accelerator maintains a certain amount of autonomy," Ricket explained. "They can operate on their own, or in parallel with the other accelerators here."

"Yes … and what I suspect happened was one was singled out, used as a model for others to be duplicated from," Granger said.

"Which mean all subsequent technology was born from that one unit," Bristol said. He scratched his chin and sniffed. "So right, an idiotic assumption was made that shouldn't have been made. How many accelerators are presently here? Twenty something? They will all need to be analyzed and measured for differences, down to the smallest detail logged. Only then can we determine what we're really dealing with."

"Agreed," Norwell said.

"The *Minian*'s AI can accomplish that fairly quickly. But she needs to be brought back online, to her full capabilities. Right now, the *Minian* is barely sustaining life support … has minimal, low-level, functionality," Ricket said.

"Why didn't you just leave the AI alone in the first place?" Bristol asked, looking at Norwell.

"I don't have clearance for reinstating the AI's full functionality. The Omni specifically wanted that AI deactivated. It was the first thing we were directed to do, once we had her here."

"Well, he should have come along too, if he was so interested in what we're doing. I'll reinstate her operating status to normal. It'll take me all of two minutes."

Norwell stood, looking hesitant.

Ricket knew perfectly well why the ship's AI was disengaged—sure, there were safety concerns, but also, more importantly, there was the issue of loyalty. After years of operating within the same structured environment, and having consistent interactions with the same crewmembers—the AI, in a very basic sense, becomes loyal. At least, in relative terms, to the extent an artificial intelligence device can experience such things. It is not uncommon for an AI to be totally scrubbed between redeployment with new crews.

"Wait. I don't think this is a good idea," Norwell said. "We should find another way."

Bristol scoffed at that. "You mean like use a pad and pencil? We're talking about trillions upon trillions of parallel transactions going on. Yes, there's the mechanical aspects happening too, but I suspect it'll be pretty much the same for each one. No … it's getting the AI working on it, or we're just wasting our time."

"My suggestion would be to use something like a portable AI device. Interface it to each unit separately. I have several such devices available for exactly that type of work. I'll need to create an interface to the accelerators, but that is simple," Norwell said.

"It's stupid, is what it is. By the way, just what is it you do here? You can't honestly think such a device is a workable solution. Look, the *Minian's* AI already has all the data … all the information's stored within the ship's core. I'm going with my idea. You can shoot me in the back, if you want." Bristol turned and headed for the exit.

"Where's he going?" Norwell asked nervously.

Again, a bemused expression returned to Granger's face. "I suspect he's heading for the bridge, where he'll have the most access to ship-wide systems."

"I should stop him. We'll be defying the Omni's orders."

Granger and Ricket exchanged glances.

Bristol walked between both guards and out the exit.

Granger continued, "Why don't you tell them the truth, Norwell?"

Norwell didn't answer.

"What *truth* is he referring to?" Ricket asked, looking at Norwell.

"The truth that Hobel has no intention of letting any of us live; releasing us, along with the *Minian*, was all a lie," Granger said.

Ricket looked to Norwell for confirmation. "Is that true?"

Norwell's silence was answer itself.

"Caldurians pride themselves in their peaceful ways ... risen above the barbaric methods of lesser races, society. But jeopardize their technological advantage over others, and their true nature becomes unequivocally clear. You've already witnessed it. Right now, they are desperate, and they are dangerous," Granger said.

"You speak as if you weren't one of us, Granger," Norwell said, sneering.

Ricket said, "So the sooner we find the problem ... fix your Zip accelerator issues, the sooner we will be terminated."

"No one will be terminated," Norwell said, emphatically. "And don't forget, your involvement here helps more than just the Caldurians ... the impending nanotech issues will affect many others ... including your friends."

"No, maybe not terminated ... but we'll be placed in permanent stasis somewhere within their MicroVault," Granger added.

Ricket's mind flashed to Leon and Hanna. Granger was right. Escape was their only hope of getting out alive.

Ricket was hailed by Bristol.

"Go for Ricket."

"AI's being initialized ... should be fully functional within the next few minutes."

"Thank you, Bristol. Please return to the Zip Farm. We only have a few minutes left in this session."

★ ★ ★

They were back within the *Parcical's* MicroVault terminal, with five minutes to spare. Hobel, dressed in his crisp white uniform, was waiting for them, looking anxious to hear how things had progressed.

Norwell was the first to speak. "We have only just started, Omni. There is still much testing to do. But we believe the answer lies in finding, first-off, what differences there are between the multiple Zip accelerators."

"That sounds promising. I knew the three of you, with your combined intellects, would come up with a solution. Is there anything else you need? Perhaps more equipment from the *Parcical*?"

"Most definitely, we'll need specific test equipment before our next session. Remember, we require a minimum of four hours down-time before entering the MicroVault again ... just to be on the safe side," Norwell said.

Hobel tilted his head and pursed his thin lips. "Understand, we all must sacrifice our own wellbeing for the greater good ... perhaps we can trim that down, say to ... two hours?"

"Four. Not a second sooner," Bristol retorted, on his way out of the compartment. He stopped and popped his head back in. "Okay if I upgrade my nano-devices to the latest version? I noticed a souped-up MediPod in Medical."

"As long as it does not interfere with the timing of your next session inside the vault," Hobel said.

Ricket, having completed the same MediPod procedure

earlier, thought Granger should probably take advantage of this down time as well.

"Where is Granger, Omni? Should we not wait for him?" Ricket asked.

"No … he will not be joining you this time."

"Where is he?"

"He is locked within a holding cell. He will be processed for long-term MicroVault storage."

"We need him … his experience—"

"No, Ricket. You will need to do without his input," Hobel said. "I also want to speak with you about the junior science officer. Young Bristol? Perhaps it would be best for him to join the others … in stasis … at least, for the time being."

Ricket was starting to really dislike this Caldurian captain. "I assure you, his contributions have already been beneficial. Together, the two of us will bring about answers, and a fix, much sooner than if we are split up." Ricket was well aware what was going on here. Hobel feared an attempted escape. The three of them together were too much of a risk.

Hobel seemed to be contemplating his response. "Fine, he stays for now … I won't waste any more of your time."

"There is one thing that would be beneficial," Ricket said.

"Anything."

"The mecher. There will be some heavy lifting and the robot would be helpful."

"Of course. Check with Norwell; he knows far more about the disposition of it than I do."

Things had progressively become more dangerous. Now that Hobel was splitting them up, an escape was looking more and more difficult. Not impossible, but difficult. He could not afford to have Bristol put into stasis—like Hanna and Leon and, soon, Granger. Probably a stasis none of them were intended to awaken from. But at least now the mecher was part of their team. Ricket's mind began to race ... *Now what? Just how does one escape from a MicroVault?* The beginnings of an idea were forming, but it was preposterous ... totally preposterous.

Chapter 18

Open Space, Nagbram System
Parcical, MicroVault Terminal

Four hours exactly had passed since their most recent return from the MicroVault. Ricket was the last to hurry into the terminal. He was happy to see the mecher standing next to Bristol. All eyes flashed in Ricket's direction, palpable tension in the air.

"We cannot have further delays, Ricket. I'm sure you understand the importance of what we are doing here."

"I'm sorry, Omni," Ricket said, holding up a portable device of some sort. "Needed to modify this test equipment … I apologize for the delay."

In truth, he had made no such modifications. He didn't even know what the item was he'd hastily grabbed off Norwell's workbench. Secretly, he'd spent the last twenty minutes within the confines of one of the ship's MediPods. The new modifications made to his internal nano-devices would be an essential component to his plan. A plan as ludicrous to him now as when he'd first thought of it hours earlier.

He tried to hide the fact that he was in pain … excruciating pain. Fortunately, he'd already been updated with the latest, next level comms interface from his initial MediPod session on board the *Parcical*. Since then, off and on, over the last few days, he'd been tapping in to the MediPod's computer. Surprisingly, since there were very few safeguards set up against intrusion to the ship from inside, Ricket was able to immerse himself in the MediPod's root-level software. The added modifications had pushed the limits of what the MediPod was designed for, if not far exceeded them. What he was trying to do was not normal.

But Ricket was not normal. Over the years, he had pushed the boundaries of just how far organic brain matter could be stretched in order to accommodate the intrusion of newer, more advanced, technology. In this instance, the addition of six times his present level of processing power; five times his present bandwidth level of communication; twenty times his present level of diagnostic capability. But adding these levels of advanced tech to oneself had a cost.

In Ricket's case, it was physically a matter of necessary brain tissue … how far could he go—how much brain matter could he sacrifice—to accommodate large additions of new technology? Granted, the additions weren't hardware, per se; they were quasi-organic in nature. Pre-matched to his DNA, rejection was not an issue. But Ricket had found nothing in him he couldn't live without. He'd already removed portions of his brain over the last few years. So the answer was simple … actually, there were two answers: First, he had programmed the MediPod to alter the size of his cranium. The alterations were minimal—barely noticeable, unless one looked for them.

He now had a bigger head. Second, he simply squeezed things in—tighter into his skull than was normal. The body is amazing at adapting. Now, standing within the confines of the MicroVault terminal, he inwardly cringed at the pain: both pain and heat. He hadn't figured on the increased measure of conduction and radiant heat that would pervade his skull with these cranial additions. Within the over-cramped cranial space, less moisture was now present. Ricket quickly rechecked his body diagnostics and saw his core body temperature had risen three degrees since he had left the MediPod.

Hobel was talking, snapping Ricket away from his inner thoughts.

"I've been thinking about this endeavor of ours, and I have decided we require far more security. That ship … the *Minian* … holds the answers to our very survival. Nothing can happen to her … she is literally our most precious resource."

Ricket noticed movement in the corridor and saw Caldurian soldiers. In fact, the corridor was packed with them, each one wearing a battle suit and armed with a unique version of a multi-gun. *This complicates things*, he thought.

"From now on, in revolving, twenty-minute shifts, there will be no fewer than one hundred armed guards on board the *Minian*. I'm certain all of you understand why I must insist on this high level of security. Oh … and one more thing. I am well aware of the reinitializing of the *Minian*'s AI. Please do not underestimate my ability to observe such things. For now, as long as its assistance is required, it can remain operational in its current state. In the future, you will first clear all such decisions through me. Is that understood?" Hobel stared directly at Bristol.

Bristol shrugged and maintained a bored expression.

"All right, you have twenty minutes. Please make the best of them."

Norwell tapped at the pedestal's virtual display and the portal appeared before them.

★ ★ ★

They arrived into the *Minian's* mess, which had been re-configured—tables and chairs now moved to one side of the large compartment. The mess was determined to be the best staging area between the *Parcical's* MicroVault terminal and the *Minian* for bringing in personnel, such as numerous armed guards, plus any equipment needing to be transported. There was also a DeckPort, in the nearby corridor, which would quickly gain them access to any other part of the ship.

Norwell moved from a companion virtual pedestal to one within the *Parcical's* MicroVault terminal. He closed the open portal.

There were no less than twenty Caldurian guards already awaiting them in the mess.

"Now there's a real sign of trust," Bristol said, eyeing the armed soldiers.

Although no guns were pointed in their direction, it was clear their armed presence was meant to keep watch over them.

One guard, in a group of four, signaled for them to follow. Norwell led the way after them, toward the mess's exit, followed by Bristol, and Trommy5—the mecher robot. Ricket brought up the rear, four guards following behind him. He used the sleeve of his spacer's jumpsuit to wipe perspiration from his forehead as a sudden wave of nausea washed over him. He slowed, but kept on walking ahead. *Things should get better ... in time.*

Ricket saw the awkward junior science officer up ahead. "Bristol? Can you hear me?"

"That you, Ricket? This is cool! Much better than that

stupid NanoTexting."

Ricket had to agree. NanoVoice, just one of the newer advanced upgrades they'd each received in their recent MediPod visits, was this comms upgrade. Prior to the upgrade, non-verbal communications was limited to a kind of ocular texting, which was time-consuming—up to the point it was rarely used by any who possessed the internal imbedded nano-device. Their new upgrade was a very welcome one.

"We cannot speak aloud what I'm about to tell you, Bristol. It is evident the Omni, somehow, is watching and listening to everything going on here."

"Yeah, and that weasel, Norwell, can't be trusted. I saw him talking to Hobel … he told him about the *Minian's* AI being reinstated. Did you know Norwell returned here two hours ago?"

"No. Why would he do that?" Ricket asked.

"Probably to jury-rig surveillance into the AI. That's my guess, anyway."

"We need to escape, Bristol."

"No shit … you come up with that all by yourself?"

"We need to do it today … this shift."

"Um, *Ohhh Kaaay* … and you have some kind of plan?"

"I think so."

"You do realize the *Minian's* AI has been compromised? We can't count on the AI, not without it informing on us to Hobel. Again … thanks to that ass-wipe, Norwell."

"I've taken that into consideration."

"And you've taken into consideration the one hundred or more armed Caldurian guards running around the ship?"

"Yes, I've had to adjust my plan for them."

"So what do you want me to do?"

"Go get me the rhino-warriors."

"Huh? Say that again."

"Once we get up to the Zip Farm compartment, you'll

come up with an excuse ... why you need to head down to Deck 11. You'll head directly to the Zoo; directly to HAB 170. Find Traveler and convey the situation. We'll need as many of the rhinos as he can pull together. Let him know they'll need to wear battle suits and they'll need to be armed."

The procession exited the Level 18 DeckPort, and filed into the Zip Farm compartment. Ricket felt dizzy—things were spinning around. *Or am I spinning?* He lost his balance, tripped, and fell to the deck, face first. Everything went black.

★ ★ ★

"Ricket? Come on, man ... you okay?"

Ricket opened his eyes to see Bristol's pimply face hovering inches above his own. He briefly wondered why Bristol's internal nanites hadn't cured the young man of such a simple ailment. There was virtually nothing the nanites weren't capable of repairing, yet this human had been plagued with a simple case of acne as long as he'd known him. Suddenly, Ricket became aware of his incredible, greatly enhanced, cognitive abilities—his brain was super-charged into high gear. He was having difficulty keeping track of the incredible amount of information now at his disposal. In an instant, he knew what caused Bristol's recurring acne.

"You need to stop ingesting Gorpin Locks."

Bristol's concerned expression turned to one of confusion. "You've picked a bad time to go crazy, Ricket."

"Your skin. You've become allergic to those candy bars you like so much ... their main ingredient is the root of Gorpin Locks. Even replicated, your internal nanites can barely keep up with all the new infections just one of its ingredients cause. Did you know that you would have died if it weren't for your nanites?"

"Fine. I'll cut back. Can you get up?"

"I think so. Thank you, Bristol."

As Bristol helped Ricket to his feet, he spoke to him via NanoVoice. "You were out for about five minutes. You still want me to go get the rhinos?"

Ricket looked around the Zip Farm, noting there were ten armed Caldurian guards standing around the perimeter of the compartment. They'd already burned through fifteen minutes of their twenty minute session. *Why twenty minutes?* Ricket reevaluated the parameters, reassessing all available data. Norwell was correct; the effects of being miniaturized were a detriment, but not to the extent the Caldurian science officer calculated. Any effect at all would take many hours— thirty-two hours, five minutes, and twenty-three seconds, to be fully accurate. But even then, such effects would be minimal. One could survive here for weeks, without it being too much of a problem.

"Yes ... do not worry about the session time. Norwell has miscalculated."

"He's an ass clown ... I'm not surprised."

Bristol spun around to face Norwell, who was almost standing on top of him. "He's had these spells before. Usually only affects Craing females. I need to get his medicine from Medical ... be right back. Watch him. Make sure he doesn't stumble and fall again. Can you do that?"

Norwell looked from Bristol to Ricket, then back again. "I didn't know he ..."

"Yes or no, can you watch him, or not?"

"Yes, yes! Of course ... go. Go!"

Bristol ran toward the exit.

Norwell continued to watch the open hatch. "Four of you ... make sure he gets to where he's going and then returns promptly."

Chapter 19

Open Space, 1.2 Billion Miles from
Sol Solar System
Assailant, Bridge

"There's no sign of them, Captain," Orion said. "They were here ... that much I know. But they're gone."

"Nothing from the probe you sent out?"

"No ... they've been retrieved. Cap, they could be any-where. Perhaps gone back into the multiverse?" Orion said.

Jason began to pace. He scratched at the scruff on his chin and tried to think. Unless something had dramatically changed, the Caldurians were no longer capable of traversing multivers-es. So how did one find a fleet of ships that were virtually invisible to both long- and short-range sensors? *You don't. You can't.* So, how then?

Jason was being hailed. "Go for Captain," he said, uncon-sciously bringing two fingers up to his ear.

"How you holding up?"

Just hearing Dira's voice relaxed the tension in his shoul-ders. "Fine ... just frustrated."

"No sign of them?"

"No."

"Come back. I'm pretty much done here."

"I thought there were a slew of injuries?"

"Everyone's stable. Much of the fleet has now returned to other parts of Allied space. There are more doctors here than needed, plus we have an addition of two MediPods from Earth."

"That is good news … something there hasn't been much of lately."

"I saw your father."

That brought a smile to Jason's face. Suddenly he missed the old man. "Does he seem like his old self?"

"Yes and no. If anything, his rough edges are a bit softer … but, otherwise, he's pretty much the same. He dropped in and talked with each of the injured. Morale boosting."

Jason nodded, suddenly chagrined. His father was always good at that sort of thing, but it should have been him, shaking hands, and giving pep talks, to those men and women.

"The dreadnaught, the *Independence*, has arrived in local space. He shuttled over to her about an hour ago. I can meet you there," she said.

Jason was staring at the forward display—the blackness—the emptiness.

"You there?"

"Yes … sorry … I'm missing something, Dira. I know I am. It's there, but I can't quite grasp it."

"I'm going to talk to you as your doctor now, okay?"

Jason had to smile again. "Okay, doctor."

"Get off that bridge. Go do something else … just for a while, anyway. You're too close and too emotionally vested in recent events. You need a change of atmosphere. For me, that's when my mind gets freed up enough to come at things from a different direction."

At this point, Jason was willing to try anything. He sure wasn't ready to return to the carnage back home in Earth space. "You know what, Doctor Caparri? I think I'm going to take your advice."

★ ★ ★

Jason found Boomer in the captain's quarters kitchen. She'd taken a monstrous bite out of a grilled cheese sandwich. He came around the corner. "Hey, little one."

Mouth stuffed to its maximum, she tried to talk—her words coming out as gibberish—but he understood what she'd said, anyway.

"I'm home because I was looking for you."

"Did I do something wrong?" she asked, looking behind her father. "Did that droid tattle on me again?"

"No … Dewdrop said nothing to me. I'm here to get my training."

Boomer took another oversized bite, contemplating what he said. "Kahill Callan?"

"Is that okay?"

"Like … right now?"

"Uh huh."

"And you'll do what I tell you to do? I won't get in trouble for yelling at you when you do something stupid?"

"I expect nothing less."

"Okay … you'll need to change. I'll replicate a *Shadick* for you. Meet me in the gym."

★ ★ ★

While Jason waited for his daughter, he loosened up by stretching his limbs. The gym compartment was a quarter of the size of the one on the *Minian,* but it seemed to serve its purpose. The recently installed mats were already turning gray and the air had the distinct smell of men's body odor. The walls were mirrored and he assessed his reflection, combing his fingers through his hair. He needed a haircut, and a shave. Dark circles were starting to form beneath his eyes—he looked as tired as he felt.

"Dad?"

Jason turned to see Boomer standing in the middle of the mat and wearing her *Shadick.* Holding out another in her right hand, she said, "Go, put this on."

Jason took the garment and headed for the locker room. Two minutes later he was back on the mat where Boomer waited. On her left arm, she wore an enhancement shield. She held another one out to her father.

"Put this on your left forearm and make sure it's snug. You don't want it flopping around while you're in battle."

He did as told and tested it for snugness.

"That's good. Now, for the next hour we're going to go over the basics ... how to generate different forms of distortion waves, and—"

Jason interrupted her. "Wait, there's different forms?"

"Don't interrupt me. I promise I'll cover everything at the right time. And you need to call me Master Tahhrim Dol ... or just Master."

Jason noticed she was having a hard time keeping the smile from her face.

"Yes, Master Tahhrim Dol."

She'd given him a low-powered training shield, and over the next hour Boomer showed him the proper positioning of the shield—in front of his chest, for both defensive and offensive opening stances. He learned the face of the shield produced different distortion waves than those from its three curved edges. He learned the shield produced the most power when he was able to tune in to it—feel the shield—make it a part of his own body. The hour passed quickly and Jason was disappointed when their time was up. He'd thoroughly enjoyed learning something new.

"Again tomorrow?" Jason asked.

Boomer stared back at him, blank faced.

"Again tomorrow, **Master** Tahhrim Dol?"

"Yes ... but tomorrow you'll be joining the group class. You won't know what you're doing, at first, but you'll catch up. Do you want to be in Billy's or Rizzo's class?"

Jason thought about that. Both would take great delight in kicking his ass. "Billy's. He's old, like me ... maybe he'll be easier on me."

"Billy's a bad-ass, Dad. You're in for sore muscles and a lot of pain."

Jason raised his brow.

"They've been doing this for months now. I feel kinda sorry for you." She made a face at him that did not convey sorrow.

"Don't enjoy this too much, little one. The day will come when I'll kick all your asses ... um ... Master."

Jason had been hearing a hail for the last minute. He waited for Boomer to excuse him, before answering, "Go for Captain."

"Captain, Admiral Reynolds has been trying to reach you," Seaman Gordon said.

"Go ahead and connect us, Seaman."

"Jason ... I'm sorry, but there's an issue you need to be aware of," his father said.

"What kind of issue?"

"The kind that requires the fleet commander's presence."

The irony was not lost on Jason: Five minutes earlier he was answering to the commands of his eleven-year-old daughter, and now his own father was his subordinate. But life was all about change, and they'd all have to deal with it.

"All right, Admiral. We should be back within the solar system within the hour."

"Jason ... there's been an accident."

"What is it?"

"It's Dira ... she was leaving what's left of Jeffer—"

"Dad! Just tell me if she's okay?"

"No, Jason, she's ... she's not. I'm very sorry, there was an explosion." Jason, hearing the tightness in his father's baritone voice, waited—purposely letting time slowly tick by, back to when things were still okay, like they were only moments earlier. Jason didn't want to ask the next obvious question, and worse, he didn't want to hear the answer.

Jason walked out into the central corridor away from listening ears and concerned eyes on the bridge. He found a bulkhead to lean up against.

"Are you still there?"

"I'm here, Dad."

"Look ... she's alive. But I won't lie to you, she's in real bad shape."

"What does that mean ... bad shape?"

"The explosion took place right outside of an airlock. She wasn't the closest to the blast. From what I've heard, it was awful ... two other crewmembers were killed instantly. Son, she's lost both her legs and most of one arm."

Jason tried to breathe, keep himself from folding. "Where is she now?"

"Still on Jefferson. They got her into a MediPod ... she has a heartbeat. Twice she stopped breathing and flat-lined. Jason, there's only so much our technology can do in cases like this."

"I'm on my way. Promise me you won't leave her side, Dad. Promise me ... not for a second."

"I promise, Jason. One more thing, son."

"What is it?"

"Ricket. It would help if he were here. He knows Medi-Pod functionality like no one else. How to make the things do more than they were designed to do. You, better than anyone, know that he's performed miracles."

Jason was well aware what Ricket could accomplish at the controls of a MediPod. Hell, he'd brought Mollie back to life. She was shot through the heart, and he'd found a way to bring her back. Jason wiped at a stream of tears that wouldn't stop falling. "I can't find him, Dad. I have no idea where the Caldurian fleet has gone."

"I want you to listen to me, Jason. This may be hard to hear."

"What?"

"Don't come here. Don't come back here and see her like this. Find Ricket … bringing him back will be the best thing you can do for her."

"I want to be at her side. I need to be there."

"No, you don't! Go ahead, get angry! Hell, get fucking angry! But stay away and go find Ricket, and the others too. That's what's needed right now. I'll keep you apprised of the situation here. I promise."

Jason didn't answer his father right away. What he wanted was to be with Dira. But what was best for her?

"I want updates on the hour, Dad. And if there is a change, good or bad, I want to know."

"You've got it. Now get out there and find that little fuck-er."

Chapter 20

Open Space, 1.2 Billion Miles from
Sol Solar System
Assailant, Bridge

Jason reentered the bridge and took a seat in the command chair. No one spoke. It was obvious word had already spread concerning Dira's accident and her dire condition. The forward display appeared as black and lifeless as it had earlier. A thought crossed Jason's mind:

"Seaman Gordon, I want you to key the ship's AI listening in to distant chatter—as far out as feasible—specifically looking for a fleet of twelve big ships."

"The Caldurian fleet, sir?"

"Yes. Their ships may not show up on anyone's sensors, but if someone's close enough, they're going to see them. Think about it; it's an impressive sight—miles and miles of advanced Caldurian assets, moving across open space. It's a shot in the dark, but ..."

"I'm on it, sir. I can have every ship in the Allied fleet conduct the same chatter search as well."

Jason hadn't thought of doing that, but the idea exponentially increased their odds of success. "Good thinking, Mr. Gordon. I want to know the moment you hear anything— anything, even if you're not one hundred percent certain it relates."

"Yes, sir."

Jason, checking the time, stood and headed for the exit. "Gunny, get the XO to return back to his duty post on the bridge. I'll be in the gym."

"Aye, Cap."

★ ★ ★

As expected, Boomer had a class in session. Jason skirted the mat, walking around the gym's perimeter, and entered the locker room. A few minutes later, when he emerged wearing his Shadick, the class was standing at attention—quietly waiting for him.

Jason bowed toward Boomer. "I apologize for the disruption, Master Tahhrim Dol."

Boomer returned the bow, along with the six others standing silently on the mat. The sad news had reached them too— he could see it in their eyes. Boomer looked as though she'd been crying. He saw Billy, standing in the front row, and they locked eyes. "I need a diversion … anyone up for kicking the captain's ass?" Jason asked them.

"Gladly," Billy said.

"We only just started, Dad," Boomer said. "Here, take my trainer. I'll get another."

Jason stepped onto the mat and took Boomer's enhancement shield, then assumed a position to Billy's right. By the time he'd secured the shield onto his forearm, Boomer had returned with a new one for herself.

"We'll do a review today. We'll practice knocking our opponents off their feet."

They broke into pairs. Billy gestured for Jason to move next to him and away from the others.

"Okay, old man … you know the starting defensive position?"

Jason got himself into position—legs slightly bent, shield positioned outward, in front of his chest. Billy adjusted Jason's shield, moving it several inches higher and in closer to his chest. "There you go—looking good," he said approvingly.

Boomer walked around and further adjusted everyone's position. "Attack!"

Billy darted to his right, while thrusting his shield forward. Jason took the full force of the training shield's disruption waves into his lower belly. He doubled over, a second stream of waves punching him in his face: The counter-force lifted him up and off his feet. Landing flat on his back, Jason scarcely knew what hit him.

Billy looked down at him. "How was that for kicking the captain's ass?"

Jason took Billy's outstretched hand, pulled himself up, and assumed an offensive position.

"Attack!"

Jason repeated the same movements that Billy had previously orchestrated—with a slight twist. Similarly to Billy's move, he darted right, but then he crouched low, firing off two forward thrusts into Billy's belly, followed by the same punch to the head. Billy blocked the first set of waves but not the second. He went down on his back with a loud grunt.

Jason stood over his friend and held out his hand. "God that felt good."

For the next two hours, both Jason and Billy held nothing back. It had been a long time since Jason felt this physically spent. Sweaty and tired, he had bruises forming on top of bruises. Boomer just called it quits when a hail came in from Seaman Gordon.

"Go for Captain, what do you have for me, Seaman?"

"I think I have something ... it might be nothing."

"I'm on my way."

Jason bowed to Billy, then to Boomer. He hurried from the gym, still wearing his sopping-wet Shadick.

★ ★ ★

By the time Jason reached the bridge, a small group huddled around the comms station.

There were several double takes at Jason's strange attire. Orion made a face as she observed the way he was walking.

"You're moving like an old man, Cap."

"You have no idea, Gunny. Bring me up to speed."

Seaman Gordon, the only one seated among the standing group, said, "Let me play it for you, sir. Tell me if you think this is what we're looking for. It's chatter between two freighters."

Jason listened to the short audio clip. Already translated by the AI, the audio sounded clear with little distortion. One of the male voices sounded throaty, while the other sounded younger, and higher-pitched.

He listened to the clip and said, "Play it again, Seaman."

Vessel 1: "... oh, for shit's sake ... they totally cut me off."

Vessel 2: "Fuckers! That's about twenty regulations they just circumvented. You just don't cross shipping lanes like that."

Vessel 1: "Almost didn't see them there ... must be fifteen of them. Damn things are huge ... as black as space itself."

"That's it, Cap. The reference to fifteen ships may be a guess. Could be our twelve Caldurian ships."

"Where did this take place?"

Orion had returned to her station and was again seated in

front of her tactical board. "I checked on that and it's another indication we're on the right track. Corian Nez system."

"Why does that sound familiar to me?"

"Alurian ... it's the planet where the Zip accelerator technology first stemmed from."

"Yes, that's right. But haven't they been gone for something like ninety years?"

"That's the story I heard as well," Orion said. "But it would be one hell of a coincidence, Cap. We have the potential spotting of a Caldurian fleet—right where Zip technology first originated."

"Seaman, request an interchange wormhole."

"Yes, sir."

Jason moved back to the command chair and sat down.

"This is odd," Perkins said.

"What's that, XO?"

"We've received a new batch of requests for Star Watch. Seems our friend Captain Oz is up to his old tricks again."

"He'll have to wait," Jason said, dismissively.

"The thing is ... Captain, it's the Manilaise system where these reports are coming from."

Jason shrugged.

"That's less than three light-years from the border of the Corian Nez system."

"Seriously?"

"He's right," Orion said. "They're a stone's throw from one another."

"Captain, the interchange wormhole is now forming, forty-five thousand miles off our port side," Ensign McNeil reported.

"Take us in, Helm."

The spatial anomaly grew in size as they approached the mouth of the multi-colored wormhole. Jason felt his heart restrict in his chest—feeling no different than were it gripped by a man's fist. *Dira! Oh God, Dira.* He was moving further and further away from her. She was light-years away and dying. He should be with her … at her side. Had he made a mistake, chasing after Ricket? What were the odds of actually finding him? *Is he even still alive?*

They'd entered the wormhole and Jason looked away. *What the hell am I doing?*

"We've entered Corian Nez, Cap," Orion said. "Um … this is a busy place."

Jason was thinking the same thing. Orion had put up the logistics screen and there were at least fifty vessels in their vicinity.

"Seaman Gordon, how about trying to find one of those freighters."

"Yes, sir. I think I have one of them pinpointed already. That gravely voice was pretty unique.

"Okay, sir. The freighter's answered my hail. On screen?"

"Put it through, Seaman Gordon."

The face was a good match for the voice. Humanoid, the bearded man would fit right in with band members of ZZ Top. He scowled. "Who the hell are you?"

"I'm Captain Jason Reynolds, from Star Watch of the Alliance. Thank you for answering our hail—"

ZZ Top cut him off: "Star Watch? Our lucky stars … we've been waiting for you guys! Listen, my name's Strorn Manning … Captain of the *Big Jugs*. But the folks you need to talk to are back in the Manilaise system. Things have gotten pretty bad there. That lunatic captain has attacked no less than ten spaceports. Man, it's good to see you guys!"

Chapter 21

Open Space, Corian Nez System
Assailant, Bridge

———————————————————————

"Captain Manning, the person … being … you referred to is called Captain Mar Oswaldo, known as Captain Oz. Capturing him, and those associated with him, is a top priority for Space Watch. I assure you … he will be stopped. But, first, I want to ask you about that fleet of black ships which recently crossed your shipping lanes. Do you know the ones I'm speaking of?"

"Of course I do! The bastards arrived acting like they were royalty or something. Granted, no one in his right mind would go up against them, but that's how to get a bad rep too. Once your rep is crap, it sticks to you like—"

Jason interjected, "Do you know where they went … where they are now?"

"Hold on."

Jason watched as the big man pushed himself from his seat and left the camera's view. A few moments later he returned.

"You're in luck. They're close, though not in a particularly friendly part of space. No legitimate shipping or commerce vessel goes anywhere near Gracow CD1 … at least, not on purpose."

"Why's that?"

"Thieves and deviants! The place is teeming with the dirge of space. Don't go anywhere near that place, my friend. You do, you'll find yourself fleeced of your purse, and your women taken into the trades." Captain Manning leaned forward and squinted his eyes. "That is one magnificent lassie behind you, Captain. Stand up, girl, and let me take a look at that magnificent backside of yours."

Jason was taken aback by the quick turn their conversation had taken.

Orion turned in her seat and looked at Jason, then up to the display. She flipped him the bird and smiled. She looked back at Jason and shrugged. "There's no way he knows what that gesture means way out here … right?" She stood and moved next to the captain's chair.

Captain Manning was all smiles. "Oh yes … that is quite a backside."

Orion lost it. "Listen to me, old man … I'm going to come over there and choke you with your own ugly beard. Then I'm going to …"

Captain Manning looked startled at first, but soon laughed uproariously. As he wiped tears from his eyes, trying to control himself, he managed to say, "I meant no disrespect, lassie, but you are indeed a fine specimen. I've no doubt you could pull my arms off, one at a time, and beat me to death with them." He continued to stare at Orion with admiration. "Just so you know, you get tired of your post over there, *Big Jugs* will always have a place for you." He patted one knee and raised his brow: "Right here, sweetheart."

Jason, looking up at Orion, thoroughly enjoyed the momentary distraction. He watched her furious expression turn to one of disbelief. She shook her head and looked down at Jason.

"So you think this is funny?"

"No."

"Yes, you do."

Jason shook his head. "Nope, not funny."

Orion returned to her station and turned her back on everyone, especially Captain Manning.

"Thank you for your help, Captain. We'll be back in touch if we need anything more from you."

Orion cut the connection before the bearded man had a chance to reply.

Jason turned his thoughts to Captain Oz. What should he do about him? He couldn't address searching for him and simultaneously finding Ricket. But his mind quickly flashed on Dira's lovely face and the decision became obvious.

"Gunny, what can you tell me about this Gracow CD1?" Jason asked.

"Well, the jerk was right about that place. It's about the worst part of space there is. The history behind it is interesting: Alurian, where we know Zip technology originally stemmed from, is still there—part of the five-planet system known as Gracow CD1. Though pretty much a blackened husk of a planet now, Alurian's still uninhabited … for the most part."

"What happened to it?"

"Alurian was the predominant power in this part of the galaxy about one hundred years ago. They were technologically highly advanced, and didn't share their tech with anyone. Few tears were lost at their demise. From what I'm reading … they were a ruthless, mean-hearted bunch. Basically, the neighborhood bullies no one wanted to cross."

"Until the Caldurians buzzed into town?"

"That's right. The Caldurians, to their credit, did try to negotiate with the Alurians for their superior technology. Offering up a deal where they would equally share in all technological advances made between those two interstellar superpowers. The Alurians wanted no part of the offer. The Caldurians, used to getting their own way, persisted ... kept trying to sweeten the deal. Kept offering more and more enticements."

"And the Alurians finally had enough?"

"Exactly. They attacked."

Jason thought about that. *The Lilly*, designed from Caldurian technology around that time, had been an amazing warship. Although not at the same level as the latest Master Class vessels, she was not a ship one would want to go up against in war—a lesson the Craing, later, were all too cognizant of. Imagining a fleet of similar Caldurian ships, Jason knew that the Alurians, in the end, hadn't a chance. His mind flashed on the very recent past, when twelve Master Class ships destroyed Jefferson Station. They were indeed fortunate Earth hadn't been destroyed in the process.

"Helm ... set a course for Gracow CD1. No phase-shifts ... we need to keep things stealthy as possible."

★ ★ ★

It took them four hours to reach Gracow CD1 at their sub-light speeds.

"Approaching the system, Captain," Ensign McNeil said.

"And we're still cloaked?"

"Aye, Captain," Orion said. "We'll need to bring our speeds down ... let the drives cool a bit. But we should go unnoticed, unless they're specifically looking for us."

Jason watched the small planetary system come into view on the forward display. Four bright red planets, plus a dusty gray planet, were orbiting a white-blue star, about twice the size of Earth's sun.

"If we're going to spot the fleet, I think we know where we need to look first," Jason said.

"Cap, there's a ton of traffic in this area of space. I'm counting close to two hundred thousand individual ships."

As they closed in on the first planet—city lights, expansive metropolises covering entire continents, shimmered up from the ruby red world. They continued on, passing an almost identical planet, which was, if possible, even more effusive with lights than the first one.

"Coming up on Alurian, Captain," McNeil said.

"Take us into high orbit, Helm."

"Aye, Captain."

Jason watched the screen carefully as they moved around the big, Saturn-sized, world. Orion magnified the planet's surface and what they viewed was startling. Not black or gray, it was more a dark shade of red. Structures were still there—partial buildings, ragged and scorched, looked as though a magnificent fireball had closely circled across every mile of the planet, ensuring nothing survived.

"Look at this, Cap," Orion said, gesturing toward the screen. "This is using an infrared filter."

The display showed the same dreary planet surface, only now there were patches of bright blue in one area, at the top of the display.

"What am I looking at, Gunny?"

"I believe what we're seeing is a city hidden beneath an old city. A subterranean civilization."

"Shit!" Ensign McNeil suddenly screamed.

Suddenly, the bridge tilted backwards—almost vertically. The crewmembers that were standing were immediately thrown to the deck. Cups and miscellaneous odds and ends flew in the air, then backward, toward the rear bulkhead.

The ship's klaxon began wailing loudly, in repetitive squawks.

"What the hell's happening, Helm?" Jason barked, barely able to stay in the command chair.

"There, Captain!"

Now Jason saw it: Almost invisible against the blackness of space, a Master Class Caldurian ship. It was directly in front of them—now taking up most of the entire display.

"We're going to hit it," Perkins said, standing at the entrance to the bridge.

"No, we're not!" McBride responded back, busy at the controls.

"We're going too fast to stop in time, Captain. We'll need to go up and over … hold on."

Jason watched, his eyes moving between McNeil at the helm, and the display, where only the top portion of the black ship was now visible.

"I think he's right … we're going to hit it!" Jason said.

"No! We're not, sir!"

Jason both heard and felt the *Assailant's* G-force dampeners being pushed to the limits. The klaxon seemed to blare even louder. "Turn that thing off!" he yelled to no one in particular. The Caldurian vessel's hull plating, which was covered with layers of nanites and almost perfectly flat, was clearly visible now. Jason yelled, "Everyone … grab ahold of something!"

The top of the Caldurian vessel came into view on the display, then only open space could be seen.

The klaxon fell silent. No one spoke. The ship leveled off and the ship's G-force dampeners again returned to functioning at nominal levels.

"All stop, Helm."

The display now showed the entirety of what they'd just missed hitting: Close by was the Master Class vessel they had

162

just missed by a hair, and eleven other ships in stationary orbit right below it.

"Any indication they know we're here, Gunny?"

She continued to study the readings on her board. She looked over to Seaman Gordon, who put several fingers to his ear and appeared to be listening to something. He shook his head.

"I think we're good, Cap," Orion said, her voice quiet, as though not wanting to speak too loudly.

Jason turned back to McNeil.

"Sorry, Captain. I didn't see them."

"It's all right, Ensign. You did some amazing maneuvering. We're alive because of your quick actions and skill," Jason told him.

"Did you see that?" Orion asked, up on her feet now.

"What?"

"That glimmer. The *Parcical* ... she's right there."

Chapter 22

High Orbit Over Alurian, Gracow CD1
System
Parcical, Zip Farm

Ricket stumbled again—apparently his most recent Medi-Pod session was still affecting him. Granted, his physiology had been dramatically altered and impacted. But he wasn't prepared for what he was now experiencing: disorientation, a massive headache, and an influx of too much data—information streaming in, both internally and externally. He already knew everything was measurable virtually, but now he was faced with the prospect of having to address each and every tidbit of data as it flooded to the forefront of his mind. What he hadn't thought of, or managed to do yet, was to have the proper cognitive systems in place, which not only prioritized the new data stream, but allocated it to the appropriate, newly-added, memory banks. He would have to do that now, before he was totally incapacitated.

Norwell, standing to Ricket's right, and holding on to his upper arm, watched him as if he were a specimen in a laboratory.

"What have you done to yourself, Ricket?"

"I just need to sit for a while, Norwell. Can you help me do that? Please?"

Norwell helped Ricket ease down to the deck. He leaned back against one of the Zip accelerators, and felt the big machine's vibration behind him. The sensation was calming; actually helped him concentrate on the task at hand.

"What have you done to yourself, Ricket?" Norwell repeated. He looked irritated and his eyes traveled upward, toward the top of Ricket's head.

Ricket didn't answer.

"Your head is … bigger … it's distorted. Did you think no one would notice? Answer me or I'll be forced to contact the Omni."

Ricket, who'd closed his eyes to better concentrate on developing close to three trillion new lines of code, opened them to find Norwell's face staring back at him. Ten paces behind him were three Caldurian guards, also taking new notice of him. That was not good. If they were preparing to contact Hobel, it would place his escape plan in jeopardy.

Ricket, who only days earlier found lying so distasteful an act that he simply never engaged in it, was now getting used to falsifying. "I knew what was needed of me, by both you and Hobel, was way beyond my capability. I'm sorry, but I needed to increase my mental capacity. I hope you are not disappointed in me."

The Caldurian scientist's face relaxed some. "I don't even know what to say to that. You look terrible." He reached out a hand and placed the back of his palm against Ricket's cheek.

"You're running an extremely high temperature." Norwell spun around to face the three guards: "One of you, fetch him some water. Go! Hurry!"

Ricket closed his eyes again and concentrated on his programming. He realized he wouldn't be able to accomplish what he'd originally intended. The concept of doing such multitasking would push him to the limit—he would be walking around in a mental fog; all connection with the outside world would eventually disappear. No, what he needed was an interface. He needed an AI to manage the *Minian's* AI. An AI who would proactively handle processes for him and work in the background. The negative aspect of doing such a thing was a possible concern, as he would, in a sense, be sharing his mind with a device, which would be disconcerting, to be sure. But then again, it could be ... *what's the word?* Nice? Comforting? He next remembered he had a usable nested object, its compacted code already stored in his memory, taken from *The Lilly's* AI years earlier. It was much smaller than what either the *Minian's*, or the *Parcical's*, AI provided. As much as an AI interface could have a personality, he liked *The Lilly's* better. He retrieved what data was necessary and mentally wrote the appropriate sub-routines, which would allow the two AIs to communicate with each other.

Norwell was shaking his shoulder. "Ricket!"

Ricket continued with the job at hand. He only needed another few moments to finish.

Something was being placed up to his lips. Water. Ricket drank ... and drank ... and drank. He hadn't realized how thirsty he had become. The quenching, hydrating sensation was overwhelming and wonderful.

"Please allocate desired nomenclature, if one is desired."

Ricket opened his eyes. The process was complete and he'd heard the familiar, somewhat feminine, AI voice speaking within his head. Norwell was looking at him, concern on his face.

Ricket had always liked the name Beatrice, but he didn't know why. *Have I ever known a Beatrice?* He didn't think so.

He said, "Beatrice."

"Beatrice nomenclature allocated. In the future, non-verbal response is sufficient," Beatrice replied inside his head.

Norwell looked worried. "Ricket, I am Norwell ... not Beatrice." He turned to look at the guards. "He's hallucinating ... he doesn't know who I am. Contact the Omni—"

Ricket stopped him. "No no ... I'm fine, Norwell. Honestly, I'm feeling much better now. Thank you for the water. It helped." Ricket slowly got to his feet. Smiling, he signaled to the guards with a raised palm that he was fine.

The tall mecher came into view. Ricket had forgotten about Trommy5, who was positioning itself between him and the guards. That was good, but hopefully unnecessary.

"Our time is up here," Norwell said. "This has been a totally wasted session and Hobel will be most annoyed. You will have to explain to him what you've done to yourself and perhaps he will keep any disciplining to a minimum. Come Ricket, time to return to the *Parcical.*"

"I'm back," came Bristol's voice from the corridor. He emerged into the compartment, sweaty and out of breath. "Get out of the way!" he yelled at the two guards blocking his path. Bristol barreled through and approached Ricket. "You're feeling better?"

"Somewhat, yes ... thank you, Bristol. Did you get what you needed?"

"Yes, I did ... and something else too. You'll need this. It will make you feel better." Bristol took one of Ricket's hands in his own and placed a small device into it.

Then Ricket noticed the small SuitPac device that hung

from Bristol's belt. The same type of device he'd placed in Ricket's palm. Bristol turned and looked at Trommy5.

"Hey ... can you catch?"

What followed happened quickly. Ricket saw the astonished look on Norwell's face—he'd undoubtedly become aware something was very wrong. Probably wondering where the guards who had accompanied Bristol up to Medical were. Suddenly Bristol threw something small and metallic into the air: a SuitPac device. "Stop them!" was all Norwell could muster, but it was already too late as the mecher caught the small device in one hand. First Bristol, then Trommy5, initialized their battle suits and immediately flashed away. Seconds later, Ricket too was gone.

★ ★ ★

Ricket hadn't gone far. In fact, he now stood just ten feet away from where he'd stood mere seconds earlier. Looking down from the top of a nearby Zip accelerator, he watched the scene below erupt in chaos. Norwell was yelling for the guards to bring in reinforcements from all around the *Minian*, and to dispatch others to their aid from the *Parcical*.

The entrance to the Zip Farm went dark as a seven-foot-tall rhino-warrior filled the empty space. His heavy hammer gripped in one fist, even wearing a battle suit, Ricket recognized Traveler. Bristol, it appeared, had successfully recruited him from HAB 170.

The guards didn't hesitate to fire their weapons. Traveler staggered back from the impact on his battle suit, then steadily moved forward. He used the integrated plasma weapon on his left wrist to return fire, while using his heavy hammer to club a Caldurian soldier over the head, then another on the back of his shoulders, when he tried to run away. The other guards ran, taking shelter behind the farthest row of accelerators.

Using his NanoCom, Ricket let Traveler know where he was standing, on top of the Zip accelerator off to Traveler's right. Their eyes met and Traveler snorted.

"Did you bring others?" Ricket asked him.

"Everyone wanted to come. Two hundred are here, and I can get more, if needed. What do you want us to do, Ricket?"

"There are Caldurian soldiers throughout the ship and more will be entering through the mess. We need to subdue them; hopefully, without killing any others. Perhaps place our prisoners into Hold 1?"

Again, Traveler snorted. He turned and spoke to another rhino, standing behind him, who then rushed off. Suddenly, fifteen rhinos rushed into the Zip Farm—five moved left, five moved right, and the last five rushed forward. They were clearing the compartment. Although they were out of sight, he heard more plasma fire, then the distinctive sound of heavy hammers pounding down on Caldurian battle suits. *So much for not killing anyone.*

Norwell dashed forward, trying to skirt around the large rhino-warrior leader, but instead Traveler caught hold of Norwell's neck and held him fast.

Ricket phase-shifted down to the deck, directly in front of the two. "Thank you for coming, Traveler."

"Tell me, Ricket, what has happened here on the *Minian*? Who are these people that look like Granger?"

Ricket explained everything as quickly and efficiently as possible. He related how the *Minian* sat within a virtual vault of a Caldurian ship, called the *Parcical*, and how, presently, they were all highly miniaturized. He also explained that Hanna and Leon and probably Granger were within the same vault—unconscious … somewhere. He further explained the underlying problem with the Zip accelerators technology—

that Caldurians were unable to cross over into the multiverse. Then, Ricket spoke of the probable, imminent issues that they might be facing over time, with their own nano-devices. Norwell continued trying to free himself from Traveler's grasp, but eventually gave up.

Ricket was well aware the Caldurians would not back down easily, but their own survival depended on them maintaining control of the *Minian*. With twelve Master Class vessels standing nearby, a force of thousands could be preparing to storm the *Minian* anytime.

Ricket noticed Bristol and Trommy5 approaching.

Ricket spoke fast. "We need to ensure that the mess is no longer accessible. Disable the virtual pedestal."

"I already did that," Bristol said. "And just so you know, disabling something that's even partially virtual is not so easy."

Ricket had to think about that for a fraction of a second. Bristol was right; he must have disrupted the phase-signal derived from the *Parcical*.

"I had to disrupt the phase-signal coming from the *Parcical*. That meant a phase-shift up to your workshop to jury-rig a portable, localized, disruptor-signal generator. It's a temporary fix, though." Bristol smiled, looking proud of himself.

"That was a good idea, Bristol. But the *Minian's* AI could have accomplished the same thing and also ensured that every part of the ship maintained the same disruption throughout. So I'll have Beatrice interface with the *Minian* and complete that task immediately."

Both Bristol and Traveler stared at Ricket, blank faced.

"Who is Beatrice?" Bristol asked, confused.

Traveler leaned over, closer to Ricket. "What is wrong with your head?"

Ricket answered them both with one statement: "I've slightly increased the size of my cranium to make room for additional processing … there's an AI *in there* I've named Beatrice."

Neither Bristol nor Traveler had anything to say to that, continuing to stare at him.

"You will not escape," Norwell spat—again trying to free himself from Traveler's grip. "Our forces will cut you down the second you return to the *Parcical*. The ship, herself, will extinguish your lives within a microsecond of your return."

"And that is why we cannot return to the *Parcical*," Ricket said. The sounds of new plasma fire could be heard in the distance.

Norwell smiled. "It is only a matter of time. You cannot defeat us. You cannot escape from the *Minian*."

"Escaping from the *Minian* would be easy, leaving through any one of the Zoo habitats. We've already proven escape is not an issue. Your MicroVault terminal is virtually the same, albeit more elaborate, as any habitat portal. But we cannot extricate the *Minian* from her position here, and that is unfortunate."

Ricket began to walk around the Zip accelerator situated behind them. He looked at the deck—how the big contraption had been mounted there, with heavy, odd-shaped bolts.

Ricket returned to the group and placed a hand on the Zip accelerator. He looked up at Traveler. "You need to get more help … we'll need to take this with us."

Chapter 23

High Orbit Over Alurian, Gracow CD1
System
Parcical, Zip Farm

"What are you talking about?" Bristol asked. "Do you have any idea how heavy that thing is?"

Ricket looked at the large device and said, "It's approximately thirty-six tons ... give or take a ton or two. But we must hurry now. We need to get out of the MicroVault as soon as possible."

"What's the rush? The Caldurians won't be able to infiltrate this space, at least not now."

Ricket looked at Bristol sympathetically. "You have forgotten one key factor: where we are located."

"What? Oh no." Bristol slapped his forehead with an open palm. "Crap ... we're in virtual space. We can be deleted."

"That is right. The simple fact, though, is that anything that was processed via the MicroVault terminal has been logged and catalogued. As you said, any item—the *Minian*, we as individuals, all of us … can be deleted with the simple push of a button."

Traveler snorted loudly and looked around the large compartment.

"Not sure what would happen to you, big guy," Bristol said. "You can't be deleted, since you came here in a different way. But without the *Minian* here, you'd probably just float around in the MicroVault for eternity."

Three more snorts from Traveler, who looked uneasy.

"Please don't taunt Traveler, Bristol. I have an idea. It's really quite simple, and I have Beatrice already working on it."

"And what is that?" Bristol asked.

"We'll build our own MicroVault terminal, right here—within the *Minian*. But there is the not-so-insubstantial issue of locking into specific, relative planes of existence—planes of the multiverse. Personally, we'll be moving items—going from a virtual plane of reality, back into a non-virtual, material plane. It's basically all math: Beatrice has completed some of the calculations."

"Hey, that's a pretty good idea. How can I get another Beatrice put into *my* cranium?" Bristol asked. Then, looking over at Ricket's distorted head, he made a face. "Never mind."

Bristol said, "Back to what you said earlier, Ricket. Hobel won't delete the ship. He knows the importance of the Zip accelerators. He would delete me … the guy never liked me."

Ricket could not refute what the young junior science officer said. "Then I must hurry to my workshop. Traveler, please find the necessary tools to remove those mounting bolts on the Zip accelerator, and let me know when that has been accomplished."

"And him?" Traveler asked, looking at Norwell.

"I will secure him within the brig," Trommy5 said, with more gusto than one would expect from a robot.

★ ★ ★

Just over two hours had passed since Ricket and Bristol entered the workshop on Deck 23. They'd made several phase-shifts back to the mess compartment, where what remained of the disabled MicroVault mobile pedestal had been re-accessed and partially hacked, code to be used as a starting place for implementing their own designs.

"I have the final batch of data for you, Ricket. Are you ready for it to be uploaded?"

Ricket almost answered verbally, still not used to speaking to an internal AI. *"Thank you, Beatrice. I believe Bristol is almost done with the last batch … please wait."*

Bristol continued entering information into a terminal in the corner of the room. Every so often he would look up and gaze out the workshop hatchway to evaluate his latest change or alteration. Although more basically designed than the MicroVault terminal compartment on the *Parcical*, Ricket, Bristol and Beatrice managed to create a remarkable facsimile in the empty compartment across the corridor. What was empty space only thirty minutes earlier now gave the appearance of a fully functioning MicroVault terminal.

Bristol slammed his fist down on the workbench. "This is really annoying the crap out of me."

"What is wrong, Bristol?" Ricket asked, getting up from his seat and going over to his side.

"I'm not used to working with this … this … *virtualware*. I mean, it's basically just fart-matter, right? Numbers—formulas that inevitably allow all known physics to be thrown out the window. Take nothingness—we give it weight and mass and the ability to physically interact with the physical environment around it. Around us! Hell, I'm used to plugging one end of a cable into connector A and the other into connector B. But here, there is no cable … there is no frigging connector!"

"Would you like me to take over for you? I am finished with my part. Beatrice has the last piece of the formula worked out."

"No … I'm doing this part by myself. Shit, the guy gets his own internal AI and he thinks he knows it all. Just take a step back so I can finish." Bristol, soon back immersed in his work with only an occasional swearword, seemed to be making good progress.

Ricket wandered across the corridor to the newly constructed MicroVault terminal, which was approximately twenty feet wide, by thirty feet long, by fifteen feet high. Like the original, a wrap-around display rested on a central pedestal—a small virtual display atop it. Everything could be controlled from this one location. The compartment was larger than the one on the *Parcical* for good reason: There were certain items on board the *Minian* Ricket wanted to take with him, such as the colossal-sized Zip accelerator unit down on Deck 18. Their plan was to phase-shift it into this compartment within the next hour, where it would then be projected out, back into the real world in its full original size. It was a good plan—they were making excellent progress, but something nagged at Ricket. He hated the thought of the *Minian* being left behind. He assumed the *Minian* could not be taken from her present location, tucked within the virtual, miniaturized space within the MicroVault, because one had to be *outside* an object—separate or apart from it—in order to achieve such a thing. But was that actually true?

He posed the question to Beatrice, but her answer didn't come back immediately. He was about to ask again, phrase it slightly differently, when he heard her voice:

"Your assumption that the newly constructed MicroVault terminal would need to be outside the virtual constraints of the Minian *is*

correct."

"Thank you, Beatrice," Ricket said, feeling disappointed. *"Well, now I know the ship must remain here."*

"That is incorrect, Ricket."

"Why is that … have I miscalculated?"

"You must keep in mind, Ricket, the MicroVault terminal is not a physical construct. It can reside virtually anywhere, including outside the ship, or within the open storage space surrounding it."

Ricket slapped his own forehead and instantly regretted doing so. His head began to throb again. Bristol was scowling at him from across the corridor. Ricket ran from the MicroVault terminal and back into his workshop. He stood and stared at Bristol.

"You're creeping me out, Ricket."

"We'll need two of those."

"Of what?"

"The MicroVault terminals."

"Dude … do you know how hard it was to create even one—" he cut himself off, realizing how stupid that sounded. "Don't say it," Bristol said, shaking his head. "I know … it's virtual … it's all virtual. To duplicate it we only need to cut and paste the code."

Ricket smiled. "Are you ready for the last batch from Beatrice?"

"Yes. Go ahead and have her send it on … I'm ready."

Ricket sat down at his workbench, pushing his mind to think about the plan's new direction. *"Beatrice, what is the maximum distance out that objects stored within this MicroVault can be extracted to?"*

"Ninety-seven miles would be within safe parameters."

That response was not what Ricket hoped to hear. He asked another question. *"Is it possible to initiate the* Minian's *propulsion system while she's still inside the MicroVault?"*

"No, there are safeguards within the vault that disallow such things from occurring."

Many of those safeguards, Ricket had observed earlier, were from the hacked code they'd taken from the disabled virtual pedestal in the mess. Truth was, there were probably justifiable reasons why such safeguards were built in. The thought of re-designing the code from scratch, only to find things should have been left as they were, did not seem prudent. So yes, they would be able to move the *Minian* from the MicroVault, out into the real world, but her drives would be shut down. And there was a distance limit—less than one hundred miles—that the ship could be projected out to. Ricket calculated the time it would take for the propulsion system to come up to speed from a cold start. The ship's anti-matter drives offered a re-turn to full operation fairly quickly ... maybe thirty minutes. Ricket played out the scenario in his head: visualizing the ship suddenly appearing close to the Caldurian fleet in open space. It wasn't a promising thought.

"Beatrice, can you determine the location of the Parcical *at this present moment?"*

"Not precisely, but based on known factors available to me, I esti-mate the Parcical *is in a stationary orbit around the planet Alurian, within the Gracow CD1 planetary system."*

Placing a mile-long vessel into space, without propulsion, was far too risky, especially with twelve Master Class warships nearby.

"Beatrice, is the phase-shift system on board the Minian *opera-tional?"* Again, her reply was not instantaneous.

"No."

Ricket, expecting another lengthy involved explanation, guessed her *no* meant no. But a new idea began taking form in his head, and his heart rate nearly doubled. *"Beatrice ... what is the estimated distance to the surface of Alurian?"*

"Between seventy-eight miles and one hundred miles is the closest approximation I can make, without more data."

That would be calling it close, but his idea was looking promising. *"One more question for now, Beatrice: Will the* Minian *maintain her ability to avoid detection, from both long- and short-range sensors, once she's projected out from the MicroVault? Specifically, from the Caldurian fleet still in near orbit?"*

"Yes, the Minian*'s shielding is still operational. Internal and external ship-wide functions, other than propulsion, are being powered by stored reserves."*

So that was that. They would project the *Minian* onto the surface of the planet and hope they would not be visually spotted. At least, not before the ship's propulsion system could be brought back online, or her phase-shift systems repaired. Either way, they needed to have a good bit of luck on their side.

"Done!" Bristol said, looking pleased with himself. "What do we do now?"

"I suppose our next step is to fetch Leon and Hanna. Are you ready to test out the terminal?"

"I think so. Maybe we can first test it with something inanimate ... like this," Bristol said, holding up a coffee cup.

"Good idea. Let's give it a try," Ricket said, getting to his feet.

Bristol, still staring at the cup and looking lost in thought, said, "Ricket, within this miniaturized vault ... there's air; oxygen to breathe."

Ricket smiled. "This particular vault is probably just one of many others set up by Norwell. Like separate folders on a storage tab, this particular MicroVault was set up with certain modifiable, virtual characteristics, including a type of virtual atmosphere that could accommodate both humans and Caldurians; a virtual physical environment that allows for navigating within the virtual construct. It is a whole lot to think about, Bristol … perhaps too much for right now."

Bristol rose and hurried to the MicroVault terminal—across the corridor—with Ricket following close behind. Bristol stood at the pedestal, and entered a set combination of commands that would open a virtual portal. When it appeared, Bristol did a fist punch into the air. "Yes!"

He moved to the open portal and, looking over at Ricket, tossed the cup forward and into the void beyond. Ricket moved over to the pedestal and adjusted it lower, befitting his own smaller stature, and quickly entered a flurry of commands. The wrap-around display came alive and after a bit of navigating, they found the cup—suspended in open white space. "There it is! It is now logged and placed within the virtual MicroVault catalogue," Ricket said.

"Cool. I guess it works. Can we now take a look for Leon and Hanna?"

Ricket, getting more accustomed to the controls, applied the designated data for the location. Within a few seconds, they could see both prone bodies; they looked as if they were fast asleep.

Ricket looked back toward Bristol and—right before his eyes—Bristol vanished. Ricket knew exactly what had happened. Back within the *Parcical*, Hobel had cut Bristol from virtual memory. The young man had been deleted!

Chapter 24

Visually, there was nothing there, but Jason could almost feel her presence. "No way to phase-shift in—"

"Inside the vessel?" Orion asked, completing his sentence. "We have nothing definitive to pinpoint exactly where the *Parcical* is physically located. All I have is a guesstimate. You could end up caught—halfway inside and halfway outside the outer hull. And that vessel is so advanced, she may repel all phase-shift intrusions, anyway."

Jason continued to watch the fleet of Caldurian warships positioned in Alurian's high orbit. He mentally weighed his options: He could attempt to phase-shift a probe, or several probes, to the spot where Gunny had seen the momentary glimmer and hope to get lucky. Once inside the *Parcical*'s hull, it would transmit the ship's coordinates back … maybe. But then again, it could alert the entire Caldurian fleet that there was a cloaked vessel within their vicinity. Alerted, their advanced technology might zero-in on the *Assailant*'s position … and that would be the end of the game.

"What in hell are they doing up here?" Jason asked out loud, staring at the display. "Somehow, it must relate to the Zip accelerator issues they're having. But all inventors of that old technology probably died off when the planet was torched, years ago."

"Then it's probably related to that subterranean city," Orion said. "Maybe there are survivors ... descendants?"

"Could be."

"Captain, we've got movement from one of the Caldurian vessels," McNeil said, gesturing toward the display.

Sure enough, a small ship could be seen emerging from the ship's flight bay.

"Looks like a shuttle," Jason said.

"It is, Cap," Orion said, "and it's headed down to the surface."

For the first time in a long while, Jason felt like they might get a break. "Whatever you do, Gunny, don't lose track of that shuttle." He hailed Billy.

"Go for Billy ... what's up, Cap?"

"Put together a team, Billy—your five best men. We're going to head down to the planet for a little reconnaissance. I'll be in the barracks in two minutes."

"Gunny, ask the XO to come on duty. Transmit the surface coordinates to my HUD as soon as that shuttle lands, and I want to be kept up to date on anything happening with that fleet."

"You got it, Cap."

★ ★ ★

Jason arrived in the *Assailant*'s cramped and somewhat smelly barrack quarters and was again reminded how much he missed the *Minian*. He found Billy and Rizzo waiting, along with two other Sharks he didn't know. He was not happy to see the fifth team member.

"What's this?" he asked as he joined the group.

"What do you mean *what's this*? You wanted my best team of five ... she's proven better in battle than just about anyone else."

"She's also eleven years old."

"You're talking like I'm not standing right here, Dad."

"Boomer, stay out of this."

But Jason knew it was true. Looking at the small runt of a girl, he knew she was by far the most battle-savvy on the ship, with the possible exception of Billy and himself, and even then ...

"I brought you this," Boomer said, holding out an enhancement shield. "Careful, this one's not a trainer."

He noticed each team member had an open duffle bag lying on the deck by his feet; inside was a plasma sidearm, a multi-gun rifle, an enhancement shield, and miscellaneous supplies.

"Listen to me, Boomer ... I'm serious now. You follow my orders to the T. No going off and doing what you want. That's how people get killed. Do you understand?"

"Perfectly."

He looked at Billy, who shrugged.

Jason gave Boomer as stern a stare as he could conjure up, but she only smiled back. He initialized his battle suit.

"Okay, I've just been updated with the coordinates for a Caldurian shuttle that has landed on the surface. We need to find out what they are doing down there, and hopefully acquire more information on the whereabouts of our missing crew members."

Billy initialized his battle suit, followed by Rizzo, Boomer, and the other two Sharks—Baldwin and Cramer. Next, every-one affixed their enhancement shields to their forearms. Jason felt a little strange following suit, since he barely knew how to use the thing.

He said, "Gunny has a phase-shift drop location for us she believes is well hidden. Although it's underground, there's a lot of movement going on down there so we need to get going now. Everyone ready?" He counted five thumbs up. In a flash, he phase-shifted them away as an entire group from the *Assailant*.

★ ★ ★

Gunny's drop location was not optimum. In fact, it was God-awful. She'd put them on top of a plateau about seven-ty-five feet from what looked to be a below-ground airstrip. Below them lay two long, parallel runways, which led at an upward angle to an opening on the surface. Hundreds of huge light fixtures, the size of minivans, hung down from chained cables. The vast space was more than a cavern—it was a com-pletely hollowed-out section of the planet. Everything, includ-ing the rock and dirt, was orangey-red. Aircrafts of varying technology were parked at odd angles, and in no particular ar-rangement, at the opposite end of the runways from the distant opening—and there also sat the Caldurian shuttle.

But what was positioned behind their backs was the prob-lem. The control, or observation, tower loomed over them—two ginormous windows peered down at them like two wide-open eyes.

Jason spun around in search of a better place to hide, then remembered their battle suits' latest tech feature add-on: sixty seconds of cloaking capability. It took him another eight sec-onds to configure out the group settings before they all disap-peared together. He waited for something to happen—like an army of Alurian soldiers bursting out from nearby buildings—but no such commotion took place. He watched as the HUD mission timer ticked past the thirty-second mark.

"How about over there, Dad?"

"Are you pointing at something, Boomer? I can't see you … remember?"

"Oh. Hide inside the shuttle. Looks like everyone's coming out."

Jason watched as a group of Caldurians, dressed in official-looking dark blue uniforms, made their way out of the shuttle and onto the gangway.

A hovercraft vehicle was making its way across the open rocky plateau. Jason watched it as it continued going past them—not seeming to be in a particular hurry.

He turned back to the shuttle. The Caldurians were now off the ramp and the back hatch secured. At the two-second mark, Jason phase-shifted his team.

Both Rizzo and Baldwin found themselves immersed within cabin seats. Their mass had displaced the seats, but they were awkwardly caught—their legs and arms sticking out of seat cushions and fabric, giving the appearance they were *wearing* the seats.

Boomer offered Rizzo a hand, but he waved her away, opting instead to use the ka-bar knife he'd just released from the pocket compartment on his thigh.

Jason's attention was on the cockpit, where, startled with his mouth agape, sat the pilot. Before a scream or yell reached the Caldurian's lips, Jason pulled his sidearm and shot him in the chest. The pilot slumped forward, onto the controls.

"Um … Captain? I think you may want to see this," Rizzo said, still looking out the shuttle's starboard observation window. Jason moved into the small cockpit and peered through the forward observation window.

"They're disgusting," Boomer said from behind them.

She was right. They had to be some of the most bizarre-looking creatures he'd ever seen. The same group of Caldurians who'd left the shuttle now stood in a huddle with five others. Most likely Alurians, the strange beings stood in a group next to them. Jason assumed they would be humanoid, but they weren't … not completely anyway.

Primarily, they appeared to be some kind of insect. Like praying mantises, light green in color, they had human-ish arms and legs; their heads looked normal enough with the exception of two bulbous, baseball-size eyes jutting out from the top of their foreheads. They had a second pair of arms, which dangled below the others, with ugly pinchers in place of hands and fingers.

Jason wondered what they were saying. Everyone seemed fairly cordial—considering what the Caldurians had done to their planet—turning their world into a burnt-out lifeless crouton.

Billy, now at Jason's side, also looked out the forward observation window. "Looks like some kind of a handoff."

That's exactly what it was. Both the Caldurians and Alurians had *something* with them. Jason recognized the uniquely shaped, long equipment locker that rested on a nearby hover cart. It held a MediPod. Now he knew what the Caldurians were offering in trade, so what were the Alurians offering up?

The answer to that, he saw, was whatever fit inside a container the size of a toaster that one of the Alurians was holding on to. But the handoff never happened. A ruckus started between an Alurian and one of the Caldurians. Heated words.

"Somebody's got his panties in a bunch," Billy said.

"I guess possessing a MediPod doesn't hold the same significance it used to. But I sure would like to know what's in the box that Alurian is holding on to. I suspect it's the answer to our, and the Caldurians', Zip accelerator problems."

"Isn't that what they wanted Ricket for?" Billy asked.

"Perhaps Ricket was their backup plan, in case something like this happened."

Suddenly, they saw more Alurians approaching from all sides … hundreds of them—one after another. Soon, countless insect-like armed creatures surrounded the group of bewildered Caldurians.

"Should we help them?" Billy asked.

"After what they did to Jefferson Station? No, I'd be more inclined to help the damn bugs. Wait here," he said, smiling. Jason headed for the rear of the shuttle and disappeared from view mid-step. A second later, a bright flash indicated he had phase-shifted away.

Jason landed on the opposite, far side of the shuttle—away from the mayhem. Now cloaked, he confidently strode back around the shuttle and made his way toward the Caldurians. They were still arguing over the little black box, but nervously watched as the army of bug people pointed weapons at them. There was something thrilling, Jason thought, about being so close to one's enemy and being invisible. He saw the black box, a mere five feet before him, tightly gripped in the arms of the Alurian. Jason brought his own arms up, hands positioned just right to snatch the box from the bug man's green arms, when one of the Caldurians suddenly stepped sideways, blocking his way.

Jason had already burned through forty seconds of invisibility. Whatever move he was going to make, he needed to do it within the next twenty seconds. *Why pussyfoot around?* Jason burst forward, knocking a Caldurian to the ground and pushing another into a furious-looking Alurian. Getting both hands on the black box, he wrenched it free. Two bulbous eyes watched in shock as the small black box flew from his arms and floated away, seemingly on its own volition. In a flash, the box disappeared from sight.

Several seconds after he flashed back into the shuttle, Jason turned visible.

"That was classic, Cap," Rizzo said. "They'll be telling stories about the flying box for the next hundred years."

"Now back to the *Assailant*?" Billy asked.

Jason nodded, but paused as he observed the situation outside. The five Caldurians were down to three—two decapitated, he suspected, by razor-sharp pinchers.

Jason said, "Shit … shit, shit, shit!"

"You want us to rescue them?"

"I guess … and I think I'm going to take their shuttle, too." Jason watched as his team, including Boomer, flashed away. He manhandled the dead Caldurian from the pilot's seat and tossed his corpse in an open rear area of the cabin. Positioned behind the controls, Jason quickly got the shuttle's drive revved up to speed, and felt its familiar vibration come up through the deck below his feet. He missed flying. Outside, new elements of bright purple were crisscrossing from many disruption waves. Boomer summersaulted into view, right in front of the nose of the shuttle. With quick, punch-like motions, she catapulted six or so Alurian bugs off their feet, sending them sprawling into the rocks. *Well, Boomer, now you're just showing off*, he mused.

Rizzo was the first one to arrive back in the cabin, his arms wrapped around a uniformed Caldurian officer. Next came Billy and his captive officer; then Baldwin, holding another. Cramer flashed into view, empty handed.

"Where's Boomer?" Jason asked, craning his neck to look out the side observation window.

"I'm right here. Dad!"

Confused, Jason looked toward the copilot's empty seat. She instantly appeared, sitting with her arms crossed over her chest. "Are we going to go, or what?"

Outside, an army of Alurian bugs had shifted their focus to the shuttle. The small vessel began taking on plasma fire from virtually every direction.

The onboard AI announced the ship's shields were down to ninety-eight percent. Jason brought the shuttle up and off the airstrip, goosing the propulsion system forward while turning in a wide arc, over the heads of the angry mob below. Halfway down the runway, the shuttle was phase-shifted away.

Chapter 25

High Orbit Over Alurian, Gracow CD1
System
Assailant, Flight Bay

Jason watched as Billy and Rizzo walked the three new Caldurian prisoners down the gangway and off to join the other three already being held within the *Assailant*'s hold.

"I'm sorry, Captain, but the *Assailant*'s bay was not designed to accommodate a shuttle of such size," Chief Petty Officer Gomez said, apologetically. "It's about three feet higher, two feet wider, and easily five feet longer than the *Perilous*."

Jason stood with his hands on his hips, looking up at the top of the shuttle. The three hanging light fixtures overhead had instantly shattered when they phase-shifted into the flight bay. He was really starting to miss the *Minian*.

"You'll have to figure something out, Mr. Gomez. That shuttle is an important asset. We all need to do our part to make any necessary accommodation. As of now, she is our only Caldurian vessel."

"Yes, sir. I suppose we can figure something out. Make room … somehow."

"That's the spirit. I'll let you get back to work." Turning to leave, Jason was hailed.

"Go for Captain."

"Captain, we have a serious situation on the bridge."

"On my way, XO."

Jason picked up his pace. Even though the *Assailant* was a relatively small ship, half the size of *The Lilly*, not having the convenience of DeckPorts on board to instantly move between decks, from the stern of the vessel—where the flight bay was located—to the forward bridge, took him close to eight minutes, jogging double-time. Tempted to break his own rule—no inner-ship phase-shifts—he resisted the urge and jogged faster.

Seven-and-a-half minutes later, Jason rushed into the bridge. "What's up, XO?"

Perkins relinquished the command chair. "That, sir," he said, gesturing to the forward display.

Jason sat down in the vacated seat and took in the logistical feed. "That's quite a fleet ... let me guess, our friend Captain Mar Oswaldo?"

"Yes, sir. I've color-coded the *Carrion* red ... she's there, in the middle of the pack."

Jason wasn't surprised to see Captain Oz and the *Carrion* in that section of space. The *Assailant* wasn't particularly far away, in relative light-year terms, from the CAP-RIM star system, where they had their last encounter with Oz.

Orion reported, "Twenty-eight warships, mostly destroyers and battle-cruisers. There are also several large vessels the AI does not recognize. In all, a formidable force."

"What has he been up to lately?"

"It looks like he's continuing on with the same directive— to reestablish the Darion Empire's boundary back to its former size."

"Boundaries that were established a thousand years ago

and spanned close to two hundred light-years," Jason added. "Can you put that section of the galaxy up, along with an overlay, showing that empire's earlier boundaries?"

Orion did as asked. Jason recognized several of the once-existing star systems, now revealed in an orange background. The former area included a vast section of the sector.

"Now put up the areas he's already retaken."

The logistical display updated. Close to the middle of the vast, orange-delineated section of space, approximately one-sixteenth of the total area, an odd-shaped octagon section was registering as light blue. It spanned a distance of six or seven total light-years.

Jason studied the display. "Gunny, show me Earth, as it relates to this perspective."

The display refreshed, and off to the left, clearly within the confines of the orange overlay, a new, added, circle appeared. Orion zoomed in on that particular section of space until the Sol solar system came clearly into view.

"At his current rate of advancement, it's estimated Oz's fleet will reach the Sol system within five to eight years." She then zoomed back out to the previous view.

There were millions, if not billions, of stars contained within that area, once known as the Darion Empire. Realistically, for Oz to take control, Jason knew they only needed to deal with civilizations capable of space travel, and those exhibiting a strong military presence. "Now, Gunny, show me the systems capable of putting up resistance."

It took a full minute before the display refreshed to show multiple, newly added, green circles.

"Two hundred and thirty-six civilizations currently maintain military space fleets. Most, if not all, would quickly fall to Captain Oz's fleet."

"Okay. Now show me the Alliance's borders."

Orion, already prepared for his request, displayed the odd-shaped borders of the Alliance, outlined in bright purple. Earth was positioned within the purple borders, but barely, as well as other planetary areas, including all of Corian Nez.

A far bigger issue than the Alliance ever realized, Jason had no idea what the current death toll now was due to the Darion Cartel's continuing space-grab—and what it had elevated to. Millions? Billions? More? It was one thing to defeat other forces in space, but it was quite another to subjugate those conquered societies, as the Craing Empire had done previously. No, it took the Craing hundreds of years of strategic planning to physically accomplish the takeover of so many worlds and to occupy vast sections of space. The Craing typically utilized the prisoners—taken from those vanquished worlds—to do their fighting for them. Jason couldn't see the Darion Cartel going to such almost-unimaginable lengths. In reality, most worlds wouldn't be impacted in the least—even aware they were now positioned within new borders reestablished by the Darion Empire.

"How could things progress to this … level so fast?" Perkins asked, his voice lowered.

"I'm not sure. I don't think the late Admiral Dixon really knew the extent of the Cartel's unhindered advancement. But it should have been recognized, and dealt with far sooner."

Perkins looked concerned. "We already have the Caldurians to deal with. We're pretty much at war with them today, yes?"

Jason nodded, bringing his thoughts back to the fleet of twelve warships here in space within the Gracow CD1 system. He felt his blood pressure rise as his irritation grew. Within weeks of their defeating the Craing, Alliance's high command quickly gutted the fleet. Warships were mothballed, service men and women sent home. Did they honestly believe, once

Star Watch was formed, that alone it could sufficiently police the vast borders within Allied space? Now, after years of hard fought war, they were once again in jeopardy.

Jason stood. "Have a seat, XO … I've got some long-distance directives to initiate that could take me a while."

★ ★ ★

Jason took a seat at the desk in his ready room. He took a moment to organize his thoughts before making the interstellar call to his father. His eyes fell on the toaster-sized black box, sitting on the deck near his feet. In an earlier rush, he'd left it there—meaning to take a closer look when he had more time. Reaching for it he hefted it up and turned it around in his hands. It was perfectly symmetrical, without seams or openings. *How in hell does one look inside the thing?* It occurred to him, he was juggling too many things—nothing getting done. He set the box back down on his desk, and pushed it aside. *One thing at a time,* he mused to himself. He contacted Seaman Gordon and prompted him to issue an interstellar comms request to Admiral Reynolds, back in the Sol system. While he waited he thought about Dira, and felt an all-too-familiar tightening in his chest. He wondered if he could ever do anything without her and didn't think so. His eyes fell back onto the black box. Without Ricket or Bristol … or even Granger around, how the hell would he know what to do with the thing?

"Jason?"

Jason saw his father, back in uniform, on the virtual display. "Dad … tell me … how is she?"

There was a pause before his father spoke again: "I wish I could give you better news. She's alive, son … but just barely. The MediPod is keeping her vitals steady, but for how long no one is really sure. Tell me how your search for Ricket is going."

"We're in close proximity to the Caldurian fleet. We're cloaked and keeping an eye on them. We believe the *Parcical* is there too, and hopefully Ricket is on board." Jason quickly reached for the box and looked thoughtful. "Son of a … it just occurred to me, I might have a bargaining chip."

"That's good, Jason. You'll need to hurry, though. You understand that, right?"

Jason could hear the tension in his father's voice. "I do. Listen, we need to change subjects here."

"I'm all ears," the admiral said.

"Gunny's going to send you what we have—what's been transpiring with the Darion Cartel, with Captain Oz, and their recent arrival here within the sector."

"Oz is there?"

"He, and a fleet of twenty-eight warships. It's a substantial force that's been allowed to run rampant and unchecked far too long. I know that the Allied fleet command since the end of the Craing war wanted to avoid future wars … and even skirmishes … at all cost, but their lack of taking Oz and his cartel seriously, taking prompt action, will have devastating repercussions for years to come."

"I've been coming up to speed," the admiral said. "Apparently, after I went into retirement, many decisions were made that shouldn't have been. The Allied forces, along with the U.S. space fleet, were disassembled. I've taken it upon myself to amend some of those decisions. I hope you don't mind. We haven't had time to speak—"

Jason cut in, "Listen, Dad … Admiral … we can talk about rebuilding our assets later. But right now, we need to deal with what's going on here and the issues at hand. You've proven yourself in battle, over and over again. No one trumps you when it comes to battle strategy. Your goal, your highest priority right now, is to defeat Captain Oz and drive the Darion

Cartel back to their own small corner of the galaxy. Re-mobilize what's left of our fleet and also talk to the Alliance leaders, in case their involvement is necessary. Whatever resources we have, I'm now putting at your disposal. But I need to be kept in the loop."

"I understand, Jason, but we can't allocate our entire arsenal toward that one enemy when another, even more powerful, has already attacked us and is looming nearby."

"Let me deal with the Caldurians. Let's be frank, Dad … we can't prevail over Caldurians using conventional weapons … the ones available to us. We no longer have *The Lilly*. We no longer have the *Minian*. Today, our forces are a mere shell of what they were even six months ago."

"Huh … you sure know how to paint a rosy picture, Jason."

"But what we do have is cunning. And, yes, we still have a few tricks up our sleeves. Take Captain Oz and his fleet off my plate—make a stand and defeat him. Let me deal with the Caldurians and getting Ricket and the others safely returned to us. Can you do that?"

"Hell … I don't know. We lost more than warships when the Caldurians barreled through here and took out Jefferson Station. We lost a good portion of our command structure. Listen, I'll do my very best."

"That's all I can ask for, Admiral."

"Good luck, Jason."

The feed went dark and Jason, feeling that at least some of the heavy load had been lifted from his shoulders, sighed in relief. He sat back and again looked at the black box. If indeed it actually were something they could use as a bargaining chip, he needed to contact the captain of the *Parcical* without divulging their own coordinates. They would be dealing with a vessel that had an even higher level of technology than the *Minian*.

Shit, who knew what they'd be up against? Jason hailed Orion.

"Go for Gunny. Yes, Captain?"

"Be in my ready room in five minutes. I want Billy, Jackson and Rizzo there, too." He was about to ask her to contact Traveler, before remembering the rhino was back in HAB 170—accessible only from the *Minian*. Would he ever see his old friend again? "Just the four of you for now, Gunny ... five minutes." He looked up and saw Boomer standing in the hatch.

"Whatever you're planning ... I'm going."

He didn't even try to argue with her. Truth was, their odds of success without her help were beyond terrible. "You'll follow my orders?"

"Yes."

"Okay, then you'll need to sit in on this meeting."

Boomer smiled. "I'll give you another Kahill Callan lesson, if you want? You're still not very good at using an enhancement shield."

"Yeah ... well, I'm not so bad with a multi-gun."

Chapter 26

High Orbit Over Alurian, Gracow CD1
System
Minian, Ricket's Workshop

For six hours straight Ricket sat perfectly still at a terminal within his workshop. Bypassing the far too slow manual input device, he'd tapped in directly, via his NanoCom, to communicate with Beatrice and the *Minian*'s AI. All together, they possessed substantial processing power for working on one particular problem. He needed administrator access to only one vault—theirs, the vault they were situated in. Undoubtedly, there were many others ... perhaps hundreds of separate vaults under the purview of the *Parcical*'s AI. Pure and simple, Ricket was attempting to hack into the *Parcical*. He only had one access point: the partially operational virtual pedestal located in the *Minian*'s mess.

Ricket and his two AI assistants were not in pursuit of the

highest executive or command-level access. That could take them days or even weeks. He simply wanted access to their present MicroVault, and class-level access would be sufficient for that.

Distracted, Ricket noticed movement. Traveler was standing in the workshop's entrance. Placing all internal processes on momentary hold, he said, "Hello, Traveler."

"What are we waiting for? We should leave this place."

"Yes, Traveler, I'm working on that. I'm trying to find Bristol ... then we can leave."

"He's still alive? You said he was ..." Traveler paused, searching for the correct word to use, "... deleted."

"He was. I determined that unequivocally."

Traveler didn't respond to that.

"But I noticed something interesting," Ricket continued. "There were alterations made to the vault's catalogue. Not like something was added to its storage area, such as a ship or another person, but the size of the vault's buffer has grown significantly."

"I don't understand anything you are talking about," Traveler said, his irritation obviously mounting.

"In simple terms, Bristol was deleted from this virtual space ... but that does not mean nothing remains of him. Like a deleted file, he still is, hopefully, in one piece—only he's now contained in a buffer, or a temporary holding space, like a trash file. If we can access that file before something is written on top of it, or the MicroVault's trash buffer is emptied, we may be able to retrieve him ... bring him back into this virtual realm."

"Just tell me when Bristol will return."

"If he can be brought back at all, it will happen within the next few minutes. Please let me continue with what I am doing."

Traveler snorted and left. Ricket resumed where he, Beatrice, and the *Minian*'s AI had left off. They were at a crucial juncture. Up until now, their presence hadn't been detected by the *Parcical*'s AI. It was imperative that their intrusion into the MicroVault only come across as one of billions of sub-processes going on in the background, which meant, at least mathematically, all checksums matched perfectly. That redundant, as well as arbitrary, security measures come back normal. Six hours and ten minutes into the hack, Ricket finally gained class-level access. He allowed himself a small smile. But their work was not quite over. With his newly acquired access, he began searching. There were trillions of parallel transactions taking place, all at the same time. The *Parcical*'s AI constantly remained in a housekeeping state of maintenance: cleanup, reorganizing, and updating. *Where is the trash bin? Ah, there you are!* He'd found it. Actually, there were thousands of trash bins, but he knew the one he specifically looked for had been accessed on a particular day and time and in a particular MicroVault— theirs. He opened the trash bin and found two separate objects: Bristol and—most surprisingly—Granger! Although the virtual files still appeared to be perfectly intact, how long did he have before the AI's maintenance protocols automatically emptied the trash? He didn't know.

Okay, Ricket reasoned to himself, this next part would be dangerous. Not only to Bristol and Granger, who still could be permanently deleted, but to all others at risk on the *Minian*. His hack may well be detected.

Ricket once again placed his, and the two AIs', intrusive hack process on hold. He got to his feet and hurried into the *Minian*'s recently built MicroVault terminal, just across the corridor. Was it ready for what was needed? Was it capable of moving more than just an inanimate object, like a coffee cup?

He wasn't sure. He stood in the middle of the compartment and spoke aloud. "Beatrice ... have I done all that I can

… have we missed something?"

"Together, we have completed all the directives you have set forth."

"Good. Then it is time I bring Bristol and Granger out of the trash buffer and back to the MicroVault proper." Ricket stepped up to the virtual pedestal and called up an access portal. It appeared and loomed before him. Ricket did one more check on what they had accomplished and felt surprisingly satisfied with all their work. *No … wait. Why's the buffer decreasing in size?* No! The trash bins! The *Parcical's* AI maintenance functions were clearing out all the trash bins—one right after another, at lightning speed. Without hesitation, Ricket moved the two virtual files from one location to another within the MicroVault's virtual storage. He didn't have time to look where he was moving them to, not specifically anyway. Mesmerized by what he was witnessing, he watched as, one after another, the *Parcical's* AI emptied out every trash bin until the buffer read zero. Had he truly gotten Bristol and Granger out in time? There was only one way to be really sure. He stepped through the open MicroVault terminal access portal.

★ ★ ★

Ricket arrived in the familiar, bright white environment of the virtual MicroVault storage area. He turned around and assessed his surroundings; feeling relieved, he knew he was standing at the same approximate drop location he'd stood at previously. Thousands upon thousands of stored objects surrounded him—everything in its place and perfectly organized. Behind him was the open portal he'd just walked through. He eyed it, double-checking it hadn't disappeared, thereby condemning him to lifelong captivity.

He continued on, following the same route as before. Eventually up ahead, he saw Leon and Hanna, lying side by side upon padded platforms within medium-sized containers, both still unconscious. He debated if he should continue on— look first for Bristol and Granger—or attempt to wake them now. The truth was, there was no guarantee he'd ever find Bristol and Granger, while these two needed rescuing.

Ricket moved to Leon's container, taking stock of what he was connected to. There was an intravenous tube coming from his arm, which led to some kind of dispensary device secured to the platform. He pulled at the tube before realizing it wasn't an intravenous tube at all, but more like an optical cable strapped to his wrist. Removing it was a simple matter of expanding the elastic band, then pulling it over his limp hand. Looking at the inside of the band, he saw fluctuating micro-pulses of light.

Ricket leaned over Leon's face—using two fingers, he pried open one of his eyelids. His pupil, although responding sluggishly, did register a level of responsiveness to the light. Leon's breathing became shallower and he opened his mouth and licked his lips. He was waking up. Ricket moved over to Hanna's container and removed the elastic band and cable from her wrist, as he'd just done with Leon. He sat down on the edge of the platform and waited. His mind, always in a state of multitasking, was still watchful of the *Parcical*'s AI and her actions. His presence within this section of the MicroVault hadn't triggered any alarms to go off.

Leon's arms and legs moved and he abruptly leaned forward on his elbows. Startled at first, he stared directly at Ricket. "What the hell is going on? Where …" Leon looked around and took in his surroundings. His gaze finally fell on Hanna's still-immobile form, in the container next to him.

"Is she?"

"She should be waking up momentarily," Ricket said.

Ricket saw comprehension in Leon's eyes. He knew exactly where he was and what had happened to them.

Hanna, more slowly than Leon, was coming around. She opened her eyes.

Leon leaned closer to her. "It's all right. You're okay, Hanna."

Slowly she sat up and she too looked around at her surroundings. She touched her head and rubbed her temples. "Freaky dreams."

"Tell me about it," Leon said, now on his feet and going to Hanna. "Can you stand?"

"I think so." She cautiously stood up and climbed out of the container. She wavered a bit and Leon held her steady. They both looked at Ricket.

"We don't have much time," Ricket said. "In fact, we could all be deleted at any second."

"Then let's get the hell out of here!" Leon said, looking ready to run.

"Both Bristol and Granger are in here somewhere. We first need to find them and bring them with us. Then we can leave."

But Leon was only half-listening to Ricket as he wandered down the virtual corridor.

"Leon?" Ricket said.

"There she is! Right there in that large container … we're not going anywhere without my ship." Leon strode back to Ricket. "What's exactly happening … what are we doing?"

"Escaping. Once we find the other two, the plan is to extricate ourselves, along with the *Minian*—"

"And the *SpaceRunner*," Leon interjected.

"Yes, and the *SpaceRunner*, onto the surface of Alurian."

"Alurian?" Hanna asked, looking confused.

"It's a long story and we haven't time to waste," Ricket said. He looked at Leon and Hanna for several beats and said, "We need to split up. I still have work to do on board the *Minian* to prepare things. You two need to look for Bristol and

Granger on your own … can you do that?"

"Without getting lost in this place? Twenty steps from here, we'll be totally disoriented!"

He was right, Ricket realized. He at least had Beatrice to guide him within the virtual constructs of their environment. An idea struck him and Ricket smiled. "Leon, you have Nano-Com!"

"Yeah … so what?"

"I want to introduce you to … um … a friend of mine. Her name is Beatrice. She'll be talking to you via your Nano-Com. She'll help direct you … keep you from getting lost."

"What are you talking about, Ricket?"

"We're out of time so just take my word for it; she's here to help."

Ricket first mentally accessed Beatrice, then opened a NanoCom channel to Leon. He would interface between the two. "Leon, I'd like to introduce you to Beatrice … Beatrice, say hello to Leon."

"Hello, Leon … we should hurry," Beatrice said.

Ricket watched Leon's face and the smile that reached his lips. "Works for me." He held out a hand for Hanna and the two headed down the virtual corridor—between the masses of strange and bizarre stored objects.

Ricket spun in the opposite direction and ran back the way he'd come only ten minutes earlier. He saw the open portal ahead—just as he had left it. He ran right through the opening and immediately found himself again standing within the MicroVault terminal, within the *Minian*.

He looked around and considered all he needed to accomplish. He heard heavy footsteps approaching, and Traveler, once again, came into view.

"Traveler. Good you are here. I think it's best if you and your team return to HAB 170."

"Go back and hide?"

"No ... not at all. It's temporary. I can't explain technically what is happening ... what will be happening, other than I will be moving the ship ... the *Minian* to a different place. While I'm doing that, you and the others need to be back in HAB 170. Please trust me; it's safer that way. I'm not completely sure anyone on board the *Minian* will survive. That reminds me, please get Norwell from the brig and take him to HAB 170 as well."

Traveler seemed to consider Ricket's words before snorting, "I will get Norwell and send him with the other warriors back into the habitat. But I will remain with you. I will stand by your side, Ricket. Nor will there be future discussion on the matter."

Ricket was touched by the rhino's loyalty and knew there was no arguing with him. He was as stubborn as he was courageous.

"Thank you, Traveler. Then go—do it now. Ensure everyone is off the ship and return back here as quickly as possible."

Traveler snorted once, initialized his battle suit, and flashed away.

"Ricket?"

"Yes, Beatrice ... have you found Bristol and—"

Beatrice interrupted him: "Ricket, objects within the *Parcical's* MicroVault are systematically being deleted."

Chapter 27

High Orbit Over Alurian, Gracow CD1
System
Parcical, Omni's Quarters

Startled, Hobel awakened from a deep, dream-filled, sleep. His second-in-command, Cloister Hann, was standing at the side of his bed, looking uneasy.

"There's been an intrusion, Omni. It was detected by the ship's AI ten minutes ago."

"Intrusion! Impossible. We're cloaked. How would—"

"A virtual intrusion. It looks to be a hack into the ship's network ... more specifically, into one or more of the virtual MicroVaults."

"It's that damn Ricket! Why wasn't he captured hours ago? My direct orders were to go in and get him."

"Somehow, he's blocking our MicroVault projection link

… some kind of firewall."

"I will not tolerate any more incompetence. I'll be on the bridge momentarily. Get out!" Hobel scrambled from beneath his bedcovers and hurried to get dressed. His mind raced. *Virtual hacking isn't supposed to be possible.*

Hacking into the *Parcical* was no small matter. In many ways, it was worse than a physical invasion by enemy forces. The *Parcical* was unique: much of the ship was nothing more than a virtual representation of actual matter. Certainly, the ship's hull was real, as were the ship's superstructure, the propulsion systems, the deck plating, and perhaps even the plumbing. But almost everything else was a mere representation—a virtual construct—that only looked and felt solid. All of it a derivative of advanced software programming. A hack into the vessel could be catastrophic. The ship was the product of the greatest Caldurian minds at work—unparalleled robust engineering and testing added years into the design, and the ultimate production of the craft. The *Parcical's* AI and network had been deemed one hundred percent impenetrable. Hobel was certain there was no finer vessel—none more technologically advanced—in the universe. *Perhaps the multiverse!*

★ ★ ★

It took Hobel less than eight minutes to go from the comfort of his bed to the buzzing, high-tension atmosphere of the bridge. Wearing the same somewhat rumpled white uniform he'd worn the prior night, he took a seat in the command chair and glared at his second-in-command.

"Speak to me!"

Hann approached the Omni, swallowed hard, and began: "It is as I said earlier. We have been hacked. But only to command level."

"Only to command level?" Hobel yelled. "Do you know what can be accomplished with command-level access?" Hobel, in reality, was not completely sure himself. He guessed with only lower user-level clearance, the ship was probably safe. Access to either propulsion, or navigation software subroutines, would not be allowed. But, whoever this intruder was—and he had a pretty good idea it was Ricket—he certainly had access to the *Parcical*'s storage systems, including each of their MicroVaults.

"So what have you done to safeguard the network?" Hobel asked, glowering at his second-in-command.

"The intruder has hidden himself well. Well enough not to differentiate himself from native programming. With that said, the intruder, or multiple intruders, will need to be apprehended manually."

"Manually? What the hell does that mean?"

"T-bots … Tracker bots. A final safeguard that was deemed unnecessary by the engineers, due to the high level of security already in place, but added, nevertheless, as another level of protection. The bots are virtual, of course. Simply put, they have the ability to find, confront, and destroy anything that looks suspicious. Five of them have already been dispatched into the MicroVaults in question."

"Just as long as the *Minian*'s Zip accelerators are left intact," Hobel said. "Their technology may still hold the only key to Caldurian survival, especially after that recent fiasco down on Alurian."

"That is understood, Omni."

"Good. Now I want Ricket found and destroyed, and that goes for the other prisoners in stasis. All terminated immediately."

"Unfortunately, Omni, they are no longer registering … showing up … as valid cataloged items."

"Does that mean they have been rescued, or does it mean your T-bots have already terminated them?"

"That, Omni … sir, I do not know," Hann said.

"Well, find out. Now! I want all of them deleted. Permanently."

★ ★ ★

Ricket was back at the workstation where Bristol, earlier, had been working. He found the assembled code for a second portable MicroVault virtual terminal and uploaded it into his own memory banks. Even with the expanded, updated nano-devices now functioning within his newly enlarged cranium, the code still contained a tremendous amount of data for him to store. He knew the data was weightless, had no mass, so maybe it was his imagination, but his head suddenly felt heavier on his shoulders.

"Your completed projector unit is waiting in the hopper, Ricket."

"Thank you, Beatrice." Ricket was already out of the chair and running down the corridor. He entered the phase synthesizer compartment and headed for the output tray. The building-sized synthesizer machine was capable of manufacturing virtually anything—from spacecraft to toothpaste. Today, it was a quasi-portable, hand-held projector, which would, if he and Bristol had designed it correctly, properly synchronize with either of the newly developed MicroVault terminals. The pyramid-shaped projector was large enough, though, to require Ricket to use both hands to heft it, and it was far heavier than he'd anticipated. Struggling to carry it even a few steps, the projector was suddenly pulled from his grasp. Traveler, returned from sending fellow rhino-warriors back into their habitat, easily plucked the device away with three fingers of one hand.

"Thank you, Traveler."

He grunted and waited for Ricket to lead on. Ricket checked his internal sensors—verifying that no other life signs showed anyone still on board the *Minian*. He saw that the mecher, Trommy5, was still there where he had been left within the Zip Farm, but that should be fine. "This way, Traveler, we must now leave the *Minian*."

Ricket hurried into the MicroVault terminal and went directly to the pedestal. He tapped at the virtual display and almost immediately the access portal appeared before them.

Traveler looked somewhat startled by its unexpected appearance and snorted a burst of snotty mist into the air over his large head.

"This way, Traveler ... we must hurry now." Ricket ran through the portal opening without hesitation, but when he stepped out into the whiteness of the MicroVault storage area, Traveler wasn't behind him.

In the stark-white brightness, row after row of stored equipment lockers, fuel cells, reactor modules, and countless other items of every shape and size were hovering weightless in their perfectly organized and allocated spaces. Now standing alone, there was an eerie, disconcerting silence he hadn't noticed before. Startled, he heard Beatrice's voice in his head. *"Ricket, I'm detecting additional security measures being implemented within this MicroVault."*

Ricket did not answer her. Still waiting, his eyes were locked on the open portal. *Come on, Traveler ... where are you?*

Upon gaining entry into the vault, Ricket's internal sensors had also detected the vault's added security measures. This added complication he hadn't anticipated. Ricket hailed Leon.

"Where the hell have you been, Ricket?" Leon asked, sounding out of breath.

Ricket said, "I was working on—"

Leon cut him off: "Listen, we found Bristol and Granger; both were unconscious. I think they're okay. But there's something else—right now, we're being chased ... hunted, by a ... I don't know what the hell it is. But it's gaining on us."

Suddenly, Ricket heard Bristol's voice added into their comms channel: "It's a fucking tracker bot! Things can shred anything in their path!"

Ricket's relief at hearing Bristol's voice was short-lived. Off in the distance he saw four figures running for their very lives. Leon and Hanna were out front—Bristol following, with Granger bringing up the rear. But what was closing in behind them captured Ricket's full attention. Bristol was correct; it was indeed a tracker bot. In this realm, where it was a requirement everything take on physical form, the bot was perfectly suited to, as Bristol so eloquently stated, shred anything within its path. It looked like a wild cluster of circular, razor-sharp, buzz saws.

Ricket stared, mesmerized.

Leon was now close enough for Ricket to hear what he was yelling: "Go Go Go! Run, Ricket!"

Then it hit him, he was standing in their path. His mouth fell open to say something, but no words escaped his lips. One by one—Leon, Hanna, Bristol, and Granger ran toward him, then past him. Ricket remained paralyzed where he stood—not taking his eyes off the fast-approaching tracker bot that was efficiently shredding everything in its path.

Ricket fumbled for his SuitPac device, hanging from his belt. Nervous fingers unsuccessfully tried to locate the two inset tabs to initialize his battle suit. He realized his actions were futile. He'd run out of time.

The tracker bot was going to churn him into dust, or whatever one got turned into within this microscopic virtual world. In that instant, he resigned himself to the fact he was going to die—and die within seconds. Seeing the approaching blades, he decided to close his eyes.

Chapter 28

High Orbit Over Alurian, Gracow CD1
System
Parcical, Virtual MicroVault

The next sensation he experienced was not exactly expected. Ricket felt himself flung, more or less, through the
air, but without any accompanying, and expected, pain. Then,
landing hard on something, Ricket did feel pain ... but a different kind of pain. He opened his eyes and found he was lying
sideways on an enormous food replicator. In full view before
him was the tracker bot, being mercilessly battered by a seven-
foot-tall rhino-warrior wielding his heavy hammer.

Traveler had obviously found the fortitude to enter the
access portal and his timing couldn't have been more perfect.
Lacerations crisscrossed both arms and his blood flowed red,
markedly contrasting with the white world around him. Un-

relenting, Traveler gave the already destroyed tracker bot a final definitive blow with his hammer. He continued to watch the wrecked bot for several seconds, as if waiting for it to suddenly come back alive. It did not.

Ricket crawled down from the top of the replicator and made his way to Traveler's side. He had no words to express what he was feeling—what words would even be sufficient? Traveler finally looked toward Ricket and simply nodded.

The other four had not gone far. Walking now, still out of breath, they approached.

"You've got more lives than a cat, Ricket," Leon said.

Hanna, saying nothing, put her arms around Ricket and hugged him close. She pulled away to gaze down at him. "Why didn't you run?"

"I don't know ... I couldn't."

Granger, looking serious, said, "There will be others."

Ricket faced Traveler and saw he was no longer holding the projector. "The projector?"

Traveler didn't answer. Instead, he turned around and pointed. Ricket, his eyes following the pointing finger, spotted the pyramid-shaped device near the opening of the access portal.

Bristol scurried over and tried to lift it up. Swearing, he asked, "Is this our projector? Why is it so flipping heavy?"

"There's a lot packed into it," Ricket said.

Traveler, ignoring his bleeding arms, took several long strides and picked up the projector.

"What now?" Hanna asked. "If there's more of those things shouldn't we get back on the *Minian*?"

As if on cue, Ricket detected two more tracker bots had entered the MicroVault. "We need to get over to where the *Minian* is stored. It's time we got out of here, once and for all."

★ ★ ★

As they passed in front of the *SpaceRunner*, reduced in size and stored in a MicroVault container, Leon said, "Whatever you're planning, this ship comes with us. That you promised, Ricket." He raised his brow, not taking no for an answer.

Ricket checked on the tracker bots' locations. They were nearly impossible to track with his internal sensors, but definitely closer; he estimated they were still several minutes away. He looked over to Leon's ship. Truth was, it didn't matter where he set up the virtual MicroVault terminal and the projector.

"We must hurry … we have limited time. Traveler, please put the device right there."

Traveler placed the projector down and stepped away. Ricket knelt down next to it, putting a hand on one of its sharply angled sides, and opened a link to the device.

"What are you doing?" Leon questioned.

"Shush!" Bristol said. "My guess is he's downloading a shitload of data right now. Let the guy concentrate."

Ricket was doing just that and it took him less than a minute. He stood and gestured for Traveler to help him. "Please clear a large space, approximately twenty feet wide, by thirty feet long."

Traveler turned to assess the area Ricket indicated. To gain sufficient open space in the virtual corridor, he'd need to move several large container items—one was some sort of flatbed hovercraft. Leon, Bristol and Granger helped, too. It took another two minutes of pushing and shoving before Ricket had his requested amount of open space available.

The next part would be tricky, and he wasn't entirely sure he'd be able to accomplish the task. *"Beatrice … I need to access the* Parcical's *AI, one more time."*

"That may be impossible, Ricket. The Parcical's *AI has institut-*

214

ed numerous new security safeguards since your previous intrusions."

"Can you work in conjunction with the Minian's AI? Find some alternative method to establish a connection? It does not have to be a permanent one ..."

"We are attempting that now, Ricket ... please wait," the AI said.

Momentarily distracted, Ricket's internal, close-proximity sensors suddenly came alive. It happened when both tracker bots had locked on to their positions within the MicroVault. They were now on a direct path, heading their way.

Beatrice was back: *"You are in. You have seventy-two seconds. We won't be able to hold off the Parcical AI any longer than that."*

Ricket wasted no time, tapping directly into the *Parcical's* internal network. The ship's AI, instantly hostile to his presence, looked for means to extricate him. Ricket noticed Beatrice and the *Minian's* AI were hard at work to keep it distracted and was reminded he had less than sixty seconds before his connection would close. He traveled to the portion of the ship's network where the MicroVault terminal processes took place, established the necessary back-and-forth handshaking, and eventually gained permission to start an external upload. Less than forty seconds remained.

With a sense of relief, the immense amount of stored data—the cloned MicroVault terminal program—transferred from his memory banks into the *Parcical's*. Suddenly, Ricket felt light-headed. In twenty seconds the upload was complete. He instantly took control of the original MicroVault terminal located within the *Parcical* and issued one simple command: Project the new, very similar to the original, MicroVault terminal to the designated coordinates.

Beatrice said, *"The Parcical AI is now closing all access to its onboard network."*

Ricket was only partially listening to her. He had already

accomplished what he'd needed to do. In the cleared space before him stood his, and Bristol's, not-quite-perfect-looking MicroVault terminal.

Bristol began throwing fist punches into the air and looked ready to burst with excitement. What they were viewing was massive amounts of data, a projected signal, coming from the *Parcical*. Extricating Ricket from the network was one thing, but not everything. Eventually, that ship's AI would discover the transmission: It could take ten minutes ... or take an hour—but her detection was inevitable.

Bristol was already standing at the MicroVault terminal's pedestal. He looked over at the pyramid-shaped projector Traveler had placed in the virtual corridor. Bristol looked at Ricket. "I think it's syncing with the thing."

Ricket was fairly certain it was going to work. *It has to.* He moved over to Bristol's side and, as gently as possible, nudged him aside and took over tapping into the pedestal's virtual display. He entered the last of the commands and looked up. He found Leon and nodded.

"What?"

Ricket pointed to the now-empty container directly behind Leon.

"My ship ... you did it! You got her out of here?"

Ricket smiled. "I did ... we did."

"And the *Minian*?" Granger asked.

"Also gone. I think ... I hope."

Hanna looked as if she were about ready to give him another hug. He held up a finger. "We still need to get out of here." He began tapping again at the top of the pedestal.

Leon said, "There they are! Two inbound tracker bots ... can you move things along, Ricket?"

Ricket saw Traveler in his peripheral vision. His heavy hammer was raised and he started moving his bulk away from the others, putting himself between them and the oncoming bots.

Bristol resumed standing at Ricket's side. "What's taking you so long? Let me do it."

"I have it, Bristol. This is a complicated process." With that, a MicroVault terminal access portal appeared. "Please, everyone … hurry into the portal!"

"You sure we're not running head first into open space?" Leon asked.

Ricket didn't answer. He was as sure as he could be, but not absolutely a hundred percent sure. If he had done everything right they would enter the portal and exit below on the planet surface, where both the *Minian* and the *SpaceRunner* would be waiting nearby.

Bristol was the first to run into the portal, quickly followed by Hanna, Granger and Leon. Traveler stood his ground while the two thrashing tracker bots rapidly approached.

Ricket said, "Traveler … we must leave now! Come with me."

Traveler shook his head. "Go. I will not run scared and hide from these mechanical demons. I will stand my ground while you escape."

Traveler would give his life to save the others and Ricket had little doubt it would be near-impossible to convince him to flee. The bots would be upon him in mere seconds.

"I am very sorry for this, my friend," Ricket said, and meant it. Traveler gave him a quick sideways glance and then prepared for the oncoming clusters of spinning buzz saws. Ricket tapped at the top of the pedestal and watched as Traveler's more than one thousand pounds disappeared from view. The pyramid projector was just as effective moving a rhino-warrior as it was a spacecraft. With any luck, he'd find himself now standing with the others. Ricket took one last glance at the approaching tracker bots and hurried into the access portal.

Chapter 29

High Orbit Over Alurian, Gracow CD1
System
Assailant, Captain's Ready Room

Jason waited for everyone to settle down. What he was about to ask Orion, Billy, Rizzo, Jackson, Boomer, and, oddly enough, Chief Horris to agree to, was tantamount to a suicide mission. But with the exception, perhaps, of Chief Horris, danger was nothing new to any of them. The truth was, he wouldn't ask them to do anything he wasn't willing to do himself, and for that reason he'd be leading the raid.

He addressed Orion, sitting directly to his left: "Were you able to obtain any more information?"

"Aye, Captain, although there was only so much I was able to do. I'm sure Ricket or Bristol could have done far more. The twelve Caldurian Master Class ships, four of which we've already come into contact with, are nearly identical to the *Minian*. Perhaps somewhat more advanced … but similar enough that I could piece things together from the nearly infinitesimal amount of sensor-scan data I was able to acquire."

"And you're sure we weren't detected?"

"Yes, Cap, I'm sure we weren't detected, since I camouflaged our scans to mimic their own, constant, virtually identical, inter-ship scans."

"So what did you see?" Billy asked, sitting on her left.

"That most of the vessels are practically ghost ships, carrying only minimal crews. One ship, as we determined before, is manned completely by droids. Another ship exhibits substantial life signs—estimated to have a crew complement of ... perhaps five hundred."

"How were you able to figure that out?" Jason asked her. "We already knew Caldurian vessels are virtually impossible to scan." He thought about verifying Orion's information with the three Caldurian captains, Larry, Moe, and Curly, still held within the ship's hold. But first hand information trumps the possible lies they'd glean from those three any day.

"I thought we were pretty clever in that regard. Chief Horris actually helped me. We've been cloaked, almost sitting on top of their fleet for some time now. Even tiny bits of data can be analyzed. So it's based on data packets, which at first seemed to be erroneous environmental data that we were able to pick up. Using that partial data, the *Assailant*'s AI calculated that the barracks section of that one ship is sucking up about twenty-four percent of the vessel's total capacity. We can compare this data to our own previous measurement stats from the *Minian*. Full capacity is close to two thousand occupants. Twenty-four percent, or about one quarter of the ship's environmental resources, is being utilized. We believe there are about five hundred Caldurians on board, mostly concentrated in the barracks of that ship ... the *Tall Spire*."

Everyone looked impressed by Orion and the chief's accomplishments. Orion continued, "But we can't get overly excited just yet. Although I can't get any readings from that cloaked ship, the *Parcical*, what I've picked up from the other ships is that she is far more dangerous than we considered. The technology utilized on that vessel is a factor of one hundred times more advanced than on other ships … frankly, more advanced than anything I've ever seen."

"In what way?" Jason asked.

"Like I said, I'm getting much of my information second-hand, so we need to keep that in mind. The *Parcical* has practically no overall mass. Sure, she's cloaked but even taking that into account, the ship is almost non-existent. It's basically a virtual ship, Captain."

No one said anything. Jason tried to determine the implications of such a thing.

"From a tactical point of view, Cap, how does one destroy … hell, even fight something that isn't really there?"

Jason shrugged. "I have no idea, Gunny, certainly not with conventional weapons." He had a quick thought and asked, "Back to the other ships … do you now know which one is the least occupied?"

"I do. Other than the ship that is manned by droids, it's the one under the designation *Quantum Lark*. Using the same measurement matrix we used for the *Tall Spire*, there are somewhere in the neighborhood of twenty to fifty souls on board her. Seaman Gordon has been monitoring bits and pieces of barely detectable comms chatter, and we've determined that the *Quantum Lark* just so happens to be the fleet's command vessel … although the *Parcical* and her captain, Omni Hobel, are higher up on the command ranking. This really gets into the area of conjecture, but we're guessing Omni Hobel is the top banana amongst the fleet but the captain, or Omni, of the *Quantum Lark*, a guy named Stanton, is the chief military guy."

"Why so few on board a command vessel?" Jason asked.

Orion shrugged. "Not sure … other ships in the fleet are fairly sparsely manned. My guess is that they left the multiverse

… wherever they came from … in a hurry."

"Captain, may I ask a question?" Chief Horris queried.

Jason looked over at the robust, somewhat befuddled-looking, older engineering officer. "Of course, Chief."

"Why am I here?" He looked around the table at the others. "I'm not a battle-hardened warrior like the rest of you."

"First of all, a warrior is just as much a state of mind as it is being a good physical combatant. But to answer your question, you're included because we are lacking talent in one particularly important area, since Ricket, Bristol and Granger are all missing. You know what that is?"

Chief Horris shook his head, still looking confused.

Orion answered the question for him. "You have an engineering degree … you know the science behind things at a level the rest of us don't."

"She's right. You're now the closest thing to a science officer we have, and you'll be an invaluable asset for the mission we're planning."

The chief sat up straighter in his seat, emphasizing his ample belly, and swiped at the few strands of gray hair left on the top of his nearly bald head. "Um … I still don't know what you plan to do, Captain?"

Boomer, sitting at the far end of the table, and looking exuberant at the future prospect, said, "We're going to steal another ship. We're trying to figure out which one … right, Dad?"

Jason nodded toward her end of the table. "I suspect this fleet's not going to hang around here much longer. They leave, the odds of finding Ricket and the others become very slim. No … we need to make a move … right away."

Horris looked from Boomer to Jason. "Seriously? We're going to steal a Master Class warship, sitting alongside eleven or twelve other warships?" He suddenly looked ill.

"We're not going to do anything we haven't done many

times before. Only this time we need your help in coming up with an idea—something to get the *Quantum Lark*, since she has the fewest combatants on board, to lower her shields."

"Why would she lower her shields?" he asked.

"Well, she wouldn't. Not normally. None of the ships in the fleet would. But in order for us to phase-shift a team into the *Quantum Lark*'s flight bay, her sophisticated Caldurian shields have to come down."

Chief Horris scratched the top of his head and shrugged. "I have no idea. None."

Everyone stared in disappointment at the chief.

Rizzo asked, "Why would any ship bring down her shields?"

Jason shook his head. "There's really no need to. Their own cleared vessels can pass through raised shields with no problem … say, to enter their flight bay."

"Why do we care if their shields are up?" the chief asked. "We can phase-shift into the *Quantum Lark*'s bay with or without their shields being up. As you said, we've certainly done that sort of thing many times in the past."

Orion held up a finger. "Because, Chief, in light of us surprising them earlier … dropping in as we did and abducting three of their ship captains, we believe they've modified their shields. They'd be crazy not to.

"Hell … a ship might explode just attempting to phase-shift in. And if we send in a probe, say to test things, there goes our element of surprise. The original plan was to phase-shift our assault team into the *Quantum Lark* using their own shuttle. The same vessel we absconded off with down on Alurian. But we just can't chance it."

The chief slowly nodded at that. "Don't we still have three of their officers locked in the brig?" the chief asked.

"Actually we have the three officers we grabbed down on

Alurian, as well as their three captains all hanging out in Hold number 2," Billy interjected.

"So maybe we bring the officers … not the captains of course, but the ones that were on the shuttle. Then if we get scanned, having those missing three also on board, maybe that could take us a step farther getting clearance to enter their flight bay. My guess, they still don't know what happened to their shuttle … or their officers, for that matter."

Jason thought about that. Could it really be that easy? Maybe this idea—to simply get clearance to fly right into their flight bay, was possible. He couldn't think of a reason not to try. If things go wonky, they could always phase-shift away.

"See, Chief," Jason said. "You're already helping us. Okay … we head out in fifteen minutes. Looks like I need to have a little chat with our prisoners. Orion, ensure we're all outfitted with SuitPacs, multi-guns, and enhancement shields."

Orion's annoyance at the latter was quickly evident.

"Oh … that's right. Sorry, Gunny, I completely forgot you still haven't been trained on the use of an enhancement shield …" Jason offered her a crooked smile.

Jason was being hailed.

"Go for Captain. What's up, XO?"

"Captain, just a heads up. Under the command of Admiral Reynolds, a U.S. fleet of forty-four warships has just emerged from an interchange wormhole near Manilaise in the next system over."

Jason was surprised his father had been able to pull together such an impressive force in so little time. "And Captain Oz and his fleet?"

"They're right there, as well, Captain."

"I want to be kept apprised of what transpires, XO. Captain Oz is as clever as they come, and he won't go down easy."

"Yes, sir … and good luck, Captain."

Chapter 30

Gracow CD1 System
Dramicus 9, Planet Surface

Oh no ... this is not Alurian, Ricket concluded, within seconds of his arrival. First of all, gone was the expected black and scorched planet surface. Although there was supposedly an atmosphere on Alurian, somewhat breathable, the atmosphere here ... was perfectly fine.

Ricket assessed his current situation. He was buried from the waist down, and, as far as he could tell, still in one piece. He felt the coolness of the soil around his legs, but something was crawling around down there, tickling his upper left thigh.

He scanned his surroundings. It was daytime under dark and cloudy skies. The terrain was rocky and the red soil was clay-like. In the far distance was a city, where spacecraft and small vessels could be seen, flying over the modern metropolis like tiny hovering insects. He didn't need Beatrice to inform him he was on Dramicus 9—Alurian's neighboring red planet. *But how could that be?* He'd configured the distance, set the projection coordinates himself. He should be on Alurian, not half buried on Dramicus 9, unless he'd missed something when programming the projector, but that was *not likely*. No, the *Parcical*, for some reason, had suddenly changed location. The pieces were coming together in his head … yes, the *Parcical* phase-shifted at the same exact time they were escaping through the MicroVault terminal. The *Parcical* was in orbit now, above Dramicus 9. It was crazy timing … whatever had happened was an anomaly and they'd ended up here, on Alurian.

Ricket's arms were uncomfortably pinned to his sides, and something was definitely moving around on his leg. He tried not to think about that. Where were the others, and the *Minian* and the *SpaceRunner*? They certainly weren't in view from this present position.

"Beatrice, please scan this planet for Hanna, Leon, Bristol, Granger and Traveler. Also, find both the Minian *and the* SpaceRunner.*"*

Her response was immediate: *"The two vessels are buried close by. Two hundred yards, directly below you … one next to the other."* Ricket's heart sank. His internal sensors confirmed her assessment.

"And the others? Are they alive?"

"Yes … all alive … four are within five miles of your current position. They too are partially or completely buried, and are trying to extricate themselves."

"You said four others. Who is missing?"

"Bristol. He is on the surface of Alurian, Ricket."

"Beatrice, what is the condition of Bristol?"

"He is on the surface of Alurian and unconscious. Due to the marginal atmospheric characteristics of Alurian, he is not getting adequate levels of O^2."

Ricket squirmed and twisted, but still could not free his arms. Using his NanoCom, he hailed Leon Pike.

"Ricket?"

"Yes, Leon, it is Ricket."

"Where the hell am I?" Leon asked. "I don't see you … or

anybody. Where's Hanna?"

"She is alive. She may be partially buried also. Since she does not have internal nano-devices, NanoCom, I cannot communicate with her. But Beatrice assures me her vital signs are strong. She is no more than a mile from your current location."

"This soil. It's impossible to move in. My head's the only damn thing above ground. I'm pinned," Leon said.

"Please stay calm. I will think of something." Ricket hailed Traveler and, receiving no response, tried Granger, but nothing was forthcoming from him either. Beatrice reassured him that both were still alive, although their vital signs were starting to fluctuate.

Something was burrowing into the top of his left boot. Again, Ricket tried to withdraw, first one arm, then the other from the tight grip of the red clay. Feeling as though he were caught in a vise, he thought, *we could all die, stuck like this. Granger, Traveler and Bristol may be dying at this very moment.* Think! Who could help them? There was no one ... they were all buried, or partially buried, on this planet. *No, think! Wait ... there's Trommy5!*

"Beatrice?"

"Yes, Ricket?"

"Can you re-establish communications with the Minian's *AI?"*

"Yes, although with your updated nano-devices you could have done so yourself."

Why didn't I think of that? Perhaps, because he was finding it harder and harder to concentrate—*something* was chewing through the flesh on his left calf. *"Beatrice, I think I'll need your assistance. Please locate the mecher, Trommy5, and instruct him to acquire no less than five additional SuitPac devices, and then phase-shift to this planet's surface—close to where I am situated. He'll also need to phase-shift over to Alurian. To get Bristol."*

Ricket waited, his eyes now brimming with tears, as the pain on his leg increased.

"Ricket, I am sorry to inform you I am no longer detecting any life signs from Granger."

"Listen, Beatrice, have Trommy5 phase-shift to Granger's location first. Tell him to extricate him quickly, and return him to the Minian, *and into a MediPod in Medical without delay. Have him help Traveler as well."*

Ricket tried to ignore the onslaught of fresh data now streaming into his mind. He knew with sudden clarity exactly which leg tendons were being severed; the specific muscle tissue being chewed on; the exact amount of blood now depleted; and, disturbingly, what the insect—a stubby, cockroach-like thing—looked like. These were all pictured in three-dimensional, ultra-high-definition resolution. The only good news was that millions upon millions of internal nanites, rerouted from their normal body-sustaining activities, were helping with the catastrophic assault being fostered on his leg. Internal dopamine levels were increasing to help with the pain, but only so much could be done to help him.

★ ★ ★

Ricket checked his internal clock. Nine full minutes had transpired.

"Beatrice, please give me an update. Has Trommy5 found Granger yet?"

"Yes, Ricket. Trommy5 has already placed both Granger and Traveler into MediPods. Traveler, with his more substantial girth, took a bit longer. Both are expected to recover."

Ricket felt greatly relieved. *"And how are Leon and Hanna?"*

"Trommy5 is extricating them from the surface now. I will ask him to hurry. I am sorry I cannot do more for you, Ricket."

An agonizing three additional minutes passed before the telltale, bright white flash, indicating a phase-shift, occurred before him. Ricket had never been happier to see anyone in his entire life. Trommy5, enveloped within a battle suit, released its handholds on soil-encrusted Leon and Hanna. As they slid down to the ground, the robot hurried to Ricket's side; he had begun to shake violently. The poisonous, highly toxic secretions spewing from the insect were saturating his wound.

Ricket watched as Trommy5's two metallic arms, like some kind of power tool on steroids, began digging a trench all around his trapped torso. In a blur of motion, the mecher scooped and shoveled the thick clay away from him. Once again, Ricket was impressed by Trommy5's apparent transition—from a clumsy, typically off-balance robot—to a higher-functioning droid unit.

Both Hanna and Leon watched with anticipation as Ricket's arms came free. He raised them up—stretching them, one at a time, over his head. In seconds, his legs and feet were freed too, and Trommy5, mindful of Ricket's injured leg, lifted him up and into his arms. Turning to Leon and Hanna, getting back to their feet, Trommy5 handed each a SuitPac device. The mecher waited for them to initialize their battle suits; then, nodding at them, in a flash phase-shifted all four directly into the *Minian*'s Medical.

* * *

Ricket, his eyes clenched shut in agonizing pain, felt his boot being pulled away from his left leg and foot. He opened his eyes and saw Hanna toss the bloodied boot away and hurry, first past Traveler in one expanded-sized MediPod, then past the next MediPod, where Granger lay, to the third available

MediPod unit. Leon initiated the opening of the clamshell top and shuffled out of the way as Trommy5 lowered Ricket into the unit.

Hanna reached inside and patted his shoulder. "You'll be fine, Ricket. Just rest and get better."

Grimacing, his jaws clenched, Ricket nodded and tried to relax. Suddenly he remembered: "Bristol!"

Hanna placed a hand on Ricket's shoulder. "Stop worrying; he's on Alurian now and we're rescuing him."

Ricket watched as they hurried away and out of Medical. Once the clamshell lid closed he heard the familiar hum as the MediPod unit began its self-diagnostic check, followed by a patient evaluation process. Within seconds, the prescribed treatment was administered. The pain, now increasing, forced Ricket to lean forward and grimace down at his leg. His pant leg had been pushed up and he studied the ragged, open tear in his calf. Putrid green slime oozed from the wound and something else: First, two small, black antennae or feelers peeked out. Then in a frantic, manic-seeming motion, the bug was out and running unrestrained up his leg. The insect-thing had several sets of pinchers, which opened and closed at a rapid rate.

By the time the creature had scurried upward to Ricket's mid-section, he was feeling something rare: pure unadulterated hatred. He hated the little beast—no, he despised it. Instinctually, Ricket knew it was coming for his face—perhaps his eyes or even his mouth. Not taking his eyes off it for a second, he timed his next move to the millisecond. He grabbed it with his right hand and squeezed. He squeezed it with every bit of strength he had. *Did I kill it?* Then, he felt a white-hot pain in his hand—almost of the same intensity he'd experienced in his leg. He screamed in agony and in terror. But he continued to hold on, squeezing the alien demon until every part of his body rigidly tensed.

It was still moving—Ricket felt the insect's incompressible strength. *What do I do?* He cupped his right hand inside his left and, pressing both hands together, hoped to increase the amount of pressure that way. Still—the pain in his hand was only increasing.

"Ricket … I will help you, if you allow me to."

It was Beatrice. She was speaking to him with a calm, almost soothing, voice.

"God, yes … please help me, Beatrice!"

And with that Ricket felt an unimaginable amount of power, perhaps a combination of adrenalin and other internal stimulants, rush through his veins and into the muscles of his upper arms; then into his biceps, his forearms and, finally, into his tightly gripped fists. He felt the insect *snap*—not once, but twice, then a third separate time. The pain suddenly ceased.

Ricket opened his shaking hand and, studying his right palm, saw that the creature was fractured into three separate sections. *"Please tell me it is dead, Beatrice."*

"It is dead. I've instructed the MediPod control program to destroy its remains and sanitize the MediPod interior. Rest now, Ricket."

Chapter 31

High Orbit Over Alurian, Gracow CD1
System
Assailant Flight Bay, Unnamed Shuttle

Jason watched as Lieutenant Grimes, sitting next to him in the pilot's seat, went through her pre-flight checklist.

"You piloted this shuttle?" she asked.

"For about fifteen seconds before I phase-shifted her into open space."

"Quite a bit of this material is new to me," she said, scrolling through the shuttle's hovering 3D-display options before her. She glanced over to Jason. "Um ... you're staring at me, Captain."

Jason snapped out of it. "Sorry, Grimes ... got lost in thought," he lied. The truth was, he was thankful she was still among the living. Feeling a bit overwhelmed, the final casualty tally had come in from the Jefferson Station attack. Close to fifty thousand beings died at the hands of the Caldurians. Close to fifteen hundred, a good many of them Sharks and SEALs, were his own people, furloughed there until the *Minian* could be fully restored. Added to that, were the abductions of Ricket,

Granger, Bristol, Hanna and Leon. And what had happened to Dira there. Oh god—his beautiful ... amazing ... Dira. No, if he let himself go there—thought about the magnitude of it all—the incredible loss he was feeling, there'd be no way he could continue on.

"I'm just glad you're still here, Lieutenant, that's all. Don't mind me."

"I fully understand, sir."

Jason turned in his seat and peered back into the cabin. The three Caldurian officers, dressed in dark blue uniforms, were seated in the front row—flanked by Billy, seated at one end of the row, and Rizzo at the other. The three Caldurians were unconscious. From the get-go, the *Assailant's* AI had been directed to ensure that these three, as well as the other three Caldurian captains, weren't able to communicate, thereby blocking all internal NanoCom signals back to the fleet. But once they left the *Assailant*, all bets would be off. The only sure-fire way to ensure that no warning messages were sent was to give each Caldurian a strong sedative.

Behind them sat Sergeant Jackson, Gunny, Chief Horris, and Boomer in the second row, while the eight rows of seats behind them remained unoccupied. All weapons were packed away into the shuttle's storage bins. The one thing they could not appear like, when undergoing scans, was a military attack team. From all appearances, their insubstantially small crew of only eight would be seen as simply transporting the shuttlecraft and officers back home to their fleet. A good faith gesture—as if to show there were no hard feelings about the recent massacre that occurred back in the Sol system. A sign of conciliation that they were at their mercy—ready to do whatever it took to keep them from attacking again.

"I think I got this," Grimes said, looking ready to go. "It's pretty much the same as the *Perilous*, with only a few more bells and whistles added." She got the propulsion system going and brought the shuttle up a foot or two off the deck. Something noisily scrunched topside, outside the vessel. *Guess more flight bay lights shattered,* Jason concluded silently.

"Phase-shift?" Grimes asked.

"Most definitely. We don't want to bring attention to the *Assailant*'s cloaked coordinates here. Put us on the far other side of their fleet."

"You really think this is going to work?"

"Sure … maybe. No … not really," he replied.

In a flash, she phase-shifted them eight hundred thousand miles into open space, to the far side of the Caldurian fleet.

Almost immediately they were hailed. Jason had few illusions—they would know his exact identity, his internal nano-devices giving him away. Undoubtedly, they also knew he was the one responsible for the abduction of their three Caldurian captains earlier.

"This is Captain Jason Reynolds of Star Watch—"

Jason's words were cut off. "Be quiet. This is Omni Stanton on the *Quantum Lark* … the *Fortitude* is now under our control. Make any attempt to redirect the shuttlecraft, or take any hostile action, and you will be destroyed."

"Hey … that's fine, Omni. We are simply returning your vessel, along with three of your officers," Jason said. He looked over to Grimes and shrugged. She shook her head, giving him a pained expression. Apparently, he hadn't sounded very convincing. At least now, though, they knew the name of the shuttle they were seated in. The other bit of good news came from the one giving out orders. If their luck held, they would be brought into his minimally crewed ship, *Quantum Lark*, versus into the *Tall Spire*—with her complement of five hundred combatants. Jason wasn't sure what he'd do in that case.

In a flash, the star-filled view of open space seen outside

their forward observation window had been replaced by a familiar-looking Master Class flight bay. One glance at the hovering display over their cockpit controls showed them that they were indeed sitting within the *Quantum Lark.*

Jason turned in his seat and faced the others. "You all know what to do. I want that ship … so let's get busy." On cue, battle suits were initialized. He caught a quick glimpse of Boomer's smiling countenance, sitting behind him in the second row, before her helmet visor obscured much of her face.

Fifteen or more Caldurian armed soldiers were presently surrounding the *Fortitude,* but it was the growing number of armed droids that made Jason do a double take. He'd seen their kind of droids before. Not so different from Teardrop and Dewdrop—but far more menacing-looking—they were ruggedized and glided over the deck with remarkable speed.

"Shit! That's a lot of droids," Billy said.

"I'm reading a total of thirty-two of them," Orion said, placing her enhancement shield on her forearm.

Boomer, shaking her head, repositioned it properly on Orion's arm. "No, it's worn like this."

Rizzo, peering out the side observation window, turned back to Jason. "Well, I'm ready for some payback, Cap … are we going to do this or what?"

Jason smiled and took the multi-gun and enhancement shield handed to him by Boomer. "We all know our jobs here. Chief and Jackson, get going into Engineering and start work on retaking that department. We'll be dealing with those fellas out there for a while."

Jackson and Chief Horris flashed away. Ultimately, Jason would need to take the bridge, but Engineering, where much of the ship's systems could be controlled from, and he was guessing was far less protected than the bridge, had to be brought under control first.

Jason took stock of his team. Five returned thumbs-up told him they were ready to go. With the exception of the three still-unconscious Caldurians, Jason phase-shifted the others out into flight bay.

★ ★ ★

They phase-shifted, appearing in a semi-circle perimeter around the flight bay and surrounding the Caldurian forces—forces that were tightly packed together and not wearing battle suits. Right off the bat, Jason knew they weren't professionally trained combat forces. What they did have going for them was their highly advanced technology—the same technology that allowed them to destroy Jefferson Station with such relative ease. Plasma weaponry was more powerful by a large factor and although things here were similar to that within the *Minian*, it was like being in a much newer model automobile. Sure, the basics are the same, but here on the *Quantum Lark*, there were far more virtual display interfaces on distant bulkheads, and even the maintenance droids looked to be more than a few iterations more advanced.

But the situation today was different than what had happened back with Jefferson Station. The Caldurian forces here, so unaccustomed to the intimacy of one-on-one battle situations, said a lot about their leadership—about the misled arrogance of Omni Stanton. And probably about the other ship captains within this Caldurian fleet of vessels as well.

The team fired into the bunched-up, completely caught-off-guard soldiers. Their plasma fire mowed them down like mere stalks of wheat. But just as swiftly as the Caldurian soldiers were dispatched to the *great hereafter*, the droids reacted with split-second efficiency. He saw them move in unison, as if centrally controlled, which they undoubtedly were. Half of them jetted into the air, establishing an immediate, overhead high ground. The other droids, still stationed on the deck, came at them with blasting, unrelenting plasma fire.

Hearing and seeing his HUD's early warnings, Jason was surprised to discover his battle suit's shields were already down to twenty percent. Not only was he being fired upon by four different droids—two from above and two on the ground— their plasma weapons were far more powerful than his own.

"Use your shield, Dad!" Boomer's voice crackled in his ear. In a blur, he saw her spinning, cartwheel-like, on the far side of the flight bay and dealing with her own droid combatants.

He'd totally forgotten it was with him. He brought up his enhancement shield and, as instructed by his eleven-year-old daughter, punched a rapid flurry of bright purple distortion waves toward two of the rapidly approaching droids. First one, then the other, flew backward and ceased firing. *Holy crap … this thing really works!* He glanced at his HUD; his shields were down to ten percent. He turned his attention upward, toward the two droids above him. "Come to Papa, you Caldurian pieces of shit."

Chapter 32

High Orbit Over Alurian, Gracow CD1
System
Quantum Lark Flight Bay

"My shields are down!" Orion said into the open channel.

"Phase-shift back into the shuttle, Gunny!" Jason urged, as he leapt high into the air, kicking in his battle suit's thrusters. He noticed that Boomer, as well as Rizzo and Billy, were all using their enhancement shields to help them leap higher into the air. He had no idea how to do that yet.

Jason knew he'd soon be joining Orion in the shuttle if he took too many more plasma hits. His HUD showed his shields were down to four percent.

The two hovering droids were circling above him when suddenly a third, one of the droids he'd stunned earlier, was now rising up, ready to resume the fight. Jason continued to fire at the droid in front of him, trying to find a weak spot in the thing's armor or shields, or a combination of the two.

Three plasma bolts hit him hard in the back, bringing his suit's power levels to zero. Falling twenty feet, Jason dropped like a bag of rocks. His head hurt and he felt on the verge of blacking out and suddenly he became very uncomfortable, as the temperature rose substantially inside his battle suit. While lying there prone on his back, he saw the three droids above him. With his shields' protection level gone to zero, he had little if any options left.

He raised his head, but his multi-gun was too far out of reach. *Damn* ... his integrated plasma guns were inoperable and phase-shifting away was no longer an option. A faded message showed on his HUD, *regeneration time required.*

What the hell am I supposed to do now? Simply lie here and wait to be deep-fried? he asked himself in frustration.

In his mind, Jason replayed Boomer's training class instruction: *"Come on, Dad, it's not a thing that's separate from you ... think of your shield as an extension of your arm ... what you feel, it will feel ... it will help you ... if you let it."*

Jason's mind flashed to Dira. He visualized her—what was left of her—lying in a coma, barely alive, vulnerable, and confined within a MediPod; then he pictured the beings responsible for putting her there. His enhancement shield came up before he knew what was happening. Multiple red plasma bolts were firing down on him from the droids overhead; several had pierced into his suit like white-hot pokers. But his shield, somehow, managed to block most of them.

Getting to his feet, Jason's inner rage took ahold of him— driving him forward to overlook the pain and ignore the overwhelming odds stacked against him. He spun left then right, unleashing barrages of his own bright violet distortion waves, one after another, at the droids. With each punch thrust forward, another equally strong recoil struck his arms. The stronger the recoil, the more painful the strike felt. But the pain sustained him, driving him into an almost manic state of frenzy. The violet distortion waves, shooting out from his shield, for a split second, changed color—turning to red, then back to violet. Apparently, that was all to the good. One of the three hovering, dodging droids exploded with such a force that the blast propelled it into the droid next to it, sending it—like a bullet—into the nearby bulkhead, where it too exploded.

But Jason wasn't paying any attention to explosions nor much else. He slowly and methodically stepped forward—pounding out distortion waves ever-increasing in strength into the last remaining droid. It moved backward, as Jason moved forward, firing continuously at Jason, but none of its shots connected with anything other than Jason's raised, always moving, enhancement shield. With teeth gritted, and a scream so loud and primal the devil would cower in fear, Jason put all his anger and rage into one final thrust. The droid disintegrated without leaving a trace.

It took almost half a minute for Jason to break free from his self-induced trance. His white-knuckled fists slowly unclenched as the battle around him came to an abrupt end. No other droids circled above them.

The deck was scattered with the remnants of destroyed droids and the fifteen dead Caldurian soldiers. Jason scanned the deck for any of his own, for a battle suit, and spotted one. Rizzo was sitting at an awkward angle directly across from him, leaning up against the opposite bulkhead.

As Jason came closer he recognized the young SEAL was in bad shape. Like his own, Rizzo's battle suit must have lost its shields. Too many blackened scorch marks to count pocked his arms, torso, and legs.

Billy was now at his side. "You look like shit, Rizzo."

Rizzo's visor was open and he was gasping for air. His words were faint. "Bite me."

Billy smiled and turned toward Jason. "We need to get him into a MediPod."

Jason nodded. His own battle suit still hadn't regenerated enough for him to phase-shift. "Can you phase-shift him into this ship's Medical?"

"Nah! My suit's dead, too."

"Mine's not," Boomer said, approaching them at an all out run.

Jason was surprised to see she had almost no damage done to her suit. She looked virtually the same as before the battle.

"Listen … there's still plenty of Caldurian combatants on board this ship … not to mention other droids. So be careful, kiddo."

Boomer smiled. "They come near me they'll need to be the careful ones." She knelt down next to Rizzo, placing a hand on his shoulder, and in a flash, both were gone.

"Have you checked on Gunny?" Jason asked Billy.

Billy nodded. "On comms. She's okay, actually taking care of Grimes. Guess she also took a few too many hits. Both are still in the shuttle."

Jason stood and looked around the flight bay. "We need to move things along. It's only a matter of time before they start bringing troops over here from their other ships. Hell, they could be readying to phase-shift at any second. This compartment is now ours so start moving Sharks over from the *Assailant*. No less than two hundred."

"I'm on it. I'll also check on Gunny and Grimes and get them into Medical if needed. By the look of things, you could use a few hours in a pod yourself, Cap," Billy said, gesturing toward Jason's blackened battle suit.

"Later. My suit's power levels have just risen far enough up into the black that I can phase-shift again. I'll go check on the boys in Engineering. Meet me there when you're done

240

here, okay?"

Jason gave a quick nod to his friend but then hesitated. In the distance, where the majority of Caldurian vessels were parked in the flight bay, were no fewer than twenty royal blue fighters, lined up like children's toys on a shelf. Now, looking again, he realized he'd almost missed seeing the three dark red two-man fighters parked farther back. He allowed himself a brief smile. They looked identical to his favorite, no longer in existence, *Pacesetter*.

★ ★ ★

Jason arrived in Engineering to find it another battle zone. Bulkheads were pocked with blackened craters and, just like in the flight bay, the deck was strewn with the shattered remnants of drones. A life-icon indication on his HUD showed Sergeant Jackson was nearby. Whatever action had taken place here was over now, as all was quiet. Jason moved to the center of the large open compartment and glanced up. Like the *Minian*, the ship's Engineering compartment spanned far upward, nearly to the top of the ship, some twenty-three decks in all. Ascertaining there were no hovering droids around, he brought his focus back toward finding Jackson and the chief.

Beneath several overturned storage bins, Jason saw two outstretched legs. He moved in and hefted the bins out of the way. Jackson wasn't moving. If Rizzo's battle suit had looked bad, Jackson's was far worse. Leaning over him, Jason peered into the sergeant's visor. His eyes fluttered open and Jason saw recognition there. He was alive and still conscious. The big man stirred.

"No no, Sergeant. You're pretty badly hurt and need to be moved to Medical."

Jackson's visor retracted back into his helmet and Jason saw him blinking away tears.

"The chief ... I couldn't protect him. I'm so sorry, Captain. It's my fault. It's completely my fault. There were too many of them. Five ... no six ... of those monster droids." Jackson's gaze turned toward the right and settled on a part of Engineering where two bulkheads converged into an inset, recessed area. Jason, following his gaze, saw a pair of legs, protruding from beneath a console. "Dead?"

Jackson simply stared in the chief's direction, and then, ever so slightly, nodded.

"What happened here?"

"The chief got a lot done ... he was amazing, really. He transferred all control of this ship here, to Engineering. Comms were disabled so no distress calls could go out and he configured the shields to only allow *Assailant*-designated personnel and vessels to phase-shift in. You were right—if we'd tried to phase-shift that shuttle in we would have exploded on contact."

Jason turned his eyes back to where the chief's body lay. He died a hero. With a heavy heart, Jason said, "He won't be forgotten."

Billy flashed into view and quickly took in the situation. "What the hell happened here?"

"Apparently, six other drones were here ... waiting. Sadly, we lost the chief," Jason said.

Billy stood quietly for several beats, then suddenly kicked the head of a nearby drone. "Mother fu—"

Jason cut him off: "There'll be plenty of time to curse the Caldurians later. For now, help me get Jackson into Medical."

Chapter 33

Dramicus 9, Gracow CD1 System
Minian, Bridge

Ricket's leg had fully healed, freed of the parasitic bug, as he made his way onto the *Minian's* bridge. Most of the ship's systems were still down and he needed to address them before getting the vessel phase-shifted from its current location, two hundred feet below the surface of Dramicus 9. The good news was the *Minian's* AI was still active and that would make things significantly easier. Plus, having Bristol and Granger there, both recovered nicely from their ordeals, would help to expedite things considerably.

Ricket gave Bristol and Granger the important task of getting the propulsion system activated in Engineering, and almost immediately, he felt the ever-so-slight vibration of the ship's two massive drives slowly coming alive.

Ricket was moving toward the tactical station when Leon

entered the bridge.

"There you are ... hey, I want to get into my ship ... get it up in space."

"I understand, Leon. I am in the process of doing that very same for the *Minian*." Ricket gestured toward the wide-open, deserted bridge. "Perhaps we can work together. Help me here, getting her systems activated, and I will assist you with the *SpaceRunner*."

"Deal. What do you want me to do?"

"Bristol and Granger are working on bringing both the propulsion and environmental systems up to their optimal states. Why don't you get comms operational—see what is going on there—while I bring tactical back online. Then we will know what we are dealing with topside."

Leon hurried over to the comms station and took a seat, as Ricket went to Gunny's open seat and brought the board before him to life. A small, projected, hovering 3D display came alive and Ricket took in all the information. At first glance, everything seemed to be as it was when he was on board the *Parcical*: Twelve Master Class warships were in high orbit, still above Alurian. But something had changed. Ricket couldn't quite put his finger on it, yet something was different. As expected, the *Parcical*, wherever she was, was cloaked. But one of the Master Class vessels was ... *broadcasting on an open channel?*

Ricket glanced over at Leon who, with his brow furrowed, was intently listening to something. When he looked over to Ricket his expression held a mixture of confusion and something else.

"I think I'm picking up U.S. comms chatter, going on above. It's encrypted ... protected, but definitely has Allied fleet characteristics."

Ricket considered that. The *Minian* had been a U.S. space vessel for years. Whoever was up there was using the most recent updated comms protocols. He smiled. "We may not be able to decipher what they are saying, but they will be able to understand us." About to ask Leon to open a channel, he stopped short, instead, opening his own NanoCom channel. A moment later, Ricket was more than a little surprised by the voice coming across.

"Is that you, Ricket?"

"Yes, Captain ... it is me."

"You have no idea how happy I am to hear your voice! Where the hell are you?"

"I am sitting inside the bridge of the *Minian* ... some two hundred feet below the surface of Dramicus 9—a planet within in the Gracow CD1 Syst—"

"I know where it is! I'm looking right at it," Jason interrupted.

"You're here? In the same system?" Ricket turned his attention back to the data being relayed from the tactical display.

"The *Assailant* is here ... cloaked. But I'm on the *Quantum Lark*, one of the Caldurian ships. Listen to me, Ricket. I don't know how you escaped from the Caldurians, we can get into all that later, but there's a lot going on you're probably not aware of."

"Yes, sir, I'm just now—"

"Be quiet ... just for a minute. Thanks to the actions of our friends up here, Jefferson Station's almost been destroyed. Ricket, Dira's ..."

Ricket listened as the captain hesitated.

"Ricket, Dira's been injured. In fact, she's barely hanging on. The truth is, there's not much left of her."

Ricket's heart sank. He loved Dira. For a brief moment he wondered if Captain Reynolds could survive her loss—be able to continue on?

"She's in a MediPod. The last I heard her vitals were stable, but she's not regenerating … The MediPod's spitting out complaints about being incapable of completing the task as there's too much damage."

"I am very sorry, Captain, but it is probably true. MediPods certainly can achieve miraculous results, but there's a limit—"

"I don't want to hear it, Ricket. You need to think of something. Come on, pull one more rabbit out of that fantastic brain of yours, you hear me? Figure something out. I don't care what it takes. Promise me you'll do that?"

Ricket sat still, listening to the desperation in his friend's voice. He was poised to tell him the very sad news that there was nothing he could do—it was beyond his capabilities— probably anyone's, when something flashed in his mind. *Could it be that simple?*

"Captain, I don't want to give you false hope. It may be impossible to bring Dira back. It may be best to let her go. I am sorry."

"What are you saying? Is there a fucking chance to save her or not?"

"The short answer is that I, under present conditions, do not have the necessary understanding, nor the knowledge, to help her."

"Oh my god—"

This time it was Ricket's turn to interrupt: "Captain. You may already have in your possession all that is necessary to save Dira."

It took several long seconds before Jason answered. "The *Quantum Lark*?!"

"Yes, sir. From what I have seen of the Caldurian vessel, the *Parcical*, there have been substantial technological advancements since the *Minian* was designed. I, personally, have taken advantage of a few of the latest MediPod advances."

★ ★ ★

And just like that, Jason felt a glimmer of hope to save Dira. Discovering, too, that Ricket, Leon, and Hanna, and also Bristol, Traveler, and Granger, were still alive was icing on the cake. But none of them were out of the woods yet, not by a long shot. There were still twelve—no, thirteen, if he counted the *Parcical*—advanced Caldurian warships out there.

The Caldurian fleet would have little trouble destroying the *Quantum Lark*—if it came down to that, but getting the *Minian* back in the fight sure would increase their odds favorably.

"Listen, Ricket. Keep doing what you're doing … I want that ship back in space as soon as possible. Wait for my cue."

"Yes, Captain."

★ ★ ★

Jason found a tarp to cover the chief's body. He laid a hand on the still form, and thanked the man for his service and dedication. He also made him a personal promise, a promise he'd die to uphold: make those responsible pay, and pay dearly.

He got to his feet and found Rizzo standing several paces behind him.

"You doing okay, Rizzo?" Jason asked.

"Much better. But you don't look so good, Cap."

"I'll get fixed up as soon as there's time. You catch me talking to Ricket?"

Rizzo nodded. "Didn't mean to eavesdrop, Cap, but that's truly good news if Dira can be helped, and that Ricket and the others are still alive."

Jason caught Rizzo staring at the chief's covered remains. "He died a hero today." The three let several moments lapse before Jason spoke again. "We still have a lot to do."

"Where's Billy?"

"Managing the forces coming into the flight bay. He says he'll have multiple teams ready to take back the ship in a few minutes."

"What's the latest with the *Quantum Lark*?" Rizzo asked.

"Good question. For the time being, we're keeping any Caldurians from phase-shifting in. As you know, the bay is secured and ... thanks there to the chief. And we have most of the ship's systems under our control, here, via Engineering. My HUD's indicating there's twenty-five Caldurians still active; most are gathered toward the bow ... around the bridge," Jason added.

"And their captain ... their Omni?"

"He's here."

"He the one responsible for the destruction of Jefferson Station?"

"That would be a good guess," Jason said. He let out a breath and stepped away from the chief's still form. "Orion and Grimes still in Medical?"

"Yes, they're there with Jackson. He should be about ready to pop out of the oven any time now," Rizzo said.

The two of them smiled at his comment. Jason said, "Then let's get up there and come up with a plan to finish taking this ship."

Chapter 34

High Orbit Over Alurian, Gracow CD1
System
Quantum Lark, Medical

Jason and Rizzo phase-shifted into the corridor outside of Medical, on the *Quantum Lark's* twenty-third deck. Entering Medical, Jason found Grimes and Gunny standing over one of the eight MediPods. Jason suddenly realized these pods were indeed different. The ones on the *Minian* had small observation portholes, placed on the top of each clamshell, while these clamshell lids were entirely see-through—composed of some kind of blue-tinted, glass-like material. He wondered if he were looking at the answer to his hopes and wishes: the technology that would restore Dira back to good health.

Orion looked up and nodded to Jason. "Cap … it's Jackson. Guess he was in worse shape than we thought."

Jason stepped up to the MediPod and saw the big man filling every inch of space within the pod. "He's okay?"

"Seems to be … he's due to come out in a few minutes."

"Good. We're going to need his help."

Grimes said, "What's the plan, Captain?"

Jason noticed she'd directed her question to him, although her eyes were locked on Rizzo. It seemed clear, in that instant, that there was something going on between the two. Usually, Boomer gave him the latest scoop on who was dating who … Jason suddenly turned around. "Hey, where's Boomer?"

Both Orion and Grimes turned and glanced around. "She was just here, like two seconds before you walked in," Orion said.

Jason hailed his daughter.

"Hi, Dad."

"Where are you?"

"Investigating."

"No, Boomer, we talked about that. When on a mission you follow orders and don't go running off on your own."

"I'm sorry, Dad. But I've found something you'll want to see."

"Where are you?"

"First tell me you won't be mad."

Jason could simply reinitialize his battle suit and find her via his HUD, but that seemed like more trouble than just playing along. "Fine … I won't be mad."

"I'm in the captain's quarters. It looks different than—"

"Damn it, Boomer, when are you going to start listening to me?" Jason initialized his battle suit and quickly found her blue life-icon on the bottom of his HUD. There were also red and yellow icons showing fairly close to her position.

"I'm OK. Geez!"

Jason didn't answer her. He caught the rest of the team's attention: "Lock and load, people … time to move." Jason waited a few seconds for Billy, Gunny, Grimes, and Rizzo to initialize their battle suits and grab their multi-guns. He made the necessary settings and, seeing Boomer's location was the kitchenette, phase-shifted the five of them to the captain's quarters living room. On arrival, they stayed still, waiting for Jason to give the next order.

With her helmet visor open, Boomer walked out of the kitchenette, eating a sandwich. "Dad?"

"What are you doing?" Jason asked in a hushed voice.

"I found the meal replicator. I was hungry."

Jason nodded to Billy and he moved past Boomer, down the hall toward the bedroom compartments. He returned several seconds later.

"All clear … no one's home."

"I could have told you that," Boomer said.

"How long have you been here?" Jason asked.

"About two minutes before you hailed me. Look at this," she said, waving for Jason and the others to follow her. They entered the captain's ready room and Jason immediately noticed that the compartment, like much else of the ship, was an updated version of the *Minian*'s. The compartment was larger, and contained something like a small theater arrangement. Several rows of seats were off to the side.

Jason shrugged. "So what? It's a theater."

Boomer smiled and moved to the bulkhead. She triggered something, and the 3D display came alive: showing—as if a still image of a video or movie had been placed on hold—what appeared to be a space battle in progress. Two Master Class Caldurian ships, and a smaller, egg-shaped vessel, were firing on another immense vessel, which Jason instantly recognized was a Caldurian Crystal City ship. The implications were troubling, to say the least. Up until then, from what Granger had told him, the progressive Caldurians were leaving the originals alone. Obviously, that was no longer the case. Adding this event to the recent massacre at Jefferson Station, it was clear they were no longer dealing with the same Caldurian progressives who were so advanced that warring was a thing of the past for them. Jason continued to study the image on the display and shook his head. What they were witnessing was sickening. *How many Caldurian originals' lives—tens ... hundreds of thousands, had been snuffed out in this one attack?*

"I wonder when this happened," Orion asked.

Before Jason could comment, a noise came from the living quarters next door. Everyone stayed still. Billy, closest to the door, eased back into the living room and disappeared from view. He returned a few moments later and shrugged. "It's the captain. I think ... he's in the shitter."

Gunny rolled her eyes and Boomer giggled.

Jason phase-shifted their group of six back to Medical.

★ ★ ★

An hour later, Jason spoke with his three other team leaders, grouped together within the flight bay. Billy, Jackson and Rizzo, along with himself, would each command fifty Sharks. It was understood that Jackson and his team would stay put, right where they were, ready to deploy when needed as backup to those problem areas encountered by the other three teams.

"There's no more than twenty-five Caldurians on board, Cap. You don't think this is a bit of overkill?" Billy asked.

"We lost one of our own today. The chief was an old friend and it didn't have to happen. I'm betting there's a reason this ship seems so sparsely manned. Yes ... I may be overreacting with a force of two hundred Sharks, but I'm sure they're all happy to do something other than play cards in the barracks." Jason turned to look at the four groups, now gathered nearby. Mostly men, but a few women, were going through their own personal routine of checking over weapons and reviewing HUD settings—the things a soldier did, prior to going into battle.

"Look, it's their technology we need to worry about," Jason said, as he turned to Orion, standing by his side.

"From what I've been able to scan, there are actually twenty-seven Caldurians on board, plus maybe twenty of the same droid variety we faced earlier in the flight bay."

Billy shrugged, as if to say, "*So what ... that's no problem.*"

Orion continued, "But there's something else."

"What does that mean, *something else?*" Rizzo asked.

Gunny made a face—like she didn't know how to answer his question. "All I can say is there's *something* moving around the forward part of this ship. The sensors in Engineering are not the same as those I had on the *Minian's* bridge, but evidently, it's something cloaked and it's something pretty big."

"How would you know that if it's cloaked?" Jason asked.

"It happened only once, while I was trying to observe it. At one point, when I detected *something* moving within the corridor, near the mess hall on Deck 7, two directly opposing hatch openings were triggered, at exactly the same moment. As we all know, you need to be standing ... like right up close ... to a hatch opening to generate a *someone's at the door*–type response."

Depending on in which section of the ship one stood, the corridors varied in width. Some, like those on the main thoroughfares leading to the mess, were very wide: maybe twelve feet wide.

"You're telling me we have a twelve-foot-wide droid ... or something else, moving around this ship. And it's invisible?" Jason asked.

She shook her head. "Yes and no. Whatever it is, it can change its size somehow. There are passageways here that are eight feet wide, while some are fifteen, like the main corridor, running down the middle of the ship, just outside the bridge.

So if that thing is twelve feet wide, it would constantly find itself stuck in narrower passageways—"

"Unless it's avoiding certain areas," Rizzo interjected.

"Or altering its ... girth," Gunny said. "I don't think it's avoiding any other area, only this one, where we are now, toward the stern section of the ship."

"Anything else about this thing you can add to that, Gunny?" Jason asked.

"Just that it seems no one, and I'm referring to the Caldurians, wants to be anywhere near the thing. They give it a wide berth. Seems they try to stay off whatever deck it's located on. But that's just a guess on my part. I mean, they never evacuate the bridge on Deck 23, no matter where the thing is ... so I'm getting it's more of a preference."

"Do you know where it is now?"

"Not really. Sorry ... it's cloaked. What I can tell you is that there are Caldurians moving all over the bow section of the ship right now. My guess, and it's just a guess, is the thing is hanging around outside the bridge."

That made sense to Jason. If it were some kind of droid, positioned to protect the ship, then that would be the place for it to be—especially right now. The Caldurians were undoubtedly aware of their movements. Aware an attack could come at any time.

"Billy, I want you and your team down on Deck 1. Split into smaller teams and clear it, then move up, deck by deck, from there. Rizzo, you'll do the same thing; I want you and your team on Deck 22. Clear it first, then systematically move downward. You and Billy will meet somewhere in the middle. Stay on open comms. While you're doing that, my team will take Deck 23 and the bridge. Jackson, you and your team are the backup and will be deployed to any one location on an as-needed basis. Orion and Boomer, you're with me."

Chapter 35

Dramicus 9, Gracow CD1 System
Minian, Bridge

Ricket stumbled and fell to his knees. At first, he wondered if the ship had somehow shifted position, even though buried hundreds of feet below the surface. Then he heard the pounding, like a distant drumbeat, that seemed to be coming from all around the *Minian's* outer hull.

Ricket and Bristol were working together, in Engineering, dealing with the latest crop of problems. Still cranky for being, *somehow,* temporarily marooned on Alurian, Bristol—tightly holding on to the closest console—snarled, "Now what?"

Ricket climbed to his feet. "The surface of the planet is being bombarded."

"Why?"

"To destroy the *Minian,* would be my guess. Or, more likely, disable her."

"No, that's not possible! We shouldn't be showing up on anyone's sensors. Shields are one of the few things still working on the *Minian*," Bristol added.

"My guess would be it is the *Parcical*—now in orbit over Dramicus 9. Her sensors are far more sensitive, at least to a focused-on area," Ricket explained. "She is zeroing in on us."

"Yeah … sounds like the strikes are getting closer."

Ricket initialized his battle suit. "Finish up here, Bristol. I need to get back to the bridge. Please join me there when you can." Ricket flashed away.

★ ★ ★

Ricket phase-shifted onto the bridge and found Leon and Hanna sitting together at the comms station, Granger at tactical, and Trommy5 standing erect near the entranceway. Everyone glanced up at his sudden appearance.

"The surface of the planet is being strafed from high above," Granger said.

Ricket joined him and looked at the small display. "We do not have much time. Maybe five minutes."

"Why don't we simply phase-shift to another location, beneath the ground?" Hanna asked.

"I thought of that, but even if we phase-shifted to the other side of the planet, the sudden displacement of matter here will most certainly be detected. And perhaps accurately enough for the *Parcical* to get a clear fix on us."

Granger stopped what he was doing and looked up at the now-operational overhead wrap-around display. The view showed nothing but tons and tons of rock and dirt. As though able to see through it, all the way to the surface, and into high orbit above it, he looked back to Ricket and asked, "How close are we to bringing the drives all the way back online?"

Ricket didn't look up from the station. "I thought we would be ready by now. Probably another ten minutes. Bristol is working on several different propulsion issues."

"We don't have another ten minutes," Granger said flatly.

Now it was Ricket's turn to stare into the wrap-around display.

Bristol flashed into view and all heads turned toward him. "Propulsion is operational. Drives need another seven minutes before they're fully online."

"Thank you, Bristol."

"Oh my god … it's even louder in here. Isn't that pounding driving you crazy?"

"It's driving me crazy," Leon said, sounding annoyed.

Ricket wasn't listening to the pounding, or to Leon and Bristol either. Instead, he was pacing and staring off into space.

He suddenly stopped and looked over at Granger. "How well do you know the operational characteristics of the *Parcical*?"

"Not very. Ships like that were still on the drawing board when I was around."

Ricket nodded at that. "How well do you know Hobel?" The question seemed to have struck a nerve and Granger turned back toward the tactical board.

Bristol took two steps closer to Granger and tapped him on the shoulder. "He asked you a question."

Abruptly, Granger spun back around. "I'd never met him before!"

Bristol raised both hands up in mock surrender. "Whoa … easy there, cowboy."

Ricket tilted his head, as if really seeing Granger for the first time. Granger stared back at him and finally said, "You can't tell me you haven't figured it out yet?"

"What?" Bristol asked.

"Hobel and I are derivatives of the same clone group."

"What the hell's a clone group?" Bristol asked.

"Be nice, Bristol," Hanna reprimanded from the comms station.

"I assumed as much," Ricket said. "The resemblance is remarkable."

Granger shrugged. "They try to mix things up a little—eye color, skin tones, hair, but skeletal structures pretty much remain the same."

"You're a clone?" Bristol asked.

Granger didn't answer.

"Do you feel any kind of brotherly bond with him?" Bristol asked.

"You mean like you did with Stalls?" Hanna asked Bristol—her brows raised. He ignored her.

"Sometimes. A clone tends to look for connections—what non-clones possess that they don't. Find some kind of familial bonds, that sort of thing," Granger added.

"Aren't we wasting precious time here?" Bristol asked.

Granger answered the question: "You want to know if Omni Hobel would have sentimental feelings toward me? If so, then perhaps use that to our advantage?"

"It is something to consider," Ricket said.

The *Minian* suddenly shook violently, which coincided with a thunderous noise from directly above.

Leon was on his feet. "We're out of time. What are we going to do?"

All eyes turned to Ricket, as he hailed Captain Reynolds. He had an idea, but it would be the captain's ultimate decision, since their comms were functioning again.

"This isn't a good time, Ricket. We're trying to take this ship."

Ricket spoke fast. "We are being attacked by the *Parcical*,

Captain. I would like to go on the offensive."

There was a pause as Ricket waited for a reply. "I trust you, Ricket … just don't screw it up. I should be able to talk more in an hour or so." The connection ended.

Ricket was well aware that they needed to do something now, not in an hour, or two. He turned toward the others. "We need to storm the *Parcical*."

No one said anything for several beats, until Bristol said, "You're crazy. We just escaped from that hell hole."

As another loud crack shook the ship, this time something shifted above them—noticeable through the wrap-around display.

"We'd need an army … it's just us," Bristol said.

"We have an army. And we have something even better— the element of surprise," Ricket replied, with the beginnings of a smile.

They still weren't getting it, so Ricket continued, "We have Traveler and his army, remember? We also have the MicroVault terminal that Bristol and I built. If I am not mistaken, I believe I can use it to get us back into the *Parcical*."

Ricket pointed to Bristol. "Please come with me. Leon, contact Traveler and ask him if he and twenty of his best warriors would like to help us. If so, have him join us in the *Minian's* corridor, outside the MicroVault terminal, as soon as possible. And have him bring Norwell along."

"I'm on it," Leon said.

"And Leon … if we do not take control of the *Parcical*, if we are unsuccessful, then get in touch with Captain Reynolds for further orders."

Ricket and Bristol flashed away.

★ ★ ★

Ricket phase-shifted both of them into his workshop. Bristol, rushing to the same terminal he'd worked at previously, said, "Phase-shifting's not an option, you know. Not with the level of tech on the *Parcical*. And that MicroVault storage area is gone. You knew that it was being deleted even as we were escaping. So that can't be our doorway in."

"You are correct, Bristol. We must work fast. What I am hoping to achieve is a direct connection between both MicroVault terminals."

"I don't think that's possible; not with our limited amount of technical specs on the *Parcical*."

Ricket, seated at his own terminal, was already accessing the MicroVault program. Bristol, joining him at his side, watched the code flash by at an impossible-to-read rate.

"What are you doing?"

"I am having Beatrice set up a new virtual terminal interface, based on the stored data within my expanded memory banks. A tremendous amount of information—actually, much of the workings of the *Parcical*—is stored there. Far more than I, personally, have been able to access and review. But now, with Beatrice's help, that too can be scanned in the background."

Bristol stared at Ricket, as if seeing him in a whole new light. He shook his head in amazement.

Ricket brought up a second virtual window. "Here you can see that the *Minian*'s AI is now tracking the precise coordinates of the plasma fire being directed toward the surface—towards us. While the *Parcical* is invisible, cloaked, the plasma energy pulses are visible. Once the AI takes into account the rapidly-moving Caldurian ship, the rotation of Dramicus 9 on her axis, and things like that, with the basic physical layout of the *Parcical* already stored in my memory and factored in, we should be set."

Beatrice was speaking. *"Ricket, I have configured a new virtual interface between the two terminals. The* Minian's *AI has completed its tasks as well, and I am ready to attempt a link between both terminals."*

Ricket said to Bristol, "Can you check on Traveler? See if he is coming."

Bristol stood. With two fingers up to his ear, he walked out into the corridor. The *Minian* was now rocking almost violently. The *Parcical* had found them and was concentrating her plasma weapons directly at her. It was only a matter of time before the *Minian's* shields weakened and fell.

Bristol was back. "On their way."

"Good, we should ready the terminal." Ricket climbed down from his seat and scurried out of the workshop, going across the corridor into the MicroVault terminal. He reached the pedestal in three strides and went about synchronizing and bringing forth a new virtual portal. He glanced up and saw the portal was indeed there, exactly where it was supposed to be. This portal was designed slightly differently from the type previously used—moving people and objects between ship and MicroVault storage areas. This was a ship-to-ship—terminal-to-terminal—portal. That being the case, he now looked directly into the matching portal within the *Parcical's* own MicroVault terminal. He hoped nobody was there, standing nearby, to notice a new portal suddenly appear.

Ricket looked up as the deck began to shake and the noise reached a new thunderous level. He realized it was the combined footfalls of at least twenty rhino-warriors, hurrying their way down the corridor.

"Do you want me to come with you?" Bristol asked, getting out of the way as the first of the rhinos entered the compartment.

"No, Bristol, stay here and help Leon and Hanna. I have asked Granger to accompany me."

Bristol, looking somewhat relieved, shrugged and left.

What moments earlier seemed to be a large compartment quickly became tight quarters. Traveler was at Ricket's side, huffing and snorting. Ricket recognized the sounds the rhino-warrior made when he was either excited or impatient, and right now he suspected it was some of both. Norwell, too, had been brought along, and was firmly clutched—in the grasp of one of the twenty-plus rhinos clustered within the compartment. Granger, looking less than enthusiastic, was the last one to arrive.

Ricket said, "We need to move fast. In fact, right now. I also suggest, if not done so already, that everyone initialize their battle suits."

Chapter 36

Jason used the main corridor, outside of Medical, as a pre-mission staging area. Jackson and his team were holding in place, back in the flight bay, while both Billy and Rizzo, and their teams, had already phase-shifted to lower decks down.

With Boomer and Orion at his side, and his team of fifty Sharks spread out—some right behind them, some covering the less-wide, parallel corridors on their same deck—they moved out and headed toward the bow of the *Quantum Lark.*

Jason no sooner took his first steps down the main corridor than Ricket hailed him. He listened to him briefly and decided to let Ricket manage whatever he was planning on his own. He trusted Ricket. It would take Jason far too long to catch up, come up to speed, on past events and still remain an effective, decisive leader in the here and now. He only hoped his decision wouldn't come back and bite him in the ass later.

He briefly thought of his father, and what he might be doing, in the next system over. He doubted the U.S. fleet had engaged Captain Oz yet, but truthfully, he wasn't certain of that. Just as he had to trust Ricket, he needed to trust his father, who, in all reality, was a far better tactician than himself in making the best situational command decisions. He made a mental note to reach out to him as soon as possible and get an update.

Jason, listening to the multiple open channels, was already hearing sounds of the first combat confrontations on the lower decks, engaging Billy's team. Each team leader had standing orders to try to take opposing combatants into custody, but deadly force was to be met with deadly force. From the sounds of things, spontaneous eruptions of plasma fire, there wouldn't be many Caldurians transported to the ship's brig.

Although numerous passageways and corridors transect a ship a mile long and many hundreds of feet wide, Jason's team focused on the four primary corridors, running the length of the vessel. They also avoided using DeckPorts, since they could still be under the influence of the ship's AI, and under the control of the Caldurians.

Orion was using her virtual notebook, over six hovering displays placed before her. As tactical officer, she would keep Jason keyed-in to everything going on—both within the ship, as well as outside, in local space.

Jason listened as he and his team of fifty moved forward with rapid efficiency, clearing compartments—one after another. It was far from an ideal situation when either side could phase-shift virtually anywhere, at any time. Thus far, the few Caldurians on board the ship were doing their best to avoid confrontations. Gunny, monitoring everything, could see if combatants suddenly appeared, moving in behind them. At that point, Jackson and his team would be deployed. One thing Jason was curious about was the lack of apparent usage of any remaining security droids. If their roles had been reversed—Jason defending the ship, with control over the ship's AI—he would have already deployed the droids to multiple decks. Why Omni Stanton hadn't done so was one mystery he was curious to uncover.

"Cap, Rizzo's yet to come across any combatants. His team has cleared three decks. Billy's team has encountered light resistance, but no droids. They've cleared two decks."

Jason looked at Orion's top-most logistical display, which showed his own team's methodical progression. They'd made good progress and were a tad more than halfway to the bridge, which, eventually, they would walk right into on this same level.

"I'm seeing the Caldurian fleet starting to move, Cap. Seems the *Quantum Lark* may be sacrificed for the good, or security, of the rest of the fleet."

"All the more reason we need to move things along here," Jason said, taking in the logistical representation of local space on one of Orion's hovering displays. Looking back up at the top display, he saw more than two hundred small blue icons spread out on various decks throughout the ship. All were his people. Any red and yellow icons showing were almost exclusively in front of them and on the same deck.

"They're making a stand there," he said, gesturing to the far end of the corridor, where movement could now be detected, still a hundred feet before them.

"Enough of this." Jason turned around, facing those on his team he could see, and spoke over the open channel: "On my signal, we're moving forward … to the bridge." He turned to Orion and said, "Phase-shift us in stages and try not to put us on top of each other." He smiled at her. "You hang back, but place our group up close and personal to the bridge."

Jason raised his multi-gun and the ten Sharks behind

him followed suit. Boomer raised her enhancement shield and nodded, letting her father know she too was ready. They phase-shifted away.

* * *

They flashed into view, about one hundred feet from the captain's quarters. To the left and right were virtual hatchways, leading into other officers' quarters; two hundred feet ahead lay access to the bridge. Between them and the bridge were the remaining Caldurians—armed with their own version of a multi-gun. They wore light blue battle suits, which gave them a somewhat friendly, unthreatening appearance. Between the Caldurian combatants and Jason's team was only a span of fifty feet and, so far, no one had fired.

Jason heard Orion's voice on the open channel. "Cap?"

"What do you have, Gunny?"

"Remember that big cloaked thing I've been trying to track?"

"I remember."

"Well, I think I've found it. It's thirty feet in front of you … and it's moving … right toward you."

Boomer was already on the move—her shield coming up, while bright violet distortion waves shot forward. Jason fired his multi-gun and within seconds the rest of the team was firing as well.

Jason noticed several things right off the bat: First of all, none of their weapon-fire was reaching the Caldurians, located at the far end of the corridor. Second, the Caldurians weren't returning fire. And lastly, Boomer's distortion waves were having a visual effect on whatever was standing there in front of them. It was still cloaked, but they could now see an outline around the thing that differentiated it from its surroundings.

Jason slung his multi-gun over his shoulder and switched over to using his own enhancement shield. Now, as both Jason and Boomer's distortion waves bombarded the thing in front of them, a clearer outline of it was becoming apparent. And, just as suddenly, Jason felt a cold chill run down his spine. He wanted to yell *retreat … get back*, but the words didn't come out fast enough. The creature was already on the move.

Chapter 37

High Orbit Over Dramicus 9, Gracow
CD1 System
Parcical, MicroVault Terminal

Ricket exited the portal within the *Parcical* at a full run and quickly stepped aside—letting Traveler and twenty rhino-warriors, their heavy hammers in hand, thunder by and out of the MicroVault terminal compartment. Ricket watched as the last one disappeared behind a virtual bulkhead, wondering if he should have given Traveler some kind of direction. Certainly, Captain Reynolds would have designated some kind of plan.

An ear-splitting klaxon sounded all around; clearly their presence was now detected. *Of course, detected!* Ricket thought, with twenty rhino-warriors running amuck inside the ship.

Ricket turned to see Granger and Norwell standing at his side. Although Granger was wearing a battle suit, Norwell was not. "What do you say we go and talk to Omni Hobel?" Ricket queried them.

Behind his visor, Granger looked even less enthusiastic than he had before, but he gave a slight nod just the same. Ricket rechecked his settings, put a hand on Norwell, and phase-shifted all three at once.

★ ★ ★

Flashing onto the *Parcical*'s bridge, Ricket immediately flinched. Loud noises were coming from all around. It seemed several rhinos found their way into the compartment, meeting armed Caldurians who fired their weapons at them. Two rhinos lay still on the deck, while no less than eight Caldurians, all with substantial head trauma, also lay strewn around the deck.

Omni Hobel was backed into a corner, his arms raised to protect his face. Before him, hammer raised high, was a rhino-warrior Ricket didn't know personally.

"Stop!" Ricket yelled.

The hammer, already descending, was diverted just enough to miss the Omni's head and career, instead, into a bulkhead. Being virtual, the damage was really more a blurring of lines than an actual bashed-in dent.

The rhino snorted angrily, as if Ricket had deprived him of something special, which probably was true.

"Thank you," Ricket said. "I need to speak with the Omni alone. And please … apprehend—don't kill—the others, if at all possible."

As the rhino stormed by him and out of the bridge, Ricket was certain that his words had fallen on deaf ears. He turned to Omni Hobel, who was straightening his still perfectly clean white uniform.

Hobel looked at Ricket, then at Norwell, and finally to Granger. "How have you entered this vessel? Phase-shifting on board is impossible; breaching this ship is impossible!"

Norwell answered his question: "You have underestimated

the Craing man, Omni Hobel. He used our own technology against us. He used the MicroVault terminal to access the ship."

Ricket watched their exchange, seeing indignant rage brewing on the Omni's face, and a resigned, tired expression on Norwell's. He realized the older Caldurian scientist was not doing well; in fact, he looked frail and ready to keel over.

Granger took a step closer to Hobel and their eyes met. Hobel was the first to speak. "How can you do this to your own people ... to your ..." he let his words fall silent.

"To one within your own clone group?" Granger asked, finishing his sentence.

Hobel said, "Stand with us now, with me, your brother."

"It was you, wasn't it?" Granger asked.

Hobel's expression turned defiant.

"It was you who gave the order to destroy the space station, Jefferson Station," Granger said, a statement more than a question.

"That station was insignificant in importance, compared to what is at stake for our people ... for your people, Granger. I would destroy a thousand space stations to ensure the survival of our kind."

Ricket watched as Granger listened, then slowly raised his arms toward Hobel. Confused at first, the Omni tentatively smiled and stepped forward toward his clone-brother's open arms. But it wasn't a hug Granger was proposing. He simultaneously fired two bright red energy bolts from his integrated wrist-mounted plasma weapons. Apparently, Granger had set the power level to maximum. Hit in the chest, Hobel's already lifeless body was catapulted across the bridge compartment and into the far wall. Again, the suddenly disrupted virtual bulkhead only fluttered, staying somewhat blurred.

Granger lowered his arms and continued to stare at the Omni's lifeless body. Ricket reached a hand out to Granger.

"I'm sorry."

"I didn't know him ... not really. As Bristol would say, he was an asshole and deserved what he got."

The ship suddenly became quiet. No more distant weapons' fire could be heard. Traveler, with two other rhinos in close pursuit, entered the bridge.

"Are any still alive?" Ricket asked.

"Four," Traveler said. "Tied up and left below."

Ricket nodded and gave quiet thanks that even those few had survived.

The two other rhinos stepped past Traveler and grabbed ahold of one of the dead rhino-warriors—one taking his feet, the other taking him under the arms. Traveler knelt down and slid his arms beneath the second one. He straightened his legs, and lifted up his fallen comrade into his arms.

Ricket said, "The MicroVault portal should still be open. Thank you, Traveler." Without further words, Traveler, followed by the other rhino-warriors, was gone.

"Why not spend some time in a MediPod, Norwell?" Ricket asked.

Norwell shook his head. "What will happen to me?"

Granger interjected, "His loyalties will always be with the Caldurians. He can never be trusted."

Ricket shook his head. "He is old ... he is—"

Granger raised a weaponized battle-suit wrist and shot Norwell in the heart.

Stunned, Ricket went to Norwell's side and checked for a pulse. He looked up at Granger. "Why, Granger?"

"Whereas I didn't know Hobel, other than that he was one of hundreds within my clone group, I did know Norwell. Quite well, actually."

Ricket waited for him to continue, part of him wondering if he would be next, also shot in the heart.

271

"With one exception, Norwell was the most intelligent being I've ever met." Granger let the implications of that set in. "But he was also the architect of systematic genocide. His technological breakthroughs were a means to an end."

"What end?"

"The end of the Caldurian originals. Sure, the progressives left this universe, for an alternate multiverse realm, years ago. Something, as you know, the originals did not go along with. They wanted to stay here. This is their home and they wanted to peacefully live out their existence here among their own kind. What you didn't know was that the progressives, although they stayed away from here themselves, sent back ten *Mechnoids* into this ... our ... multiverse realm."

"I don't know anything about what or who they are," Ricket said, getting to his feet.

"They are the result of years and years of genetic cross-breeding."

"Cross-breeding? Of what?" Ricket asked.

Granger's eyes fell on Norwell's remains. "That was Norwell's pet project: The cross-breeding of one of the universe's most wretched, ungodly, creatures, with the most highly-advanced droid technologies. Technology, and a creature hybrid, capable of destroying thousands, perhaps millions, of lives: self-sufficient, self-motivating, and totally unstoppable. Capable of traveling vast distances across space, Mechnoids are completely invisible. Their programmed mission is to track down originals' Crystal Cities. Once found, they land and literally devour the populace."

"That's horrible. Unimaginable." Ricket looked at Norwell's body. "Is that why you left?"

"Partially. Mostly, I suppose."

Ricket looked up and out through the surrounding wrap-around display at the open space beyond. "I have to hope that they did not bring any of those creatures along with them here. What did you call it … a *Mechnoid*?"

Chapter 38

High Orbit Over Alurian, Gracow CD1
System
Quantum Lark, Deck 23 Main Corridor

-

Jason yelled into the open channel, "Billy … Rizzo, get your teams up here!"

Even as the rest of Jason's Sharks on Deck 23 rejoined his group, they were being forced backward. He watched in astonishment as fifty or more multi-guns, along with his and Boomer's enhancement shields, fired at the steadily approaching beast.

The thing twice momentarily lost its cloaking ability so twice Jason saw exactly what it was they were up against. It was white—perfectly white, and also possessed a bizarre combination of both mechanical and organic aspects. It had six, multi-jointed, spider-like legs—each capable of altering its position, where it joined with its main body. The legs were in constant motion, never idle, which was more than a little disconcerting. The main body reminded Jason of a sickening, bloated tick. He watched as it grew and shrunk width-wise, while also expanding and contracting lengthwise—all at different rates of speed. Currently about the size of a standard city bus—Jason, not now focusing on its disconcerting legs, or its organic, shape-shifting central body, stared in amazement at the thing's heads. There were three. Like its main body, the heads were also of organic origin, while its three long extendable necks were mechanical. And like its six legs, its three necks were not locked on to any particular point on the main body—so its necks and heads were in constant movement.

Billy's team of Sharks began to appear on the other side of the beast. Five Caldurians were sent flying into side bulkheads as more and more Sharks phase-shifted into position, right on top of them.

"What the hell is that thing?" Billy yelled into the open channel.

Before Jason could answer, two of Billy's men charged forward, firing their multi-guns—attempting to bring near point-blank fire into the thing's belly.

Two of the creature's heads swung around on their extendable necks and, at exactly the same time, both heads grew—expanding to the size of small Volkswagens. Jaws opened wide and both Sharks disappeared into the beast's dual gaping mouths. Almost as rapidly as they'd first expanded, the heads lifted up and began to shrink down. The segmented necks expanded outward to compensate for the not-yet-swallowed soldiers. As the Sharks were pushed along, down the thing's gullet, some kind of auto-muscular reaction was ongoing. Jason could hear continual screaming over the open channel. Within seconds, both Sharks were totally devoured. At that exact point, Jason

realized the creature's bulbous main body was actually somewhat translucent. He could partially see the outlines of the two
Sharks—frantically trying to escape—then moving about less
and less as their forms disappeared. They were quickly being
digested alive.

Rizzo's Sharks appeared, joining in the fight, some
phase-shifted in behind Jason's team, and others behind Billy's. The beast was becoming more and more aggressive, beginning to pluck soldiers, one after another, off their feet,
then swallowing them whole at an astounding rate. Their
combined, tremendous amount of plasma fire didn't seem to
show much result.

"Rizzo ... Billy ... Enhancement shields seem to have
more of an effect," Jason said, as Boomer moved precariously
close to the beast. "Get back, Boomer. Now!" he yelled, not
wanting her anywhere close to those constantly moving, biting
heads.

Boomer did as told for all of several seconds, then began
edging closer again. She was now firing off a constant flow
of reddish-violet distortion waves into the beast's belly. Jason
moved closer to her and concentrated his own distortion waves
on the exact same spot.

Something was happening. Their combined distortion
waves were altering the thing's belly, turning it to an ugly
brownish color. Jason and Boomer exchanged quick glances.

Billy suddenly phase-shifted directly to Jason's left, while
Rizzo flashed into view on Boomer's right. Then all four, their
enhancement shields held high up in front of their chests, concentrated combined distortion waves at the same dark brown
spot, now increasing in size and color.

The beast's three heads solely focused on the four attack-
ers holding on to enhancement shields. Each time an open-
mouthed head began to descend down toward any of them,

plasma fire from the Sharks located behind it increased—forcing it to pull away, dodging and weaving like a boxer in a ring.

It was clearly apparent the thing was in agony. *Why doesn't it just phase-shift away?* Jason wondered. It had obviously been created using highly advanced Caldurian technology. *What the hell is it waiting for?*

As they continued their unrelenting attack, Jason saw something splatter high into the air and land on the deck, not far from their feet. Steam or smoke, or a combination of both, rose into the air.

"Look, we made a hole in it!" Boomer exclaimed. "See … there's an open tear and stuff's coming out."

She was right. There was now a clear-cut rift in the beast's belly and yellowish-brown gunk was seeping out—stomach acid.

"That shit's burning right through the deck," Billy said.

"Hey! Boomer, get back! I'm not going to tell you again!" Jason barked.

She moved back, just as a slop of *something* landed where her feet had been. It was a partially digested arm, most of a battle suit sleeve eaten away.

"Ywey! That's beyond disgusting!" she said.

The half-mechanical, half-organic beast became totally preoccupied with its own ever-expanding-in-size wound. Like a wounded animal, its three heads kept trying to get close enough, their long tongues extended, to lick its torn open carcass.

Now Jason knew why it hadn't phase-shifted away: It was overwhelmed—so completely thrown into survival mode it could think of nothing more than staying alive for another minute, one more second. Jason was fairly certain the thing had never fought for its life before. It was taken completely and utterly by surprise by the effects of the distortion waves on its body.

The rest of the thirty-five Sharks who'd been taking part in Boomer's ongoing Kahill Callan classes now joined them; holding their enhancement shields up high, they pressed to the front ranks, moving through and past those using their multi-gun weapons. Soon Sharks on both sides of the corridor were using their enhancement shields exclusively.

Two of the beast's heads suddenly dropped, hanging lifelessly down to the deck. Only two of the mechanical legs seemed to have any movement left in them, and all they could manage to do was drag their open, seeping, carcass a few feet in any one direction. More steam wafted into the air as the singular live head lazily drifted back and forth sideways, as if floating; then it, too, abruptly fell forward, lifeless, onto itself.

Everyone stopped firing. Visibility had become nearly impossible, due to the ever-rising caustic steam. Jason swiped at his visor with a gloved hand—only smearing it worse. He wondered how soon before this stuff ate its way all the way through his suit.

"Boomer, I want you to get back. All the way back, near Medical."

"Why? It's dead."

"Do it. And I want you out of that suit as quickly as possible. Go now!" Jason heard her protesting again before she phase-shifted away.

Billy and Rizzo took tentative steps closer to the thing's carcass. Jason reached a hand out to hold Billy back, when suddenly something creaked and shuddered in front of them. In a swoosh, the deck beneath the beast disintegrated.

"Holy shit!" Billy said, just as startled as the rest of them.

"Get back ... away from the opening," Jason ordered. More steam rose up from the now-open thirty-foot-wide void between them and the officers' quarters on the other side.

Orion was at his side. "That thing's already fallen through

five decks and there's no sign it'll stop falling through more decks."

"Let it," Rizzo said. "I'd be happy to see that thing floating off in open space just as soon as possible."

"How many did we lose, Gunny?"

"Sixty-seven Sharks. Five Caldurians got caught in the crossfire."

Jason finally looked across the open deck before him, and caught sight of a grouping of light blue battle suits, standing on the far side of the void.

"I'm on it, Cap," Billy said, phase-shifting right into the midst of them.

"Rizzo and Gunny, you're with me." Jason then phase-shifted them into the corridor, directly in front of the entrance to the bridge.

Chapter 39

High Orbit Over Alurian, Gracow CD1
System
Quantum Lark, Bridge

Jason, Rizzo and Orion stormed onto the *Quantum Lark*'s bridge, their weapons held high. Every station was manned by a Caldurian bridge crewmember and there was an armed security detail, outfitted in their light blue battle suits, standing at the ready. They stood between the entrance and the three, centrally located, command chairs. Omni Stanton was visible, sitting in the most forward seat.

Jason, annoyed at his continued blurry vision, raised his visor. He lifted his enhancement shield a little and said, "All of you … drop your weapons."

Two of the armed Caldurians turned back toward the Omni, as if looking for guidance. The other four guards held their ground, one even raising his multi-gun toward Jason's now-exposed face. Omni Stanton had yet to swivel his chair around. Apparently, he didn't want to deal with the fact he was about to lose command of his vessel.

Jason gave Rizzo a subtle nod. Using a sweeping motion, Rizzo engaged his enhancement shield, and, like being hit by a colossal ocean wave, the six Caldurians were sent flying—three to the right and three to the left. All hit the deck hard, and none got back up. It was an impressive move. He'd have to ask Rizzo later how he did it.

Jason stared at the back of the Omni's head. Even in light of the injury, if not death, of his security detail, the captain still faced forward. *Is this guy for real?*

Jason took three long strides forward and, using the sole of his right boot, kicked the corner of the Omni's chair—abruptly spinning him around to face him. Why hadn't he noticed it before? Jason knew he'd wonder about it for days to come. It certainly seemed obvious now: Captain—or Omni—Stanton was not Caldurian. He was human.

Orion was at Jason's side, her virtual notebook projected out in front of her. "He's definitely human, Cap."

"Of course I'm human," the man said, getting to his feet. Tall and broad-shouldered, he looked to be middle-aged, with salt and pepper gray hair and a mostly gray goatee.

"Before we get into that, which I'm more than a little intrigued to hear about, I must formally inform you that I'm taking command of your ship. You can either resist, and face the consequences, or work with me to make this an amiable transition. Up to you."

Stanton's eyes bore into Jason with burning hatred. Eventually, he turned and glanced around the bridge at the many nervous-looking faces of his, waiting-for-orders, bridge crew. When he looked back at Jason there was slow resignation.

"The ship is yours. How you defeated that … that demonic, god-forsaken, *Mechnoid-thing* out there, well, it's nothing short of a miracle. Hell, maybe you deserve the damn ship."

Jason raised a brow. *Wasn't that thing a Caldurian creation?*

"Don't get me wrong," Stanton continued. "I like the Caldurians. I am, for all intent and purpose, one of them … I'm accepted by them … but that doesn't mean I like everything they do … or all of their methods. The Mechnoids' presence here comes from the highest levels of Caldurian command and they are not here solely to protect us."

Jason didn't say anything to that. "Inform the AI of the change of command and set the new protocols."

Stanton hesitated, let out a long breath, and walked over to the closest console. It took him no more than two minutes to do as ordered. "The AI is now cleared for new command parameters," he said.

Orion shooed a Caldurian crewmember out of the tactical seat and went to work at the station. That took her another sixty seconds. "We have full command of the *Quantum Lark*, Cap."

Jason said, "Get me a logistical feed of the local surrounding space, Gunny."

The wrap-around display adjusted, the new logistical feed now positioned at the front. As Omni Stanton moved to sit back down in the command chair, Jason grabbed him by the nape of his collar and physically manhandled him up and over into Rizzo's waiting grasp.

Jason sat down in the command chair and assessed the situation. Eleven Master Class vessels, identical to the *Quantum Lark*, were now in relatively close proximity. "Gunny, what's the status of those ships?"

"We're being targeted. They're all at battle stations with weapons charged."

"Eleven to two odds—if we figure in the *Assailant*. That's still not good … not at all," Jason said.

The display changed and two more icons appeared.

Gunny said, "Eleven to four, Cap. Both the *Minian* and the *SpaceRunner* have phase-shifted into local space."

Jason's heart leapt at the sight of the *Minian*. "Hey, it's getting better."

One more vessel appeared.

"Cap … incoming hail from Ricket. He has control of the *Parcical*."

"Eleven to five. Now things are getting interesting." Jason turned toward Stanton. "Give the command for those eleven ship captains to stand down."

Stanton shook his head. "Only the fleet Omni can make that happen."

"I thought you were the fleet Omni?"

"I simply direct the day-to-day military consignments. Only Omni Hobel has that level of command. Think of his rank as more like fleet admiral."

Jason pursed his lips and, to move things along, hailed Ricket directly.

"Go for Ricket."

"Ricket … I want Omni Hobel, in whatever condition he's in, phase-shifted to the coordinates Gunny is about to provide you."

"Yes, Captain, but—"

Jason cut the connection. He turned back to Orion: "Give Ricket the coordinates to that open space, at the front of the bridge."

"Aye, Cap."

Billy entered the bridge and looked around. Eventually, his eyes fell on Stanton.

Jason shrugged. "I'm still waiting to hear what his story is. What's the status of the ..." Jason queried Stanton, "What is that thing called?"

"A Mechnoid."

"Status of the Mechnoid?" Jason asked Billy.

"The thing finally came to a stop on Deck 3. It left quite a mess; won't be an easy clean up."

"See what they have in the way of maintenance droids here that can get started on that."

Billy nodded and left the bridge.

The bridge flashed white as Ricket and Omni Hobel appeared at the front of the bridge. Ricket stood still, whereas Omni Hobel lay sprawled on the deck ... apparently dead.

Jason was more than a little happy to see Ricket alive. In fact, he'd never been happier to see anyone. He was tempted to order him to go back to the *Parcical* and make his way back to the Sol system at once ... to help Dira. But unfortunately, that would have to wait.

Looking at Ricket, he thought there was something different about his appearance. He looked *weird*.

"Hello, Captain, it is very good to see you again," he said as he retracted his battle suit. Jason noticed he was wearing stained and soiled clothes.

"Good to see you too, Ricket. How are the rest ... Bristol, Leon, Hanna and Granger?"

"All are fine, Captain." Ricket gestured toward Omni Hobel's still form on the deck. "I tried to tell you that Omni Hobel is dead."

"What happened to him?"

"Granger killed him."

"Good. One less problem to deal with," Jason said, knowing it was Hobel who had ordered the attack on Jefferson Station, in turn causing Dira's horrific injuries. He only wished he could bring him back to life—long enough to shoot him again.

Jason turned to Stanton. "As you can see, Hobel is dead. That would put you in charge of the fleet … correct?"

Stanton, up on his feet, looked at the dead Omni on the deck. Stanton looked back to Jason and teetered his head back and forth, and side to side.

"What the hell does that mean? Are you in charge or not?"

"It's not as easy as that, Captain. The command structure was determined before we left our home—an alternate realm within the multiverse. Safeguards were put in place to ensure we complete our mission: to bring back the *Minian* and … him," Stanton said, gesturing toward Ricket. "Thus all the Mechnoids."

"I don't understand," Jason said.

Omni Stanton smiled, then began to laugh uncontrollably.

Jason, signaling for Rizzo to deposit the Omni into one of the secondary command chairs, turned in the command chair to face him, feeling his anger go hot. He leaned forward and slapped Stanton hard across the face.

"Listen to me, you traitorous shit; thousands of good men and women are dead because of the Caldurians … and in no small part because of you. What I really would like to do is pull your arms and legs off, grind them up, and feed them to you … like dog food. So I suggest you take me very seriously."

Omni Stanton composed himself and sat straighter up in the chair. "What you don't understand, Captain, is that I most certainly can issue the order for the other fleet captains to stand down. But those very same captains will have a dilemma on their hands: face off against you, or a Mechnoid that sees them as deviating from high command's orders. There are eleven other Mechnoids—one on board each Master Class vessel. Understand, even Omni Hobel would not have been able to reassign the Mechnoid's orders. That's how high of an importance the Caldurian central command placed on this mission."

Jason was stunned. His mind flashed back to the recent battle against the Mechnoid here, costing the lives of sixty-seven Sharks. Sure, it now lay dead on Deck 3, but the cost had been extreme. Going up against eleven more of the things would be nearly impossible.

"There's no way to update their orders?"

"We've been trying to figure out how to do that for weeks. Do you think I wanted to attack Jefferson Station?"

"Captain … perhaps I can assist," Ricket said.

Jason hadn't noticed that he'd moved to his side. Seeing him now, closer up, he was even more perplexed by Ricket's looks—his altered cranium. "What's left of the Mechnoid is down on Deck 3. Can you have a look at it? Perhaps look for potential weaknesses. We could be fired upon within seconds."

Ricket said, "I have the specs for the hybrid creature already contained within my memory banks, Captain. Beatrice is looking for a way to breach the Mechnoid's core."

"Who is Beatrice?"

"I installed *The Lilly*'s AI into my expanded nano-devices, Captain. It was necessary for our escape."

Jason stared at his small Craing friend in wonder. The bridge suddenly went quiet as Ricket, seeming deep in thought, stood very still, gazing up towards the wrap-around display. Thirty seconds later he looked back at Jason.

"Apparently, Captain, the Mechnoids are highly advanced from a technical aspect. Reissuing it new orders is not possible. Their orders have been hard-wired into place to avoid exactly what we are trying to do. They will protect their assigned ships to the death. Nothing will make them leave their … post, for lack of a better word, and they will die protecting it."

"We found that out," Rizzo said.

"And you should also know that there are other Mech-noids, operating under different orders, here within the gal-axy," Ricket said.

"So what's the answer?" Jason asked.

Ricket had the beginnings of a smile. "It is almost too sim-ple, Captain."

Jason raised his brows. "Well?"

"Each hybrid was given orders: protect their designated Master Class ship, as well as ensure its captain and crew fol-lowed certain, pre-determined, orders. Orders, such as the one given that resulted in what happened, I heard, to Jefferson Sta-tion. Other orders included finding and acquiring the *Minian*."

Omni Stanton said, "He's right. Caldurian high command has taken no chances. The mission of this fleet was of the high-est priority. The Omnis, both myself and Omni Hobel, faced dire consequences for not following high-command directives. More than one ship's Omni has ended up in one of those things' bellies. Until recently, I was only this vessel's XO."

"Cap, the Caldurian fleet is changing formation," Orion said.

Omni Stanton stood and hurried over to Orion. He looked at the board and turned back to Jason. "They are moving into a standard *Lazmoth* formation. They are preparing to attack us now."

If that wasn't enough of an emergency situation, Jason was receiving an incoming, high priority hail from his father. He ignored it—would listen to the recorded message later. He could only handle one dire emergency at a time.

"So you say you have an answer, Ricket? Now would be a good time to share it."

"I have figured out how to give one singular Master Class vessel eleven different name designations."

Jason shook his head, his frustration growing. "Explain. Why would you want to give one vessel eleven names?"

"We cannot change the Mechnoids' hard-wired orders ... their directives. The Mechnoids are assigned to one—a specific—vessel. The mistake made by the Caldurians was that the Mechnoids are assigned to the ship's name, not the actual vessel itself. Knowing that, we can hack each of the ships' cores and change every ship's designation ... its name. We can now change all eleven ships' name designations."

"So what? I'm still not getting it."

"We will take all eleven ship designations and assign them to just one of the ships. One ship will have eleven different name designations," Ricket said.

"What will the Mechnoids do when they discover the ship they are on suddenly has a different name than the one assigned to it?" Orion asked.

"The Mechnoids are all equipped with the capability to phase-shift. I believe, once it realizes it is no longer on its assigned ship, the one with its pre-designated name, each Mechnoid will phase-shift ... immediately, to the ship that does have that name designation," Ricket replied.

"So let me get this straight: You'll simply change the name of the *Quantum Lark* so she'll be given, instead, all eleven of these Master Class ships' names?"

"Yes. I am ready to do that now."

"And then ... ?" Jason asked.

"Then all eleven Mechnoids will phase-shift onto the *Quantum Lark*," Ricket said.

Everyone just stared at Ricket—still not getting it.

"Within a matter of seconds, all the Mechnoids will be together in one place. But we ... everyone on board, will have left. Be away from here. You could fire on the *Quantum Lark*, destroy her, along with all the Mechnoids."

Jason's face went from confusion to a broad smile. He reached over, grabbed Ricket's odd shaped head, and kissed him on the cheek. "You truly are a genius, Ricket!"

Ricket looked uncomfortable with the compliment and the kiss.

"Listen up, everyone, I don't know if Ricket's plan is going to work, but it's the only one we've got right now. A lot has to happen in a very short amount of time." Jason looked at Orion. "Gunny, I want everyone on board the *Quantum Lark* to phase-shift over to the *Minian* ... like immediately!" He then looked over to the Caldurian at the comms station: "Who are you?"

"I am Darlain," she answered.

"Darlain, phase-shift over to the *Minian*. As soon as the Mechnoids start phase-shifting onto the *Quantum Lark*, you'll hail each of the other ships' captains ... their Omnis. Let them know what we're doing and that they are to let loose ... have everything they've got aimed at this ship, the *Quantum Lark*."

"When should they fire?" she asked.

"As soon as they see the *Minian* start firing. That will be their signal. Someone give her a SuitPac device." Rizzo retracted his battle suit, giving her his own small SuitPac device. Darlain looked at it with a confused expression; apparently, SuitPac technology wasn't utilized on this ship.

Orion took the SuitPac from her, clipped it to Darlain's belt, and compressed the two inset buttons. Within two seconds, Darlain was standing within a battle suit.

Jason turned to Ricket. "Who's manning the *Minian's* bridge?"

"Bristol. Granger is on the *Parcical*. Hanna and Leon are on the *SpaceRunner*."

"Let them all know what's happening and to expect Darlain."

"Yes, Captain." Ricket immediately put two fingers to his ear and made his NanoCom hail.

Jason noticed that Orion was also on her NanoCom, undoubtedly directing everyone off the ship. He turned back to Darlain and gave her a forced smile. Giving her a thumbs-up signal, he used his HUD to remotely phase-shift her onto the *Minian*'s bridge, using the coordinates Orion sent him.

Jason turned to Omni Stanton. "You ... I want you also on the *Minian*'s bridge, helping Darlain. The other eleven captains may require you to backup what she's asking them to do." He pulled the SuitPac device free of Ricket's belt and placed it on Stanton's belt. As soon as the suit initialized, Jason phase-shifted him to the *Minian*.

"Incoming!" Orion yelled.

Jason looked up to the logistical feed on the display. Missiles. Hundreds of them. *Shit!* "Who's firing? ETA?"

Orion shot back, "All of them ... first impact's coming in forty-six seconds."

That'll at least make Darlain's job easier, Jason thought. "Okay, Ricket ... go ahead and change over all the ships' name designations to the *Quantum Lark*. Right now!"

Ricket nodded and quickly turned away, two fingers up to his ear.

"Gunny, what's the status of the *Quantum Lark*'s crew and our Sharks?"

Barking off orders herself, Orion lowered her fingers from her ear and faced Jason. "Except for a few stragglers, all are back on the *Min*—"

Her words were cut short as several bright flashes simultaneously occurred—one in the corridor, right outside the bridge; another, close by, at the front of the bridge. A highly compressed Mechnoid stood where Omni Hobel's body had lain, just seconds earlier. Three heads, their jaws open wide, moved lightning fast toward a few fear-paralyzed crewmem-bers. They were rapidly plucked up, one after another, from the two forward consoles. Their terrified screams filled the confined space.

"Fifteen seconds, Cap!" Orion hurriedly backed away from a newly arrived Mechnoid.

Jason glanced up at the display and saw the icons of quickly approaching missiles. "It's time to go!"

Rizzo reached for his SuitPac device, then remembered he'd given it to Darlain. Orion grabbed on to his arm and, together, they flashed away.

Jason could see three terrified crewmembers huddled together, as well as Ricket, who no longer had a SuitPac device on his belt.

The Mechnoid from the corridor was now squeezing its way into the bridge, its three heads jutting around, looking for new prey. Its bloated belly showed the outline of several beings, still moving around and frantically trying to escape their horrific, deathly, confine.

Jason grabbed Ricket up with one arm, and took ahold of the sole remaining Caldurian crewmember with his other. The other two were quickly seized and were now finding their tortuous way down the expandable necks of the on-the-move, fast-approaching, Mechnoid.

Jason phase-shifted the three of them away.

Chapter 40

High Orbit Over Alurian, Gracow CD1
System
Minian, Bridge

As Jason flashed onto the *Minian*'s bridge he released his hold on Ricket and the Caldurian crewmember. He hurried over to the bridge's command chair and placed his full attention on the overhead display. The *Minian*'s spatial location was such that he could clearly see several other vessels, including the *Quantum Lark*. The ship was being bombarded—from a constant barrage of missiles, as well as from massive amounts of plasma fire. It surprised him that the ship had survived the assault so long. He looked around and then over to his right, noting Orion was back on tactical. Darlain and Omni Stanton were seated at the comms station, both fully engaged in conversations—undoubtedly with other ship commanders. Bristol was at the engineering console, doing something or other.

"Status, Gunny?"

"We have everyone from the *Quantum Lark*, all those that survived, here on the *Minian*."

"And the Mechnoids?"

"Impossible to actually see them with our scans, with their cloaking capability," she said. "We saw two of them on the bridge and there were reports of no less than five others from our Sharks, just prior to them leaving the ship."

Omni Stanton held up a hand and said, "All fleet Omnis have reported that their vessels are free, one hundred percent free, of Mechnoids."

As if on cue, the *Quantum Lark* exploded into a bright yellow ball of fire that quickly dissipated in the vacuum of space.

Jason heard a high-priority NanoCom hail and he again ignored it. He stood and approached Omni Stanton. "I want the other eleven ships, all of them, to surrender their command over to me immediately. Get on the horn and tell them to be prepared to be boarded."

Stanton looked unsure how to respond to that. "I'll try, but … I have to tell you, they still outnumber you. They—"

"Just do it," Jason told him. He hailed Billy.

"Go for Billy."

"What's our Sharks situation?"

"We still have close to a hundred on the *Minian* and another three hundred are still back on the *Assailant*."

"Be ready to deploy assault teams to eleven ships."

"At once?"

"All at once," Jason said, cutting the connection. He turned back toward Stanton, who told him, "The answer's no, Captain. They appreciate the extrication of the Mechnoids, but … there's no way."

"Cap … the Caldurian fleet are charging their weapons

again," Orion said.

Jason felt something pulling on his sleeve and looked down. "What is it, Ricket?"

"I suggest you and I phase-shift over to the *Parcical*."

"Now … while eleven enemy vessels are charging weapons?"

"Trust me, Captain."

Jason spun around, remembering his XO, Perkins, was commanding the *Assailant*. He looked at Orion. "You have the bridge, Gunny, and somebody please give Ricket a SuitPac."

★ ★ ★

After a brief NanoCom conversation with Granger, instructing him to have the *Parcical's* shields temporarily lowered, Ricket and Jason phase-shifted directly into the smaller vessel's bridge. Immediately, Jason was taken aback by the ship's ultra-modern-looking interior. Without exception, with its clean lines and muted, almost glowing, bulkheads and consoles, she was the most beautiful ship he'd ever seen. Whereas the *Minian* had a three-hundred-and-sixty-degree, 3D overhead display, this ship possessed both an upper and a lower wrap-around, three-hundred-and-sixty-degree, 3D display. The bridge appeared to be floating in a blue-tinted bubble that seemed to offer unhindered visuals all around them.

But his admiration was quickly quelled, with the sight of blood and a large severed hand lying on the deck—one so big that it must have belonged to a rhino-warrior.

Granger, seated at a console, looked up and acknowledged Jason's presence.

Ricket moved quickly to an adjacent station and rapidly went to work. A minute later, apparently finished with what he was doing, he looked over to Jason. "Captain, this ship …

the *Parcical*, is highly advanced. More so than even her previous captain was aware of. I believe the only way we will avoid a horrific space battle between this many warships will be through a definitive show of force. You must destroy one of the Caldurian vessels. We have mere seconds to do this, Captain."

"You're asking me to arbitrarily just murder untold numbers of Caldurian crewmembers, without trying, at least, to further negotiate?"

Granger cut in, "Ricket is right, Captain. These Omnis are unaccustomed to ever surrendering. Caldurian technology has given them an inflated sense of superiority. No. They most definitely will calculate the odds and destroy the *Minian*, along with other opposing ships. They're charging their weapons at this very moment to do just that."

Jason stared at the wrap-around bubble display and thought about what Granger'd said. He suddenly turned back to Ricket: "I remember one of their ships is manned exclusively by bad-ass droids. No Caldurian crewmembers. I know that because I mistakenly dropped in and witnessed it for myself."

"Which one was it?" Ricket asked.

"Ask Gunny. She was in charge of phase-shifting the teams."

Granger spoke for several moments in lowered tones, nodded, and then turned back. "I have the ship, it's the *Lorial*." Granger pointed to a lone ship, visible off in the distance.

Ricket raised his brow and Jason nodded. "Go ahead ... do it!"

Ricket returned to working on the station.

Jason quickly surveyed the bridge again, which was surprisingly similar to the *Minian*'s, though more the same size as *The Lilly*'s. He seated himself into the padded command chair.

The bridge brightened as four blue continuous plasma bolts flashed into sight, coming from above and below, and right and left, of the *Parcical*'s bridge. Off in the distance, the energy streams converged into a single plasma bolt.

"Can you zoom in?" Jason asked. The *Lorial* now filled the forward part of the display, the vessel's shields beginning to glow from excessive heat.

"Her shields are failing," Granger said.

A moment later, with her shields gone, the *Lorial* first glowed orange, then red. Almost anticlimactically, the ship dis-integrated before their eyes: No explosion—no indication that the *Lorial* had actually occupied space mere seconds earlier.

"Open a channel to the other fleet Omnis, Granger." He did as asked and nodded.

"This is Captain Jason Reynolds, aboard our newly-ac-quired Alliance Star Watch vessel, the *Parcical*." He briefly let his words sink in. "You will cease any and all aggressive ac-tion. The next Omni to bear its weapons will only live long enough to bring about, and experience, the same fate as the *Lorial* upon his own ship. Now prepare to be boarded. Each captain will then be relieved of his command."

Jason leaned back and looked out where the *Quantum Lark* had once sat in open space. He wondered what he was feeling now. Relief? Probably. His thoughts turned back—to the mad rush of getting everyone off the ship. Boomer! He'd sent her away—back to Medical on the *Quantum Lark*—out of harm's way. *Oh my god … I forgot about Boomer. Did she get out safely?*

Chapter 41

High Orbit Over Alurian, Gracow CD1
System
Parcical, Bridge

Jason sat forward in the command chair and listened to Billy over his NanoCom.

"You know Boomer. She wanted to stay on board until you left, but rest assured, I watched her phase-shift off the *Quantum Lark* and verified her arrival onto the *Minian,*" Billy said.

"I can't believe I didn't check on her myself." Jason shook his head.

"When was the last time you slept? I'm betting it's closing in on twenty-four hours. Cut yourself some slack … you've had more than your hands full, Cap."

Jason rubbed the stubble on his chin and, indeed, suddenly

felt the lack of sleep closing in on him. "There are some things I need to take care of first. I'll catch some sleep in a few hours. How's it going with all the Caldurian vessels?"

"I have security teams locking things down on each one. So far, no resistance; in fact, everyone seems fairly happy to have us on board. Not sure what that's about. Have you given any thought to who's going to command those ships?" Billy asked.

Actually, Jason had. "It's next on my list. I'll be back in touch with you within the hour." Jason cut the connection, sat back, and thought about Boomer again. He was glad she was safe. His thoughts turned to Dira.

"Ricket!"

Ricket, seated next to Granger, and in a deep discussion about something, looked up. "Yes, Captain."

"I need you to head back to the Sol system right away."

Ricket looked across at Granger, then back. "What is it? Have I done something wrong?"

"No, absolutely not. You've been extraordinary. It's Dira … she's … she's not doing well. She was caught in a secondary explosion on Jefferson Station."

Ricket's face fell and his eyes filled with moisture.

"They managed to get her into a MediPod and stabilize her, but there was too much damage. She's lost too many body parts to repair. She's going to die. It's just a matter of time, if it hasn't happened already." The words caught in Jason's throat. He was suddenly hit with the full weight of losing her—all over again. That, and sheer exhaustion, made it hard for him to talk—to keep himself together.

"I do not know if I will be able to help her. I am not a doctor, Captain."

"The admiral suggested that if anyone could help, it would be you. Perhaps you could use one of the newer MediPods on this ship? Hell, everything on board here is far more advanced."

"I can try, Captain."

"I'd like it if you'd hurry. Go now—take whatever you need."

"I can ask Leon to take me back in the *SpaceRunner*, perhaps have one of these advanced MediPods phase-shifted into its hold," Ricket replied, already getting to his feet. On his NanoCom, and speaking in low tones, he began making arrangements.

Jason sat back and tried not to think about Dira. There was still too much to do here, before he could personally return to see her. *I'm sorry, Dira … I'm so, so sorry.* Feeling his eyelids get heavy, he shook himself awake. He heard a familiar soft *ding* in his head—his NanoCom messages awaiting playback. Then he remembered the urgent incoming hail from his father. *Shit!* He played back the message.

There was a clattering of sounds and then his father's out-of-breath baritone voice came across: "Jason … I don't know where you're at or if you'll even get this message in time. We arrived in the Manilaise system and everything was fine—until the shit hit the fan. Maybe I've been gone too long, or I'm too old to command. Captain Oz has outsmarted me at every turn. We came into this system outnumbering his fleet two to one, now we're getting our asses handed back to us. With so much that was mothballed, there's not much left of our military within the Alliance that I didn't bring with me. It's a bad situation here, son. I'm not sure what you'll even be able to do, what with the *Minian* gone. We're being picked off like ducks in a pond … we need help. We need help *now!*"

Jason immediately tried to hail his father, but without success. He left him a NanoCom message: "I'm coming, Dad … I'm bringing help." He replayed his father's message again and felt the effects of too much adrenalin coursing through his veins.

Ricket, now gone from the bridge, left only Granger.

"Granger, quickly bring me up to speed on this ship."

"She's highly advanced. I've been looking over her capabilities and I'm having a difficult time absorbing everything. There are five primary decks and several sub-decks. She's roughly the size of *The Lilly*, at approximately three hundred and eighty feet long, but she's taller, and meaner."

"Meaner?"

"Her weapons systems, as you witnessed with the destruction of the *Lorial*, are quite powerful. This is a warship like no other. First of all … she's mostly virtual." Granger used his knuckles to knock on the panel in front of him. "Yes, it all seems solid, but it's really not, which makes this vessel incredibly light and fast. The ship can be cloaked from virtually all external scans and sensors, and she is invisible to the naked eye."

Jason nodded in appreciation.

"There's more … a lot more. Similar to *The Lilly* and the *Minian*, the *Parcical* has a large flight bay that spans the width of the ship. Inside are three shuttles, three two-man fighters, and ten one-man fighters. There are also seventy-five unmanned drone fighters. The ship has an advanced phase synthesizer on board; a habitat Zoo—not nearly the size of the *Minian*'s, but since so much is virtual, there are actually more habitats available: close to five hundred, accessible via four portals, which access any and all habitats. There are various laboratories, and also something called a MicroVault, of which I have first-hand knowledge. It's for storing an unlimited amount of *anything*—including items as large as the *Minian*."

Halfway through Granger's monologue description, Jason had already decided she'd be the ship he was taking into battle. "Thank you, Granger. I need you to learn everything about this vessel, as quickly as possible."

"I figured as much. I better get back to it."

Jason looked around the empty bridge. He hailed Orion. "Go for Gunny."

"I have a simple question for you; answer me honestly."

"Sure, Cap … I'm always honest with you."

"Do you want your own command?"

"You mean command of my own ship? Like one of those ten Master Class ships, sitting out there?"

"I mean exactly that."

"I don't have the appropriate rank for that. I'm not an officer."

"You're the most qualified person I know to skipper a vessel."

He waited for her to answer, knowing it was a complicated situation. She had Billy to consider, who was as close to being her husband as possible, without actually being married. There were also the dynamics she and Jason had on the bridge. They were a good team—an amazing team. There was no one else he could count on to the same extent.

"Are you staying on … the *Parcical*?"

"Yes. It's the best option for me."

"Well, then the answer is no. Put me on dual-duty—tactical and as your XO. And make sure Billy is on the *Parcical* too."

Jason smiled at that. "Don't you think you're getting a little pushy at this point?"

"You want the best?"

"I do. Okay, XO Orion, come over and help me figure out who should command the other ships."

"I'm on my way."

★ ★ ★

Jason was well aware the U.S. fleet could already be destroyed, or be very near so. His father might even be dead. It took all his resolve not to rally the fleet of Caldurian warships and charge headlong into battle. He also knew that Captain Oz was in a league all by himself. If he didn't think things through thoroughly first, get his fleet prepared for the upcoming battle to the best of his ability, he'd potentially be handing the enemy a fleet so powerful, it would change the course of billions of lives, including those on Earth. No … he needed to be smart. Maybe smarter than ever before, and if that meant sacrificing what was left of the U.S. fleet, and his own father, then so be it.

It took Jason several minutes to find the captain's ready room on the *Parcical*. It was one deck up from the bridge, at the top of the vessel, accessible via a DeckPort. It was also unique—not similar in the least to the ones on the *Minian* or *The Lilly*. Although it adjoined the impressively appointed captain's quarters, it also had the largest onboard conference room he'd ever come across. The vessel was clearly designed to be a command ship—one that facilitated big meetings with other fleet officers. The glass, or facsimile of glass, conference table could seat up to forty personnel. There were virtual displays, inset along much of the curved bulkhead around the compartment, and something else: a massive viewing window, or portal, that looked out to vast space beyond. An identical matching portal was on the other side of the ship, where the captain's living quarters were situated.

★ ★ ★

Every seat within the *Parcical*'s ready room compartment was filled. Several late arrivals stood along the bulkhead. Heads were turning this way and that, taking in the accommodations, and, of course, the floor-to-ceiling window view, which was impossible not to be mesmerized by.

Jason said, "We need to move things along." As all heads turned in his direction, he continued, "I'm sure you are all aware of recent events, when we brought the Caldurian fleet of thirteen vessels, now eleven, under our control. What you may not be aware of is that Admiral Reynolds, and the bulk of the U.S. fleet's some forty-four warships, has come up against a powerful adversary, in the nearby Manilaise system."

"You're talking about the Darion Cartel and Captain Oz, Captain?" Lieutenant Grimes asked.

"That is correct. We need to come to the admiral's aid ASAP. But before we can do that, we need to place our own officers, some permanently, some temporarily, on board our new Caldurian warship acquisitions."

As if anticipating what was coming next, the atmosphere in the ready room had grown even tenser.

"The *Parcical* will take over, becoming my primary Star Watch command vessel. I've designated the ten remaining Master Class vessels new names. If you don't like them, blame Boomer … she came up with them."

All heads turned toward Boomer, seated at the far opposite end of the table, across from her father.

"Lieutenant Grimes, you will take command of the new U.S. warship, *Gemini*. You have been promoted to captain. Is that acceptable, Captain Grimes?"

She flashed a quick surprised smile and nodded. "Yes, sir. Absolutely, sir!"

"Good. You will also assign three others as temporary captains, which may turn to permanent rankings in time. Select three of your fellow senior fighter pilots. Their vessels will be the *Pisces*, the *Aries*, and the *Leo*. You are dismissed, Captain Grimes. Please assemble your selected commanders and get them situated onto their respective vessels. Also note, you will have existing Caldurian bridge crews, as well as ship crews, on board and under your command. Former Caldurian bridge captains will be providing backseat support. See my new XO, Lieutenant Commander Orion, after this meeting; she'll be everyone's point of contact for this transition."

Jason waited for Grimes to hurry from the room before continuing: "Ensign McNeil, you will temporarily be promoted to the rank of Commander and will captain the *Virgo*. Do well and we'll talk about making this a permanent position."

"Yes, sir … I won't let you down, sir."

"I'm sure you won't. Okay, Lieutenant Commander Perkins, please have the *Assailant* closed up and parked in open space. You are promoted to the rank of Captain and you will be commanding the *Minian*."

"Thank you, sir," Perkins said. He stood up and hurried from the ready room.

Jason turned to the one Caldurian still seated at the table. "Granger, you have proven yourself loyal and are an extraordinary asset. You are promoted to Captain and are assigned to the *Aquarius*. Is that acceptable?"

"Yes, sir. I am honored."

"Stay seated, Captain Granger, for just a moment." Jason then called out, "Bristol."

Bristol nervously scratched at his face, looking uncomfortable being the subject of everyone's attention. "Um … yeah?"

"No, you are not promoted to captaincy rank."

Bristol instantly relaxed and laughter broke out around the table.

"But you are highly valued. You will remain under my direct command, on the *Parcical*, promoted to Ship's Engineer."

"Captain Granger, you will make yourself available to Bristol, on an as-needed basis, to bring him up to speed with any Caldurian tech that may be new to him."

Bristol nodded and then said the title aloud, "Ship's Engineer. I like it!"

"You are both dismissed." Jason continued on, "Leon Pike is scheduled to return from the Sol System any time now. Temporarily, he will be captaining the *Libra*. That leaves three warships—the *Scorpio*, the *Taurus* and the *Sagittarius*; we still need to find captains for all three. Rest assured, by the time we move out, we'll have those positions filled. We have a lot to do, people, in a very short amount of time. Let's get going."

Chapter 42

Sol System, Jefferson Station
Auxiliary Space Platform, Hospital

Ricket awoke, feeling somewhat disoriented. Looking around the *SpaceRunner's* comfortably appointed cabin, it took him several moments to remember where he was … what he was doing there. The vessel jostled, a sensation Ricket was familiar with. The small ship was being locked into place onto a spaceport. He sat up. *How long have I been asleep?* He knew in an instant—four hours. It was the most sleep he'd had at any one time in weeks. He stood and made his way down the forward passageway, where he found Leon, Hanna, and the mecher, Trommy5, on the bridge. All three rose to their feet.

"Have a nice nap?" Hanna asked, with a sympathetic smile.

"Yes, I believe I did. Thank you, Hanna."

Nearby, out the forward observation window, Ricket could see one of the many Auxiliary Space Platforms, or ASPs, that flanked Jefferson Station. They were typically located twenty to fifty miles out. The platform itself was nondescript; a utilitarian assemblage of pre-engineered light-gray modules. Ricket was aware of at least thirty of these large support ports.

Some were designated specifically for spacecraft maintenance and repair; others were off-station barracks for crews and military personnel; and several others, such as this one, were designated as space hospitals. He saw the familiar large Red Cross emblem stenciled onto the platform's hull.

Leon said, "I've ordered a flatbed hover cart and several grunts to transport the equipment. We've got this. Why don't you go on ahead?"

Ricket nodded. "Thank you. I will see you all soon then." He went out the same passageway he'd just entered. Once back in the passenger cabin, he descended the circular stairway to the lower level.

The *SpaceRunner's* side access hatch was just in the process of opening up. Beyond it lay one of the platform's numerous connecting narrow causeways. Without hesitation, Ricket proceeded forward and followed the slightly curved passageway—first left, then right. Ahead in the distance he saw another open hatch, where the causeway opened up wide into the primary platform concourse. He saw movement ahead—busy people, scurrying from one place to another.

He stepped into the open concourse, uncertain which direction to go. There were five large passageways, branching off from the concourse, which was temporarily filling in as a reception area for those arriving. In the middle of the expansive compartment was a small grouping of several couches and chairs. Ricket stopped in his tracks when he saw who was seated there.

"There he is—Ricket!"

It was Mollie Reynolds, Captain Reynolds' daughter, Boomer's identical sister. Seated next to her was Nan Reynolds, the acting-president of the United States. Both were already on their feet and hurrying forward, looking thrilled to see him. The feeling was mutual. He opened his mouth to say hello, but words wouldn't come, due to the large lump in his throat. The emotions of the moment hit him with surprising intensity—he hadn't realized how much he'd missed them both.

Mollie was the first to reach him and her arms wrapped around him before he could properly react.

"That's enough, Mollie," Nan said with a smile, "let him breathe." Mollie no sooner stepped away than Nan moved in, giving him an equally tight squeeze.

"You look … different, Ricket," Mollie said. Dressed in light blue leggings, pink sneakers, and an over-sized white T-shirt—her long hair parted on one side—she looked quite different from her warrior-like sister. Mollie maintained an innocence that Boomer had lost over the past year—battling aliens in the far outer reaches of space. No, Mollie was still a little girl in every sense of the word, and Ricket couldn't be more pleased to see her and her mother again. Nan, to him, looked pretty, the same as always.

"Thank you for the warm reception," Ricket said.

"We heard you were coming and we wanted to be here," Nan said. "We've been coming every day to see … to see Dira." The lightness in her voice was filled with trepidation.

"How is she doing?" Ricket asked, not certain he wanted to hear her answer.

Mollie and Nan exchanged glances. "Well … she's alive. That's about all I can say," Nan responded.

"Mom doesn't let me see her," Mollie said. "She says I should remember her as she was—vital and alive."

Ricket could see the weight of Dira's dire situation pressing down on Nan's shoulders. She clutched a wadded-up tissue in her fist, dabbing it frequently at the moist corners of her eyes.

"Oh God … you'd think I'd be all cried out by now."

"Perhaps you can take me to her?" Ricket asked.

Nan nodded. "Stay here, Mollie … I won't be long."

Mollie nodded herself, and headed back to the couch where she picked up a small tablet and started to read.

"She loves to read," Nan said, gesturing toward the leftmost passageway that exited the concourse.

They made their way into the main hospital proper where nurses and doctors scurried about, moving into one patient's room and out of others'.

"Since the attack, this hospital, and two other space hospitals, have become crazy busy. Many patients have been ferried down to the planet's surface."

Ricket did his best to keep up with Nan's quick pace. Up ahead were four large observation windows that looked out to space beyond. As he got closer, he realized he was looking at Jefferson Station—or what was left of Jefferson Station. What once was the Alliance's spectacular, ultra-modern space station, spanning many miles in circumference—was now little more than a clump of ragged metal—a small fraction of its previous size.

"I know … shocking, huh? I find it hard to look at. I avert my eyes when I walk past," Nan said. "It's not far … this way."

Ricket tore his eyes away from the wreckage and followed Nan down a passageway, off to their right, then directly into a medium-sized compartment. A woman nurse was standing beside a MediPod, checking the display and making some kind of adjustment to its settings. She looked up as Nan and Ricket approached and, nodding, offered up a perfunctory smile. "The poor thing's holding on." She looked directly at Ricket. "You'll need to prepare yourself for what you're about to see. It's quite disturbing the first time. I'll leave you two alone. Call if you need anything." The nurse gave Nan a pat on her arm as she left the compartment.

Before Ricket could approach Dira, Nan reached out a hand to him. "Hey … I know Jason is hoping you'll be able to perform some kind of miracle here. He's not one to give up. But we've all come to terms with the inevitable. No less than ten doctors have examined her and the majority of those doctors are borderline outraged that we've kept her alive in her state. Dira deserves the dignity of a swift passing. Your presence here is only symbolic … you have to know that."

Ricket did not know how to respond to that. He was certain she was right. Nothing he had learned, through scanning and rescanning his expanded database of the most advanced Caldurian medical practices, had led him to believe he would be able to help save Dira.

"I'm going to step out and sit with Mollie for a while." Nan tapped her temple. "NanoCom me when you're done." She glanced in the direction of the MediPod, hesitated, and then left.

Ricket moved closer to the MediPod. Nearly at eye-level, he looked into the small portal window sited on top of the clamshell. The nurse was right. He was not prepared for what he saw: Her face, with the exception of a few minor scrapes, was untouched and as beautiful as ever, although her violet skin had lost much of its color. She looked to be sleeping. Ricket leaned in closer, noticing Dira's lips were moving ever so subtly. A paper sheet lay crumpled by her side—perhaps it had been placed on top of her? Had she awakened enough to pull it away? That should not be possible. *Has she been suffering all this time?*

Her injuries were as described. She'd lost both legs and most of one arm. What Ricket hadn't been told was that damage occurred to her torso as well. She'd been sewn-up, as any conventional doctor would do, unaware how a Medi-

Pod worked. If anything, that was a detriment and would have hindered her chance of recovery within the pod. Ricket next took it upon himself to visually examine every inch of her exposed body.

"Beatrice ... I will need your help."

"I understand, Ricket. But Dira's injuries are beyond the capabilities of medical, even Caldurian medical, practices."

Ricket slowly nodded; his heart heavy, he felt as if it were going to literally break in two. He was startled when two technicians entered the compartment, jockeying a large hover-cart into the suddenly confined space. As the two techs unloaded a newer, far more advanced MediPod—taken from the *Parical*—Ricket made sure all the ancillary cables and support equipment were there also. Satisfied, it took about ten minutes for Ricket and the techs to remove the protective packing material from the new MediPod and position it next to the older pod where Dira, still unconscious, resided. Then Ricket went to work connecting all the ancillary cables, and getting the device properly configured via the newly attached display terminal. All the while, his mind continued to work the problem. He knew why the older MediPod had failed to repair Dira's injuries—failed to start the regeneration process of her two missing legs and one arm along with her various internal torso injuries. MediPod computers operate under the influence of an algorithm—an algorithm that utilizes a set baseline. Dira's injuries, obviously extreme, exceeded the acceptable baseline parameters. From first hand experience, Ricket knew the capabilities of both MediPod devices. Sure, the newly designed MediPod was capable of cramming even more and higher tech within someone's cranium, such as his own. But the only way to make the determination if the new pod's algorithm or baseline was more accepting, even marginally, for these kinds of catastrophic injuries ... well the only way was to try it and see.

Things were probably that close … that marginal. He needed to get Dira out of the older pod and into the newer one right away.

"What the hell are you doing?"

Ricket turned to see a human—a male with a bald head and thick glasses—standing in the doorway. By the way he was dressed—a white coat and a stethoscope draped around his neck—he was clearly a doctor.

"I am in the process of assembling this MediPod device."

"No … you're not. I am Dr. Carl Lowell, the hospital's chief of surgery, and no further extraordinary life-saving measures are to be taken for this patient. I do appreciate the new hardware, though. It will undoubtedly save many lives. Unfortunately, not Dira's. She has suffered far too many indignities here. It is time to let her go."

Ricket looked back to Dira, cocooned within the Medi-Pod, then over to the entrance into the room. He saw Nan standing behind the doctor. Her eyes were brimming with tears.

Chapter 43

High Orbit Over Alurian, Gracow CD1
System
Parcical, Bridge

Things were moving at a far slower rate than Jason wanted. Readying a fleet of alien warships for battle, with green command personnel, had been a taxing undertaking. Still, going on thirty-six hours without sleep, he made his way to the Omni's quarters on Deck 5—stumbling onto, he surmised, Omni Hobel's former bed. Four hours later he was awakened by a NanoCom hail from his father.

"Dad … are you all right? What is happening?"

"We've got him on the run, Jason."

"What do you mean?"

"When we came out of the interchange wormhole … when was that? Yesterday? Anyway, it didn't take long for the attacks to start happening. I guess you'd call them guerrilla tactics. Our fleet of forty-four Craing light and heavy cruisers, plus two dreadnaughts, was attacked. Not all at once, but along our periphery—one here, then one there. All very chicken-shit. You know, clandestine bullshit. We would no sooner divert our assets to one location than they'd come at us from someplace else with another attack. It took us a while to wise up to their strategy."

"Is the fleet still viable ... still intact?"

"We're down to twenty ships, to their eighteen."

"That's half the fleet, Dad!"

"You think I don't know that? I've never come up against this kind of ... cunning before!"

"Where are you now? What's the situation?"

"He—Captain Oz and his fleet—is on the run and we're in pursuit. I'm going to get that bastard this time and when I do—"

Jason cut him off mid-sentence: "Stop! It's a trap, Dad. It's the same damn trap I fell for at the CAP-RIM star system. He's playing you."

Jason heard his father talking to someone else, probably the helm commander on his bridge. When he returned, he sounded angry, as if Jason had taken something important away from him—*revenge*.

"Will you listen to me, Dad ... Admiral? For a few minutes?"

"Go ahead."

"We can no longer play his game. He will finish you off. I guarantee it. Whether it's beyond the next cluster of planets, or in an asteroid field. He'll get you, and what's left of the U.S. fleet, right where he wants you. Then it's lights-out time."

"What do you suggest?"

"We beat him at his own game."

"I'm listening," the admiral said, his interest seemingly piqued.

"Hold on a quick second, Dad." Jason was out of bed and moving through the Omni's quarters. He moved down the passageway between the other bedrooms and stopped at seeing an open door. Looking in, he saw Boomer sprawled across a bed, sleeping. He heard the same little snoring sounds he'd heard a thousand times before. He partially closed her door and continued on, now entering the living room area. He noticed the magnificent observation window, which mirrored the one in the ready room conference area, on the opposite side of the ship. He'd been so out of it earlier, he hadn't noticed how nicely appointed these Omni's quarters actually were. He exited the quarters and headed toward the nearest DeckPort.

Jason continued speaking: "Dad ... you need to slow your speed down and then, as if you've given up the chase, head the fleet in the opposite direction. Let Oz think you've come to your senses and you're now running scared."

"To what end, Jason? What difference does it make if we fight him here, or twenty light-years from here?"

"Because I've got the Caldurian fleet."

The dead air between Jason and his father lasted a full five seconds.

"You have the fleet? All twelve Master Class warships?"

"Well, it's down to ten now, but yes ... and the *Minian* too. As well as another warship, called the *Parcical*. But we can't get cocky. Oz nearly defeated the *Minian* when I engaged him earlier, remember? And he may have significantly more assets on hand than any of us think. I'm betting he does. He's probably drawing you into a trap. Hell, he could possess two to three times as many ships as you think he has. As I said, if we're going to defeat him, we need to be smart and beat him at his own game."

"Where do you want me to take the fleet? I've already given the order to hold up."

"Good. Let me work out first our own reception party for Oz. Get moving away from him … and don't let him get in front of you or flank your assets. You'll need patrols—outer periphery scout ships—"

"I still know how to command, Captain," his father barked.

As Jason entered the *Parcical*'s bridge, he was tempted to remind his father to start calling him Admiral, but he let it go. "We'll be in touch, Dad. Orion will reach out to you soon." He cut the connection.

He was happy to see the bridge nearly fully manned. Orion was seated at the tactical station, and Bristol was off to the left, at the engineering console. One of the Gordon brothers sat at the forward right-hand comms station. Also, five Caldurian crewmembers, manning various other boards, were there as well. Jason gave Gunny a wary glance.

"We're keeping an eye on them. But we need their help, Cap."

Jason didn't reply to that. He turned forward, unsure at first who was stationed at the helm station, directly in front of him. A tall female, sporting a crew cut, Army Ranger Sergeant Gail Stone, turned quickly in her seat, her long platinum bangs, swinging like a silky curtain, drooped across her eyes.

"Good evening, Captain."

"Evening, Sergeant. You're qualified for the helm station?"

"Yes, sir … fully qualified on all bridge posts."

Jason, catching Orion nod her head as he moved to the command chair, said, "Fine. Welcome to the bridge."

Orion stood and moved closer to him, sitting down in the closest secondary command chair. "Here's where we're at: All ten … eleven, counting the *Minian*, have crews and commanders."

"What about the *Scorpio* and the *Sagittarius*? We hadn't assigned anyone to them yet."

"We're keeping their original Caldurian commanders in place, instead, as well as on the *Libra*."

"The *Libra*? Isn't that Pike's assignment?"

"He hasn't returned; apparently he got held up, back in the Sol system. I've been in contact with him ... there were, um, some negative issues—"

Jason's heart missed a beat. He knew where this was going and didn't want to get into it. "Fine, he can catch up to us when he arrives in this system. So we're a go ... ready to move out?"

"Yes ... as best as can be expected, considering how green our commanders are, and our own inexperience with some of these ships' newer technical advances."

Jason thought about Ricket. It sure would be advantageous to have him back on board. Undoubtedly, he was with Leon and Hanna and he'd see him when the *SpaceRunner* returned. He gestured toward the forward part of the wrap-around display. "Can you bring up a logistical feed of that system? We need to stage a welcoming party for Captain Oz and his friends."

Chapter 44

Lorchire 555 Planetary Chain, Gracow
CD1 System
Parcical, Bridge

Jason had found what he was looking for: a planetary system comprised of twenty-three large worlds. There was also an asteroid belt, which snaked through the long chain of uninhabitable planets. Here, high levels of radiation streamed from three nearby stars, which would disrupt long- and short-range sensors. It seemed a perfect place to hide from a determined adversary in hot pursuit.

With spatial coordinates provided, Jason had watched as the U.S. fleet moved into the system, where he headed for the middle of the planetary cluster. Once there, they broke into four groups. There the fleet currently sat in hiding on the far sides of the planets.

Separate feeds from his new fleet commanders were currently on view up on the wrap-around display. So far, they'd asked a lot of questions, some Jason couldn't answer.

"Captain, how do we know which direction Oz's fleet will approach us from?" Captain Grimes asked.

"We don't. We need to strategize as he would, but he'll definitely want to trap the admiral's U.S. fleet—make it impossible for his ships to escape."

Orion joined Jason at his side and said, "Let's look at the logistical feed. The admiral's twenty ships will be moving into position here, among those planets in the middle of the cluster. There are only three ways in or out of here: the way they entered this planetary cluster; over there, on the opposite side; or here, by skirting this closest star."

Captain Granger asked, "What about right there, between those two moons?"

"No, that's inaccessible, due to that asteroid belt. He'd lose half his assets moving through that mess of rock," Jason said.

"Captain, why are you positioning so much of our fleet so far out? Can't we tighten up some, bring those five vessels in closer somewhat?"

"Know that our Master Class vessels will be totally undetectable to Oz. With that said, they are huge ships and can be visually spotted … although even that is unlikely. We've got five warships eight hundred million miles out, in a circle around the planet cluster. Once the enemy fleet, or multiple fleets, move into position, we can tighten things up a little and bring those five vessels closer in somewhat."

"The other five Master Class ships will be placed here, here, and here," Orion added.

"Wait. That's within the asteroid belt, isn't it?" Captain Perkins asked.

"Hiding as close to it as possible, without actually being in the belt," Jason said.

"And where will the *Parcical* be?"

"The *Parcical* has the most advanced cloaking capabilities. Even now, we're over two light-years away from the rest of you that are lying in wait for Oz and his fleets. The *Parcical* will wait for the enemy fleet to pass by us, then we'll come in, following right behind them."

Jason next observed a new logistical feed, appearing up on the display, as Orion pointed at four clusters of icons, each many millions of miles from one another. She drew in a sudden breath and said in a lowered voice, "That's one hundred and fifty inbound warships total, Cap."

That large a number was unexpected—and Jason thought it a truly sobering sight. He continued, "As anticipated, we see Oz has multiple fleets in motion. Four of them are converging on the Lorchire 555 planetary cluster. They obviously know that the U.S. fleet is trying to hide there. And now we wait to see what they do—watch how they plan to trap the admiral's fleet."

"So we just wait here?" Captain Grimes asked.

Jason smiled. "Yes, we wait. No one moves. We will keep all communications, from this point on, down to the barest minimum. We cannot give Oz the slightest indication he is moving into our own trap. Is that understood?"

The ship captains all said yes.

"One more thing, Captain." The final question came from Perkins again. "No offense, but three Caldurian captains are part of our command team … how do we know they'll really fight with us; or worse, that they won't warn the approaching Darion Cartel fleet?"

It was Billy, on his own display feed, who answered the question: "We've carefully selected three Omnis—not only willing to fight for us, but motivated to do so. They also, literally, have guns pointed at their heads."

Jason had to swivel around backward in order to catch Billy's feed. He had several days' worth of stubble on his face and was chomping on the stub of an unlit cigar. He looked as tired as Jason had ever seen him.

"If that answers everyone's questions, wait for further orders. Good luck to each of you."

One by one most of the overhead feed segments closed down, allowing an open view of local space to take their place. All except Billy's feed, which had moved around, now in front of the display.

"You holding up, buddy?" Jason asked.

"I'm fine. I wanted to talk to you one on one … any chance you can go to your ready room?"

"Sure. Give me a minute."

Billy's feed closed down.

★ ★ ★

Jason planted himself behind the desk in the Omni's ready room, which was adjacent to the large conference room next door. Billy's holographic feed was already waiting for him, hovering several inches off the desk.

"You look like shit, Billy."

"Well, have you looked in a mirror lately?" Billy retorted.

Jason had to laugh at that. "So what was it you needed to talk to me about in private?"

"I saw that secondary logistical feed Gunny put up … one hundred and fifty warships inbound."

"Yeah, that took me by surprise too."

"How does something like that happen? When a potential adversary, like the Darion Cartel, can produce such an immense military buildup without the Alliance having a flipping clue about it?"

Suddenly, Jason felt more tired than he could remember. He threw his hands up in mock resignation. "Geez ... I don't know, Billy. What do you want me to say? Space is big ... it's so fucking immense ... there's no way to keep tabs on everything that's going on everywhere. But to answer your question, since the end of the Craing wars we basically stopped looking. We thought with the defeat of the Craing we'd finally changed minds. That beings on all planetary systems had finally learned their lesson—that war truly was ... *is* hell, and that we could, perhaps for one damn minute, stop and take a breath; that we could all actually live peacefully together for a little while."

Billy, smiling now, said, "Well, I guess the folks—the ones you're talking about—need to learn one more lesson."

Billy's sudden fatalistic and humorous attitude was somewhat contagious. Jason returned the smile, then turned serious again. "You know, Billy, things right now aren't looking so good." Jason mentally swatted away thoughts of Dira—that most likely she wasn't alive anymore. "I don't care how advanced our Caldurian fleet of twelve warships are, when you have one hundred and fifty inbound enemy warships under the command of a strategic genius ... well, you know we're in deep trouble."

"We've been in worse situations," Billy said. "Well, maybe not," reassessing what he'd said. "Hell, I don't know, you've always pulled a rabbit out of your ass ... some kind of miracle that inevitably saves the day."

Again, thoughts of Dira tried to weasel their way into the forefront of his mind. *Do I even care if we win anymore? Why even try?* Before Jason could respond to Billy, he saw movement at the entranceway and Boomer, sleepy-eyed, wandered into the ready room, yawning, as she weaved her way over to him, and plopped down onto his knee. She leaned against him, her head against his shoulder.

She said, "I'm hungry, Dad."

In a rare moment, Boomer was an eleven-year-old child again. Jason kissed the top of her head and with that answered his own question. "Why don't you go and find where the kitchen is in these quarters and I'll join you in a minute."

Nodding into his chest, she stood and, yawning again, padded off.

Billy's smile was there again and Jason could only shrug.

"We need to take the offensive," Jason said. "We may not be able to defeat Oz, come an all-out face-off in limitless space, so we'll take the battle to him instead; fight him on a better-controlled playing field. I suspect with the head of the snake thus neutralized, the Darion Cartel fleet will lose much of its fight."

"I like it," Billy said. "We'll keep it small … maybe get the boys in the band back together again; you, me, Rizzo … along with that thousand-pound rhino?"

Jason laughed at that, hesitating before answering. After all, he was commander of the entire operation—the Omni. It would be irresponsible of him to go off and lead a small assault team, while an incoming battle of such magnitude would take place elsewhere. "I'm in," Jason said. "First, I'll need to talk to the admiral and bring him up to speed. Go assemble a team of our best and be ready to leave within the hour."

The channel closed and Billy was gone. Jason sat back and began to formulate a plan.

"Where we going?" Boomer asked, chewing a mouthful of something.

Chapter 45

Lorchire 555 Planetary Chain, Gracow
CD1 System
Parcical, Bridge

Jason entered, for the first time, the *Parcical*'s flight bay. His initial impression was that it was similar to that on the Master Class vessels, but closer in scale to *The Lilly*'s. His eyes went to the cluster of two- and one-man fighters, somewhat disappointed that he didn't see anything like the dark red fighter, the *Pacesetter*, he'd noticed back on the *Quantum Lark*. But there were three sleek, dark purple, two-man spacecraft that suddenly caught his attention. He'd have to investigate them further, when he had more time.

Jason was listening to Orion talking in his ear—giving him an update on the position of the quickly approaching Darion

Cartel fleet of four groupings.

"You were right, Cap … it looks like they're moving as-sets—readying to block the three access points where the U.S. fleet is in hiding within that planetary cluster."

So much for finding a hiding place hidden by high radiation levels. "Well, that alone tells us they have more advanced tech than we'd assumed. Any indication they are detecting the presence of the twelve Caldurian ships?"

"No, we're invisible, as far as they're concerned, Cap. They only see twenty light and heavy Craing cruisers and two dreadnaughts. That's it."

Jason watched as the admiral's newly arrived shuttle slowly settled down onto the flight bay's deck and cut its engines. It reminded Jason of something he needed to deal with—and deal with right now.

"Gunny … I want you to put out an announcement to all Alliance and U.S. fleet officers …"

"Okay, Cap, what's up?"

"I'm updating my rank status."

"Making it official now, Admiral?" Orion asked, sounding like she already knew that old news was coming out.

"No. It's changed to the new designation of Omni."

"Omni?"

"That's right. Maybe I'll explain why later, but for now … that's what my title is."

"I think I get why. It may take me … any of us … a while to get used to it, though."

"No worries. It's more a title designation for official encounters than something I expect to be called on board. Either way, I'm fine with what the crew calls me."

"Got it, Cap … um … Omni."

Jason cut the connection and approached the stern of the shuttle, where Admiral Reynolds now strode down the gangway. He had two fingers up to his ear, a NanoCom conversation in process. Noticing Jason he gave him a cursory wave, as Jason held up and waited.

"What's this Omni bullshit I'm listening to?"

"Good to see you too, Admiral. To answer your question, do you feel comfortable calling me Admiral? Does that seem … appropriate to you?"

"I don't know. Actually, I don't give two shits what I call you."

"Uh huh … well, it's done; you can call me Omni Reynolds, or Jason, or hey you, but I think taking on an Admiral rank doesn't work."

"That's fine. Do you want to talk battle strategy or keep jabbering on about ranks all day?"

There was something surprisingly comforting about his father's no-nonsense attitude. Jason gestured forward and they headed for the nearest passageway out of the flight bay. "Welcome to the *Parcical*, Dad. This ship and the *Minian*, along with two of the newly-acquired Master Class warships, now comprise Star Watch."

His father stopped, looking irritated: "So you've just assigned yourself three more warships, Captain?"

"Omni."

"Whatever."

"Yes. Star Watch was a brilliant idea … on your part, Dad. But it's grown into a much bigger undertaking than you have any clue about. It requires far more presence than a lone warship can provide, policing the entirety of Allied space. If you think about it, you'll realize what I'm saying makes sense."

"And the others? What about the other eight Caldurian warships?"

"They're now U.S. fleet assets," Jason said, "and we now need to move it along." The two men began hurrying toward a nearby DeckPort. "My question to you, Dad, is … are you coming back to duty, or returning to the scrapyard and the '49 pickup?"

"I told you, I'm now working on a Studebaker, a Commander convertible." The admiral pursed his lips and then continued. "Look … I'm not fully one hundred percent yet, Jason."

"Understood. Only you know what you're able to manage. Also remember, you've got help."

"What does that mean?"

"Just that not everything sits on your shoulders anymore. You have a boss now," Jason said, pointing a finger at himself: "Omni Reynolds."

When they had reached the *Parcical's* bridge, the admiral looked around the ultra-modern, ultra-sophisticated surroundings and nodded. He glanced at Jason as he took a seat in the command chair. "Let's see how this clusterfuck turns out … then I'll let you decide."

"Listen up, everyone. Admiral Reynolds is *temporarily* in command of the *Parcical.*"

Jason spent the next few moments introducing his father to those he didn't know on the bridge. Orion and Bristol he already knew and he acknowledged them with a nod.

"Don't you have a mission to run off to?" the admiral asked.

"That I do. You're clear on what the plan is?"

The admiral simply stared at Jason with a blank face.

"Fine," Jason said, and turned toward Orion. "I want constant updates on what's happening with the fleets—both theirs and ours."

"Aye, sir."

As Jason hurried from the bridge, he whispered to Orion, "Watch him."

★ ★ ★

Jason left the bridge and immediately phase-shifted direct-ly to the flight bay. Billy, Rizzo, and Jackson, as well as Traveler, were in a tight huddle, talking in low tones. It wasn't until he got closer that he saw Boomer standing there, too, on the other side of Traveler's bulk.

As Jason approached, they each reached for their SuitPac devices—initializing their battle suits. Billy turned to Jason and said, "Nice of you to join us, Omni Reynolds."

Traveler snorted, which Jason knew was one of the rhi-no-warrior's ways of snickering. "You'll get used to it," Jason said. "Listen up … Orion's just updated each of your HUDs with the phase-shift coordinates of Captain Oz's command vessel. As far as he's concerned, he's closed any possible escape route for the U.S. fleet and he's moving in for the kill."

"Why is he doing this?" Boomer asked.

"It's a long story, Boomer. Let's leave it to say he and the Darion Cartel believe this part of space belongs to their people."

"Well … does it?"

"No. At least, it hasn't for a very long time. Over a thou-sand years. And even if the cartel did have some kind of claim here … the answer shouldn't involve the mass murder of mil-lions of beings on so many alien worlds across space. That's what negotiations are for. The cartel never even attempted to discuss the matter."

Boomer seemed to understand and went quiet.

Billy said, "So we're at war with the cartel?"

"They've taken out over twenty U.S. warships, killing thousands of our men and women. But are we officially at war? No, that would take a majority vote from within the Al-lied planets. Something they are already considering—against the Caldurians—for what transpired on Jefferson Station. The truth of the matter is, we can't effectively engage in any war right now, with the recent mothballing of our fleet, let alone engage and simultaneously manage two war fronts. That's why we need to take this battle directly to Oz—engage him personally—one on one. We need to nip his tyrannical striving in the bud ... right now."

Jason hailed Orion: "You have the phase-shift coordinates for the command ship?"

"I do. The problem was finding you a suitable location on board that gives you an element of surprise. I'm putting you in the engine room, at the opposite end of the vessel from the bridge."

"That's fine. Go ahead and phase-shift us over now."

Jason turned to the others. "Lock and load." After another full minute, Jason hailed Orion again. "What's going on?"

"Sorry, Cap ... the cartel fleet just initiated their attack from three different fronts."

"That was expected. Listen, my father knows what to do; we discussed how this would play out. He should be bringing in our outlying ships now ... closing the noose around Oz's fleet any moment."

"Yes ... he just gave the orders. I'm phase-shifting you over to the command ship now. Good luck."

Chapter 46

Lorchire 555 Planetary Chain, Gracow
CD1 System
Parcical, Bridge

Admiral Reynolds watched the logistical feed on the overhead display. A part of him felt guilty, leaving his fleet stuck there in the middle of a battle. Twenty U.S. warships that appeared, for the time being anyway, nothing more than captive bait: an offering up for imminent slaughter. But Jason's plan was sound. Oz wouldn't be expecting such an outlandish, borderline-irresponsible strategy.

"Admiral, our five outlying Master Class ships have moved in, now holding inside a perimeter of two million miles," Orion said.

The admiral watched as five bright blue oblong icons moved into position. He also noted another five identical icons running along the outskirts of the asteroid belt that was woven in between the same planets where the U.S. fleet currently waited. The *Parcical*, also a bright blue icon, but more egg-shaped, was slowly making her way through one of three Darion Cartel fleet groups. Earlier, there were four. The plan was for the *Parcical* to invisibly make her way, staying within firing distance of Captain Oz's own command vessel. Soon, Oz would be faced with attacks, coming from both within it, as well as from nearby open space. For Admiral Perry, this was far more than another space battle. A failure here and he would officially be done: too old, or too mentally incapacitated, to further command any fleet, even a fecal waste management barge, somewhere out in the far reaches of the galaxy.

"We have visuals on the command ship, the *Carrion*, Admiral."

The admiral stood and stretched his back. The command ship looked like fairly new construction. Thin and tubular, she looked more like a seafaring vessel, similar to a gigantic submarine, than a spacecraft. Whereas most Caldurian vessels were rounded and had totally smooth hulls, this ship was all angles and protrusions, including numerous rail cannons, too many plasma guns to count, and varied types of what looked liked communications gear. The ship managed to look both old-fashioned and menacing at the same time. The admiral stared at the vessel, doing his best to temper his growing anger. Here was the ship … the captain … responsible for the deaths of so many. He thought of the small planetary system, located at the edge of Sector 22—tranquil and peace-loving Airigo 5. The admiral once spent weeks there, and had even briefly fallen in love with a native female. She would be dead now. His thoughts turned to General Jonathan Taft, an elderly emissary from Earth, and probably his closest friend. He too was dead at the hands of Captain Oz.

"It's a heavy destroyer class vessel, Admiral," Orion said. "I've never seen more weaponry on one vessel. It's a killing machine."

"Distance?"

"Close. We're at thirty miles and holding."

"Captain ... or should I say Omni Reynolds?" he corrected himself, rolling his eyes.

"Not in position yet ... needs another minute or two, sir."

"We may not have—"The admiral's words were interrupted by the equivalency of all hell breaking loose.

He heard Orion report the obvious: The attack had commenced. Captain Oz hadn't even given the surrounded U.S. fleet an option to negotiate, or even to surrender.

You've made your bed, asshole ... now sleep in it, he thought to himself.

"Omni's in position ... he's given the order to attack," Orion said.

"Contact every fleet commander to move into attack position. All ships are to open fire!"

★ ★ ★

Jason listened to Orion's voice, giving the passed-along orders to all fleet commanders. The battle was on. Jason felt something on his left arm and, looking down, found Boomer adjusting his enhancement shield.

"There. That will give you more accuracy."

"Thanks, kiddo." Jason noticed Traveler studying his little three-sided shield. "Play your cards right, big guy, and I'll get you one of these sometime."

Traveler snorted his disapproval.

They currently stood within the narrow confines of the engine room. It was loud there, everything slick and over-glistening with oil. Jason wasn't sure what the propulsion technology on this vessel was, but it certainly wasn't clean. Four *Carrion* crewmembers lay dead on the deck. They'd been taken by surprise, but had acted quickly, drawing their sidearm weapons. Unfortunately for them, they weren't quick enough.

"Let's head out," Jason ordered, hurrying toward the compartment's open hatchway. He halted before what appeared to be a central passageway. His HUD showed at least twenty *Carrion* crewmembers ahead in this passageway alone. He called up the pre-loaded ship's layout—a best-guess schematic the *Parcical*'s AI put together that, thus far, was pretty accurate.

Jason spoke into the open channel: "There's another compartment fifty feet forward, along this same passageway. I'm going to move us over there." Everything flashed white as he phase-shifted them as a group.

"We're in jail! You put us in jail, Dad."

She was right. Jason had phase-shifted them into one of ten confinement cells. Their cell, and the others too, was empty, so no one had noted their sudden appearance. Jason reached a hand out to check if there was an invisible energy field. There wasn't one. "Come on," he said, and they moved to the open hatch entry and looked out into the passageway. His HUD showed this part of the ship to be pretty much deserted, though up ahead, there were hundreds of red icons—some stationary—others moving about. A barracks.

"That's a bigger bite than we can chew … get ready for another phase-shift." He looked for another compartment to flash into, one closer to the bridge. He'd originally intended to phase-shift directly onto the bridge, but had discovered there were an inordinate number of security droids—both on the bridge itself, as well as stationed nearby—at the bow of the vessel. To find themselves disarmed or disabled before actually confronting Captain Oz wasn't acceptable. The problem, though, was that there wasn't another unoccupied compartment between them and the bridge.

He was being hailed. "Go ahead, Orion."

"The U.S. fleet is taking a brutal beating, Cap. No damage to our Caldurian vessels, but the U.S. fleet is down to seventeen ships. Two more are about to lose shields."

"And the *Carrion*?"

"We're firing on her and she's returning fire … her shields are taking a beating … she'll be in trouble shortly. There's something else you need to be aware of … I'm detecting an old style fusion reactor on board. Outdated drive technology that's looking like it may soon go critical. It blows … it could take everything in local space with her … including us over here. You need to get out of there, Captain, and we need to get far away from that ship."

"I need a few more minutes. We'll get out in time, I promise. Let me talk to the admiral."

A moment later the older man's voice was on the line. "A bit busy here …" the admiral grumbled.

"Dad, go ahead … have three Master Class vessels phase-shift directly into the U.S. fleet's fray; seems they'll need more firepower."

"Do you know what one hundred and fifty enemy warships look like? Hell, there's not a Master Class vessel that's not already fully engaged."

"I'm more interested in protecting our current assets, than in destroying theirs. It's not about retribution, Dad."

The connection went dead. Jason did manage to get that one point across, now he'd just have to trust that the commander standing on the *Parcical*'s bridge would make the right decision. He turned to his team: "Things are heating up … time to take the direct approach. If we don't get to Oz quickly enough, we'll have his barracks, full of security, moving in on us from behind."

"How we doing this, Cap?" Rizzo asked.

"I want to draw the security droids on the bridge out and away from Captain Oz. So we're heading straight up Central Avenue. It's time to storm the bridge. Jackson and Traveler, I want you two on point ... plow us a clear path into the bridge. It's about two hundred feet forward, at the end of this passageway. Rizzo and Billy watch our six. Boomer, stay with me in the middle of the pack. Let's move."

They headed into the central passage and soon were running flat out. Almost immediately, klaxon alarms sounded from overhead. As expected, security droids began to stream out from the bridge, as well as from two adjacent hatchways, on both sides. *So far so good.*

"Cap ... we've got company coming from our six."

"Keep them at bay; that's your job, Billy," Jason retorted.

Plasma fire erupted—forward and behind them—and Jason could already feel the effects of crossfire on his battle suit. The security droids were three-legged affairs, with revolving plasma-gun-turret torsos, minus heads or arms. The damn things scurried about so quickly, it was hard to get a beat on them.

Jackson's and Traveler's forward progress slowed. To stay there, even another minute, would result in certain death for all six. But Jason's plan had already worked. No more droids stormed from the bridge entrance, and icons on his HUD showed all but five had been drawn out of the bridge. "Get ready for a phase-shift," Jason said. Two seconds later they were standing within the *Carrion's* bridge compartment.

A quick glance at his HUD told him there were fifteen combatants on the bridge—five were security droids.

"Secure the damn entrance ... no one gets in here!" Jason yelled, as he raised his multi-gun and let loose a constant barrage of plasma fire at a quickly approaching security droid. He saw Boomer had found herself in the worst possible position, standing right in front of three droids that were letting her have it with all the firepower at their disposal. She took some hits before leaping up and out of the way. Her enhancement shield simultaneously emanated purple disruption waves down at the droids from above.

Jason's droid erupted in a small ball of fire, while its revolving gun turret began to spin, uncontrollably, around and around. And then Jason spotted Captain Oz, standing at the back of the bridge. He was tall and clean shaven, had sandy blond hair—and the brightest green eyes Jason had ever seen. Green eyes that held their steady gaze directly on him. Two bridge crewmen stood before him, their sidearms drawn. Jason shot them both and waited for them to fall to the deck.

Oz seemed far calmer, considering his current situation, than Jason expected. In fact, he looked more bemused than nervous.

"Captain Reynolds, I presume?"

"I go by Omni these days—but sure, captain works, too."

Jason heard his father's voice in his ear ... "We're about twenty seconds from blowing that tin can up ... her shields are falling. Get the hell out ... get out now, Jason!"

Jason approached Captain Oz and said one word: "Gotcha."

The smile briefly left the captain's face—his seeming façade of confidence broken.

"Time's up, asshole. You lost and this ship is about to become space dust. Surrender now and I won't destroy the rest of your fleet."

Captain Oz looked as if he were weighing his options. Suddenly, having regained his composure and looking cool as a cucumber, he said, "Omni Reynolds ... go ahead and enjoy this little victory. Savor it. Truth is, I've been looking for an opponent with a glimmer of intelligence. It seems I've found one."

"Get ... out ... of ... there!" Jason heard the admiral's nervous voice in his ear.

Jason could see the bridge was relatively still. It was now theirs. Boomer, now standing at his side, was taking in the interaction between the two enemy commanders. Jason wanted her, and the others, phase-shifted away now, before the ship blew apart.

The entrance to the bridge was still a battleground, with Billy, Traveler and Jackson firing their weapons pretty much non-stop, but holding their ground.

The deck shifted beneath Jason's feet. He nearly lost his balance, but managed to regain his footing. He asked one final time, "What's it going to be?"

Captain Oz took a casual step backward.

"Don't move—don't move an inch."

But it was too late; Oz did move. He backed himself into a curved, tubular inset part of the back bulkhead. It seemed so nondescript Jason hadn't even noticed it. Captain Oz leaned backward and crossed his arms over his chest. In a blur, he was spinning away, gone from view. Next came a loud *clang*, and Jason saw the newly-made opening where Oz stood mere seconds before. Oz, off in the distance, was climbing into an escape pod. By the time Jason raised his multi-gun, the pod had gone from sight, and the vacuum of space had begun to suck out all existing atmosphere from the bridge. "Damn!"

Jason phase-shifted his team away.

Chapter 47

Lorchire 555 Planetary Chain, Gracow
CD1 System
Parcical, Bridge

Jason entered the *Parcical's* bridge. One glance up at the display told him the battle still raged on ... was raging on ... on multiple fronts. The admiral, seated in the command chair, was currently barking off orders to one of the newly assigned, and highly nervous-looking, ship commanders up on the display.

"No! Hold your position, damn it, Perkins. You've got help on the way. Concentrate your fire on those three ships on your stern ... protect your backside, man!"

The admiral noticed Jason and started to get up. Jason placed a hand on his shoulder. "No, no ... stay where you are. You've obviously got everything well under control." Jason took a seat in one of the secondary command chairs. The admiral, so engrossed in his command, didn't even look at Jason before turning to bark off another command, this one to the captain of the *Sagittarius*. Jason was having a hard time recalling just who that was. He looked over to Orion who, like everyone else on the bridge, seemed pulled in multiple directions. She glanced at him, then surprised him with a quick wink and smile.

Apparently, things really were under control. Jason leaned back and took in the logistical display above him. He counted fifteen U.S. warships, clustered in the middle of the fray. They'd lost two more warships, but still seemed to be holding their own. It sounded like the *Minian* was having some difficulty, but the other Caldurian warships were still active ... and accounted for. The Darion Cartel fleet was not doing nearly as well. Oz's three attack groups were facing tremendous firepower from the Master Class warships. Jason's plan had come together surprisingly well. He estimated, after doing a quick count, that the enemy had lost nearly forty warships and those remaining were taking on heavy fire from all sides.

Seaman Gordon abruptly turned in his seat. "Sirs ... I'm getting multiple hails ... requests coming in: Five enemy ship commanders want to surrender."

The admiral suddenly stood and punched a fist into his other open palm. "*Yes! Yes! Yes!*" He spun around and, looking surprised at seeing Jason sitting nearby, held both arms out wide, in a dramatic gesture—as if to say ... *did I handle this or what?*

"You did good, Dad. I can't say I could have done any better."

The admiral sat back down and was immediately engrossed in the happenings of the battle before him.

Jason's only regret was not capturing, or killing, Captain Oz. That would have to wait for another time. He was fairly sure Oz was already light-years away by now. The good news was his fleet was pretty much toast, which meant the Darion Cartel's land grab was completely upended. *All in all, not a bad day's work.*

"Cap?"

Jason spun toward Orion. She had two fingers to her ear and told whomever she was speaking to to hold on. "Cap … heavy injury reports are coming in from all ships … both ours and the enemy's. Overflow casualties are coming into the *Parcical. Also* … Boomer's got minor injuries."

★ ★ ★

Jason left the bridge, knowing things there were pretty well in hand. If he didn't catch a few hours of sleep he'd literally crash and burn, sheer exhaustion finally catching up with him. First he wanted to check on Boomer and Rizzo; although both had experienced first- and second-degree burns from plasma fire, they would be fine. About to enter Medical he saw something that didn't make immediate sense … didn't add up. Why was Hanna down the hallway, talking to someone? She wasn't here. She was on the *SpaceRunner*, light-years from here. He blinked twice and she was gone. *God … I really need sleep.*

"Dad? Are you just going to stand there?"

Jason turned back to the entrance of Medical and saw Boomer sitting on a rolling stool, her arm being attended to by a med-technician. A white bandage was already on her other arm.

"Where's Rizzo?" Jason asked, glad to see Boomer looking no worse for wear. In fact, she appeared downright giddy.

"He's come and gone …" the med-tech said, now turning toward Jason.

It wasn't a med-tech.

"Are you just going to stand there, or can a girl get a kiss from her fiancé?"

Jason stood there, his mouth ajar, unable to speak or move.

Dira patted Boomer's head and said, "You're fine." She smiled and walked up to Jason, so close he could see those incredible little flecks of amber and violet in her wide open beautiful eyes.

"Yes, my love … I really am alive." She slipped her arms beneath his, pulling him closer to her. She kissed him, kept on kissing him, for a long time. Eventually, she pulled away. "Are you okay?"

"How …?"

Dira took in a long breath and began, "Well, I was unconscious. Truth is … I never knew what happened to me. Not until I woke up."

"He did it," Boomer said, pointing her finger toward the small person entering Medical.

Jason turned to see the familiar little being, with his odd-shaped head. He too was smiling.

"Ricket? You managed this?"

Dira said, "Apparently, they were about to pull the plug. Even your ex-wife was chafing at the bit to yank the thing right out of the wall."

As if on cue, Hanna and Leon appeared, entering Medical arm in arm. Hanna said, "But then, just in the nick of time, Ricket had one more grand idea up his sleeve."

Ricket said, "I'm glad I was able to help, Captain. I'm glad I was able to bring her home to you."

Epilogue

It was late. Except for a limited night shift crew, the ultra-modern *Parcical* was running as quiet as a whisper. Ricket liked it like this—he was alone with his thoughts. Alone with his tinkering.

He sat patiently at the workbench. The only light present within Norwell's workshop was coming from a sapphire beam coming from high above. Ricket contemplated the square, glossy-black device situated right in front of him. He turned the device and looked at its backside. No difference. He let out a breath, feeling stumped. He wondered if this thing was, or was holding within it, the answer to a very important problem; the worsening degradation issues occurring with cloned Zip accelerators. The captain had described the subterranean meeting between Alurians and Caldurains. How the Alurians were prepared to offer this ... this thing, to the Caldurians. *Was it a ruse?* Perhaps this is simply an empty box—and the Alurians never had any intention at all of working again with the Caldurians, their past enemies.

Ricket sat back and let his mind wander. It had been a mere twenty-eight hours since the battle with the Darion Cartel, and Captain ... *Omni* ... Reynolds had ordered the slow process of transporting all warship assets, including the newly acquired Darion Cartel vessels, back to the Sol System. It saddened Ricket that so many had lost their lives here … and he briefly wondered if he'd ever witness true peace within his lifetime. He certainly hadn't in the more than two hundred years he'd been alive thus far. He let out a weary breath and brought his attention back to the issue at hand. The issue that had brought the fleet of Caldurian warships back from somewhere within the multiverse in the first place and, undoubtedly, would keep them coming back until it was no longer possible. Again, he turned the black box around.

"Any luck with that thing?"

Ricket jumped at the sound of Dira's soft voice behind. She came up beside Ricket and leaned her elbows on the workbench. She stared at the box with a furrowed brow.

"Could you not sleep, Dira?" Ricket asked.

"No. I think I'm all sleeped out. Thought I'd do a little exploring … see what all the hubbub is about with this new ship."

"Warm milk, I hear, can be of help to humans unable to sleep."

She turned and looked at Ricket, her expression now serious. "So, how did you do it?"

"How did I do what?"

"You know … get me into the other MediPod. Save my life. You never told me the whole story."

Ricket suddenly looked like he'd swallowed a canary and his cheeks flushed.

"Ricket? Tell me … tell or I'll stay here and bother you all night."

"I … I lied."

"You never lie."

"I did not know of any other way to get the doctor to comply."

"You mean to get what was left of my body into the new MediPod?"

Ricket nodded.

"So? What did you say to him?"

"I told him that the new MediPod was equipped with a small but powerful antimatter power unit. Which is true. One that I had just initiated a five-minute countdown on."

"Countdown?"

Ricket didn't answer. Then Dira's eyes went wide. "Like a bomb? Like you set it to explode or something?"

Ricket gave the slightest of nods.

"Why would he believe that? It's an obvious bluff … right?"

Ricket slowly shook his head. "It wasn't completely a bluff. It took me several minutes to show him what I had done. He was intelligent enough, quite familiar with technology. And once he saw the descending numerical countdown, he knew, without a doubt, I was serious."

"You would have blown up the hospital with all those innocent people? The patients?" Dira asked.

Ricket smiled. "The explosion would have only been enough to destroy the MediPod itself, nothing more."

Grinning ear to ear, Dira hugged Ricket and kissed the top of his distorted head. "Well, I'm glad you did that for me, Ricket. You saved my life, and I'll never forget that." Suddenly, she picked up the black box and held it up in front of her. She spun it around from front to back and then shook it like a child would do with an unopened Christmas gift. She held it up close to her ear. "There's something in there. Do you hear it?"

Ricket reached for the box but Dira raised it a bit higher, out of his reach. She moved her hands and held it now by its sharp corners. Dira spun the box a half-turn between her fingers and something made a loud click. She stopped spinning the box and looked at Ricket. "Oh crap, did I just break it? I'm so sorry."

Ricket took the box from her and carefully placed it back down on the workbench. He saw what the click had been caused by. One side, a panel, of the box was ajar. He lifted the panel and looked inside.

"What is it? What's inside, Ricket?"

He stared into the box for several seconds before looking up at Dira. He smiled. "I think we found our answer."

The End.

Thank you for reading RICKET, Star Watch, Book 2!

If you enjoyed RICKET, please leave a review on Amazon.com — it really, really helps!

To be notified of the next book in this series, Star Watch, Book 3, *and other books of mine, please join my mailing list. I hate spam and will never, ever share your information. Jump to this link to join:*

http://eepurl.com/bs7M9r

Thank you, again, for coming along with me on these Sci-Fi romps across space.

Acknowledgments

I am grateful for the ongoing fan support I receive for all of my books. This book—number eleven, Star Watch, Ricket—came about through the combined contributions of numerous others. First, I'd like to thank my wife for her never-ending love and support. She helps make this journey rich and so very worthwhile. I'd like to thank my mother, Lura Genz, for her tireless work as my first-phase creative editor and a staunch cheerleader of my writing. I'd like to thank Mia Manns for her phenomenal line and developmental editing ... she is an incredible resource. And Eren Arik produced another magnificent cover design—maybe his best yet! Thank you Lazar for the incredible website warship floor plans ... it ads a whole new dimension to reading these books. Thank you Taryn Ikenouye for and amazing website experience ... you've outdone yourself. A special thanks goes out to L.J. Ganser, who produces the audiobook versions of my books. Anyone looking for a truly immersive, not to mention 'fun' reading experience—with all his wonderful character voices ... you have to try the audiobook version. I'd also like to thank those in my Tuesday writer's MeetUp group, the *Writer's Idea Factory*, who have brought fresh ideas and perspectives to my creativity, and elevating my writing as a whole. Others who provided fantastic support include Lura and James Fischer, Sue Parr, Stuart Church, and Chris Derrick.

Other books by MWM

Scrapyard Ship
(Scrapyard Ship series, Book 1)

HAB 12
(Scrapyard Ship series, Book 2)

Space Vengeance
(Scrapyard Ship series, Book 3)

Realms of Time
(Scrapyard Ship series, Book 4)

Craing Dominion
(Scrapyard Ship series, Book 5)

The Great Space
(Scrapyard Ship series, Book 6)

Call To Battle
(Scrapyard Ship series, Book 7)

Mad Powers
(Tapped In series, Book 1)

Lone Star Renegades
(Lone Star Renegades series, Book 1)

Star Watch
(Star Watch series, Book 1)

Find Ricket
(Star Watch series, Book 2)

Made in the USA
Middletown, DE
27 July 2021

44811212R00195